Praise for *Danger Sector*

2012 Independent Publisher Award for Best Regional Fiction
Midwest Book Award Finalist 2012

"It was a summer delight to get a copy of *Danger Sector,* second in Jenifer LeClair's intelligent and well-written "Windjammer" series . . . The strong, smart protagonist is Minneapolis homicide detective Brie Beaumont. In Brie's first outing, "Rigged for Murder," she joined the crew of the *Maine Wind* to recover emotionally after her partner was shot . . . Sailors will enjoy LeClair's vivid depictions of navigation and sailing, and those who don't know a jib from a halyard get help from a glossary of sailing terms at the end of the book, [but] LeClair never lets the nautical stuff get in the way of her exciting story."

—*St. Paul Pioneer Press*

"If you love sailing, grab this title and prepare to be immersed . . . A strong sense of place and a fine little closed-room drama make this seafaring read a real pleasure."

—*Library Journal*

"Brie Beaumont is a heroine who is fun to cheer for, as she's been wounded and is working her way through her experiences to try to move forward. LeClair has an impressive knowledge of sailing, which makes for a great backdrop for a mystery. There is something compelling about the sea, particularly when it claims a murder victim. LeClair weaves a yarn that draws in the reader from the first page."

—*Midwest Book Review*

"Homicide Detective Brie Beaumont is back . . . in another top notch action adventure. LeClair combines police procedure, finely-honed investigative skills, psychological insights, and suspense . . . in this haunting story of unrequited love, deceit, and murder . . . LeClair is articulate, convincing, and involves all five senses . . . Her characters become clearly identifiable as believable . . . A creative imagination, a love for sailing, and gifted communication skills combine to make Jenifer LeClair a top notch storyteller. *Danger Sector* insures the success of the Windjammer Mystery Series and a growing fan base of readers fascinated by stories of the sea and the coastal islands of Maine."

—Reader Views

"Homicide detective Brie Beaumont and the crew of the *Maine Wind* sail to Sentinel Island, where they help repair an old lighthouse . . . After a prominent artist who lives near the lighthouse disappears, Brie's investigatory genes kick in, and she begins to nose around. The residents aren't pleased but Brie persists, digging for clues . . . The discovery of a secret journal complicates matters further, exposing a 30-year-old mystery involving the black-market art world. Will Brie wrap up the case before a nor'easter hits? Recommend this agreeable mixture of adventure and crime to fans of Chris Knopf's nautical mystery series starring Sam Acquillo."

—*Booklist*

Praise for *Rigged for Murder*

2009 Independent Publisher Award for Best Regional Fiction
2009 RebeccasReads Award for Best Mystery/Thriller

"A winning combination of psychological thriller, police procedural, and action adventure. It's a five-star launch for [LeClair's] aptly named sea-going series . . . Tightly written and intricately constructed, LeClair's *Rigged for Murder* is first-class storytelling in a setting so authentic you can hear the ocean's roar and taste the salt from the sea."

—*Mysterious Reviews*

"An engaging New England whodunit . . . Readers will believe they are sailing on the schooner and waiting out the storm at Granite Island as Jenifer LeClair vividly captures the Maine background . . . With a strong support cast including the capable crew, the battling passengers, and the eccentric islanders to add depth, fans will enjoy *Rigged for Murder*."

—*Midwest Book Review*

"Brie [Beaumont] is smart and competent, and she uses her brain and not her gun . . . Jenifer LeClair offers another appealing main character in *Rigged for Murder*, first in her Windjammer Series."

—*St. Paul Pioneer Press*

"A strong plot, non-stop action, and first-class character development combine to make this an exciting, page-turning adventure novel. Adding to the tension, intrigue and mystery is the meticulous care in researching the details and terminology of sailing, lobstering, and the Maine coastal islands and communities . . . I have added Jenifer LeClair to my list of "must read" authors."

—*Reader Views*

"A debut mystery that is so well written you will hunger for more . . . well-developed characters and superbly good writing."

—Once Upon a Crime Mystery Bookstore

"*Rigged for Murder* is an exciting mystery with a little romance thrown in. The setting for this novel is unique and gives the reader insight into life aboard a sailing ship."

—*Armchair Reviews*

"The story develops logically, with interesting twists . . . The setting and the weather are well-handled and provide strong context without obtrusiveness. The characters have depth and movement . . . LeClair gets the sea and the sailing just right."

—*Books 'n' Bytes*

"The author did a good job of hiding who the killer was . . . I recommend [Rigged for Murder] to anyone who likes mysteries and has an interest in sailing . . . This book is a great combination of the two."

—*RebeccasReads*

ALSO BY JENIFER LECLAIR

Rigged for Murder
Danger Sector

COLD COAST

The Windjammer Mystery Series

JENIFER LECLAIR

Conquill Press

This book is a work of fiction. Names, characters, places and incidents either are products of the author's imagination or are used fictitiously. Any resemblance to actual events, or to actual persons living or dead, is entirely coincidental. For information about special discounts for bulk purchases contact conquillpress@comcast.net.

COLD COAST

Conquill Press
387 Bluebird Alcove
St. Paul, MN 55125
www.conquillpress.com

Cover Design: Nicole Aimée Suek
Cover Photograph: Steven Hayes/Getty Images

Library of Congress Control Number: 2013930734

LeClair, Jenifer.
Cold Coast: a novel / by Jenifer LeClair – 1st edition

ISBN: 978-0-9800017-6-1

Printed in the United States of America

10 9 8 7 6 5 4 3 2 1

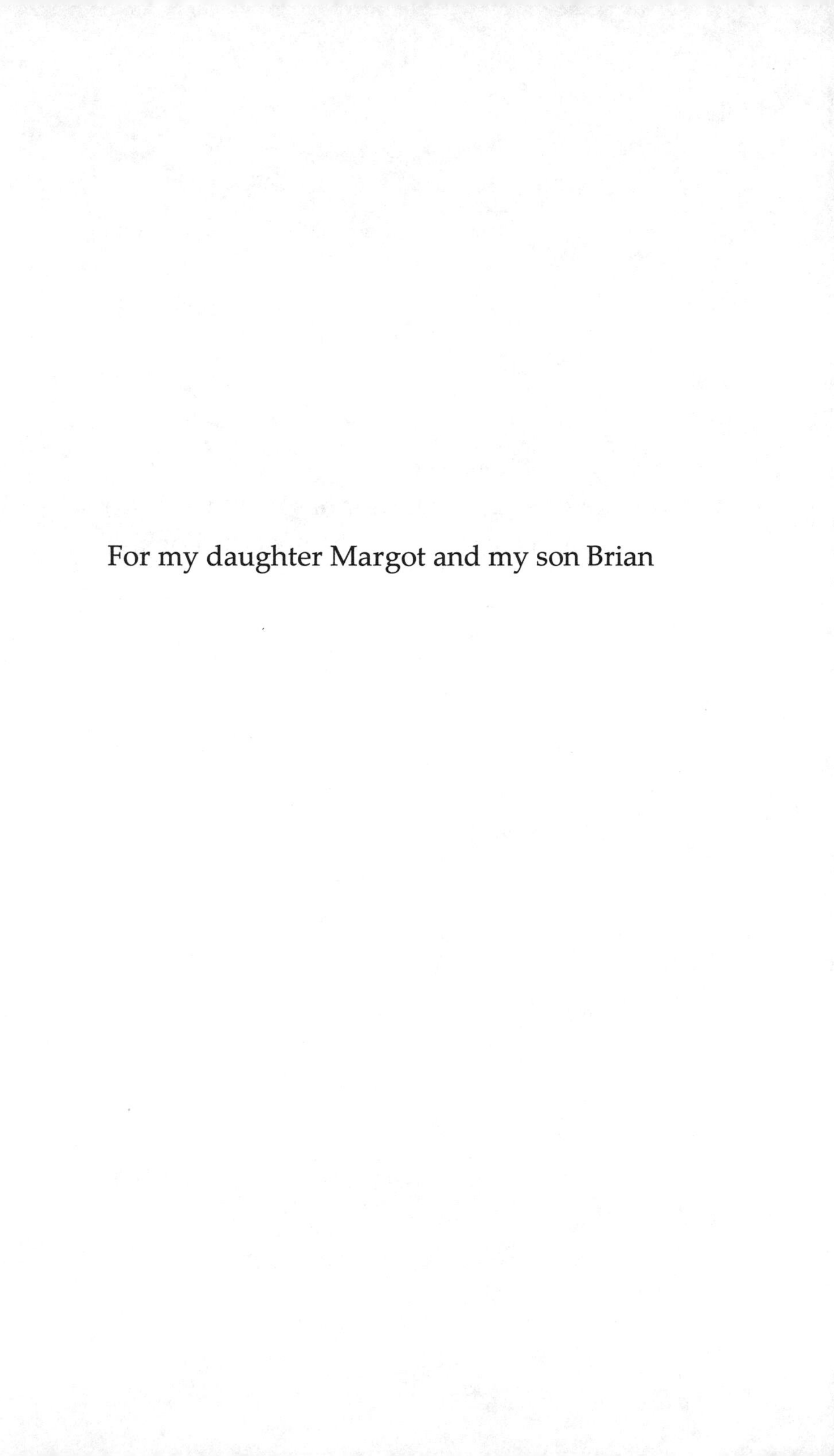

For my daughter Margot and my son Brian

For your reference, the author has included a glossary of sailing terms in the back of the book.

Out of the earth to rest and range
Perpetual in perpetual change,
The unknown passing through the strange.

—John Masefield

COLD COAST

Chapter 1

The *Maine Wind* felt its way along the coast on a heading east by northeast. Brie Beaumont zipped her jacket, turned up the collar of her wool sweater, and made her way to the bow of the ship to man the fog horn. The sun—a constant companion in the early part of the day—was now a fickle friend. They had weighed anchor in Southwest Harbor for their long day's voyage northeast along the coast to Tucker Harbor, Maine. Cadillac Mountain, the crowning glory of Acadia National Park, had worn a cap of golden light as they'd sailed beneath it and across the mouth of Frenchman Bay, where spruce-covered islands rose like green pleasure domes from the blue Atlantic.

They were now off Schoodic Point, which drifted in and out of fog like the mythical land of Brigadoon. Over the last half-hour, Brie had witnessed all the elements on display here. A large cloud would open and send a wall of rain over the point. The sun would blaze out and shoot a rainbow across the rockbound shore. Then the fog would roll back in and the dance would begin anew, as if Mother Nature couldn't decide how to attire herself.

After Bar Harbor and Acadia National Park, the last vestiges of hardcore tourism fell away. Beyond Schoodic Point, the Atlantic opened up, sheer cliffs rose from the sea, and the tides ran in and out of the Bay of Fundy with a vengeance. The Bold Coast, austere and wildly beautiful, awaited.

A few hundred yards ahead a thick fogbank rolled toward them. Brie cranked the old Lothrup foghorn and let out a long blast followed by two short blasts, the signal for a sailboat underway. She checked the second hand on her watch, cranked again, and two minutes later let out another blast—one long, two short. This scene replayed itself over and over until they sailed free of the fogbank forty minutes later.

Beyond Schoodic Point, the wind was building, stirring up the sea and hurling spindrift across the bow of the *Maine Wind*. To the northeast, a leaden sky lurked on the distant horizon, a potential omen of trouble brewing away Down East. Brie turned the phrase over in her mind as she snugged the jib sheet, ran it around the belaying pin in a figure eight, and made it off. *Down East* was an expression born in the golden age of sail when mariners would be sailing downwind, traveling east along the coast of Maine, where many of the ships' captains lived. And so, Maine came to be known as Down East.

Over the past five months, going with the wind had become a metaphor for Brie's existence. On leave from the Minneapolis Police Department Homicide Division since March, her present life aboard the schooner *Maine Wind* had everything to do with chance and the unpredictable.

She turned as first mate Scott Hogan approached.

"Brie, we need to check the reefing on the mainsail."

"Let's do it." She followed him along the starboard deck. Scott was a few inches taller than she was. He had the broad shoulders and strong build that came from hauling on sheets and halyards for a living. But he was also a fine musician and somewhat of a scholar. No surprise there. In meeting other ships' crews from around the windjammer fleet, Brie had learned they were a multi-talented, multi-faceted group of men and women who shared one commonality—a deep love of the sea.

"That must be Petit Manan Light." Brie gestured toward a low, barren island off their port bow. "John told me to watch for a tall gray lighthouse."

"That's it, all right. Second tallest light on the Maine coast," Scott said.

"I've read about the wildlife refuge there. I'd hoped we'd be sailing closer and I might see some puffins."

"Maybe the captain will take us in closer on the return trip. He's eager to get up the coast to Tucker Harbor before the weather deteriorates. He also likes to stay well south of Petit Manan Bar. The tidal currents there and the depth of the bottom can create some wicked confused seas."

The two of them climbed onto the cabin top and started checking and tightening the reefing knots along the mainsail boom.

"We sure haven't needed this reef so far," Brie said.

"I think we're about to, though." Scott nodded his head toward the east just as the rain started to fall. "And there's more wind forecast where we're heading."

The *Maine Wind* had caught the tail of a squall, and as they finished their work, a steady drizzle turned Brie's long, pale hair to dark, wet strings. She gathered them together, winding them into a knot at the nape of her neck. As soon as they finished their work, she jumped off the cabin top and headed forward to go below for her foul-weather gear.

She went down the companionway to the galley. To the right of the ladder the black cast-iron woodstove chugged out a welcome wave of heat. George Dupopolis, the ship's cook, was busy clanging pots around, getting the dinner prep started. A number of passengers were below decks staying out of the elements. They were huddled around the large table that fit the shape of the hull and were knitting, reading, and playing cards. A kerosene lantern, hung from the foremast, swung gently on its hook, keeping time with the sea.

Brie ducked behind a curtain at the back of the galley. Her berth was tucked back along the hull on the port side of the ship. A couple feet further along, she stepped through another curtain and flipped on the small battery-operated reading light next to her berth. The crew berths were tucked into odd little nooks and crannies around the ship.

She had unexpectedly become the second mate aboard the *Maine Wind* following an unfortunate occurrence on Granite Island in May. She had been sailing on the ship as a passenger, and at the end of the cruise, Captain DuLac had asked her if she would like to take over as second mate for the rest of the season. She had grown up sailing, and because she wasn't ready to return to the department, she had decided to accept his offer. She and the captain had grown close on that first voyage. Adversity has a way of bringing people together, and there had been no shortage of adversity on that trip.

Brie hoisted her sea bag onto her berth and foraged in it for a dry jacket. She ran a brush through her wet hair a few times and turned to look in the small mirror at the foot of the berth. Her face was red from the cold air, which made her blue eyes even bluer. She rubbed her face with hands that seemed to have no color at all. *Red, white, and blue,* she thought to herself. *Very patriotic.* She ran her fingers down the back of her head, making a part, worked the damp hair on each side into a braid, and secured each with a hair band. She ferreted in her sea bag again and pulled out her navy blue watch cap that bore an embroidered patch of the *Maine Wind* under sail. Even though she hailed from Minnesota, it seemed odd to be donning a stocking cap in August, but such was the climate in the North Atlantic.

She grabbed her foul-weather gear—pants and jacket—off a peg at the foot of her berth and stepped out into the galley to put them on. George had cut up a pile of beef and was now chopping a mountain of mushrooms.

"What's for dinner, George, if I might ask?" The passengers stopped what they were doing and craned their necks.

"We're having beef stroganoff tonight," he answered.

Brie heard a couple *oo's* and *ah's* from the shipmates.

"Oh, and Brie, there'll be egg noodles under the stroganoff," George said. He looked up and a smile lit his dark eyes.

George knew about her fondness for egg noodles, so he tried to work them into the fare now and then. He went back to his chopping, feet spread wide to counterbalance the motion of the ship, which was always more extreme below deck. George Dupopolis was of Greek lineage, and his curly black hair shone in the light from the lamp as he moved about his work area in the corner of the galley.

Brie climbed into her suspendered bib overalls and rain jacket and went topside. She stood at the port rail surveying the coast. They were headed for the Bay of Fundy, which boasted tidal changes as great as fifty feet—the highest tides in the world. She turned to face the wind and the sea, thrilled by the prospect of the voyage. Bound for the waters of New Brunswick and Nova Scotia to do whale watching, it was to be their longest cruise of the season—fourteen days out. And since this was the Bold Coast, or as Captain DuLac liked to call it, the Cold Coast, they had left extra days in the schedule for inclement weather that might maroon them for a day or two at anchor.

Brie turned and walked aft. The captain was at the wheel, and even though sixty feet of deck separated them, she could feel the warmth in his gaze. He wore a *Maine Wind* ball cap that concealed his dark hair but highlighted his brown eyes. Since their trip to Sentinel Island in July, things had been good between them, and even though crew protocol prohibited much contact, they had managed to find their moments.

"Hey, you," he said as she approached.

"Hey." She stood next to him at the helm for a few seconds without speaking, her five-foot-seven a good match for his six feet.

"I think we escaped the fog," he said. "Hard work at the foghorn for a while there."

"I like that old foghorn," Brie said.

"Do you. Why?"

"That sound is so much a part of the sea. Melancholy calling to emptiness. Long, low, and lonely. I know it sounds weird, but I love it."

John smiled. "It sounds like you're where you belong, Brie."

"This trip should be a real adventure." She stepped closer so they could communicate.

John slipped an arm around her waist and drew her close. "You know, I read somewhere that adventure is the result of incompetence. Maybe we should be careful what we wish for."

"Hmmm. So, unless man marches in, ill-timed and ill-prepared, we can't have one?"

"Something like that, I guess."

Brie took a step back and studied him for a second. "See now, I believe nature is the catalyst for adventure. The wind can change, the temperature can drop, a storm can blow up, or a wild animal can appear. Think Jack London."

"I am," John said. "I'm thinking about a guy building a fire under a snow-laden tree with his last match. Incompetence."

"Ahh. Or maybe the possibility of the unexpected."

"No, I think it's incompetence, or at least human error, if you feel you must give the guy the benefit of the doubt, even though he's dead. Death by stupidity."

"Such a cynic," Brie said.

"No, Brie, a realist. I sail a ship on the ocean. There are dangers. Death by stupidity is an ever present possibility."

"So, danger, or the possibility of it, goes hand in hand with adventure."

"Danger is the kissing cousin of adventure, don't you think?" He gave her a long steady look.

"An element of danger, maybe, but it differs from out and out danger." She knew about out and out danger, and she knew it had nothing to do with adventure. "Adventure is usually seen in a positive light," she said. "Out and out danger is something very different." As a cop, Brie was intimately acquainted with the difference.

"Well then, let's hope we're not in for any out and out danger this trip," John said.

"Let's hope," Brie said.

The problem with her background was that, even here in Maine, she got pulled into things, like the trouble at Granite Island, and the intrigue on Sentinel Island. It reminded her of that saying, "Everywhere you go, there you are." She took a deep breath of salt air and felt a twinge in her side from the bullet wound. Cold, damp weather sometimes made the spot ache. It was an ever present reminder of Phil's death and all that she had felt compelled to escape from back in Minnesota. In her mind, though, she was still a cop and knew she would soon have to make a decision about whether to stay in Maine or return to her former life. But for today and the next couple of months, her world was the ship, the sea, and her crewmates.

Brie saw Ed Browning heading aft. He was in his early thirties, tall and lanky with a full beard that made him look older than he was. He had served as first mate on the *Maine Wind* for five years before Scott took over the job. He had recently returned to the coast of Maine and had met with John to see if he might like an extra deckhand aboard for this cruise. John was delighted to bring him aboard, and Brie had thoroughly enjoyed hearing his stories about his time on the ship.

"Hey, Ed," John said.

"Captain. Brie. Thought I'd grab the glasses and check out Great Wass Island and Moose Peak Light." He picked up the binoculars, walked over to port, and trained them on the large island due north of their position.

Brie took the second set of glasses from the cuddy and headed over to the rail to join him. She adjusted the focus and surveyed the shoreline. Gray granite, sea-smoothed over eons of time, sloped down to the water, and tightly huddled spruce guarded the island's interior. It was so reminiscent of the north shore of Lake Superior that for a moment Brie thought she was back home sailing on the big lake.

After a few minutes, Ed walked back and put the binoculars away. "I'm relieving Scott on bow watch. Any messages for him, Captain?"

"Tell him to check below and see if George needs any help."

"Aye, Capt'n." Ed Browning headed forward along the sloping deck to the bow.

"Brie, why don't you take the helm," John said. "I need to run a plot."

Brie took the wheel, something she could never get enough of. For the next couple of hours the rain and fog came and went sporadically. She and John took turns at the helm, with the other one reading the chart, checking their position in relation to the passing islands, or running an occasional plot in order to mark their position on the chart. They carried on an easy banter, here and there laced with periods of silence—a cadence that marked their relationship, at least in Brie's mind, as an honest and comfortable one.

There was a growing sense of isolation the farther Down East they sailed. The seas were higher, the air colder, the shoreline wilder. Brie had gotten used to the mid-coast where seaside cottages and camps and small lobstering villages decorated the coastline. Charming, quaint, and picturesque were all descriptors that came to mind. But here, wildness trumped picturesque.

"This part of the coast sure has a feel to it," she said. As if timed to her words, a strong gust hit the *Maine Wind*, carrying a burst of spray with it.

"Nature unchained."

"I'll say. It'd be a great place to come to if you were flying below the radar." Brie lifted the glasses and studied the shoreline.

"You mean running away?" John asked.

Brie gave him a look, noting the irony of his comment in relation to herself—wondering if it had been intended.

"Or hiding," she said. "Looking not to be scrutinized."

"Well, going back to your flying below the radar comment, there's a rich history of smuggling along these far reaches of the coast."

"Oh, yeah? What kind of smuggling?" she asked.

"A variety of things going back to the early eighteen hundreds."

"Really?" Brie studied John's face with interest, waiting for him to elaborate. She loved all the pieces of Maine history she was acquiring from him and the crew as they plied the coastal waters, visiting new bays and islands. Bit by bit she was assembling these pieces into a sense of place to which she felt an increasing connection and attraction. She was aware that she already knew more about certain remote parts of Maine than she did about what might be their Minnesota counterparts. She found it interesting that she could have lived in a state her whole life and not have learned more about it.

"Why the far away look?" John asked.

"Just thinking about home, and how I could know more about my own state."

John was silent at that, and Brie felt the old thread of tension go taut between them. Since May, they had been feeling their way forward in a relationship fraught with uncertainty. It didn't take much to raise the specter of questions and decisions that would soon have to be addressed.

"Tell me about this smuggling," Brie said.

"Well, like I said, there's a history of smuggling along this part of the coast. It all got started back in Thomas Jefferson's time, with the Long Embargo that prohibited shipment of goods to England and France."

"So the Mainers were against the embargo?"

"Their livelihoods depended on ship building and transport of cargo by sea. Anything that hurt those industries led to hardship."

"So what did they do?"

"Found clever ways to circumvent the rules. The Mainers and the Canadians in the Maritimes were pretty much in cahoots, and a vast flour smuggling operation was born."

"You're kidding. Flour?"

"Shiploads of it. Tens of thousands of barrels came into Eastport, Maine. There were no warehouses, so they'd just drop the contraband along the shore or on forest-bound points near the border. Jefferson kept sending federal agents in an attempt to stop the smuggling. Pretty soon the woods were crawling with sentries and deputies. But the flour just kept disappearing over the border and across the bay to Canada."

"And from there it was shipped to Europe?"

"Right."

"Wild."

"The wild nature of the coastline had a lot to do with it, Brie. And the maverick character of the people."

"So how was it during Prohibition?"

"Just as crazy. Rum-running was rampant. And lots of hard-working lobstermen—well, you might say they had a day job and a different night job. Both on the water."

Brie was smiling. She studied the coastline, imagining those bygone days. The whole thing tickled her imagination. She probably shouldn't have been so entertained by it all, being law enforcement, but she knew there was a side of herself that liked to color outside the lines. She had to admire the cleverness of those colonial Mainers. And the rum-running lobstermen? That had been the problem with Prohibition. Right or not, enterprising humans had taken advantage of those opportunities.

"We're not far now," John said. "See those radio towers in the distance?" He pointed toward the coast.

Brie picked up the binoculars and focused in on them. "What are those?"

"That's the naval transmitter array near Tucker Harbor, where we're headed."

She walked to the port rail and trained the glasses on the towers. "There's a lot of them," she said. "What are they used for?"

"That antenna array is the most powerful VLF, or Very Low Frequency transmitter in the world. It's comprised of twenty-six towers and is used for communication with the North Atlantic and the Arctic oceans."

"You mean underwater communication? Like with the nuclear subs?" Brie asked.

"Exactly," John said. "It's one-way communication only —just a sending station—and the signals are encrypted, of course. The station sits on a large isolated peninsula southwest of Tucker Harbor."

"But why build it up here?"

"Well, it was constructed in 1961 during the depth of the Cold War. The installation required a lot of land right on the ocean. This part of Maine was so remote, there would have been large tracts of land still available. Also, Maine's coastal waters would have been a likely point of first contact in the U.S. for Soviet subs. But of even more importance than the transmitting station was the naval listening post at Winter Harbor. Its function was to intercept the Russians' encrypted transmissions in order to locate on and track their subs."

"How intriguing," Brie said. "Like a page out of a Clancy novel."

John reached into the cuddy for the extra glasses and trained them on the antennas. "I've heard the array can transmit as far as the Mediterranean Sea."

"So there must be a large naval base up here."

"There was, but the base closed in the late nineties. The towers are still operational and the station is manned with personnel, but transmissions are sent remotely now. I think from Virginia or maybe Pennsylvania."

"It's quite a landmark. You could take a bearing off those towers from a long way out at sea."

"Brie, not to change the subject, but would you go roust Scott? We're still quite a ways offshore, but we should be nearing our harbor in about forty-five minutes."

"And not a moment too soon." Brie pointed to the eastern sky, where a massive anvil-shaped cloudbank was making a steady advance on their position.

"I hope we get anchored before that hits," John said. "I think it's gonna be dinner in the galley tonight."

"I think you're right," Brie said.

She headed forward to find Scott. When she descended the galley companionway, she saw him helping George cut up green beans and peaches. They were sailing without a messmate this season, so Scott and Brie pitched in when needed, and sometimes the passengers even got into the act.

"Hey, Brie," George said as she came down the ladder.

"I bet those peaches are for some kind of wonderful dessert," Brie said.

"My lips are sealed," he quipped.

"So, Scott, the captain said we're within about an hour of the anchorage. We can start some prep on deck."

"I'll be up there in two shakes," Scott said as he cut the last few beans into thirds and tossed them in the bowl.

"I'll get started on the halyards."

Brie headed up the companionway and walked aft. She hoisted the throat halyard down from the rigging and began ballantining it, or coiling it into a large pile shaped like a three-leaf clover. Ballantining kept the line from fowling when the sail was lowered. When Scott came topside, he headed over to port to prep the peak halyard. They went forward and repeated the process on the foresail halyards.

After the lines were set for striking sail, they went aft to talk to the captain.

"Are you planning to lower the yawl boat, Captain, or bring 'er in under sail?" Scott asked.

"I think we'll sail her in," John said. "The harbor mouth is wide enough, and we'll have the wind pretty much dead astern as we enter the harbor. There's plenty of room farther in to make the turn upwind and drop anchor." He shifted his gaze to starboard. "I don't like the looks of that sky. We're in for a blow tonight."

"We'll be in the perfect spot for it," Scott said.

"Why's that?" Brie asked.

"Tucker Harbor's sheltered from all winds," Scott said. "With its high rocky shores and a small island at the entrance to the harbor, you can ride out just about any storm there."

"If the weather holds and we want to take the passengers ashore tonight, we can lower the longboat," Brie said.

"I think you're being an optimist," John said.

Brie knew he was right. She'd been aboard long enough to spot the signs of an impending gale. The wind marching counter-clockwise around the compass, taking on muscle, the barometer dropping, and the seas starting to roll. She looked up at the sails, her gaze travelling to the tops of the masts—a dizzying view. Occasionally the canvas would let out a loud crack, like the bed sheets of a giant snapping in the wind.

They were close-hauled now, really ripping along, and heeled enough to be taking seas through the scuppers. Brie smelled a burst of salt each time spindrift was blown off the surface of the sea and across the deck. The wind in the sails had increased to a roar. If you like a little drama at sea, you've got to get the wind up to 30 knots. They were nearly there.

They were quite a distance from shore, but the naval transmitter towers John had pointed out earlier were now off their port beam. The large peninsula the station occupied was stripped of all vegetation, and the antennas, which had to be a thousand feet high, looked as out of place on the spruce-forested Maine coast as an alien encampment might have.

"Brie, take the glasses and go forward. As we approach the entrance to the harbor, keep a lookout for red nun 2. It marks a ledge. We'll want to keep that nun to starboard as we enter the harbor. Give me a signal when you see it."

"Aye, Capt'n." Brie took the binoculars from the cuddy and headed for the bow.

Within fifteen minutes John brought the *Maine Wind* onto a westerly heading for their approach to Tucker Harbor. Ten minutes later Brie raised her left arm and pointed to port to let the captain know she'd located the nun and that they needed to steer to port to put more water between the ship and the ledge on their starboard side. Before she knew it they were entering the mouth of the harbor, with Little Beaver Island to port and red nun 2 to starboard. Ed Browning had taken up his position in the bow and was starting to unlash the starboard anchor. Scott joined him there.

"Prepare to jibe. Tell the galley," the captain called out.

Brie yelled down the companionway to George. "Prepare to jibe."

"Aye," came the reply from below decks.

"Jibe-oh!" the captain called as he spun the ship's wheel. The *Maine Wind* came up into the wind, and the main and foresail booms swung across the deck with a loud "WHOOMP" and enough force to knock off any number of heads that might have strayed carelessly into their path.

The *Maine Wind* coasted silently, gracefully to a standstill.

"Drop the hook," the captain shouted.

Scott and Ed released the quarter-ton anchor from the starboard rail. It hit the water and the massive chain thundered through the hull, following the anchor down to its sticking place. The *Maine Wind* tugged at her anchor chain, and they played out plenty of rode so there'd be no chance of dragging the anchor.

John sent word below for all hands to come topside and furl sail. Ten shipmates quickly appeared on deck, and with the help of the crew, lowered and furled the sails. Halyards were coiled, headsails were furled and lashed off, and soon things on deck were relatively shipshape.

Brie now had time to survey the harbor and the small village that sat directly astern of them. The harbor was part of a long inlet carved between granite-fringed shores. Rocky hills crowded with spruce encircled the waterway, closing it off almost completely from the sea beyond. The ebb tide had left behind a dark green tide line—a wide stripe nature painted twice daily below the granite shoreline.

She walked aft and looked toward the village. Except for the road running through the village, there was no seam between the lobsterboats in the harbor, the village docks and wharves, and the modest Cape Cod and two-story houses that huddled near the shoreline. It all existed as one cohesive picture. Well-maintained lobsterboats—clearly the pride of the community—with freshly painted hulls in a variety of colors from blues to reds to yellows played an interesting counterpoint to the weathered gray of the village docks, wharves, and storage buildings.

The surface of the harbor, broken by a slight chop, was calm compared to the seas beyond, but a low ceiling of clouds advanced toward the ship. The shore near the mouth of the harbor had turned almost black beneath the threatening sky, and Brie felt the first few drops of rain.

"Brie, we need to get the canopy up over the deck so the passengers will have a dry spot if they want to sit topside," Scott called. The three mates rigged up the heavy canvas, running it over the boom of the foremast and tying it off to the ratlines so it covered the galley companionway and the foredeck.

After they finished, Brie walked aft again. The small lobster fleet faced stiffly into the wind before the blackening sky —a platoon of floating sentries, guarding the village. Like skittish race horses, the boats tugged uneasily at their moorings, their windshields like eyes, vigilant of the gathering storm.

A sudden downburst of wind rocked the ship and ripped open the dark sky. Rain struck the wooden deck like a thousand fingers hitting a drumhead in a persistent rhythm. Brie pulled her hood up and ran for cover under the canopy. The gathering nor'easter would put an end to the usual evening activities. It had been a long day underway. She had a feeling the ship would be buttoned down soon after dinner, with crew and passengers early to bed.

George rang the brass ship's bell at seven o'clock to call everyone to dinner. The passengers and crew filed down the companionway, shed their raingear, and hung it on pegs behind the ladder. Everyone slid onto a bench behind the table, and the presence of all that humanity seated close together provided a warming comfort even before the food appeared. The thick trunk of the foremast ran through the deck overhead and down through the center of the galley. George had lit two hurricane lanterns and hung them from either side of the mast. They cast a soft golden glow on the wooden interior. It was as if George had divined the storm ahead of time. His meal was perfectly suited to the blustery weather playing out topside. He had prepared a decadently rich beef stroganoff. The gravy, thickened with sour cream, surrounded mushrooms and strips of sirloin tender enough to melt in the mouth. Brie hoped if she had to die somewhere down the line, it would be after a meal just like this.

George sent bowls of egg noodles and stroganoff down the two sides of the table and went to get the rest of the fare. The vegetable was green beans in an herb butter sauce, and he had baked loaves of sourdough bread that he placed on the table on two cutting boards.

John arrived in the galley last, carrying several bottles of wine. The passengers all applauded as he set them on the end of the table. "Oh, so this is all I have to do to gain approval," he joked as he took off his rain slicker and hung it up.

George got out the glasses, and the two of them uncorked the wine. John sat down on the end of the bench next to Brie. The wine was passed down the table and then everyone tucked in, as they liked to say in New England.

Brie took a glass of red wine. She loved the taste of wine with food, especially a good red with beef. And she liked how the names sounded when you said them—Pinot Noir, Chenin Blanc, Merlot, and Shiraz—seductive-sounding names like secrets being whispered. But sadly, wine didn't like Brie, and if she drank more than a glass, a blinding headache usually ensued. But in the spirit of camaraderie this evening, she was willing to risk it.

The shipmates lingered over their dinner, and outside, the elements roiled, powerless to affect ship or sailors, safely anchored and tucked below decks. Rain beat on the cabin top above them, and wind whistled around the shrouds and slapped the halyards against the masts. Thunder echoed down the companionways and rumbled percussively in the low-ceilinged galley. One by one passengers and crew finished dinner and leaned back. Conversation picked up, and George rose to make coffee.

"I got the weather report just before dinner," John said. "Usually a nor'easter like this will hang in for a few days, but this is a fast-moving front. It's predicted to clear out by early morning." He looked around the table. "I think we'll wait till noon to get underway, though. The seas will still be rough out beyond thc harbor."

"If it stops raining by morning, Scott and I can take the longboat ashore," Brie said. "Any of you who want to row in with us can take a hike or walk around the village."

"There's a trail that goes out to the end of Heron Head," Scott said. "It's a nice hike and just a short ways from the west end of the village."

"I'm game for that," Hurley Hampden said enthusiastically. Hurley was a round little man in his mid-forties who wore sandals with wool socks and wide-brimmed hats. He worked as an accountant in Hartford, Connecticut. John had told Brie that he was a regular on the *Maine Wind* every season. He had already surprised Brie by taking the head of the line on one of the halyards when they raised sail. The farther forward on the line, the heavier the work. Hurley wouldn't have been Brie's first choice for head of the line, but he handled it like a champ, teaching her once again never to presume.

"Well, that's one oarsman for the longboat," Scott said. Several other folks spoke up and said they'd like to go ashore if the rain stopped by morning. But just then the group was distracted by George opening the door on Old Faithful. The aroma of warm fruit and pastry dough filled the galley as George carried a bubbling peach cobbler over to the end of the table and set it on a board.

"George, you delightful scoundrel," John said.

Brie knew John loved a good dessert as much as most guys. And like all of George's fare, his desserts were more than just good. On every cruise he delighted passengers with a surprising diversity of pies, cobblers, coffeecakes, muffins, scones, and cookies. Whether the woodstove added its own bit of magic, as George claimed, or he was simply a chef extraordinaire, as Brie suspected, George Dupopolis did not disappoint.

George scooped the cobbler into bowls and topped them with vanilla ice cream that the passengers had taken turns hand-cranking in the afternoon. Down the table the bowls went along with mugs of hot coffee that John poured out. There was no weather that could break the post-cobbler euphoria. Brie knew that George was John's most valuable asset aboard the *Maine Wind.*

After dinner John got out a small green volume that she immediately recognized. On stormy nights he sometimes read from *Cold as a Dog and the Wind Northeast,* a salty little collection of ballads written by Ruth Moore, a 20th century Maine writer. John started with one of the longer ballads, titled "The Night Charlie Tended Weir," about a herring fisherman who, a little too into his cups one night, has a falling out with a sea serpent and a mermaid.

When the captain finished reading, Scott brought out his guitar and, to carry out the evening's theme, played a collection of maritime folksongs and ballads about following the sea—an expression that meant making one's living at sea, he told them.

At nine o'clock Brie donned her raingear and went topside to take the first watch. John always set deck watch when they were anchored in a harbor with passengers aboard. By nine-thirty the last of the passengers filed up from the galley and headed for their cabins in the amidships or stern compartments. Scott and Ed took to their berths to get some sleep before their watches, and John stayed below with George to help him finish up in the galley. Brie could hear them joking around as they made the coffee for the watch. Later, John spent an hour with her on deck talking about the trip before he turned in. The last hour she was by herself, but the *Maine Wind,* with her wood deck, masts, and hull, creaked and groaned so much Brie felt like she had a companion. Had the old ship been a living, breathing entity, her feelings for it could not have been stronger. When she'd come aboard three months ago, her life had been a storm-tossed sea, and the ship had immediately felt like a safe haven.

She looked toward the shore, now shrouded in darkness, and felt the isolation of this part of the coast. The fog horn on Little Beaver Island wailed its solemn warning. Here and there a light in the village glowed too dimly to penetrate the rain and fog. Brie took another turn around the deck, eager for the warmth of her berth and the shelter of sleep.

Chapter 2

Jake Maloney stood at his window listening to the lobsterboats rumble to life and one by one ghost out of the harbor in the dark. When the call came, he slid out the door and took the back way through the village to Tara's place. The predawn darkness felt like a shroud for his shame, but he couldn't stop himself. It had been four months since their last time together. Nancy was almost never gone overnight, and Steve never went anywhere except out to sea every day at four a.m. to haul his lobster pots. A job he returned from by mid-afternoon. Tucker Harbor, like any other Maine lobstering village, was buttoned down and sleeping by eight o'clock at night.

When Jake got to the highway, he crossed it and walked down the hill. He cut behind several properties and made his way to Tara's back door. She was waiting for him, wearing nothing but a sexy bra and panties and a pair of spike heels—something it was hard to find a use for in Tucker Harbor. He decided this was the perfect use for them. Tara led him to the bedroom while he enjoyed the view. She was voluptuous and totally unashamed of it, and for some reason that turned him on. She shut the bedroom door, undressed him, and playfully pushed him onto the bed. Then she climbed on top of him and started to work her magic.

* * * *

Jake woke with a start and looked over at his lover. Tara was sound asleep. He lifted his watch off the bedside table. Seven-fifteen. He'd been there almost three hours. He slid silently from her bed and stood there for a moment, wanting to kiss her goodbye, but not wanting to wake her. He knew she would want to talk, but he just couldn't talk about any of it. He walked quietly through the house and slipped out the back door.

It was an unusually dark morning, the clouds overhead thick as porridge. A day as colorless as his mood. Fog crawled up the shore and into the village, swallowing a house here or there before moving on. Jake didn't want to go home to his empty house, where he would be forced to reflect on his failures. Instead he headed around the curve of the highway and down past the village docks where the lobsterboats pulled up to unload their crates at the end of the day. A large schooner cloaked in fog lay at anchor in the harbor. Tucker Harbor was a little off the beaten path for the Maine windjammers, but occasionally one of them made it this far Down East.

He passed a row of abandoned shops. The structures were vacant and starting to decay from the relentless weathering of the salt air. After the Navy base closed down in the '90s, Tucker Harbor's handful of shops, restaurants, and inns had folded. Except for Varney's Diner, the Whale Spout Inn, and a few support services—library, post office, general store—the only industry here was lobstering.

Being a truck driver, Jake had always felt on the outside of things, out of sync with the rest of the village, out of sync with the lobstermen who were all comrades in fishing. At least he didn't have to feel guilty about sleeping with a friend's wife, since he and Steve French had no commerce with each other.

Jake followed the road along the fogbound harbor to the other side of the village. He stood for a moment debating and then continued a ways further on the highway, turned left, and headed down Final Reckoning Road. He shook his head.

What a ridiculous name. He was sure there was a story behind the name, but he had never bothered to find out what it was. He increased his pace as he neared the end of the road. He thought about the rough trail that ran through a dwarf spruce forest all the way out to the end of Heron Head. Generally, he didn't like hiking and he didn't like being in the woods. But one day, after being with Tara, he had walked all the way out to the end of the trail and had found he liked the peace of the spot.

He left the road and climbed toward the trailhead, wanting the closeness of the forest around him. It wasn't any failing in Nancy that had driven him toward Tara, but a feeling of desperation and futility. For three years, as his transport business fell off, money had become more and more of a problem. Then a few months ago he had finally gotten a break. But he should have been more careful at the outset. Now he wasn't sure what he'd become involved in. There were some questions he needed to get answered.

He kept on going up the trail, thinking about his situation. He planned to contact the transport companies next week, see if he couldn't pick up some other work . . . Jake stopped. He thought he heard a sound. He turned and tried to stare through the thick fog that now obliterated both the village and the trail behind him. Probably a deer.

He pressed on up the trail, replaying his lovemaking with Tara again and again in his mind, savoring every remembered touch, smell, and feeling. He knew he was treading on dangerous ground, that sooner or later their affair would be discovered. In a village the size of Tucker Harbor, he was amazed they hadn't been found out already, and he knew that was part of the thrill. He knew if he'd lived with Tara instead of Nancy all these years that Nancy might be the one he'd be cheating with. He wondered why he couldn't just be satisfied—why some people just can't be satisfied.

The trail was climbing now, and Jake looked down as he went, focusing on his footing. The path was all roots and rocks. It would be easy to trip and fall. He stopped when he heard a rock slide down the embankment near him and splash into the water. He held his breath for a moment, listening, feeling oddly vulnerable in the tight cocoon of fog that surrounded him. It was an unfamiliar feeling, and after a moment he laughed at himself. He was a powerful man. Shadows didn't scare him. His mind must be playing tricks on him. He was thinking about being caught with Tara, and that had translated into thinking someone was following him. "Hah," he scoffed at himself and continued up the trail.

With his physical strength Jake, had always felt immune to fear of his fellow man. Unconsciously, he tightened his fists at his sides, flexing his biceps as he slogged along. But the presence of the fog was starting to irritate him. He couldn't see anything around him, and he wouldn't be able to see anything when he got to the end of the headland. Why had he come out here, anyway? *Why am I always making stupid choices?* But then he thought about Tara again, about the feel of her hair and her skin. About how her breasts looked as she moved her hips up and down on top of him in a more and more urgent rhythm.

Suddenly tears came to his eyes. He wasn't sure why. He felt confused, angry. And he hated the fog. It was claustrophobic. He flailed his arms at it like it was a swarm of gnats he could shoo away. He broke into a run, stumbling up the rough trail. Spruce boughs that overgrew the path emerged without warning from the fog, tearing at his hands and arms and face. Everywhere slender roots broke the ground like bony fingers clutching at him, grabbing his feet, tripping him. He finally stopped to catch his breath, his face sheened with tears, his body with sweat. Something was wrong. He knew it now.

What Jake Maloney didn't know was that his moment to act, his chance at defense, had already passed. An arm like an iron bar locked onto him from behind, and a blinding flash of white-hot pain sliced across his throat. He dropped to his knees, saw the blood squirting out and put his hands to his neck to stop it. As his face hit the cool damp ground, he had one moment of regret before everything went black.

Chapter 3

The day rose cold and gray as a corpse. At six o'clock Brie crawled out of her berth, dressed quickly in the chill air, and crept up the companionway to the deck. The *Maine Wind* was locked in an impenetrable fog. It was as if their world now consisted of the ship alone, and nothing existed beyond it. Even the blasts from the fog horn at the entrance to the harbor seemed oddly distant. So detached was the feeling that they could have been in Tucker Harbor or on an alien world comprised solely of dense fog and water.

She saw George heading forward with his arms full of wood for the stove.

"Hey, George, need some help?" she asked as he came up to her.

"No, this is my last load. I'll have the stove chugging and the coffee going in a few minutes. The captain gave me a little reprieve this morning, so I got up a half-hour later than usual."

"No reason not to. We're not going anywhere in this." Brie waved an arm at the nonexistent world beyond the rail.

George started down the ladder to the galley with his load of wood, and Brie followed behind. She ducked into her quarters, grabbed her toiletries bag, and went to use the head in the amidships compartment. When she came topside, Scott and Ed were there getting out the buckets and mops to swab the deck, and Brie headed over to help out. Washing down the deck with salt water was a regular morning ritual. It kept the deck clean, added traction, and caused the boards to swell, keeping the deck tight.

"Ed and I can get this, Brie, if you want to help George in the galley."

"Fine by me," Brie said and headed forward. With Ed aboard this trip, the crew duties could be rearranged a little, and she knew George always welcomed her help in the galley. She descended the ladder. "We've got one too many swabbies on this trip, George, so I get to help out down here."

"Great," George said. "Let's get started."

She put her toiletries away and came back out to the galley, carrying a wool sweater that she pulled on. "Need an extra layer until the stove gets going," she said.

"We'll have coffee soon. That'll warm you up. I'm making corn beef hash and scrambled eggs for breakfast, so we need to peel and slice these potatoes and chunk up the cooked corn beef."

They waded into the large pile of potatoes George had out, and in a half hour the job was done and the coffee was brewed. They each got a cup o' joe, and Brie started cutting up the corn beef while George cracked the eggs into a large bowl. Then George prepped the corn beef hash on top of the stove, put it into two large baking pans, and slid them into the oven.

"Next course, something yummy," George said.

Brie rubbed her hands together in anticipation. "Okay, George, don't keep a girl guessing."

"All right then, how about blueberry muffins?"

"Yes." Brie pumped a fist.

George put the fresh blueberries in a pot on the stove. "Add a couple large spoons of sugar to that, Brie, and let them cook down a bit." He got going on the batter, and in no time the muffins were heading into the woodstove.

By half past seven the passengers were coming on deck. Brie took a tray of mugs and a pot of coffee topside for them. She returned to the galley and got the table set while George started scrambling the eggs in batches. On a nice day they'd have been eating topside, but it was cold and dank this morning, and Brie knew the passengers would welcome the warmth of the galley.

At eight o'clock, Brie went topside and rang the ship's bell for breakfast. Before long, everyone was seated below decks in the galley, and George was sending steaming platters of corn beef hash and scrambled eggs down the table. He set two bowls of fruit containing bananas, peaches, blueberries, and raspberries on the table, and passed around baskets of warm blueberry muffins.

George's breakfast created such a sunny mood that when Brie looked up the companionway, she saw blue sky breaking out of the fog.

"I guess we can lower the longboat after all, if anyone wants to go ashore," the captain said. There were some takers, and he told Brie and Scott to prepare to take the group ashore. He kept Ed aboard to help him get ready to raise anchor later in the morning.

Brie and Scott lowered the longboat, taking care not to let it swing into the hull of the *Maine Wind*. They put the boarding ladder over the starboard side, and Scott went down and got the oars set up. Brie went below to grab her camera, and in ten minutes, the passengers who were going ashore were on deck ready to load up. One by one they climbed down to the longboat and took their seats. There were eight oars, and counting Brie and Scott, there were eight oarsmen. They pushed off, and in unison pulled for shore. Fog still cloaked the shoreline out near the entrance to the harbor, and the foghorn still broadcast its melancholy warning, but the village was completely visible now.

There was a spot along the shore where they could land, and within a few minutes the boat struck sand. Brie was in the bow, and she hopped overboard. Scott made his way forward, stepping on the thwarts, and jumped out. He and Brie pulled the boat a bit farther up onto the beach and helped the passengers climb ashore. Brie snapped a few pictures of the harbor and the *Maine Wind* lying at anchor and then slung her camera over her shoulder.

Two of the passengers, the Rileys, a married couple in their late forties, decided they'd walk around the village. The other four passengers said they'd like to take the trail out to Heron Head with Brie and Scott. So the group split up. Scott checked his watch. It was just past nine o'clock, and he told the Rileys to be back at the longboat in an hour or so to head back to the ship.

They had landed the longboat near the edge of the village, so the trail hikers didn't have far to go to pick up the road that ran out toward the trailhead. As soon as they came to the junction, Hurley Hampton pointed to the street sign. "Hope you've all got your affairs in order," he said. "We're headed down Final Reckoning Road."

"What lugubrious type came up with that?" Scott asked. He pointed to the lone house along the road. "Doesn't really encourage a rush for development, now does it?"

Final Reckoning Road dead-ended in about a quarter of a mile, and the group climbed up a small embankment to the trailhead. There was a marker carved on a piece of wood that gave the length of the trail—three quarters of a mile—and asked hikers to be respectful of the fragile habitat along the trail. Hurley took the lead, followed by Judy Corbett, a writer for an outdoor magazine who was on an assignment to do an article on the Maine windjammers. Next came her friend Sarah, a nature photographer. Hurley's friend Dan was next in line, and finally, Brie and Scott brought up the rear. Brie took her camera off her shoulder and caught a shot of the group as they wound up the trail into the spruce forest.

She surveyed her surroundings as they followed the trail upward. Except for an occasional cedar tree, the vegetation ran to spruce that was stunted in size. "This reminds me of the dwarf forests on some of the headlands along the far north shore of Lake Superior, where I've done a lot of hiking," Brie said.

"The islands and coastal areas used to have a much more varied habitat before all the virgin timber was logged off back in the eighteen hundreds," Scott said. "When the land was stripped bare, it destroyed the microclimate. After that, nothing but the hardiest species could grow. Spruce became the dominant forest in those decimated areas. They were the only trees that could survive the harsh conditions of cold and continual salt spray."

"Interesting but sad," Brie said.

"On lots of smaller islands the forests are gone for good," he said. "Except for low ground cover, nothing grows."

"That's not unlike Minnesota's history. The virgin forests were white pine. Now they're largely balsam and jack pine. Whatever conditions the white pine needed to regenerate were destroyed by the logging."

They continued up the trail in silence. Droplets of water, remnants of the morning fog, beaded the spruce boughs, and spider webs near the ground glistened with micro-droplets. The trail was rocky and root-woven. Except for an occasional wave lapping the shore or a distant gull's call, the forest was quiet as a graveyard—no squirrels chattering, no birds chirping—just muffled silence. The pungent smell of spruce, mixed with the salty tang of the ocean, filled the air and Brie's senses. She breathed deeply, enjoying the sensory experience of the hike.

The farther the group progressed out the headland, the more visibility became an issue. The fog played hide and seek in the forest, hiding the trail, making them seek it. Their pace slowed a bit as they picked their way along, gradually climbing higher.

"Hopefully we'll have time to make it to the end," Brie said to Scott.

"I don't think there'll be much to see even if . . ."

"Ahhhh!" Hurley's terrified cry came from the front of the line.

"Oh my God," Judy screamed. "Oh my God!"

Brie knew a cry of fear when she heard one. She pushed past the hikers, rushing toward the front of the group where Hurley stood frozen, staring at the ground. Brie made her way up to him. The body of a man lay in the prone position at Hurley's feet, blocking the trail. The dead man's face was pale as the underside of a halibut, and one dull, glazed eye stared fixedly into the forest beyond the trail. The man's throat had been cut from ear to ear, so deeply that the head lay at an odd angle to the neck below the wound.

"What do we do?" Hurley's voice had moved to a higher range. "We need to get help."

"I need to ask everyone to just stay very still for a second," Brie said, looking from one to the other of the four passengers. "Okay, now before anyone moves, could you all look down at the ground around you. See if you see anything unusual, anything that seems suspicious—that looks like it doesn't belong in the forest. I know you are all upset, but please look carefully before you move." It was all she could do at this point to preserve a death scene that had already been trampled. Everyone obediently looked down and around for a few moments but no one noticed anything.

"All right. Does anyone have a cell phone on them?" Brie asked. But, as she suspected, everyone had left them aboard the ship. "Scott, I'm going to stay here. You need to go down to the village and call 911. Give them the location of the body." The passengers were looking at her quizzically. Brie sighed and looked from one to the other of them. "Until this spring, when I came to Maine, I was a homicide detective for the Minneapolis Police Department."

They looked at Scott for confirmation.

"It's true," Scott said. "And since she's only out here on leave, she still is a homicide detective."

They looked back at Brie, waiting for instructions.

"You all need to be very careful and observant going down the trail. If you see anything, anything at all that you think might be evidence, don't step on it, and please don't touch it." With that caveat, they turned and followed Scott slowly down the trail.

Brie knew she would have a few minutes to study the scene before the craziness began. And while she had no jurisdiction here and would not be involved in any unfolding investigation, she couldn't help observing and analyzing what she was sure was a crime scene. There was no doubt in her mind that this was a homicide. Had it been a suicide, the knife would be present somewhere near the body. She squatted down next to the body and touched the man's bare arm. The body was cool, but rigor had not begun to set in. There were no animal marks or bites. She guessed the murder had taken place within the past two to three hours. It would have been daylight, although the heavy fog earlier in the morning would have reduced visibility out here to near zero.

Because the victim was lying face down, there was no way to inspect the wound on his neck to tell if it was angled, which might indicate whether the perp was right or left-handed, or to see if there were any hesitation marks. The cut was clean, not jagged, which indicated that a smooth-bladed knife or razor blade had been used, and probably a very sharp one, judging by the depth of the wound. There was dried blood between the man's fingers. Brie guessed he had brought his hands to his throat to try and stanch the flow of blood before he passed out.

There were no defensive wounds on the backs of the man's hands or arms. Without turning the body, she couldn't see if there were defensive wounds on the palms of his hands or forearms. But she suspected he had been taken by surprise and attacked from behind. The victim was a good-sized guy—not overly tall, but muscular. Someone knew what they were doing here, she thought. When the killer uses a knife, there is often some kind of violent emotion involved, and often there are multiple stabbings. This murder was precise and calculated—almost surgical. She wondered if the killer might be ex-military. Few people were capable of killing in this fashion. One of the advantages—knives are silent, no gunshot to attract attention or be heard by someone in the village.

Brie stood up and looked carefully around the ground. There were no signs of a struggle, and unfortunately, since the trail was such a network of roots and granite, the chance of finding shoe impressions was greatly reduced. She looked at the alignment of the body and walked off the trail to where she thought the assailant might have stood. She looked around carefully and now saw blood castoff from the knife on the surrounding foliage. She took her Nikon off her shoulder and snapped a number of close-ups of the body from different angles, and then rotated the lens back in for some wide-angle shots of the broader scene. She could hear multiple sirens in the distance now, which meant the 911 call had gone through. She knew several law enforcement agencies would be responding. It was about to get very busy in these woods. She took one last look at the victim and headed down the trail to meet the responders.

A Washington County Sheriff's patrol was the first to arrive, followed closely by two Maine State Police troopers in their sky blue cruisers.

"I'm Brie Beaumont." Brie held out her hand as the officer from the sheriff's department came up to her.

"Sergeant Jeff Starkey," he said, extending his hand. "You the one who found the body?"

"It was a group of us, actually, from the schooner *Maine Wind*. We anchored in the harbor last night." Starkey had pulled out his notebook and started scribbling. "I'm in Maine for the summer on leave from the Minneapolis Police Department Homicide Unit." Brie tried to state it as if it were the most normal thing in the world, but Starkey's head came up suddenly, and he studied her like she might be making a joke.

"Do you want to wait till the ME and the crime lab folks arrive or head up the trail to the scene?"

If he had any doubts, her question seemed to dispel some of them. "I think we should wait for the crime lab guys."

"Good idea," Brie said. She didn't want to be making suggestions, but if the first responders had been intent on trampling the crime scene some more, she might have tried to dissuade them.

"The ME radioed in when the call went out. He was about twenty minutes away, so he should be here shortly," Starkey said.

At the sound of the sirens, a number of Tucker Harbor residents had started down Final Reckoning Road to see what was going on. The Maine state troopers had strung crime scene tape across the trailhead and now went forward to meet the villagers and keep them at bay.

The medical examiner pulled up. He got out with his kit and headed toward Sergeant Starkey. Brie placed him at mid-forties. He was about five-foot-ten, handsome, and unmistakably Native American. His hair was black as a crow's back, and he wore it in a braid that hung to his shoulder blades.

"Dr. Wolf," Starkey said as he approached.

"Sergeant Starkey."

"This is Brie Beaumont, Doc. She was with the group that found the victim. She's in Maine this summer on leave from the Minneapolis Police Department Homicide Unit."

Wolf extended his hand. "Pleased to meet you, Brie."

"Dr. Wolf," Brie said, shaking his hand.

"Call me Joe. So, what have we got here?"

"The victim's up the trail about half a mile. Throat's been cut. My guess is he's been dead two, maybe three hours."

"Let's head up there," Wolf said. "The Evidence Response Team should be here soon. Sergeant, would you stay here and direct them up the trail when they arrive?"

"Will do," Starkey said.

With that Brie led the way up the trail with Joe Wolf following behind. They climbed in silence for a few minutes. Finally, Wolf broke the silence.

"So, tell me what brought you to Maine, Brie. Sergeant Starkey said you were with the Minneapolis PD."

"I was shot in the line of duty, and my partner was killed."

"Ahh. I'm very sorry," Joe said.

"I struggled with Post-traumatic Stress Disorder for a year after being shot. I've had a particularly difficult time with it. Ultimately, I took a leave and came east to try and get my head straight."

"But why Maine?"

"My dad was a Mainer, so I spent a lot of time here as a child. Since being back, I've decided that putting some geographic distance between me and my problems was a good thing. Living among strangers, well, there's an anonymity to it. And the sea's a wondrous thing. Very healing."

"I can understand that. I'm from the Penobscot Nation—the Native Americans have a tradition of using solitude and the natural world to deal with loss."

Brie turned and nodded. "That's it, I think. It's about the solitude. When you're out on the ocean, you're in a world apart, and that world is a balm for the spirit. It's almost as if earthbound problems can't jump that gap."

"You speak poetically about it. I like that," Joe said.

"My dad was a sailor. I think it's in my blood."

Within ten minutes they came around a bend in the trail and saw the body up ahead. Joe Wolf swung into his ME mode, making sure the body was just as they had found it.

"COD appears obvious." He bent low and looked at the wound. "The carotid artery was severed. He would have bled out in minutes and probably lost consciousness very quickly." He was still squatting down, looking over the body and recording his observations in a small hand-held recorder, when the Evidence Response Team from the Maine State Police arrived and began photographing and processing the scene. The investigator in charge set up a zone search and assigned each member of the team to a sector.

Brie stood off to one side, watching them work, feeling like she'd slipped through a wormhole and was suddenly back in Minnesota in the midst of a crime scene. From her vantage point, she had a view down the trail, and within fifteen minutes she saw a familiar figure climbing toward her. She'd met Maine State Police Detective Dent Fenton on Sentinel Island in July, when she became involved in a missing person's case there while she and the crew were visiting John's friend Ben on that island. Detective Fenton was about six feet tall and well put together. A prominent brow bone added a bit of drama to his intelligent face. There was a vitality about him that suggested he took good care of himself and that stamina would never be an issue. Brie recalled that he had intensely blue eyes.

Dent Fenton surveyed the activity as he approached the crime scene, and before long, he spotted her and waved. Brie moved toward him and now noticed he was followed by another detective she had met named Martin Dupuis.

"Brie Beaumont. Well, I'll be," Fenton said as he approached. "I heard a group off a ship had discovered the body."

"Hi, Detective Fenton. Good to see you again. Bad circumstances, of course."

They shook hands. "Call me Dent," he said to her. "I think you've met Marty Dupuis here."

"Detective Dupuis," Brie said, extending a hand.

"Good to see you again, Brie."

Marty Dupuis was quite a bit shorter than Dent. He had black hair and a mustache and a powerful build. For some reason he reminded Brie of a small piece of earth-moving equipment. She had met him when she'd visited the Maine State Police headquarters to file a report after the goings-on on Granite Island in May.

"You keep finding crimes for us," Fenton said. "We need to give you some kind of honorary designation."

"How about Detective Stumbles-on-Stuff-She-Wishes-She-Hadn't?" Brie said.

Dent laughed, and his blue eyes sparkled like sunlight hitting a glacier. "Despite all the ugliness I see, I still like to believe things happen for a reason, Brie."

She shrugged noncommittally, but his words hit home.

He walked over to the body. "So, what have we got here, Joe?" he asked the ME.

"Hello, Dent," Joe Wolf said. "Well, the victim's throat was cut. No weapon so far, which would rule out suicide. Looks like the vic was attacked from behind." Wolf looked up. "No signs of struggle. It happened fast."

"Killer knew what he was doing," Fenton said, squatting down next to Joe to study the victim.

The body had been turned over, and Wolf continued recording his observations while the crime lab photographer snapped more shots of the victim face up.

"Any guess on time of death?" Dent asked the ME.

"Two, maybe three hours. Although the cool temps would keep rigor at bay longer."

"What were conditions like out here this morning?" Fenton looked up at Brie.

"Pea soup fog," she said. "Out on this point the visibility would have been almost nil."

"Killer used that to his advantage, I bet," Detective Dupuis remarked.

"Yup," Brie said.

Dent Fenton stood up.

"We're ready to bag the body," Wolf said. He called over two men from the Evidence Response Team.

"I'll wait for your ruling, Doc," Dent said.

Joe Wolf nodded. "I'll be doing the autopsy today. I'd say all the evidence points to homicide." He turned to Brie. "Nice meeting you, Brie."

"Nice meeting you, too, Joe," she said.

"Marty, go with them and see if any of the townsfolk down at the foot of the trail know who this guy is," Fenton said.

"Yes sir, Lieutenant," Marty said. He turned and followed Joe Wolf down the trail.

Dent turned to Brie. "Could I talk to you for a minute?" he asked, drawing her off to the side of the activity.

"Sure," Brie said. "Say, Marty called you 'Lieutenant.' Did you receive a promotion?"

"Just a few weeks ago," Dent said.

"Congratulations."

"Thanks," Dent said, but Brie sensed he was uncomfortable with the praise. This guy was not about bravado. It was one of the reasons she liked him and had felt comfortable working with him during their brief contact over the case on Sentinel Island.

They walked down the trail a bit out of earshot of the Evidence Response Team. "I'll come right to the point," Dent said. "Would you have any interest in working this case with us, Brie?" Before she could respond, he continued. "You'd have official status. I'd see about having you deputized."

"But why?" Brie asked. "Don't you have plenty of detectives?"

"Actually, we're stretched really thin right now. Our division, CID II, covers a lot of territory—Maine's eleven northeastern counties—with our eighteen detectives. At the best of times we're stretched pretty thin, but this month there've been a string of homicides in Washington, Penobscot, and Aroostook counties." He paused and studied her for a moment. "But beyond that, I think you're a heck of a detective. That case out on Sentinel Island might easily have gone cold without your investigation. What's more, I have a funny feeling about this case."

"Why?" Brie asked.

"I'm not sure. Just a gut feeling that this might be a tough one."

Brie was silent for a moment. She knew that feeling. Sometimes, before you even start into an investigation, you have a sense about it. There's no way to explain it to someone outside the profession.

"I have a job, though, aboard the *Maine Wind*. I'm the second mate. So, even if I wanted to work the case, I'd have to leave my job . . ." Brie paused mid-sentence. She suddenly remembered that they had an extra deckhand aboard this trip. Theoretically, Ed Browning would be able to step in for her.

"What is it?" Fenton asked. "You seem to be having a thought."

"This guy that served as the first mate for a number of seasons is aboard this trip. I guess I could ask Captain DuLac if he could fill in for me."

"I don't want to jeopardize your place on the crew, Brie, but working this case with us would give you an insider look at the Maine State Police. When we met on Sentinel Island, it seemed like you weren't sure whether or not you were returning to your job at the Minneapolis PD."

"It's true. I haven't made that decision yet. I took a leave, and the clock doesn't run out until October."

"Working with us on this case would give you a chance to explore an alternative."

"I know from our contact on the missing person's case on Sentinel Island that I'd feel comfortable working with you," Brie said. "And Marty—Detective Dupuis—is a great guy, too."

She looked up at the sky for a moment. She knew John wouldn't like it, but she also knew he probably wouldn't stand in her way. She had looked forward to this long cruise aboard the *Maine Wind*, but here was a hand-engraved invitation to explore a possible career option—one that might make her decision in October easier.

"Let me talk to the captain," she said. "The ship is supposed to get underway this afternoon, so I'll have an answer for you fairly quickly. You would need to clear it with the Minneapolis Police Department."

"Of course," Fenton said. "I'll talk to them right away."

"Lt. Frank Henderson is my boss in the homicide unit."

Dent Fenton wrote the name in his small notebook and gave Brie a card with his number on it. "We should head back down and see what Marty found out from the townspeople. See if anyone knew the victim."

With that they started down the trail. Brie wondered what she was about to get involved in. The thought of the investigation intrigued her, as it always did. Somehow, she was hardwired to be a detective. But there was an accompanying uneasiness in her. She looked out at the ship in the harbor and then around her at the cool, green anonymity of the forest, feeling the remoteness of this place. She felt safe aboard the *Maine Wind*. But here, there would be no safety net. She'd be subject to all the dangers attendant with tracking down a killer. She knew that territory, that landscape. It was unforgiving of mistakes.

Chapter 4

Within fifteen minutes Brie and Dent Fenton emerged from the spruce forest and walked down the embankment to the small parking lot. Two more sheriffs' cars were there and another Maine State Police trooper. There were about thirty or forty residents of Tucker Harbor milling around. They were mostly women, children, and seniors since the men were all out on their lobsterboats at this time of day. The expressions of the villagers ranged from horrified and distressed to mildly elated. The latter group undoubtedly liked a little drama in their lives. Brie wanted to tell them they didn't want this kind of drama.

Dent Fenton gestured across the parking lot. "There's Marty talking to one of the troopers," he said. "Let's see if he got a name on the victim."

They headed toward Detective Dupuis, and when he saw them coming, he stepped away from the trooper. "I got a name on the vic," he said. "A couple of the older guys here, with strong stomachs, identified him from the crime scene photos the ERT guys took. His name's Jake Maloney. He lives in the village here. Works as a trucker."

"Next of kin?" Dent asked.

"His wife's name is Nancy. A neighbor of the Maloneys said she went to visit a friend yesterday morning. I sent a trooper up to the house, but no one's home."

"Can you point out the neighbor you talked to?" Dent said. Dupuis turned and motioned toward a thin middle-aged woman a few yards from them.

"Lieutenant," Brie said, "I'd like to get back to the ship and talk to the captain if you don't need me here."

Dent took her by the elbow, and they stepped away from Marty Dupuis. "That's fine, Brie. I'll talk to the victim's neighbor and see what I can find out and fill you in later if you decide to come on board."

"The *Maine Wind* is slated to weigh anchor around noon, so you won't have to wait long for an answer."

"Thanks, Brie. I'll talk to you soon."

Brie headed back along the road to the village. She was glad Dent Fenton hadn't pressed the issue when they signed off. There was an aura of extreme professionalism about him that she liked. But she sensed that businesslike attitude was coupled with a deep humanity, the kind that grows strong in good cops.

She checked her watch as she walked back to the village where they'd beached the longboat. It was eleven-twenty. They'd come ashore a little after nine, with the intent of staying about an hour. That hour had stretched to more than two. As she came down the hill toward the water, she saw Scott waiting for her with *Tango,* the ship's small dory.

"What happened to the longboat and the passengers?" she asked.

"People wanted to go back to the ship, so we rowed back. Ed helped me haul up the longboat and lower the dory so I could come back for you. He's busy helping the captain get ready to weigh anchor."

"What time does the captain plan to get underway?" Brie asked.

"I think about half past twelve if possible. Quite a kettle of fish, eh?" Scott nodded toward Heron Head where they had found the body. "Do they know who the guy is?"

"He's a man from the village. That's all they know so far. They're trying to locate his wife." Brie stepped into the dory and moved to the stern.

Scott pushed off, hopped aboard, and sat on the center seat to row them back to the ship. Brie had nothing else to say as they made for the ship. She didn't want to answer any more questions. She was busy framing up what she was going to say to John. In a few minutes they came up on the starboard side of the *Maine Wind,* and Brie caught the boarding ladder.

"You climb aboard, Brie. I'll row over to the port side and you can help me haul *Tango* up on the davits."

"You know what, Scott? Why don't you leave the dory tied up here for a few minutes. I need to talk to John about something, and I may need to go ashore again."

"No problem," Scott said.

Brie climbed the ladder, swung a leg over the gunwale and stepped onto the deck. Scott came up the ladder next and stepped aboard. She glanced around the deck but didn't see John. She had little time to broach the topic of leaving the ship, so she went to look for him. She headed down the aft companionway and found him just coming out of his cabin.

"Can I talk to you for a minute, John?"

"Sure. Let's go up on deck. The passengers told me about the terrible situation you came upon out on the Heron Head trail. A couple of them were pretty shaken up. Do you think it could possibly have been suicide?"

"All signs point to homicide." She didn't elaborate on the why. "Which brings me to what I wanted to talk to you about." She looked around to be sure no passengers were nearby. She cleared her throat. It felt dry as toast. "So, you remember Ben's friend Dent Fenton who we met in July."

"Of course. He's the detective with the Maine State Police."

"Well, he arrived at the scene with another detective, Marty Dupuis. I guess I'll get right to the point," she said, looking him in the eye as she spoke. "He asked if I would be able to work this case with the Maine State Police. He said he thinks it's going to be a tough one and that they are stretched pretty thin right now, since there have been an unusual number of homicides in the northeastern counties this summer. He said I would be deputized if I come on the case, so I'd have official status."

John studied her for a moment without saying anything, then looked toward the sea. Brie could see him weighing his words carefully, as if the wrong ones might have the power to scuttle their relationship.

"You're a member of the crew, Brie. Have you forgotten that?" He continued looking away from her, and she wondered if there was anger in his eyes or maybe just hurt.

"I know that, John, and it's the first thing I told him. He said he was impressed with my work on the case on Sentinel Island. He thought working this case would give me an insider look at the Maine State Police, in case I might want to consider an alternative to returning to the Minneapolis PD in the fall. While we were talking, I remembered that Ed Browning was aboard and thought maybe he could fill in for me on this cruise." She paused for a moment, wishing he'd look at her. "But I don't shirk responsibility, John. I think you know that. And if you truly need me aboard, then that's the end of the discussion."

John looked back now, and what she saw in his eyes was puzzlement more than anything, either at her request or at his own uncertainty about how to handle it.

"It's a light passenger manifest on this trip, so maybe with Ed aboard you don't really need me," she offered.

John held her at arm's length and looked her up and down. "Somehow, I detect a difference between you and Ed."

"John, we're just talking about having enough hands on deck."

"I know that, Brie. Don't be so strictly business."

Brie studied him for a moment. "You were looking forward to taking this cruise with me, not just having me aboard as crew." She stated it as a fact, not a question, because she could already see the truth of it in his eyes.

"Of course I was. Does that come as a surprise somehow?"

"Well, aren't you the romantic." She stepped closer to him and rubbed the palm of his hand with her thumb.

"I can be," he said, his voice suddenly thick. He looked her in the eyes. "How can you compartmentalize things so much, Brie? Do you really have John and Brie, the crewmates, in a different compartment from John and Brie who are romantically involved?"

"Sometimes." She thought for a moment. "Yes, I guess I do."

"But why?"

"Because of my work, John. I have to. I'm a cop. I have to keep my personal and emotional life separate from my work. At least I have to try. I'm hardwired to do that."

"But you're not a cop aboard this ship. You're Brie, the second mate."

"You can't change the spots on a leopard, John. I don't mean to sound cliché, but once a cop, always a cop."

He sighed, and Brie knew it was a sigh of acceptance, or at least recognition of what she was saying.

"I'd like to work this case, John."

He looked past her, and Brie could feel him struggling, maybe believing the wrong decision would break what they had together. Finally, he looked back at her. "Why, Brie?"

"I guess because I see a need."

"But you're needed here, too."

"Haven't we already covered this, John? You know, Ed Browning and all." Brie studied her feet as she collected her thoughts. A strong gust of wind came over the stern of the ship. She could feel the pressure of it between them, pushing them apart. Finally, she looked up at him. "I guess I'm feeling my way, John. I have been for the last year and a half. After I was shot, I lost that cop sense of trusting my gut. It was like being at sea with no compass, no chart. I lost my way."

John reached up and rubbed his hand up and down her arm—a gesture that told her he was listening, and not just with his ears.

"Coming to Maine where I have family roots, it was the right thing. I wasn't sure when I did it, but now I am." She saw John's expression change at that, as if her words had just infused him with hope. "And working this case with Dent Fenton—it somehow feels like the next step, the right step."

Now it was John studying the deck beneath his feet. After a moment he looked up. "Then you need to do it, Brie. I won't stand in your way."

"Thank you, John."

"I'll miss you this trip, though."

"I'll miss you, too, and I know I'll miss a wonderful adventure."

John looked forward to see who was around. Brie followed his gaze and saw Ed and Scott faced away from them at the far end of the deck. The passengers were all below. John pulled her into his arms and, putting a hand on her head, brought it to his shoulder. "You promise me you'll be careful," he said.

"I will, John."

"I don't like leaving you here alone."

"There are good people here, John, just like everywhere. I'll be okay. And I'll be working with Marty Dupuis and checking in with Dent Fenton daily, I'm sure. What's more, I'll have official status, which means a gun and a badge."

"I'm happy about that. Especially the gun," John said.

"I should go below and put my things together." Brie stepped away from him but kept her hands on his arms.

"I'll see you before you go ashore." He pulled her close and kissed her lightly on the lips. He held her eyes for a moment, then turned and walked forward.

Brie felt a sudden tightness in her chest as he walked away, as if part of her vital essence had left with him. She looked around, suddenly hating the decision she had made. She reached out and took hold of one of the spokes on the ship's wheel, feeling the familiar curve of it, remembering the joy of taking the helm on days as windy and blue as freedom itself. But she knew that juxtaposed with that runaway Brie was the Brie who always answered the call of duty. And she thought Dent was probably right about this being a tough case. It was going to require someone with a singular focus. Brie had been a cop too long not to respond to the call when she was needed. She let go of the wheel, took one last look around the deck, and headed forward to pack her things.

She descended to the galley, where George was busy prepping the lunch. He didn't notice her. She ducked into the crew area so she wouldn't have to talk to him right then. Her emotions already felt raw as a skinned fish. She couldn't handle any more disclosure right now. She turned on the light above her berth, picked her sea bag up off the cabin sole, and emptied the contents onto her berth. She reminded herself to ask Dent Fenton if there was an inn in the village. She took her smaller duffel off a hook over her berth and packed her camera, her pocket recorder, a notebook and pen. She ferreted among the clothes and located her cell phone, which she stuffed in the back pocket of her jeans. She packed socks, underwear, and pajamas. She surveyed her clothes, deciding what she needed. She had one nice pair of black slacks that would serve for official visits. She packed several of her newer scoop neck tee shirts that would go well with the slacks. She added a couple pairs of jeans, a lightweight wool sweater, a cotton sweater, a couple long-sleeved shirts, her running shoes, a set of sweats and a pair of leggings for running, her rain slicker, and her toiletries.

She was reading a book about a man who had sailed a small boat around the world in what mariners call the Roaring Forties—an area between 40 and 50 degrees south latitude with strong westerly winds and high seas. She stuck that in the bag, switched off her light, and turned to leave. She stopped and flipped her light back on and grabbed a long thin length of line, grayed from lots of handling—her lucky rope. She coiled it up, put it in her duffel, and headed out to the galley.

George had disappeared temporarily. She climbed the companionway ladder and spotted John near the boarding ladder with Scott, George, and Ed. From their expressions she knew the captain had filled them in on the news, and she was grateful for that. George had a look of mild panic on his face. He was a status quo kind of guy who didn't cotton easily to change. Scott looked like he got it, and that didn't surprise Brie. Ed wasn't part of their little fraternity, so his face was pretty much neutral. John was in his strictly business captain's mode.

"Give me a minute, guys. I have to make a call." Brie walked a little ways aft. She pulled her phone and Dent Fenton's card from her back jeans pocket and punched in his number.

He answered on the second ring. "Brie, hi. What's the prognosis?"

"I've got the go-ahead from the captain to work on the case. How about at your end?"

"I've got the green light from the Maine State Police. I also talked to your lieutenant at the Minneapolis PD and got an okay from him."

"All right, then." Brie hesitated and looked toward the sea.

"You there, Brie?" Dent said.

"I'm here. Just getting ready to leave the ship. Do you know if there's an inn in Tucker Harbor?"

"There's a place at the north end of the village right on the highway. I think it's the Whale Spout Inn."

"Well, call me Ishmael," Brie said.

"Okay. Ishmael," Dent joked. "I've got a few loose ends to tie up here, but I'll meet you at the inn in about an hour and a half and get you sworn in. Marty—Detective Dupuis—is on the scene there. We're still trying to locate Maloney's wife. Marty talked to the next door neighbor and got a cell phone number for her, but she's not answering. Once we get a bead on her, she'll have to come in and ID the body. Marty will take care of transporting her."

"Got it," Brie said.

"And Brie, I'd like you to go with Marty to give notification to the wife and to do the initial questioning. I'll put him on notice about that."

"Yes, sir."

"You okay with all this, Brie? I sense a bit of hesitation."

"No, I'm good. I just don't shift gears quite as easily as I used to."

"I know what you mean. I've been there. As I told you before out on Sentinel Island, being shot changes everything."

"I think what's worse is dealing with survivor's guilt. I still struggle with those feelings and sometimes still wish it had been me that died, not my partner. But we'll talk about it some other time. Right now, it's time to focus on the case at hand."

"That's what I like to hear," Dent said. "I'll see you in Tucker Harbor at about a quarter of two."

"See you then," Brie said and ended the call. She walked forward to where her crewmates were waiting for her on the starboard side of the ship, next to the boarding ladder.

"You go down the ladder first, Brie, and I'll hand down your bag," John said.

She climbed down to the dory.

"Be careful, Brie," George said. "We'll miss you."

"Ditto that," Scott said.

"I'll see you guys soon." She tried for a tone that said this is all just great but knew she couldn't fool either of her crewmates. They'd already seen that detective work and danger walk hand in hand.

Chapter 5

John pulled for shore, and Brie watched Scott and Ed moving around the deck of the *Maine Wind* prepping the halyards and unlashing the mainsail. Her heart twisted in her chest, and she stared toward the mouth of the harbor and the sea beyond. An eagle was rising from the water, a fish in its talons. An osprey circled, deciding whether to do battle with the eagle over its take.

John was either at a loss for words or her decision had hurt him more than she knew. But then he surprised her by breaking the silence. "It's hard to be between two worlds, isn't it, Brie?" The gentleness of his tone told her he understood far more than she gave him credit for.

"I'm really trying to figure out the next step, John. To be conscious about what I'm doing. And as Dent said, this will give me a chance to explore another option." She could see he was listening. "What you just said about the two worlds. It's true. There's a battle going on inside me. My life has followed one track since I was twenty-two. I've lived and breathed law enforcement. I've loved it and I've hated it, but it's been my constant. I'm struggling to see where I fit outside of that picture, or if I even do." She looked into the water gliding past the dory's hull. "Phil's death and dealing with post-traumatic stress . . . well, terrible as that year was before I came out here, it created an opening in my life. It upended everything to such a degree that I got to start over.

So, I think it was a blessing in ways. How many people get that chance?"

"Lives of quiet desperation," John said.

"Yes," Brie said, looking into his eyes. "I guess when something rocks your world like that, it's a kind of gift. But it's a scary gift. Like a present left on your doorstep and you don't know whether to open it or call the bomb squad."

"Give it time, Brie. It'll come clear. You know, life at sea teaches you that there's a rhythm to things. Storms come along and disrupt that rhythm and sometimes dictate a new course. You may curse those storms, but then, lo and behold, you discover some wonderful new spot, some new territory you would have missed had it all been clear sailing."

"So, I guess it's all in how you look at things," Brie said. "See the threat or see the possibility. Or maybe see the threat as possibility."

"I think that's why you came here, Brie. To figure out how to see things differently. You're trained to see the threat, and you should never lose that instinct. But it seems to me if you go through life seeing only that, it'll eventually eat you up."

Brie thought about the eagle and the fish. She hoped she could somehow learn to be the eagle. To rise above and take the broad view—not just swim in fear.

"You're closing a wound, Brie. It takes time, but you have to close it or it won't heal. And you know what?"

"What?" she said.

"Your struggles have helped me see certain things in my own past differently. Helped me make sense out of them."

"So, we're okay then?" Brie asked. "Still friends?"

"Still more than friends, I would hope," he said, and gave her a look that made the breath catch in her chest.

The dory struck sand, and John hopped out and pulled it up on the shore. Brie picked up her duffel, came forward, and climbed out.

"Thanks, John, for being so smart," she said.

"You're the smart one, Brie. Make no mistake about that."

"I'm not so sure." She set her duffel down and stepped into his open arms.

"You'll keep me updated, won't you?" he asked.

"You bet," she said. "I hope we can wrap this up in a few days. If so, I might go visit my grandma in Cherryfield until I can meet up with the *Maine Wind* again."

"I'll let you know what day we'll be back here," John said.

"I'll look forward to that." She kissed him briefly, picked up her bag, and stepped away from him.

John walked back to the dory, pushed off, and hopped aboard. He rowed toward the ship, and she watched him for a couple of minutes. After raising her hand in a final goodbye, she turned and walked up through the village. The docks were quiet as she passed. It was too early for the lobstermen to be back in with their catch. Brie walked past a row of abandoned shops that looked like they had been closed for years. She remembered what John had told her about the naval base near Tucker Harbor shutting down and wondered if these might have been thriving little enterprises back then. Clearly, the main industry in the village now was lobstering. As she approached the north end of town, the road turned. She came around the bend and saw the Whale Spout Inn anchored halfway up the hill.

A rather nineteenth-century representation of a whale spouting water graced the wooden sign in front of the inn. *Hmmm,* she thought, *Herman Melville might have liked it here.* She walked up the hill, passing the town library on her right, and came to a stop at the base of the flagstone path leading up to the inn. She stood for a moment studying the modest structure that appeared well cared for. As she started up the path toward the front door, a tall, wiry man came around the side of the inn, pushing a large wheelbarrow filled with dirt. Brie placed him in his late forties to early fifties. He had salt and pepper hair and a gray mustache.

"Can I help you, miss?" he asked, setting down the wheelbarrow and walking toward her. As he came closer, Brie could see that his nose was not quite straight and guessed it had been broken at some time.

"I'm looking for a room," Brie said.

"Are you visiting someone here in the village or just passing through?" he asked. His serious gray eyes shone with curiosity.

"Oh, I'll be here a few days," Brie said noncommittally.

"Well, I have just the room for you, Miss . . ."

"It's Beaumont," Brie said. "My name's Brie Beaumont."

"Pleased to meet you, Brie. I'm Atticus Kane. I own the inn here. Come on inside and we'll get you registered."

"Atticus . . ." Brie said. "I like that name. You don't hear it often."

"I think everyone likes the name. After all, Harper Lee made it famous, and who didn't like Atticus Finch?"

"It's true," Brie said. "There probably is a subconscious connection."

"I'm afraid you've arrived on an unfortunate day," Atticus said as they climbed the front steps and crossed a wide porch. He opened the front door and let Brie enter first. "There's been a terrible incident. It's all over the village."

Brie hadn't wanted to show her cards quite yet, but Atticus had pretty much just forced her hand with his comment.

"As a matter of fact, I know about it," she said.

"News travels fast, I guess. Especially bad news."

"Well, actually, I was with the group who found the body. We were from the schooner *Maine Wind* that anchored in the harbor yesterday."

Atticus studied her now, confusion in his smoky gray eyes, and suddenly the small entryway they were standing in felt too small to Brie. She walked into the hallway beyond and turned back to Atticus. "You're wondering why I'm here and not on the ship," she said.

"I guess I am, but we Mainers don't like to ask a lot of questions. We figure people have their reasons."

"Well, as it turns out, I'm a homicide detective on leave from the Minneapolis Police Department and here in Maine for the summer. I actually became acquainted with Lieutenant Fenton from the Maine State Police earlier this summer. He was at the crime scene this morning and, to make a long story short, he asked me if I'd work on this case with them."

"You said crime scene. Do they think Jake was murdered? We all—the people in the village—thought it must be a suicide."

"Do you have a reason for thinking that?" Brie asked.

Atticus hesitated. "Well, no . . . it's just that murder seems so unbelievable. I mean this is Tucker Harbor, Maine, not New York City."

"I've never found that murder respects any particular geographic boundaries," Brie said. She studied Atticus for a moment, realizing that he probably knew everyone in the village, as well as everything that had happened here going back for who knows how long. She guessed he might be a valuable resource in their investigation.

"Why don't you follow me into the study." Atticus said. "You can sign the guest register, and I'll get you set up in a room."

They walked into the room to their left. Brie had visited or stayed at a few inns in Maine since she had arrived, and they all seemed to share a certain comfortable hominess, she thought. Like Great Aunt Mildred's parlor might have looked, if she had had a Great Aunt Mildred with a parlor, that is. The Whale Spout Inn did not disappoint with its pine floors and colorful throw rugs. An antique sofa with rose-colored velvet upholstery sat near the fireplace. A pale green knitted throw lay across one of its arms. Opposite the sofa, two high-back chairs covered with a multi-colored tapestry flanked the other side of the fireplace. The back wall of the room was covered with dark wood bookcases filled with books and a variety of maritime objects and ships' models. The inns she had visited always had lots of books, something that particularly delighted her. Maine seemed to be a bookish place—at least the coastal areas she had visited.

Atticus walked over to a roll-top desk in the corner and turned on a small lamp with a red fabric shade. He flipped open the guest register and turned it so Brie could sign in. "I'll put you in one of our front rooms, Miss Beaumont. They have a nice view of the harbor."

"That will be fine," Brie said.

"Breakfast is included, of course. It's served from seven to ten o'clock in the morning." He took a small slip of paper with a number on it from the desk drawer. "Here's the pass code for the internet should you need to use it. We have a wireless connection for our guests."

Brie took the pass code from him and put it in her pocket.

"I'll show you up to your room. Is this all you have?" he said, looking at the small duffel she was holding.

"I'm travelling light," Brie said.

Atticus walked with her back into the hall and up the stairs, which creaked as if Georgie the Ghost might be in residence. The stairway was divided by a broad landing halfway up. A window seat backed by a leaded and stained-glass window graced the landing. Brie paused to look out at the hills that lay in the distance. "You have a lovely place here, Atticus." She thought about asking him about Jake Maloney, but decided she'd wait until she had met with Dent Fenton. She checked her watch. He'd be showing up in a little over an hour. She suddenly realized she was quite hungry. A lot had happened since breakfast. She wished she had made a sandwich before leaving the ship.

"Is there any place in the village to grab a light lunch?" she asked.

"Varney's Diner is at the other end of the village. Just a five-or-ten-minute walk from here, depending on how hungry you are," Atticus said.

Brie smiled at that. "I remember seeing that place when we came ashore this morning. I think I'll check it out after I see my room."

They continued up the stairs, and Atticus led her across the hall and opened the first door to the left of the stairs. He set her duffel on the floor. It was a simply appointed room about ten by fifteen feet. Two windows on the front wall looked out over the tops of the village docks to the harbor and the open sea beyond the lighthouse. An antique dresser stood between the windows. There was a queen-sized bed against the back wall. An off-white quilt with a wedding ring design topped the bed. There was an arm chair and ottoman near the windows and a small writing desk with a cranberry glass lamp against the adjacent wall. The room was decorated with pink-and-gray-striped wallpaper, and simple lace curtains hung at the sides of the windows. A door next to the desk led into a small bathroom.

Brie turned to Atticus. "It's a very nice room. Thank you."

"You're the only guest till the end of the week, so you'll have the run of the place until then. But let me know if you need anything, Miss Beaumont."

"Thanks, I will," Brie said.

Atticus left the room and closed the door behind him.

Brie set her duffel on the bed and pulled out the small zipper case with her toiletries. She went into the bathroom, washed her hands and splashed some water on her face. She brushed her long blonde hair a few times and returned it to a ponytail. She went back to her duffel, pulled out her wallet and took out a couple of bills. She stuck them in the front pocket of her jeans and looked around for the room key. She walked over to the door. There was a bolt on the door that could be turned from the inside, but no key in evidence. She had a funny feeling there wasn't going to be a key, either. Nobody seemed to worry much about locking up in these out-of-the-way spots in Maine. She headed down the stairs and caught Atticus as he was making for the kitchen. "I didn't get a room key," she said.

"Oh, we don't bother with them," Atticus said. "We're on the honor system here."

"I see," Brie said, trying for a level tone. Even though it bugged her, she didn't want to burn any bridges, antagonize anyone at the beginning of an investigation. She had a feeling that, as a guest of Atticus Kane, she might be in a position to acquire a wealth of information about the villagers.

"Well, I think I'll try that diner. Varney's, you said—west end of the village?"

"That's right," Atticus said. "Varney makes a really good Reuben."

"Good to know," Brie said. "Thanks, Atticus." She headed for the front door.

Chapter 6

Brie followed the highway down through the village. At the far end of Tucker Harbor, the road bent north and up a hill. She spotted Varney's Diner partway up the hill on the right. There were windows across the front that faced the harbor, and as she got closer, she thought the place looked pretty empty. She figured that was because everyone in the village was down at the end of Final Reckoning Road rubbernecking around the edges of the crime scene. The door was on the left side of the diner. Brie stepped inside and looked around.

A middle-aged man in a white apron was working a meat slicer behind the blue-and-white-speckled lunch counter. A fringe of brown hair wrapped around the back of his otherwise bald head. He turned and seemed almost startled to see her. He walked to the end of the counter, picked up a string mop that sat fanned out on the black and white linoleum floor, and disappeared into the back room to jettison it. She thought he had a slight limp. He came back out and picked a menu off the counter. "Would you like a booth, miss?" he asked.

"Sure," Brie said. She was the only one in the place, and he led her to one of the booths along the front of the diner next to the windows. She noticed there was indeed a hitch to his walk.

"Coffee?" he asked, his glance travelling out the window and then back to her.

"That would be fine, thanks."

"You one of the officials, here because of what's happened?"

Brie was surprised he would think that. She was wearing jeans and certainly didn't look official in any way. Or maybe she did. She wasn't from the village, so maybe he'd just assumed.

"As a matter of fact, I am. My name is Brie Beaumont. I'll be working with the Maine State Police. Are you Varney? Atticus Kane at the inn recommended your diner for lunch."

"Varney Simms at your service," he said, and gave her a little salute. "I'll go get that coffee for you." He turned to go, and Brie watched him move away.

She studied the menu while she waited and decided on grilled ham and cheese. When Varney came back with the coffee, she put in her order.

"Would you like a cup of soup with that?" he asked. "It's tomato bisque today, and it's wicked good." His brown eyes warmed momentarily.

"Hmm, that does sound good. Sure, why not?" Brie said.

Varney scooped up her menu and headed back behind the counter.

She watched him go about the business of assembling her lunch. There was no flow to Varney. With staccato movements he collected the sandwich ingredients from the refrigerator and bread keeper. He plucked a knife from one of the silverware containers and spread mustard on the bread with quick tiered movements. At every pause in his work, his eyes would dart about the diner like balls in a pinball machine. There was a kind of pent-up energy about him. An unexpected image of an insect caught in a spider's web came to mind as she observed him.

Varney slipped the sandwich onto a panini press and went over to a big stainless steel soup kettle and dished up a bowl of tomato bisque. Within ten minutes of taking her order, he delivered the soup and sandwich on a heavy diner-style plate.

"So, what will you be doing with the police?" he asked as he put her plate down.

"Well, I'll be helping them with the investigation, trying to find out what happened to the victim."

"He has a name. Everyone knows who they found out there. You may as well just call him Jake." Varney seemed affronted by her generic reference to Maloney as "the victim." It made her wonder what connection he might have had with the guy.

"It's always sad for a small community like this to lose one of its own," she said, trying for a more compassionate tone. "I'm sure everyone in the village knew him."

"Oh, everyone knows Jake. Nice guy. Drives a truck for a living. Or did." Varney's glance moved to the window as he corrected himself.

"He wasn't a lobsterman?" Brie asked, though she already knew this.

"Nope. Drives truck." Varney pulled at the underside of his chin the way some men like to. "He stops here twice a week with supplies for the diner. Or he did, I should say."

"It's hard to talk about someone in the past tense. Someone who was just here," Brie said.

"Do you know if they've found Nancy yet? Nancy is Jake's wife. Ned said she's not in the village."

"The police are trying to locate her. Do you know if she works?"

"Nancy? No, she stays at home. Tends to the house. More coffee?" he asked, noticing her cup was low.

"Sure," Brie said.

Varney walked around the counter to the coffee maker, returned with the pot, and filled her cup.

"I notice you have a slight limp," Brie said. "Did you hurt your leg?"

Varney's eyes turned wary, and he took a step backwards. "It's an old injury. Happened in the service."

At that moment the door to the diner opened, jangling the bell. Varney quickly moved away from her. *Saved by the bell,* she thought. But it was too late. She had already noted his unease and placed it in her mental file labeled with one single word—*Why*?

She turned to see who had come in. Three elderly men stood just inside the door to the diner. Varney greeted them by name and seated them in a booth at the far end of the row from where Brie sat. She felt a little disappointed. She would have liked to tune in on whatever they were saying. She wondered if that was why Varney had put them down there. *Don't get ahead of yourself, Brie,* she thought.

She finished her soup and sandwich and checked her watch. Still half an hour till Dent would arrive at the inn. She had time for another cup of coffee, and the next time Varney looked her way, she held up her cup to give him the message. When he came with the pot, she asked him for the check.

"Did you like the soup?" he asked.

"Yes I did," she said. "Thanks for recommending it. Everything was delicious."

"Thank you, miss," he said, pausing long enough in his frenetic movement to actually look her in the eyes. Brie saw something there that surprised her. It was a searching look, almost as if he were reaching out to her. Like most glimpses into the soul, it was gone a second later, which didn't matter. Even though Brie had no idea what lay beneath the look, she had taken note of it. And in that same moment, she had felt both sadness and affinity for Varney.

"I think I'll be a regular here the next few days. I look forward to trying some more of your fare, Varney."

Varney nodded and stroked his neck. "We've got a different special every night. Tonight it's Swedish meatballs," he said and pulled her ticket out of his apron pocket.

"I think I'll be back for that," she said. "So what time do you open in the morning, Varney?"

He studied her for a second. "I open the door at six-thirty. Won't you be having breakfast at the inn, though?" Varney's shrewd expression told her he wouldn't be easily fooled by subterfuge.

"Of course. What am I thinking?" She thumped her forehead with the butt of her hand. She let it go at that, not wanting to sound like she was interrogating him. If for any reason the investigation led back to him, it would be high time then to question him. For now, she wanted to keep the lines of communication open. She sensed he could be a valuable source of information in the investigation. She was willing to bet that no one heard more village gossip than Varney as he fried eggs and assembled sandwiches.

"Well, it's been nice talking to you, Varney." She gave him some cash and told him to keep the change. She lingered over her coffee for a few more minutes and then slid out of the booth and headed for the door. She wanted to get back to the inn in time to change into her better slacks, in case Dent had any official business for her to attend to once she was sworn in.

Brie left the diner and started down the road that ran through the village between the shore and docks on one side and the houses on the other. Narrow as it was where it came through the village, the road was actually part of the highway that continued east along the Bold Coast, all the way to Lubec, Maine. Near Lubec, the famous West Quoddy Head lighthouse—the easternmost point in the U.S.—stood watch over the Bay of Fundy from its high cliffs. She would have gotten to see it from the ship during this voyage. That opportunity had been lost when she'd came ashore to work the case.

As she came in view of the harbor, she saw something that caught at her heart. The *Maine Wind* was just sailing out of the harbor toward open sea. She stopped in her tracks and watched, feeling the oddest sense of displacement. She hadn't thought the ship would be weighing anchor so quickly. She had intended to watch it get underway. Taking stock of how she felt now, though, maybe it was better she hadn't. She watched for a couple of minutes more as the ship—her home for the past four months—sailed east out of view, taking her sense of security with it.

Brie turned back to the road and noticed a teenage girl sauntering toward her at a pace that said: *I hurry for no one.* She was wearing a blue waitress uniform, and it didn't take much of a detective to see that she was heading for Varney's Diner. The girl had shoulder-length black hair—way too black to have come from anywhere but a bottle. The hair on top of her head stood up in spikes. She had unusually pale skin, which played up the whole vampire look even more. Her eyes, sinister with black liner, studied Brie with some interest. But when Brie made eye contact with her, she looked away. So typical of youth, Brie thought. They are genuinely interested in things and people, but they can never let on. She smiled to herself, thinking that she found most adults far more of an enigma than kids. She wondered if that meant she'd be a good mom, and an image of John at the helm of the *Maine Wind* crossed her mind.

As the girl passed, Brie said her friendliest, "Hey."

The girl returned the greeting in a tone that said: *I'm going to my death.*

Brie immediately liked her.

The morning's fog had totally evaporated, and a salty breeze came ashore as Brie walked back to the inn. It felt good to walk, and she fell into a long, swinging stride. Within five minutes she rounded the bend, and as the road inclined, she pushed herself to keep up her pace until she got to the inn. She went up the flagstone path to the door and stepped inside. There was nobody around, and she headed for the stairs and took them two at a time. By the time she got to the top, her calves were feeling a pleasant burn. She walked into her room and over to the bed, where her duffel sat. She took her black cotton slacks and white tee shirt with the three-quarter-length sleeves. She went in the bathroom, washed her hands and face, and changed her clothes. She asked herself how she felt about putting on a badge and gun again. She got no answer.

Brie headed down the stairs and walked out onto the front porch of the inn to wait for Dent Fenton. She paced back and forth, feeling a tinge of anxiety. New experiences were always hard now. It still amazed her how much she had changed since the shooting. Thinly veiled fear clouded every new situation, as if she were looking into a very old mirror and could no longer get a clear image of herself.

Chapter 7

Dent Fenton pulled up in front of the inn in an unmarked Chevy Impala. A second car—an SUV—pulled in behind him. Dent got out and headed for the porch. The man in the other car stayed put.

"Hello, Brie. Hope I didn't keep you waiting."

"Hi, Lieutenant, and no, you didn't. I just came out here a couple minutes ago to wait for you. Is that another one of your detectives?" she asked, nodding toward the second car.

"It is. He followed me down here so I can leave a car for you. You'll need one once the investigation gets going."

"Thanks, Lieutenant," Brie said. "Any success reaching Maloney's wife yet?"

"Nope. But her neighbor said she's due back this afternoon. The neighbor has Marty's number and is going to call if Mrs. Maloney gets home. I cautioned her not to talk to her. Told her we have detectives on hand and that they will break the news to her. I'm leaving you and Marty on the scene until we get a bead on the wife. Once you talk to her, call and fill me in. Until then it's a waiting game."

"If she doesn't show up, that would cast a different light on things," Brie said.

"That it would," Dent said. "That it would."

Brie could see him mulling over the possibility.

"Well, let's get you sworn in." He had her raise her right hand, and he read the oath. Afterwards, he produced a shield with a belt clip, and an ID wallet with photo. "I got your picture from the Minneapolis PD." He gave her a pancake holster, two clips filled with rounds, and an H & K .45 USP—the universal service pistol used by the Maine State Police. "Your lieutenant in Minneapolis said you're current on your range certification." Finally, Dent gave her a few business cards he'd printed up with her name on them.

"Well, I'm as official as can be," Brie said, taking them and putting them in her pocket.

"Nothing takes long in the electronic age," Dent said.

Brie loaded the weapon and clipped the badge and holster over the belt on her slacks. Actions that felt familiar, even comfortable, which told her she was in a different place psychologically from where she had been a few months ago.

"Oh, I brought a jacket for you as well," Dent said. Brie walked down to the car with him, and he pulled out a navy blue jacket with the Maine State Police insignia on it.

"To make me look more official?" Brie asked.

"Something like that," Dent said. "Although the badge and ID are really all you need. The jacket may come in handy on cool nights, though." He introduced Brie to Detective Tim Coughlin, who was waiting in the other vehicle, and then gave her the rest of her instructions. "There's an onboard computer. I also brought a laptop for you. You can use either of them to access any police databases, as well as file reports with the department.

"We've started a case file—the number's on a sticky note inside the laptop case. I've entered your badge number into the system and assigned a password, which you can change once you log in. So you're all set to go. There's a Kevlar vest, a bootie box, and a box of latex gloves in the trunk." He handed her the keys. "Why don't you check in with me later, after you and Marty get started on the questioning? I'll plan to be back down here tomorrow."

He produced a warrant for the Maloney property and handed it to her. "You'll need this once Mrs. Maloney returns home. It's nice to have you on board, Brie." With that, Dent walked over to the SUV, climbed into the passenger seat next to Tim, and they headed out of the village.

Brie had seen Detective Marty Dupuis near the trailhead where the townspeople were gathered. She decided she'd head down there and talk to him. She locked the extra clip for the HK in the trunk of the black Impala, climbed behind the wheel, and tossed the jacket onto the seat next to her. She turned on the car and headed for the other end of the village, where she hung a left on Final Reckoning Road and pulled up next to one of the trooper cars. The Evidence Response Team's vehicle was still there, which meant they hadn't finished processing the scene yet. Brie got out of her car and walked toward Marty. When he saw her coming, he disengaged from the Sergeant Starkey, with whom he was talking, and headed in her direction.

Brie had met Marty Dupuis in May when she had filed a report on a case she had gotten involved in on Granite Island. She had liked him immediately. He had a thoughtful, quiet manner about him, and Brie sensed he was both intelligent and self-possessed. She suspected he would be slow to panic —the kind of officer who would keep his head in a crisis. In other words, the kind of officer she would want by her side. Marty was a bit shorter than Brie, and his dark features attested to his French Canadian lineage. There was a spark of humor in his discerning brown eyes.

"Welcome to the ranks, Brie," he said, nodding at her badge as he came up to her. "I had a feeling when we met in May that I'd be seeing more of you."

"I'm going to enjoy working with you, Marty. Dent filled me in. I guess we're kind of in a holding pattern for the moment."

"That's right. Just waiting on the wife's arrival. I've collected a little general information from some of the Maloneys' neighbors. Jake Maloney and his wife Nancy have lived in Tucker Harbor for about ten years. No kids. He drives a truck;

she stays at home." Marty consulted his small notebook. "The next door neighbor said they are good neighbors—keep to themselves, but they're helpful. No reports of any fighting or raucous behavior coming from the Maloneys', and there have never been any domestic calls to their address."

Brie nodded. "I wonder how Maloney fit in in a village where almost everyone hauls lobsters for a living?"

Just then, Marty's phone rang, and he pulled it out and looked at it. "It's the neighbor." Marty answered, "This is Detective Dupuis." He listened to what she had to say and then responded. "We'll be right there, Helen. Thank you for calling. Please don't speak to her," he cautioned. "We'll take it from here." Marty put his phone away. "Let's take your vehicle, Brie. I'm boxed in down there." They climbed into the Impala and headed up the road toward the west end of Tucker Harbor.

Like many Maine villages, the houses of Tucker Harbor were tiered on the hill that rose behind the harbor. At Marty's direction, Brie took a left onto Third Street, and at the fourth house, pulled into the driveway of a modest two-story walk-out-style house. There was a dirty Ford pickup in the driveway with a red Honda Civic next to it. Both were older models. The house had cedar siding and a dark brown roof. It sat on the hill, two streets above the main road that ran through the village. Aside from a very nice view of the harbor, there was nothing remarkable about the residence. The yard was bare of trees or plants. There was a deck that ran along the front of the upper level. On it sat an old grill, two lawn chairs with blue plastic webbing, and a square metal table that needed painting. There was an entry door on the lower level.

"Let's try there," Brie said, pointing to it. "I see a door bell." They got out of the car and walked to the door. There was an outer metal door with a glass in it. The inner door was slightly ajar, and Brie could hear the TV. Marty rang the bell and followed up with a knock on the outside door. Within a few seconds a thin woman appeared at the door. She was wearing baggy pink sweats. The sweatshirt had a couple of stains on it. She had a sallow complexion, and her straight brown hair hung to her shoulders and needed a wash. Brie guessed she was in her late thirties. Jake Maloney's driver's license had revealed that he was forty, so it was a fair guess that his wife was about the same age.

"Can I help you?" she asked, but then she noticed Brie's badge and took a step back. "Are you from the police?" Her dull eyes woke up a bit. "What's this about?"

"Mrs. Maloney? Nancy Maloney?" Marty Dupuis asked.

"Yes," she said guardedly, looking from one of them to the other.

"I'm Detective Dupuis, and this is Detective Beaumont. We're with the Maine State Police. May we come in and talk to you for a few minutes?"

She glanced to her left at the room next to her, and Brie could see that she was not eager to let them in. "I guess so," she said. She pushed the storm door open, and Brie went in first. The room needed a makeover as much as Nancy. The dark blue carpet was covered with white hair, and Brie spotted the culprit in the corner—a large white cat desperately in need of grooming and a work-out regimen. The sofa was covered in brown plaid Herculon, and the tan recliner that sat at right angles to the sofa had a tear in the back. The sofa was strewn with bags of candy, potato chips, and cheese puffs; food groups Brie suspected contributed to Nancy's unhealthy-looking complexion and physique. Nancy walked to the sofa, picked up the remote and turned off the TV.

Detective Dupuis broached the topic. "Mrs. Maloney, would you like to sit down?" She sat on the edge of the sofa, her eyes on Dupuis.

"We are very sorry to have to tell you this, but your husband is dead."

"What do you mean?" Nancy stood up, and a red blotch started to form on her right cheek.

"His body was found this morning around ten o'clock by some hikers out on the Heron Head trail. We've been trying to locate you since then."

Brie was studying Nancy closely as Marty gave the news, and she could see that what they were saying did not compute. Nancy's mouth opened but nothing came out, and she looked from one to the other of them like it might be some kind of practical joke.

Brie took her by the arm and guided her back onto the sofa. "Let's sit down, Mrs. Maloney," she said.

"What you're saying, it's just not possible. Jake is on the road. He had a load to pick up in Ellsworth today."

"No, Mrs. Maloney," Marty Dupuis said, sitting down next to her. "Several people from the village identified him. We're very, very sorry."

Tears welled up in Nancy's eyes. "But that doesn't make sense. Why would he be out there and not on the road? Unless it happened last night."

"I gather you weren't here last night, Mrs. Maloney," Brie said. "Can you tell us where you were?"

"I went to visit a friend in Bangor. I see her two or three times a year and usually stay overnight so we have a couple days together. Jake always encourages me to go. Says it's good for me to get away. I started for home about eleven-thirty this morning."

"Could you give us your friend's name, address, and phone number, please?" Brie said.

Nancy recited the information, and Brie wrote it in her notebook.

"I don't understand what would have made him go out to Heron Head. That's just not like him."

Brie heard a combination of fear and confusion in the comment. "Might he have been taking a walk before he got on the road?"

Nancy shook her head. "Jake never did anything like that. Years ago I used to try to get him to take walks with me.

He never would." She looked at her hands, and both Brie and Marty let her take a few moments to collect her thoughts. Finally she asked, "How did he die? Was it a heart attack? He didn't take very good care of himself."

Brie now wondered if the bags of junk food belonged to Jake, and she'd made a wrong assumption.

"His death was not from natural causes," Marty said.

"What does that mean?" Nancy looked at Brie, and it was clear she truly didn't understand.

"It means his death was either a suicide or a homicide," Brie said gently.

"No! Oh my God. That can't be. What do you mean? Are you saying he killed himself? Or somebody actually killed him? No, that's just not possible."

"Mrs. Maloney, his throat was cut. It was either self-inflicted or someone attacked him," Dupuis said.

Nancy suddenly went pale and bolted off the sofa toward a door across the room. Brie and Marty heard her throwing up. Brie looked at Marty and shook her head. Worse than any part of an investigation, worse than the crime scene—gruesome as that might be—worse than the often unsavory suspects that peopled the world of the homicide detective, was the job of notifying next of kin. It was a blow that could never be softened, and reactions to this most terrible of news were always telling.

With couples, detectives often got a sense of the guilt or innocence of the spouse or partner based on his or her reaction to the news. Brie knew there was no way to fake Nancy's reaction to what they had told her. She decided Nancy Maloney was innocent of any involvement in Jake Maloney's death.

She heard the water running in the bathroom now, and after a few minutes Nancy came back into the room. She was hugging herself tightly as she walked toward them.

"I'm sorry," she said as she sat back down between them.

"Mrs. Maloney, there is no reason to apologize," Marty Dupuis said. "We are both sorry to deliver such terrible news."

Brie could see that Nancy was shaking. She took a crocheted afghan off the back of the sofa. It was made of granny squares and so was about fifty percent yarn and fifty percent holes. Brie doubled it over and placed it around Nancy's shoulders.

"Thank you, Detective . . ."

"Beaumont," Brie said. "It's Detective Beaumont."

"I don't know what to say," Nancy began. "You said it was either suicide or homicide. When will you know?"

"The medical examiner will be doing an autopsy to determine that," Brie said. "As soon as we have his ruling, we will let you know." She paused and looked at Nancy. "Do you think your husband could have been depressed?"

"I don't know," Nancy said. "I don't think so. I don't really know what the signs of that would be, but he didn't seem to have changed. He was worried about money. But who isn't these days? After the recession hit, he lost some of his freight jobs. You know, businesses closed and fewer goods were being shipped. He was always looking for extra work, and the last six months or so things seemed to pick up a little."

"Do you work, Nancy?" Brie asked.

"No, I tend to things around home." She looked around the room sheepishly, as if she had just realized the absurdity of the statement.

"Any children?" Brie asked.

"No, we couldn't have any." Nancy looked at her hands. "I suppose you must think I'm kind of a loser?"

"It's not our job to think anything of the sort," Brie said. "It's our job to find out what happened to your husband. Period."

Nancy looked relieved at that. "Thank you," she said.

Brie wasn't sure what was missing from the Maloney household—maybe hope, maybe love—but something was missing. It was possible that both Nancy and her husband had been suffering from some degree of depression. *Quiet desperation,* she thought, remembering John's words as the two of them had rowed ashore earlier. She understood what it was to grapple with a loss of hope. But she had learned that sometimes terrible things can create an opening for good things. Maybe that would hold true for Nancy Maloney somewhere down the line. But right now they needed to learn what had led to Jake Maloney's violent death.

"Mrs. Maloney, was Jake right-handed?" she asked.

"No, he was left-handed," Nancy said.

Brie thought about the wound on Jake's neck. It had been deeper on one side—the left side—which would indicate that it was inflicted by a right-handed assailant.

"Why do you ask that?" Nancy said.

Brie didn't want to say anything until the autopsy ruling came through. "Just gathering basic information," she said. "Did your husband have any enemies? Anyone he might have had trouble with? Maybe in his business?" she asked.

"I can't think of anyone," Nancy said. "Jake was pretty reliable. He always got to his pick-ups and deliveries on time. Oh, my goodness." She suddenly looked alarmed. "He would have been picking up freight today. I have to call the customers and let them know what has happened."

"Is there someone who can help you with that, Mrs. Maloney?" Marty asked. "Someone you could call to come over?"

Nancy shook her head. "I'll make the calls. I handle that part of the business."

"So you do have a job," Brie said. "You help your husband run the business."

"I guess," Nancy said. "I never thought of it that way." She glanced at Brie shyly. Then something seemed to occur to her. "You know, I almost forgot. Jake had a partner in the business for a while. But that ended over a year ago."

"Do you know why?" Brie asked.

"Jake never wanted to talk about it. One day he just told me they were going their separate ways. That it wasn't working out."

"Do you have contact information for that person?" Marty Dupuis asked.

"I'm sure his address is still in my phone ledger. I'll go check upstairs." She got up and headed for the stairs at the other end of the room.

Brie looked at Marty. "Well, it's a place to start if the ruling comes in homicide," she said.

"There's little doubt of that now," Marty said. "We both saw the wound. It was inflicted by someone right-handed."

"I have to agree with you," Brie said.

In a couple of minutes Nancy came back into the room with a piece of paper in her hand. "I wrote down the address and phone number I last had for him. His name's Dan Littleton," she said, handing Brie the paper. "He lives in Machias."

"Thank you," Brie said.

"Mrs. Maloney, we will need you to identify Jake's body," Marty said. "He's at the medical examiner's office. I'll be escorting you."

"All right," Nancy said, but Brie saw a look of panic in her eyes.

"Mrs. Maloney, do you have someone who can stay with you tonight?" she asked.

"My brother lives nearby," Nancy said. "I'm sure he will come over. He probably won't have heard the news yet."

"Would you like one of us to call him for you?" Brie asked.

"No, I'll go call him now," she said.

"That's fine, Mrs. Maloney. Can you give us your brother's name, address, and phone number? And can we also get contact numbers for you—both home and cell?"

"My brother's name is Nate Freeman. Freeman was my maiden name." She gave Brie and Marty the contact info for Nate, as well as her phone number. "I'd like to go see Jake now. If it's all right, I'll call Nate and then change my clothes."

Before she left the room, Brie produced the warrant that Dent had given her for the Maloney property. "We need to collect certain records—freight manifests, phone bills, and Jake's mileage log, for starters. We'll also need to check his email and the contents of his computer. Could you sign the warrant, please, Mrs. Maloney? We'll leave you a copy, and also a list of anything we take into evidence."

Nancy signed the warrant and led them to the office that was off the family room. She took out the documents they had asked for. "Take whatever you need," she said. "But his mileage log is in his truck, which he parks at my brother's place. If you want I can take you there on the way to see Jake."

"That'll be fine, Mrs. Maloney," Marty said. "And again, we'll leave you a list of anything we take." He and Brie each took out one of their cards and gave it to her. "Feel free to call us anytime if you have a question or concern."

Nancy took their cards and left the room. They heard her climb the stairs. While they waited for her, Brie and Marty collected the documents they needed to review and put them into evidence envelopes. In fifteen minutes Nancy came back downstairs. She had pulled her limp hair into a ponytail and put on clean jeans and tee shirt. They asked her if all the doors were locked and then left the house.

Brie drove Marty back to his car. It was a black Impala identical to hers. *Obviously the model used by detectives on the force,* she thought.

"Thanks, Brie. We'll be in touch." He and Nancy got out and headed for his car.

After they drove off, Brie pulled out her phone and put a call through to Dent Fenton. He picked up on the second ring.

"Lieutenant Fenton. What's up, Brie?"

"Marty's headed to the ME's office with Nancy Maloney. We just got done talking to her."

"How'd she take it?"

"Not well. From her reaction I think it's a fair bet she's not involved in any way. She said she was visiting a friend overnight in Bangor. Someone will have to interview the friend."

"I'll do that," Dent said. "I'm up here in Bangor. Give me the contact info on the friend."

Brie pulled out her small notebook and read off the name, address, and phone number for Nancy Maloney's friend.

"Did you learn anything else from Maloney's wife that might be useful?" Dent asked.

"Well, one interesting fact. Jake Maloney was left-handed, and considering the depth of the wound on the left side of his neck, it's a sure-fire bet that the assailant was right-handed."

"That would rule out suicide," Dent said. "Have you called Joe Wolf with that info?"

"Not yet. Could you give me his number? I was just going to call him and see how the autopsy is proceeding."

"Sure." There was a pause while Dent located the number. Brie pulled out her small notebook. "Here it is," Dent said.

She wrote down the ME's number. "Thanks, Lieutenant."

"Did you learn anything else?"

"Just one thing. Apparently, Jake Maloney had a partner in his trucking business for a while. They went their separate ways a little over a year ago."

"Did she say why?"

"All Jake told her was that things weren't working out."

"Hmm," Dent said.

"I got a name and address on the guy. I'm just waiting on the ME's ruling. If it's homicide, I thought I'd follow up on this Dan Littleton, the former partner."

"If they parted in a less than amicable way, there could be a motive there."

"My thinking exactly," Brie said. "And at the very least, he may have some info that will give us a lead."

"Sounds like things are on track. Good work, Brie. I'll let you get that call in to Joe Wolf."

They ended the call and Brie punched in Dr. Wolf's number. She got his voice mail and left him a message about the victim being left-handed. She asked him to call her and let her know how the autopsy was proceeding. She left her number and signed off.

Brie walked down to the shore and looked back across the harbor at the village. The lobstermen were starting to motor back in with their catch, and boat after boat pulled up at the town docks to unload their crates of lobsters before heading to their moorings in the harbor. She imagined by this evening the town would be buzzing with the news of Jake Maloney's fate, and she wondered if a killer in their midst would be playing along, thinking, as all killers do, that he had gotten away with murder.

Chapter 8

Brie turned toward the trail that led out to Heron Head. She was in a holding pattern until Joe Wolf returned her call. She decided she'd take another look at what she was certain was a crime scene. She knew the Evidence Response Team would have gone over the area thoroughly, but she wanted to visit it by herself and take in the lay of the land without the distractions that had been present that morning. She climbed the embankment, ducked under the crime scene tape, and entered the silence of the forest.

The scent of spruce felt comforting and calmed her mind. She thought about the tall pine forests she had hiked in Minnesota, where sunlight filtered through the trees like rays sent down from heaven. And she remembered the redwood forests of northern California where her family had vacationed once when she was a teenager. There was a sacred feeling in an ancient forest. If God could be in a place, it would be there, not inside four walls. That's what she had always felt, anyway.

She knew it would take about fifteen minutes to reach the scene. The trail made a gradual ascent for most of the way out the headland. She paid careful attention to the lay of the land as she approached the spot where they had found Jake Maloney. There was a short but steep incline and then the trail bent sharply to the left, toward the harbor. She paused and looked around. The killer had picked the perfect spot to strike. Both the incline and the bend would have decreased a hiker's ability to see very far ahead of him on this part of the trail. And with the thick fog this morning, it would have been nearly impossible for Jake to detect a person hiding along this section of the trail.

She looked around to see if she could determine where the assailant might have hidden. She walked to the spot where the body had lain. It had been angled slightly to the right across the trail. If Jake had dropped to his knees when attacked and fallen forward, the killer could have been hiding to the left of the trail. She walked off the trail in that direction and looked carefully for any signs that a person had waited there. There was simply nothing to see—no disturbance in the foliage or the ground cover. It was like an avenging angel had swooped down on Maloney, leaving no trace of his dark mission.

The whole scenario was troubling. It didn't make any sense. She thought about what Nancy Maloney had said about Jake never taking walks. Why was he out here this morning instead of being on the road on the way to his pick-ups? What had led him to do something so out of character? Could he have been meeting someone? Or was he suffering from a troubled spirit and needed to get away, however briefly, from the familiar world of his house and his job?

"What brought you out here, Jake?" Brie asked aloud. "And what happened here?" She squatted down and touched the ground where his body had lain. "I know you can't answer, but I hope to find the truth and, in that way, be able to speak for you."

She stood back up, thinking about Nancy Maloney, wondering how she would go on from this point, knowing the fear she must be feeling. Before Brie was shot, she had never thought much about the survivors. Until she had become one of them, she had never realized how desperately hard it was to go on.

She started back down the trail and hadn't gotten very far when her phone rang. She pulled it out of her pocket. It was Joe Wolf. She answered the call, "This is Brie Beaumont."

"Hello, Brie. Joe Wolf getting back to you."

"Thanks, Joe. I imagine Lieutenant Fenton has informed you that I'm working on the Maloney case."

"Yes, he has, and welcome aboard."

"I was calling to see how the autopsy is proceeding. There's someone I'm hoping to interview yet today, but I'm waiting on the ruling."

"I just finished the autopsy, and Maloney's death will be ruled a homicide. It comes as no surprise, I'm sure. All the signs pointed to it, but I know you have to wait for the official verdict."

"I found out from the victim's wife that he was left-handed."

"I just got that information from Dent—Lt. Fenton. It all jibes with my findings. There was no weapon found at the scene and no hesitation marks that would indicate a suicide. The neck wound was considerably deeper on the left side, which suggests a right-handed attacker. There was blood cast-off on the foliage to the right of the body at the crime scene, which would indicate the same thing, but also tell us that the vic was attacked from behind. The absence of defensive wounds on the victim tells us that he was taken by surprise and easily overpowered."

"Anything else of interest?" Brie asked.

"Really nothing. No other trauma to the body. We ran a tox screen, but that will take at least a week to get back. I'd guess the attack on Maloney happened so fast he wouldn't have known what hit him. Poor guy."

"And your estimate for time of death still holds?"

"Yes, I believe he died between six-thirty and nine-thirty a.m."

"Well, that's all I need to know, Joe. Thanks for getting back to me."

"Good luck with the investigation. Keep me apprised, okay?"

"Will do, Joe." Brie ended the call and continued down the remainder of the trail to her car. When she got there, she pulled out the piece of paper Nancy had given her and punched in the number for Dan Littleton, Jake's former partner in his trucking business.

A woman answered on the third ring. "Coffee Commons," she said.

Brie was a bit surprised not to have reached his residence. "Is Dan Littleton there?" she asked.

"He just left to get some supplies," the woman said. "Can I take a message?"

"No, I think I'll just stop by. How late are you open today?" Brie asked.

"Till five."

"Will Dan be there till closing?"

"Yes. Oh, I have a customer."

"Can you give me your address quickly?"

"Sure, it's 220 Main Street."

"Thanks," Brie said and ended the call.

She was glad Littleton wasn't there. It was always good to take any potential suspect by surprise, since initial encounters were sometimes telling. She climbed in the car, entered the address into the navigation system, and headed toward the main road. She turned left onto Highway 191 that ran northwest toward Machias.

The road climbed steadily after leaving the village, and Brie soon found herself in the midst of a surreal landscape. It was low tide, and the mudflats seemed to stretch for miles. The extreme high tides of the Bay of Fundy create a reciprocal effect when the tide is out, as it was now. Vast mudflats spread out from the coastline as far as the eye could see. There was an onshore breeze today that carried with it the smell of thousands of acres of organically and biologically rich ooze—the smell of low tide, the smell of the flats.

But even more startling was the landscape Brie witnessed out the right side of the car. The undulating land rolled toward the horizon—land where nothing grew but a bluish sea of low-lying vegetation. Brie had studied geology in college, and she could spot a glacial landscape. The terrain she saw before her was devoid of trees and punctuated only by large rocks and the occasional giant boulder that loomed out of the ground like some misshapen leviathan—remnants of the Laurentide Ice Sheet, the last glacier that had covered North America from Maine to Montana and had retreated some 20,000 years ago. These were the great blueberry barrens of Down East Maine that produced almost all of the world's wild blueberries. She had read about the barrens, but nothing could prepare her for the starkness and scope of the landscape. Brie had always been drawn to things that felt larger than life, and there was a beauty to the vast emptiness she saw to the east and west of her. The tides, the mudflats, the barrens—it was the beauty of things untamed.

Brie continued along the highway, mentally formulating some questions she wanted to ask Dan Littleton. She thought about what Nancy Maloney had said in their interview about Littleton and her husband working together in some kind of a partnership that had ended on less than amicable terms. There certainly could be animosity there, which could translate into motive.

In a little over a half hour Brie arrived at the outskirts of Machias. She drove through East Machias and followed the highway as it turned and ran next to the river for a short way. She passed a number of small businesses on the outskirts before coming to the center of town. Her navigator directed her to a storefront location up ahead on her left, and she soon spotted The Coffee Commons in a row of buildings about a block before the road crossed the bridge over the river. She could see a campus up on the bluffs on the other side of the river. This was obviously the center of town, and it was buzzing with activity at this time of the day. She turned to the right and came around a couple blocks and back onto the main road, where she got lucky and found a parking spot across the street from the coffee shop.

Two students with knapsacks were just exiting when she walked in, and the place was now empty. She spotted a man behind the counter, and his eyebrows went up as she approached—a subtle cue that he found her attractive. *Good,* Brie thought. *Maybe he'll drop his guard a bit.* But then she saw him notice her badge and his expression changed.

"Dan Littleton?" Brie asked as she approached. She placed his age at around thirty-five. The man wore black-framed glasses, and his sandy blond hair looked disarranged in a very arranged way. He wore a snug tee shirt that said *Coffee Commons,* and Brie guessed from his physique that he worked out.

"Yes," he said, studying her. "What can I do for you?"

Brie produced her ID. "I'm Detective Brie Beaumont with the Maine State Police."

"What's this about?" he asked. Brie noted that he looked more guarded than surprised.

"I'm here to ask you some questions about Jake Maloney."

"What about him?" Littleton asked, a hint of irritation in his voice. He took the towel from his shoulder and started drying a coffee mug. Brie noted that he was right-handed.

"He was found dead this morning in Tucker Harbor. It appears he was murdered."

Dan's head came up and he studied Brie for a moment, his expression unreadable. "Jake's dead?"

"Yes, he is."

"Wow. Did you say he was murdered? How do you know that?"

"It's the medical examiner's ruling."

Dan shook his head. "That's terrible."

Brie noted that he didn't display the degree of disbelief that such news usually triggered. Judging from his appearance, he might just be playing it cool, or there might be another reason.

"How did he die, if I might ask?"

"In a violent manner," Brie said. "His throat was cut."

She thought she saw a shiver pass through Littleton. "How horrible," he said. "Who would do such a thing?"

"That, of course, is what we are investigating." She pulled her small notebook and pen from her back pocket.

"Jake's wife, Nancy, said you had worked with Jake for a while in his business."

"That's right. I worked for him for about fifteen months. It was a couple of years ago, though. How's Nancy doing?" he asked, not looking up from his cup drying. "This must be terrible for her."

"It is, of course," Brie said. "What was your job when you worked for Jake?"

"It was a part-time arrangement. I drove the truck two days a week on pick-ups and deliveries. They were usually long days, so it equaled about twenty to twenty-five hours a week. Jake used that time to phone and call on potential customers to try and line up more work. The recession had hit and he had lost a percentage of his business. Lots of businesses closed during those couple of years. He was always trying to find another angle to work."

Brie jotted notes. "Nancy said that the two of you parted on less than amicable terms. She didn't seem to know much about it. Apparently, Jake had told her simply that it wasn't working out between the two of you. He wouldn't tell her anything else, but she remembered that he seemed upset about it. So what happened?"

"To be brief, Jake accused me of taking work on the side. Hauling goods and pocketing the money. Of course, I wasn't doing any such thing, but he somehow got this idea in his head, and there was no getting it out." Littleton looked her straight in the eyes now and said, "Frankly, I think Jake had a mildly paranoid side. He was always guarded when talking about the business or any new clients or prospects. I don't know what he thought. I wasn't going to buy a truck and steal his business. It got to the point where I just wasn't comfortable working for him. And then for no apparent reason, he up and lays me off one day. No notice or anything."

"Were you angry?"

"Of course I was. I needed the job."

"Did he give a reason?"

"Just said he'd gotten a new contract and that he'd be doing all the driving from then on."

"Did he say what the contract was?"

"Are you kidding? The guy never told me anything. I had to wonder if he treated his wife the same way. If so, it wasn't a formula for a great marriage."

"So, that's when you started working here?" Brie asked.

"My girlfriend and I had wanted to open this coffee shop, and when this space came up for lease, we jumped on it. It was just a few weeks after I quit working for Jake." He stared past Brie and out the front window. "I guess things have a way of working out."

"So, if you needed the job with Maloney and the money it provided, where did you get the funds to open this place?"

Littleton looked at her with narrowed eyes. "You don't miss a beat, do you?" he said with a hint of irritation.

"It's my job not to," Brie said, holding his gaze.

"It's really none of your business where I got the funds," he said.

"Actually, it is. Especially since a man you used to work for has been murdered."

Littleton let out a sigh. "Fine," he said. "My girlfriend had some money from her family. Her grandmother had left it to her. She bankrolled the start-up here."

Brie had no reason to disbelieve him and decided his reluctance to reveal where the funds had come from had more to do with male ego than any kind of subterfuge.

"I need to ask where you were between six-thirty and nine-thirty this morning?"

"I was here with Molly—that's my girlfriend—opening up and taking care of the morning rush."

"Is your girlfriend here right now?"

"No. It's been slow this afternoon, so I told her to go home. That I could handle the afternoon clientele."

"Please give me her name, phone number, and your home address," Brie said.

Littleton did as she asked, but began fidgeting with things behind the counter. Brie could see an escalating irritation in him at her questions. Finally, he looked her straight in the eyes. "If you're looking for someone with a motive, I think you should look closer to home," he said.

"You mean his wife?"

"No. I think he was having an affair with someone."

"Why do you think that?" Brie asked.

"We were on a large delivery together one day, up in Calais. He got a call on his cell phone. We'd been talking, and he didn't check to see who it was before he answered. He seemed happy to be talking to whoever was on the other end, but flustered at the same time. He ended the call rather quickly, saying, 'I can't talk now, Tara. I'll call you later.' Then in his usual cryptic way he turned and said to me, 'You didn't hear that.' He tried to make light of it, but he seemed uncomfortable for the rest of the trip."

"Huh," Brie said. "You know anyone named Tara that lives around here?" She jotted the name in her notebook.

"Nope. Doesn't ring a bell."

"Is there another number you can be reached at other than the coffee house?"

Littleton gave her his cell phone number, which Brie wrote down. "I think that's all for now," she said. She gave him one of her cards. "If you think of anything that might pertain to the case, please give me a call."

He agreed, and with that Brie turned to leave. Along the back wall on a shelf about five feet off the ground was a group of trophies for some kind of martial arts. She walked over to them and saw they were championship trophies for mixed martial arts. They bore Dan Littleton's name. She turned around. Littleton was looking at her with an air of cockiness. "I see you are quite adept at the martial arts," she said.

"That's right," was all he said. His expression was unreadable.

Brie studied him for a moment. "Good for you," she finally said. "We'll be in touch." She put her notebook in her pocket and left the coffee shop. She knew, with his martial arts training, that Littleton would make the list of those physically capable of killing Maloney.

She walked back to her vehicle and got in. The day had turned out warm and beautiful, with temps around seventy-five degrees. She opened both front windows and sat there for a few minutes, thinking about the interview. Then she pulled her notebook out and put the address for Littleton's girlfriend in her GPS. She pulled out of her spot, took a right at the corner, and headed up the hill to the upper part of the town.

Molly Harrigan lived in a vintage saltbox-style colonial on a quiet, tree-lined street. It was an awfully nice house, and Brie thought maybe Grandma had been *very* good to her. The door opened just as Brie was preparing to ring the bell for the third time. The young woman was bleary-eyed, and Brie guessed she'd been taking a nap. Brie placed her age at around twenty-four or twenty-five years old. A mane of wavy black hair framed a face with flawless alabaster skin and intense green eyes. "Molly Harrigan?" she asked.

"Yes," she said, rubbing her eyes. But she came around quickly when she saw the badge and gun. "What's going on?" she asked.

Brie filled her in on the situation and told her she'd already interviewed Dan Littleton.

"Maybe you should step in," Molly said.

"That might be best."

Molly moved back and let her in the door. Brie asked her how the routine had gone at the coffee house that morning. Molly confirmed that Dan had been with her during the timeframe of the murder. Of course, in the time it had taken Brie to find the house, Littleton could well have called Molly and told her what to say. But Molly was also able to provide the names of two or three customers who'd been in the coffee house that morning and who could attest to Dan's being there during the three-hour period in question. Problem was, they were only first names, but Brie wrote them down. Molly Harrigan thought they were students at U Maine Machias, just on the other side of the bridge.

If necessary Brie would attempt to track them down. But it looked to her as if Dan Littleton, while he may have had motive and means—the martial arts training would have given him the strength and the stealth needed to commit the murder—he hadn't had opportunity. She thanked Molly Harrigan for the information and gave her a card. "If those students come back in, would you get their full names and a cell phone number where they can be reached?" Brie said.

"Sure. No problem," Molly said. "They're regulars. I'm sure they'll be back in in the next few days."

Brie headed for her car on the opposite side of the street. She made her way slowly out of town. By the time she got back to Tucker Harbor, it would be time to think about dinner. She decided she'd give Varney's Swedish meatballs a try. In a village the size of Tucker Harbor, there couldn't be too many Taras, assuming she lived in the village, and assuming the story Littleton had told her was true. Brie decided she'd ask Atticus Kane at the inn if he knew of anyone by that name. He seemed like a discreet person. She didn't want conjecture flying around the village before she'd had a chance to uncover the key persons of interest.

The investigation was underway, and it felt good to have another lead. *Forward momentum,* she thought. "Who are you, Tara?" she asked aloud. "And how do you figure into this?"

Chapter 9

Brie followed the road back out of Machias the way she had come in. Once outside the town limits, she mentally reviewed the interview with Dan Littleton—both what he had said as well as her conjecture about what the real truth was. At this point she had no reason either to believe or disbelieve what he had told her. She had learned long ago that she seldom got the whole truth from a suspect or person of interest, but rather a version of the truth. Therefore, she didn't take testimony at face value. In her book, the truth was always discounted. Once you had stripped away the layers of embellishments, half-truths, and outright lies, the truth was what you had left. It was a process of distillation, with the detective as alchemist.

Dan had told her that Jake Maloney had basically accused him of stealing—of taking extra deliveries and pocketing the money. Certainly a possibility. Littleton wanted to open a coffee house. He could have used the extra capital. Littleton had also said that he thought Jake was a little paranoid. He based that assessment on Jake's accusation that he was stealing from him, but maybe there was a half-truth there. Something to think about. And maybe if Maloney *was* paranoid, he had had good reason. After all, he'd been murdered in a violent way, which might indicate that he did indeed have something to be paranoid about.

Brie also thought about Littleton's demeanor during the interview. He had shown little emotion, either shock or disbelief, at the news of the murder. That in itself didn't mean a lot. Not everyone showed emotion at such news, and clearly Littleton and the victim had not gotten along. Brie had actually found that the most common reaction to such news was fear. When someone connected to a person is murdered, it often triggers a fearful reaction. Fear of being accused; fear that he himself may be a target. The person often asks if he is in danger—a question she could seldom answer, especially early in an investigation. She tried to assuage such fears by reminding people that, except for a madman on the loose, killers always have a motive.

Finally, she thought about what Littleton had told her about the phone call, the name Tara, and Maloney's discomfort at being overheard. The story could be true, or it could be Littleton's attempt to deflect the focus from himself. But if she could believe Molly Harrigan, Littleton had an alibi for the time of the murder.

Brie had been so wrapped up in her thoughts that she had forgotten to look around at the remarkable vistas as she drove back toward Tucker Harbor. She rolled her driver's window all the way down, and the scent of sun-ripened blueberries from the barrens was almost overpoweringly sweet. For whatever reason, that seductive scent set up an acute longing for John and the *Maine Wind*. She looked south toward the ocean and wondered where he would be anchoring tonight and what George would be cooking. But before she knew it, she was descending into Tucker Harbor, and her mind returned to the business at hand.

She could see Varney's diner on the left as she came down the hill. She pulled into the parking lot in front of the diner and turned off the car. She sat there for a few minutes jotting down thoughts that had come to her on the drive down. She planned to call Dent Fenton after dinner and also write up a report of what she and Detective Marty Dupuis had accomplished so far. She checked her watch—almost six-thirty. Time to eat. She reached over to the passenger seat and grabbed the Maine State Police windbreaker Dent had given her. She stepped out of the car and slipped on the jacket. It covered her gun. She headed into the diner and paused at the small hostess station next to the door. Varney looked up from his grill through the serving window behind the lunch counter. He gave her a little wave, then went back to his cooking.

Brie saw the pale young woman with the jet black hair, whom she'd encountered on the road earlier, coming toward her with a menu in hand. Her fingernails were painted black, and she wore blue lipstick. When she got close, Brie could see her name tag. It said Amber. "Hey," Brie said, smiling at her.

"Hey," Amber replied in a tone that said: *I might just make it till tomorrow*.

"Do you have a booth, Amber?" Brie could see that there were a number of empty ones. The only other diners were two older couples at the far end of the establishment. As Amber seated her Brie saw the girl studying her badge. Finally, curiosity got the best of her.

"Are you a cop?" she asked. "You weren't wearing a badge when I saw you earlier."

"You're quite observant, Amber." Brie thought about explaining, but it was too complicated, so she just said, "I was off duty."

"Oh, I get it," Amber said. "I suppose you're here about Jake Maloney."

"As a matter of fact, I am," Brie said.

"Jake was a nice guy," Amber said, almost to herself. "He didn't deserve what happened." She drifted off, leaving Brie with the menu as well as the impression that she had both known and liked Jake Maloney. Brie decided Amber might be a valuable source of information.

She opened the menu and studied the dinners. She had been going to try the special—Swedish meatballs—but what caught her eye was the pan-fried halibut with sautéed summer vegetables. Except for lobster, there is nothing better than fresh halibut from the coast of Maine. She closed her menu, and when Amber came back she asked her if the halibut was good.

"It's Varney's specialty," Amber said. Then she dropped her voice. "And a lot healthier than those meatballs."

"Thanks, Amber, I'll take your advice. One halibut dinner," she said, handing over her menu.

Amber nodded and the corners of her mouth almost lifted into a smile, but she quickly got them under control. She jotted the order on her pad and headed back to the serving window to tell Varney.

For a few moments, Brie watched Varney Simms scurrying back and forth at the grill prepping her dinner. Then she turned and gazed out the front window. The parking lot below the trailhead was now clear of townspeople and police cars, but the crime scene tape still cordoned off the entrance to the trail, discouraging anyone from entering the woods. Brie looked toward the harbor. The lobster fleet was all in for the day. Her gut told her that even if she found information on the woman named Tara, this evening would not be the best time to seek her out. But she planned to be on it first thing in the morning, assuming she got a lead.

After dinner she would head back to the inn and set up the laptop Dent had given her. She needed to log into the Maine State Police and write up a report on the questioning of Nancy Maloney and Dan Littleton. She also wanted to download the pictures she had taken of the crime scene and have a closer look at them.

In a few minutes Varney came out of the kitchen and delivered her dinner personally. "The halibut was just caught today," he said. "It should be good."

"Thanks, Varney. It looks delicious."

Varney lingered for a moment and then headed back behind the lunch counter. She again noticed his limp. As he worked, Brie cast surreptitious glances at him. Varney was nervous energy personified. His eyes were constantly on the move, surveilling the interior of the diner as well as the guests. Brie always found the eyes telling. Varney's eyes weren't shifty like a felon's, but instead reminded her of a trapped animal. If she were to venture a guess, it might be that he was an unhappy man. She wondered why. It was her job to wonder why, and she slipped seamlessly into the role as easily as slipping on comfortable shoes. *Gumshoes,* she thought and chuckled inwardly.

Her halibut dinner was delicious, and she savored every bite. Amber checked in with her partway through, and Brie ordered coffee. When she was finished, Amber came back to get her plate and sang the praises of their blueberry pie—it was more of a dirge than a jingle.

"Okay, you've convinced me," Brie said. "You didn't steer me wrong on the halibut, so I know I can trust you. Blueberry pie it is."

Amber nodded glumly and headed for the pie.

I think this girl deserves a nice tip, Brie thought to herself. She had a soft spot for teens who struggled—especially the girls. She hadn't forgotten how hard it was to grow up, but especially to grow up feeling different. Even as a child, Brie had seen the world from a different and unusual angle, which had always made it hard for her to fit in, especially with the hip crowd. She realized now that her way of looking at things, of seeing the world, while not common, was what had made her so successful at her job.

When it was time to go, Brie did indeed leave Amber a very nice tip. As she walked past the front window toward her car, she saw the girl standing at the table, looking a bit nonplused. She looked up and caught Brie's eye and gave her a little wave.

Brie got in her car, took a left out of the parking lot, and headed toward The Whale Spout Inn. At the far end of the village, she headed up the hill and turned into the driveway for the inn. There was a small guest parking lot in the back, and Brie pulled in there. She reached across the seat and grabbed the case with the laptop. She got out of the car and headed around the path and in the front door. Beyond the entryway she stuck her head into the parlor on the left, where she had signed in. No one there. The inn seemed empty. *Atticus Kane must be off on an errand,* she thought.

She walked across the hall and into the other front room, which was much larger than the parlor. This was obviously the main gathering room for the guests. While not as lavish as Snug Harbor Bed and Breakfast, where she'd spent time during the case on Granite Island, the Whale Spout Inn was extremely homey. The room was filled with comfortable chairs and sofas in a variety of warm but muted colors. Hand-knitted throws lay here and there, and tables with lamps made each spot conducive to reading. A decorative bowl of candy or nuts sat on each table, along with some kind of a book about Maine. Brie walked around picking them up and checking the spines. Some were hiking guides or guides to coastal villages. Others were about ships or Maine's history.

The focal point of the room was a large fireplace flanked by built-in bookcases. There was a French-style window above each bookcase. Brie walked over and looked at the collection of photographs along the top shelf of the bookcases. There were family pictures going back several generations. Pictures of Atticus with his parents and in school, and pictures from his time in the service that showed him in his Navy whites with groups of his buddies.

"That's my rogue's gallery." Brie jumped at the sound of Atticus' voice.

"Hi, Atticus," she said, turning around. "I didn't hear you come in."

"Sorry, I didn't mean to startle you."

"Don't worry about it. I was just checking out the place. You've made this room wonderfully comfortable."

"Thanks," Atticus said. He looked like he didn't know what to do with the compliment, so he stuck his hands in his pockets.

"So you were in the Navy." Brie said. "Where were you stationed?"

"Actually, I was on the nuclear subs—Los Angeles Class—stationed out of Groton, Connecticut. I did my active duty back in the eighties."

"It's quite a leap from a nuclear sub to a Down East inn," Brie said.

"I guess so," he said. "My dad was in the Navy, and he thought I should do a stint in the service. I don't regret that experience, but running an inn is more my style. I've got a funny thing about seeing the sky every day, especially since my time spent on the subs. And I'm kind of a pacifist by nature—more into gardens than grenades."

Brie picked up her laptop, which she had set on the floor next to the bookcase. "Well, I've got some work to do, so I guess I'll get settled in upstairs."

"Feel free to come down here and work if you wish. It's a little more comfortable."

"Thanks, Atticus." She headed for the stairs and then remembered about Tara. "Atticus," she said, turning back to him, "Do you know of anyone in the village or surrounding area with the name Tara?"

Atticus thought for a minute and then his face lit up. "Why, yes. There is a Tara in the village. Tara French. She and her husband Steve live out Back Bay Road, which is just down the hill a bit and to the left. It's the third house. You can't miss it. It's a gray Cape Cod with a bright red door." He paused and looked at her. "Does this have to do with the case?" he asked.

"I'm not sure," Brie said. "Anyway, I'd appreciate it if you didn't mention my query to anyone."

"No problem with that. I'm the original tight-lipped Mainer."

"Perfect," Brie said. "Thanks, Atticus. I think I'll go grab a shower and get to work." She headed up the stairs, pausing to gaze out the window on the landing for a few moments. Then she continued on up to her room. She locked her door and laid the laptop case on the small desk.

She checked her watch. It was almost seven-thirty. It had been a long day—really long. She thought about the fact that this morning she'd been aboard the *Maine Wind,* going about her duties, looking forward to their voyage to New Brunswick. Here she was twelve hours later, installed in an inn and wearing a Maine State Police badge and gun. *This is crazy,* she thought. She took off her gun and badge, laid them on the desk, and headed into the bathroom. She reached in the shower and turned on the hot water, went back to the bedroom for her toiletries, then climbed out of her clothes and stepped into the shower. The hot water felt wonderful. As she washed her hair and her body, she emptied her mind of the details of the case and enjoyed a nice long steam under the large showerhead.

After about fifteen minutes, she climbed out of the shower, toweled herself off, and headed out to her duffel. She pulled out a set of cozy sweats and put them on. The air was already cooling off, and with the onshore breeze, it would only get more so as the evening wore on. She pulled on a pair of thick cotton socks, combed out her hair, and brushed it into a ponytail. She had the original low maintenance hair. It was blonde and straight as an arrow, and she wore it long, so it looked nice down or up in a ponytail. She never had to mess with styling irons, so there were no tedious stints in front of the mirror. She considered herself lucky.

She went out to the desk and took the laptop out, plugged it in, and booted it up. Within a couple minutes a stack of bars appeared on the lower right toolbar. *Huh. Good strong connection 'away' Down East,* she thought. She took her notebook and phone out of her pants pocket, along with a slip of paper Dent Fenton had given her with the login information for the department. She hung her slacks and shirt on hangers and put them in the closet, then sat down at the desk to get to work.

She logged onto the site using her name, badge number and the password that Dent had given her. She first encoded a new password and then entered the case number that had been assigned to Jake Maloney. She started writing a detailed report of the interview with Nancy Maloney that she and Detective Marty Dupuis had conducted. Next she moved on to her interview with Dan Littleton. She worked on the reports for about forty-five minutes, and when she was done, she picked up her cell phone and called Dent Fenton.

He answered on the second ring. "Fenton here."

"Hello, Lieutenant, it's Brie Beaumont."

"Hello, Brie. How's it going down there?"

"Just fine, I think. After Marty—Detective Dupuis—left with Nancy Maloney for the morgue, I went into Machias and interviewed Jake Maloney's former partner. I've just finished writing up a report of that, as well as the Nancy Maloney interview."

"Great. I'll take time to look at those tonight."

"You'll see from the report that Littleton mentioned a woman named Tara. He thought Maloney might be having an affair with someone by that name. I've got a lead on a Tara French here in the village. I thought I'd wait till morning to follow up on that. These lobstering villages tend to roll up the sidewalks by eight o'clock. Also, the husband will be out on his boat in the morning, which will give me a better opportunity to approach her."

"Good thinking, Brie. I'm sending Marty back down tomorrow to interview some of the neighbors."

"Nancy Maloney mentioned having a brother. I thought I'd go interview him after I get done with Tara. Do you want Marty to go along on that?"

"Why don't you go ahead and follow up on that lead, Brie. Marty can work the neighbors and business contacts."

"Copy that, Dent—ah, I mean, sir."

"Don't worry about it, Brie. We're not all that formal, and Dent was how you first knew me. I know Lieutenant or sir is protocol, but I rather like it when you call me Dent."

"Okay, sir," Brie said. She heard a chuckle from the other end of the connection. "I'll check in tomorrow."

"Copy that," Dent said and ended the call.

Brie stood up and stretched her arms over her head and leaned slowly to the left and right. Then she bent over and touched her toes and hung there for a few moments before rolling slowly back up. She went over and leaned against the dresser and began stretching her calf muscles. It was nearing eight-thirty, and she decided she'd get a run in before dark. Life aboard ship wasn't conducive to a daily running regimen, and even though she tried to fit in a run whenever they went ashore, she was sure she'd lost some of her aerobic strength. She finished stretching her legs, slipped on her running shoes, and tied them up. She picked up her gun and her car key and went downstairs.

Outside the breeze had come up. It was a beautiful night for a run. She locked her gun in the trunk of the car and zipped the key into the pocket of her sweatpants. She headed down the main road and past the harbor. By the time she reached the end of the village, her heart was pumping and she felt warmed up. She passed the turn for Final Reckoning Road and started up the hill. There were still a couple of diners seated at the front window of Varney's establishment. Brie ran on by and continued up the hill for another mile or so before she crossed the road and headed back toward the village. She hung a left at the street above Varney's diner and ran past Nancy Maloney's house. Her car was in the driveway, and there was a newer pickup truck next to it. Brie figured that belonged to Nancy's brother and felt glad she was with family tonight.

She followed Third Street all the way across until it intersected with the highway again on the far side of the village.

She'd run about two and a half miles, and aside from the older couple in Varney's diner, the sidewalks were indeed rolled up and the village was abed. Brie smiled and shook her head. It felt like a ghost town. But when you're on your lobsterboat heading out of the harbor at four in the morning, there's not much choice but to turn in by seven-thirty or eight o'clock at night.

She turned right at the highway and ran past the Whale Spout Inn and down to the next street, which was Back Bay Road. She looked both directions, then ran across the highway and down the street where Tara and Steve French lived. The third house was a gray Cape Cod with a bright red door. Brie ran by the last two houses on the road. She stopped and turned around and went through the motions of stretching her legs as she studied the Frenches' house. She thought about where it was located in relation to Jake's house, but other than that she got no particular vibe here. The houses on this street were spaced out a bit from one another. But someone coming or going could certainly be seen easily enough, unless it was dark or there was heavy rain or fog. If there was something going on between this Tara and Jake Maloney, Brie guessed there were others in the village—possibly including Tara's husband Steve—who were privy to the situation. *And that could lead to a motive,* she thought. *In fact, the most common of motives.*

She straightened up and headed back toward the inn. She guessed she'd run a little over three miles, and she wasn't as winded as she had expected. When she got to the inn, she retrieved her gun from the trunk of the car, walked around front and climbed the steps to the porch. She turned and looked out at the ocean. It was dusk, and the harbor was silver in the evening light. The salty breeze came off the sea and made her think of John. After a few moments, she headed in the door and up the stairs to her room to place a call to him.

Inside her room, she flipped the wall switch, which turned on a light in the center of the ceiling. She set her gun on the bedside table and locked the door. Then she walked to the desk, picked up her cell phone, and brought up John's number. She got his voice mail and figured that wherever they were anchored, there was no cell reception. She left a brief message telling him how she had settled in and then signed off, saying she missed him and her shipmates. She'd taken a shower before working on her reports, but she'd worked up a sweat while running and so hopped in for another quick one. She climbed out a few minutes later and went to her duffel for her PJs. Then she picked her camera up off the bed and removed the SD card, went over to the laptop and inserted it. When the menu came up, she clicked "Open Files" and sat down to go over her pictures from the crime scene.

Brie brought the pictures up to full screen size and clicked through them slowly, studying each one. She had taken lots of shots of the body from different angles, along with some close-ups of Jake's head and neck that partially showed the wound. She'd also taken pictures both up and down the trail from the scene of the crime, and pictures of the vegetation and lay of the land immediately around where the body lay. She'd gone back to the scene before heading to Machias to interview Dan Littleton, and she had hoped that taking that second look, coupled with studying the pictures, might trigger some thought or conjecture, or even better, that she might notice some clue that the killer had left behind. But there was nothing. The scene was as clean as if Jake had been deposited there by a UFO. And then something occurred to her—something she'd forgotten to check with Joe Wolf, the medical examiner. She looked at her watch. It was almost ten o'clock—way too late to call him. She opened her small notebook and wrote herself a note to call Joe in the morning. Then she removed her SD card and shut down the computer.

She sat there, stretched her arms over her head and leaned back in the chair. She experienced a bout of yawning so extreme that her eyes started to water. "For heaven's sake, go to bed," she told herself. She mustered the energy to brush her teeth, and when she came out of the bathroom, she shut the window. It was going to be a cool night. She stowed her duffel on the floor by the dresser and flipped off the wall switch, plunging the room into total blackness. She felt her way over to the bed, climbed under the covers, and passed out.

Chapter 10

Trees sway in the March breeze, casting winter-worn limbs across the Crow Moon. Brie and her partner Phil approach the gaping door. Guns drawn, they take the steps in silent stride and pause on either side of the door. The darkness within is black as the portal to hell. Brie hears her heart, feels it beating against her chest. It is so loud she fears, knows, if they enter, it will give away their position. She turns to stop Phil, but he disappears into the darkness beyond. She tries to shout, "No Phil," but the words freeze in her throat. She plunges into the blackness, knowing what's coming—desperate to stop it. As she passes through the portal, the house and room disappear. She stands in a cemetery filled with black umbrellas. The rain drives down, obscuring everything. The people beneath the umbrellas begin to hum just one note, one minor note. Suddenly she is transported without walking and stands before the headstone. It bears her name and two sets of Roman numerals. Her heart pounds so loudly now she thinks it will burst. She tries to work out the dates, but she is being pulled away by some invisible force.

Brie woke with a violent jerk. Her heart was pounding, and she was soaked with sweat. The air around her seemed to vibrate with a strange sound—a steady, low tone that alternated with a single heartbeat. Bits of the disturbing dream filled her mind—Phil, the cemetery, the umbrellas, the people humming that one note—that one terrible note. She sat up on the edge of the bed, fighting off a wave of nausea. After a few moments, she stood up and, reaching out in the darkness, moved toward the opposite wall. The tone and the heartbeat still filled her head. She found the window and shoved up on the sash to let in the night air, and just like that, the sound stopped. She stood next to the window, feeling the cool damp air on her skin, and breathed deeply for a few minutes until the nausea passed.

The nightmares had gotten so much better in the past few months. She wondered if being away from the *Maine Wind,* her safe haven, had reactivated her PTSD. Post-traumatic Stress Disorder was an odd and terrible creature. Just when she thought she had backed it into a corner—gotten it under control—it would pounce on her, and with all its fangs and claws bared, take her down once more. The worst part was that the disorder played tricks with her mind—made her think she saw and heard things that weren't there. The strange sound in the room when she had awakened, for instance. Was it a remnant of the dream, or had it triggered the dream? Even though she was sure of the answer and the cause, she decided she'd ask Atticus in the morning if he had heard anything strange in the night.

She made her way back to the bed. She felt chilled now, but that was so much better than the nausea. She crawled under the covers and curled up. She shivered for a few minutes before her body started to feel warmer. Finally her muscles began to relax. She tried to empty her mind by listening to the night sounds outside her window. She could hear crickets and the faint sound of a wind chime on the front porch. An owl hooted off in the woods. Brie found that lonely sound comforting. Somewhere out there was another creature, like herself, alone in the night.

She woke to the sound of the foghorn at the entrance to the harbor. She lay for a few minutes listening to its mournful call. Out the windows of her room a soft, gray world had replaced the one with sharp edges and definition. The fog seemed a metaphor for her mood this morning. After the nightmare last night, her future again felt obscure and confusing, the way it always did when she was visited by PTSD—when she was visited by the ghosts of her past.

She lay for a few minutes, waking up, and then got up and went to the bathroom and brushed her teeth. She turned on the hot water in the shower, and after the small room began to warm up, she climbed out of her pajamas and stepped in under the spray. She let the hot water beat down on her head and her back as she tried to organize her thoughts about the day ahead. After breakfast, she wanted to call Joe Wolf with a question about the body, and then she planned to head down the road to seek out Tara French. Brie climbed out of the shower, dried off, and wrapped the towel around her. There was a hair dryer in a cradle attached to the wall. She blew her hair dry and brushed it out. She put her pajamas in the wash bowl with some hot soapy water and hand-washed them. After her episode in the night, they had been soaked with sweat. Atticus had a clothesline out back. She'd hang them out there after breakfast so they could dry in the afternoon sun.

Brie dressed in her black slacks and pulled out a long-sleeved knit shirt in a pale blue color. It was a cool morning, and the long sleeves would be welcome. She clipped her badge onto her belt and put on her gun and holster. She had packed a cotton cardigan sweater in her duffel. She put that on and went down for breakfast.

The clock on the mantel read eight oh-five when Brie walked into the dining room. Atticus was clearing off a table and straightened up when she came in.

"Morning, Miss Beaumont, or should I be calling you Detective Beaumont?" he asked.

Brie smiled. "Why don't you call me Brie," she said. "That'll be just fine."

Atticus nodded. "Would you like to sit by the window? Not much of a view this morning with the fog, but folks seem to like the windows."

"Sure," Brie said and headed across the room to the table he had indicated. The tables—there were six of them in the dining room—were covered with cloths of a maritime blue and set with almond-colored china and napkins. A variety of painted seashells decorated the outer edge of each plate, and the flatware was heavy and ornate.

"Would you like coffee?" Atticus asked on his way back to the kitchen.

"Yes, please," Brie said. She was the only one in the dining room so she didn't have to worry about making chit-chat with anyone. *Good,* she thought. *I'm not in the mood.*

The breakfast was blueberry buckwheat pancakes. They were wonderfully thin, packed with wild Maine blueberries, and served with whipped butter and the best maple syrup. Three thick strips of applewood smoked bacon were included and fresh fruit—bananas, peaches and strawberries served in a lovely parfait glass. It was delicious and made Brie miss George's cooking a little less.

She lingered over breakfast just enough to savor the wonderful food and down three cups of coffee, which she needed after the night she had put in.

The next time Atticus came back into the dining room, Brie called him over to her table. "Atticus, could I ask you a question?"

"Sure," he said, setting down the cups in his hands and coming over to where she sat. "What's up?"

"It may sound like an odd question, but did you hear any kind of an unusual noise in the night?"

"Can't say as I did." He looked a bit concerned at her question. "What did it sound like?"

"It sounded like some kind of vibration. Kind of like a heartbeat, I guess."

"Really? That's very strange. I have to say I didn't hear anything, and I tend to be kind of a light sleeper. How loud was it?" he asked.

"It seemed pretty loud to me," Brie said. But she was starting to feel a bit foolish. "You know what?" she said. "It was probably nothing." She certainly wasn't about to tell him that the cause was connected to the dream she'd had and to her own psychological struggles. The mind is a powerful thing, and once compromised it can play all kinds of tricks on a person.

"Well, let me know if you hear it again," Atticus said. He paused, and then something seemed to occur to him. "You know, it got quite cool last night, and I did hear the furnace kick on." He turned and gestured. "These old radiators can make some pretty odd sounds. This time of year there's probably enough air in the pipes to cause some thumping."

"That might just explain it," Brie said. She was pretty sure what she had heard wasn't pipes creaking, unless the pipes were in her own head. She stood up and thanked him for the breakfast, telling him how fantastic the pancakes were. She headed back up to her room to collect her phone and notebook.

Up in her room she walked to the window and looked out at the harbor. She was feeling disheartened. She wondered if she would ever be free of the symptoms of post-traumatic stress. It wasn't just Phil's death or the violent form it had taken, or the fact that she had been right next to him when it happened. It wasn't that he had been her partner and her friend, or that he had left behind a wife and a little boy. And it wasn't just the guilt she felt that he had taken the bullet first—that he had died and she had survived. It was the sum total of all of these things that had indelibly marked her psyche.

She was suddenly glad she had decided to work this case. Painful as it might be, it was a way of testing the waters. If putting on a badge and gun again propelled her right back to where she'd been eighteen months ago, then what point would there be in returning to her job. She decided that this assignment would be a kind of litmus test of her psychological stability. What had happened during the night might just be a minor setback. She decided to adopt a wait-and-see attitude. *Just work the case,* she thought. *Just work the case.* She put her phone and notebook in her pocket, exchanged her sweater for the Maine State Police jacket, and with all the resolve she could muster, headed out to find Tara French.

Brie decided to take the car—more official. Anyway, she planned to go interview Nancy Maloney's brother after she got done with Tara. And if she turned something up in this first interview, she'd have to talk to Tara's husband later in the day. But he wouldn't be back in from pulling his pots until afternoon, so she thought that, in between, she'd stop in to visit Nancy Maloney and then head out to talk to her brother, Nate Freeman. If Jake Maloney was fooling around with someone in the village, that would give the husband a motive and possibly Nancy Maloney's brother as well.

Brie climbed into the car and lowered the driver's window. She took out her phone and brought up Dent Fenton's number. He answered on the second ring, and she told him what she had planned for the morning and that she'd check in with Marty Dupuis along the way. Marty was going to be questioning neighbors today as well as some of the customers that Jake regularly delivered to.

She remembered she had a question for Joe Wolf. She brought up his number. She thought about his Native American heritage and wondered if he had grown up on the Penobscot reservation. She recalled his dark eyes and black hair, which he wore in a traditional braid, and she wondered why he had decided to go into forensic pathology. *I bet he has an interesting story,* she thought.

Joe answered on the third ring. "Hello, Brie. How's the case going so far?" he asked.

"So far, so good, Joe. I've got a couple leads and a few people to interview today. It's too early to know where this is headed."

Joe Wolf hesitated. "Is everything all right, Brie?"

His question took her by surprise. "Yes," she said. "Why do you ask?"

"It sounds like something rests heavy on your heart," he said.

Brie was struck by the gentleness of his query. She paused for a moment, deciding what she wanted to say. "I had a bit of a harrowing night last night. I told you about being shot and that I struggle with PTSD. Well, sometimes I have really bad dreams—often they take the form of flashbacks. I know what's coming—that my partner is going to die, but I can't stop it. Last night was a doozy."

"I'm sorry to hear that, Brie." There was compassion in his voice. "It's a tough condition to deal with. Really tough. You're wrestling with ghosts—memories, fears, regrets—none of it substantial or real in any physical way. Although the symptoms certainly are physical and very real."

"Putting on a badge again may have been the trigger," Brie said. "I'm hoping I won't have continuing problems as I work this case."

"Remember, Brie, those dreams, terrible as they are, can have meaning—symbolism that may relate to the case. The subconscious mind tends to combine things in odd ways."

When he said that, Brie suddenly flashed back to the part of the dream where she was standing in front of the headstone with her name on it. There had been numbers there—Roman numerals, but she couldn't remember them.

"Thanks, Joe. I'll keep that in mind. And thanks for listening."

"Anytime, Brie. Were you calling with a question?"

"As a matter of fact, yes. I forgot to ask what the lividity showed when you did the autopsy. Whether there were any signs that Maloney's body had been moved?" Brie knew that lividity, or the pooling of blood in a corpse due to gravity, can be a clue to whether the body has been moved after death.

"No signs that he was moved post mortem," Joe said. "Lividity was consistent with the prone position the body was in when discovered. The Evidence Response Team also ran an LCV test on the ground where he fell."

Brie knew that Leucocrystal Violet is used to detect blood that is not readily visible. When the chemical is sprayed on a surface, blood will turn purple. "And what did the test show?" she asked.

"It showed a large concentration of blood in that spot on the ground."

"So I guess we can remove any question mark about where the murder occurred."

"Yes."

"Well, thanks, Joe."

"If any other questions come up, give me a call."

"Will do." Brie ended the call, stuck her phone in her pocket, and turned on the car. She took a right out of the driveway and headed for Tara French's house.

She turned left onto Back Bay Road, and when she got to the Frenches' house, parked across the road. She took a couple of minutes to collect her thoughts and jot a few notes for the interview in her notebook.

Brie got out of her car and headed across the road to the gray house with the red door where the Frenches lived. She took her ID out of her pocket and rang the bell. In a few moments a woman opened the door. She had thick reddish-brown hair that seemed to have a mind of its own. She had secured it in a number of ways, but still the hair had gotten loose and wisps of it hung here and there around her face. The effect was quite sexy, or was at least Brie's idea of what a guy might find sexy.

"Tara French?" Brie said. She saw the woman's eyes travel to the badge on her belt.

"Yes," she said hesitantly.

"I'm Detective Brie Beaumont with the Maine State Police. Could I ask you a few questions?" Brie said, opening her ID up for Tara to see.

Tara just nodded and opened the screen door. She didn't try to feign surprise, and Brie gave her points for honesty based on that. "You've come about Jake, haven't you?" she said in a resigned way.

"Yes," Brie said.

Tara showed her into the living room. "I have some cookies I need to get out of the oven," she said.

Brie could smell the cookies and decided Tara wasn't using them as an excuse to bolt out the back door. "Go ahead," she said. "I'll wait here."

Tara hurried for the kitchen. She was carrying some extra weight—maybe twenty or twenty-five pounds—but she glowed with vitality. She seemed in every way the antithesis of Maloney's wife, Nancy. Brie thought she could understand Jake's attraction to her.

Brie looked around the room. Tara kept a nice house. The tables glowed from being waxed, and the wood floors shone. The room was filled with thoughtful touches that make a mere house into a home. The furniture was new, and the largest piece—an overstuffed leather sofa—looked like it had cost a pretty penny.

Tara came back into the room with a plate of cookies. "Would you like one?" she asked. "They're oatmeal scotchies."

"Thanks, but no," Brie said. "I just had breakfast a little while ago."

Tara set them down on the coffee table in front of the leather sofa. "Please sit down," she said.

Brie sat on the sofa. The leather was so soft she had to stifle a moan of pleasure. "Tara, I'll get right to the point. Your name has come up in connection with Jake Maloney, who was found murdered yesterday out on the Heron Head Trail. Can you tell me about your relationship with the victim?"

Tara lowered her head, and Brie saw her eyes fill with tears. She wondered if this was the first time Tara had cried, if maybe she had been desperately trying, as some women do, to keep that grief at bay with a marathon stint of house cleaning and baking.

"Jake and I were lovers," she said almost in a whisper. She didn't beat around the bush or sugar coat it. She just put it out there.

Brie again admired her honesty and drew some immediate conclusions about her character. As to the affair, Brie had learned over the years that women usually have very specific reasons for such behavior—loneliness being chief among them.

"When did you last see Jake Maloney?" Brie asked.

"Yesterday morning, early. About quarter past four. After Steve had left the harbor."

"And how long was he here?"

"I'm not sure exactly. I fell asleep about quarter of seven, after we made love. He was still here then, but when I woke later, around eight o'clock, he was gone."

"Can you tell me about the relationship? How and why you got involved?" Brie asked.

Tara let out a sigh of resignation. "I left Tucker Harbor when I was eighteen, thinking I never wanted to come back here. I went away to college in Bangor. I did come home in the summers, of course, like all students, but I always felt like a visitor. I guess that surprised me. Maybe even scared me a little—that you can grow up in a place, as part of a family, and so quickly detach from it. But my friends at school said they felt the same thing, so I figured it was normal.

"I hadn't set anything on fire in high school, but I found I really liked college. I'd always liked reading books, so I majored in English. The problem was I had no idea what I wanted to do. I really didn't want to teach, so when I graduated, I ended up doing an odd assortment of things. I worked in an office for a while taking phone calls and doing filing, but

I always felt like I was smarter than the boss, and eventually I left that job. Then I worked in a coffee house and I liked that better. I enjoyed making something, even if it was only coffee drinks. I decided I was a more hands-on kind of person." Tara looked at Brie to see if she should go on, and Brie just nodded.

"It was around that time that I started thinking about moving back to Tucker Harbor. I'd had this crazy idea that maybe I'd try writing a book. *The Perils of a Twenty-four Year Old Who Knows Nothing About Life* might have been a good title. So I moved back to the homestead, and soon after that Steve French—whom I'd gone to high school with—started calling me.

"He'd enlisted in the service for four years. When he got out, he came back home and bought his own lobsterboat. I was pretty impressed with that. What's more, he had a house. I guess it was pretty easy to fall in love with him. He was nice looking—successful. I hadn't realized at that point that I was a restless spirit. That I got bored with things easily. Looking back, I don't know how I could have missed it. I think we're just stupid in our twenties. Maybe in our thirties, too. Then I guess you finally start to figure things out, but you've planted these landmines along the way. So you tiptoe through life hoping you won't step on one."

Brie was fascinated by what Tara was saying but wanted to move the topic back to Jake. "So, how did the thing with Jake Maloney get started?" she asked.

"Jake and Nancy Maloney moved to the village about ten years ago. I really didn't know either of them very well. Then about three years ago, I got talking to Jake at a community get-together. As to how the affair started—maybe we were both just bored or lonely or depressed. I don't know.

"Our encounters over the three years were few and far between. Usually when Nancy would go to visit her friend for a couple of days. Jake and I never thought about being together in any permanent way. We just liked having sex. I guess it brought something unexpected to our predictable lives. I think the fact that there was no way to plan the next encounter made it seem exciting."

"Did you talk about ending it?" Brie asked.

"Not really. I think we both felt guilty about it, but not guilty enough to end it. It's a lot easier to get into something than to get out of it, I guess."

A lot like a lobster trap, Brie thought, and reflected on the various traps people fumble into in life without ever considering an exit strategy.

"Do you think anyone knew you were having an affair with Maloney?"

"I wouldn't be surprised. In a village this size it's hard to keep any kind of secret—especially one so big."

"Weren't you afraid your husband would find out?" Brie asked.

"I guess," Tara said noncommittally.

"But that wasn't enough to make you think twice about the relationship."

Tara sighed. "I don't know," she said. Her vitality was ebbing almost as rapidly as the tide leaving the Bay of Fundy. She sat back and put her head against the soft leather. "Maybe a part of me wanted him to know—wanted him to feel jealous. Maybe some part of me wanted him to notice something but the nice house and the tasty meals on the table, before he fell asleep every night. I don't know." She stood up and walked over to the window. "You know, as Steve's wife, sometimes I feel like the background music, like I'd only be noticed if I disappeared."

Brie raised her eyebrows at that. *Lives of quiet desperation,* she thought.

"You know that we'll have to question your husband," Brie said. "He has a motive."

"I know that, Detective. And I know there's no point in begging you not to. It's your job."

"Do you think your husband could have committed such an act?"

"No, of course not." Tara walked back and sat down. "At least I don't think it's possible. Who ever knows what a person is capable of, though, I guess."

"He's your husband. I would think you'd have some gut sense about it."

"Steve is not a violent person. He's never laid a hand on me. I'm lucky in that. Maine has no shortage of spousal abuse."

"No state does," Brie said. "It's a sorry statement on the human condition." She moved on to the next question. "Did your husband go out on his boat at the usual time yesterday?"

"Yes. He's always heading out to sea around four in the morning."

"Did he seem in any way different yesterday morning or when he returned at the end of the day?"

"I don't think so. We had dinner. He went out to mow the yard while I cleaned up. We watched a couple hours of TV and went to bed. It was pretty much like every other night."

"What branch of the military was your husband in?" Brie asked.

"The Army," Tara said.

"Do you know if he had any Special Forces training?"

"Why do you ask that?"

"Because of the nature in which Jake Maloney was killed."

"How did he die?" Tara asked, and her eyes filled with tears again.

Brie hesitated for a moment. "His throat was cut."

She saw Tara recoil.

"That's what people said. I couldn't believe it."

"What time does Steve usually get back from pulling his pots?"

"Between two and two-thirty in the afternoon," Tara said. "I suppose you'll be questioning him today."

"That's correct," Brie said.

"I'd like to talk to him first," Tara said. "Own up to what I've done. Would that be all right?"

"I can't stop you from doing that, but I'd prefer you didn't," Brie said. "From what you've told me, it's quite possible he already knows. Do you have any reason to believe your husband might become violent or hurt you when he finds out about the affair?"

Tara waved that away. "I can't imagine that. I think he'll be hurt, though."

Brie sensed there was something on her mind. "Is there anything else you'd like to say?" she asked.

Tara hesitated for a second and then looked Brie straight in the eye. "Do you really think our affair could have caused Jake's death?" she asked.

"It's quite possible," Brie said. She saw no point in sugar coating it. Tara would have to live with the consequences of her actions. Anyway, Brie sensed that Tara French wasn't the type to hide from the truth. She had owned up to her actions. Because of that fact, there was a chance she might, emotionally speaking, survive this terrible detour in her life.

"Oh, God," was all Tara said. She seemed to draw into herself, possibly wondering what she would ever do with such a burden of guilt.

"I should be going," Brie said, standing up and putting her notebook away. Tara walked her to the door without saying a word and let her out.

Brie crossed the road and got into her car. She sat for a few minutes thinking about the interview she had just conducted. It wasn't clear to her whether loneliness or boredom had led to Tara's affair with Maloney. Maybe both. One thing she was sure of, though; Tara French was a smart woman. Brie's experience with the human race had taught her that smart people are restless. They become easily bored, and when that happens, they usually look around for a way to allay their boredom. Jake Maloney had been Tara's way. Those thoughts aside, though, Brie felt that Tara's comparing herself to the background music was very telling.

She guessed that Tara would rebound from this and probably be all right. She wasn't so sure about Nancy Maloney, though. She wondered if Nancy knew about the affair. If others in the village knew, there was a good chance she did as well. Brie hated to bring it up and certainly hated the thought of telling her. Murder investigations dig up ugly truths—truths buried just below the surface, like tree roots that form such a tangled web that finally nothing else can grow. She wondered if Jake's behavior was what had choked off the hope in Nancy Maloney's life.

Nancy had mentioned her brother. Brie pulled out her notebook and found the name. Nate Freeman. She wondered if the two of them were close. If so, he would have a motive for killing Jake. *Anger*. Anger that escalates to hatred can be a powerful motive for murder. Brie decided she needed to talk to Nancy again, and that she'd also have to interview the brother. Steve French wouldn't be back in from lobstering until afternoon. She could use the time to follow up with Nancy Maloney and question her brother.

Brie started the car. The morning fog had crawled back out to sea, and the air was warming up. She thought she'd stop back at the inn and hang the pajamas she'd washed out on the clothesline behind the inn. She made a U-turn in the road and headed back to the Whale Spout. She parked behind the inn, headed in the back door and up to her room.

She decided she'd fill out a report on her interview with Tara French while the details were fresh in her mind. She sat down and turned on the laptop, logged into the department, and brought up a report form. She entered the case number, her name and badge number and started filling out the report. She spent about a half hour on it and then read back through it to be sure she had included all the information. She logged off, went in the bathroom to collect her wet pajamas, and headed down to the backyard to hang them up.

The fact was that Tara existed. What Jake's former partner, Dan Littleton, had overheard that day in the truck with Maloney had led to uncovering the truth about the affair. It was a big break—one that suddenly opened up the case. Now there were three persons of interest. Tara's husband, Nancy Maloney's brother, and the former partner, Dan Littleton. He wasn't off the hook just because he'd given them another direction in which to look. While he supposedly had an alibi, she hadn't fully corroborated it. She needed to get the names of the students who were in the coffee house during the timeframe of the murder. Dan Littleton was definitely still in the running.

Brie headed for her car. She wasn't looking forward to it, but it was time to go back and talk to Nancy Maloney.

Chapter 11

The inn's parking lot backed up to Third Street. Brie turned left and drove toward the other end of the village till she got to Nancy Maloney's house. She pulled into the driveway next to the red Civic, went to the lower door, and rang the bell.

She noticed that this time the inner door was not open. She heard Nancy fumbling with the lock just before the door opened. Nancy Maloney was wearing the same limp hair and the same pink sweats as yesterday. The stains were still in place.

"Hello, Detective . . ."

"Beaumont," Brie said. "Detective Beaumont. Could I have a few minutes of your time, Mrs. Maloney?"

"Of course." She unlocked the storm door that separated them.

Brie took note of that. *Yesterday, everything wide open,* she thought. *Today, locked up tight as a drum.* She wondered if Nancy Maloney was afraid. It certainly seemed so.

"How are you doing?" Brie asked as they walked into the family room. The snack bags had been removed, but everything else looked pretty much the same.

"All right, I guess," Nancy said, but Brie heard a tremor in her voice. "Have you learned anything yet? Anything that might explain . . ." She didn't finish the sentence. Couldn't bring herself to say the words.

"There's been a little progress. Are you up to a few questions?"

"Certainly," Nancy said.

Brie decided that not knowing why or by whom Jake had been murdered would be far worse than any unseemly business she might have to ask about. Still, she hated to be the one to deliver another wound to Nancy Maloney's heart.

"It's hard to talk about some things that turn up in an investigation, Mrs. Maloney, but we have to do it." Brie tried to read her face, see if she knew what was coming.

"I understand," was all Nancy said.

She reminded Brie of a neglected ragdoll. She wished she could give her a hug but knew she had to keep some distance, keep her objectivity. "Did you ever think there was anything your husband was keeping from you?" she asked. "Either relating to his business or maybe on a more personal front?"

Nancy sat there silent, and Brie could see the question troubled her. "I'm not sure what you mean," she finally said. "I suppose there are always little things people don't tell each other." She shrugged her ragdoll shoulders. "I think Jake was a pretty honest, hard-working man."

Brie noticed the qualifying *pretty honest*. "Did you ever suspect he might have been involved in a relationship?"

"You mean with a woman?" Nancy looked at her, and Brie actually saw a little fire in her eyes. It was the first substantial sign of life she had seen in this woman who seemed as insubstantial as a specter.

"Yes, with a woman," Brie said.

The fire went out as quickly as it had been kindled, and Nancy seemed to melt into the sofa like a rapidly disintegrating life form. "If that's true, it's my fault," she said.

"Why would you say that?"

"Just look around you. I could do a better job of being a good wife."

"Or it may be that Jake's actions have nothing to do with you at all, and everything to do with him," Brie said. She could see Nancy considering this.

Suddenly, Nancy looked her straight in the eye and said, "It's Tara French, isn't it?"

Brie studied her for a moment. "Yes," she said.

"How long?"

"About three years, but according to Mrs. French, their meetings have been few and far between."

"Why would she need my Jake? She has such a great life. Nice house, her husband makes a lot of money as a lobsterman. He's one of the most successful in the village. You should see his boat."

"Those things don't always lead to happiness," Brie said. "Not that I'm defending her actions. One thing I've learned in my line of work is that people have great capacity for sabotaging their lives. It's almost as if humanity is hardwired to screw up."

Nancy had lowered her head, and Brie saw that her hands were clenched in tight fists.

"Could I ask how you knew it was Tara French?" Brie said, going for a redirect.

"I guess it was something my brother said about a year ago."

"Yes?" Brie encouraged. She pulled her notebook out of her pocket.

"Nate, that's my brother, said, 'If I was you, I'd keep an eye on that bitch Tara.' " It just came out of the blue one day when I stopped by to visit him at the airstrip—that's where he works."

"Did you ask him why?"

"Sure. But then he kind of changed the subject. Wouldn't say anything else. I paid closer attention to what Jake was doing for the next few months, but I never saw anything to make me think he was on the prowl. So I wrote it off to Nate being Nate."

"Meaning what?" Brie asked.

"Meaning that growing up it was pretty much just me and Nate. He was my older brother. Our dad was Canadian, and when Nate was ten and I was seven, he up and left the family and moved back to Canada. Our mom just slowly fell apart. She worked a job—worked hard as a waitress—but at night she took to drinking. Nate was pretty much taking care of me from the time he was ten years old. He'd help me with homework, make meals when Mom wasn't there or when she was . . . you know. Nothing special—sandwiches and soup, or mac and cheese. He learned to make pretty good eggs. He tried really hard to make things seem normal."

"So, he was protective of you?"

"Oh, yeah. I never took any grief from anyone. Sometimes I wonder if I'd have been stronger if I'd had to fend for myself a little more."

"How did he and Jake get along?"

Nancy did the ragdoll shrug again. "Okay, I guess. They never got to be friends though. Nate was always critical of Jake. Used to say he didn't work hard enough. Nate was in the Navy when I met Jake. I don't think that ever sat well with him."

"Why's that?" Brie asked.

"By the time he came home and met Jake, we were already engaged. I guess he never got to put his stamp of approval on it."

"Huh," Brie said. She knew there was a fine line—nearly invisible sometimes—between being protective and being controlling.

"Nancy, do you think Nate would be capable of killing Jake?"

"Physically—yes. He was in the SEALs. But he'd never do anything that would hurt me so badly." Nancy shivered, and Brie could see her processing the thought. After a few moments, she looked Brie straight in the eye for the first time since they'd started talking. "He could never do such a thing," she said emphatically.

Brie regarded her silently for a few moments. *Unless he decided he was doing you a favor,* she thought. She knew one thing. Jake had been murdered by someone with strength, skill, and the confidence to kill another human being up close and personal. To her that had military training written all over it.

Brie put her notebook back in her pocket and stood up. "I think that's all for now, Mrs. Maloney. I know this is a very hard time for you. Thanks for answering my questions."

"You can call me Nancy," she said. "I just need to know why Jake died. I'll never be able to be at peace unless I know. Do you understand?"

"Of course," Brie said.

"I suppose you'll be questioning Nate?"

"Yes. He's next on my list, actually. And I'd appreciate it if you didn't call and tell him I'm coming."

Nancy Maloney looked conflicted at that, but she finally nodded her head. "Okay, I'll do as you say."

"Thanks," said Brie. "We'll be in touch as we proceed with the case."

"Thank you, Detective." Nancy walked to the door with her and showed her out. Brie could hear her double locking the door behind her.

She climbed into her car and called Detective Marty Dupuis to check in. She filled him in on her interview with Tara French and also what she'd just learned from Nancy Maloney.

"I'm on my way to the airstrip now to interrogate Nate Freeman."

"Think there might be something there?" Marty asked.

"Hard to say. He was in the SEALs, though. And he's extremely protective of his sister. So, in my book, that's means and motive," Brie said. "What about Jake's clients? Turn up anything on that front?"

"Not so far," Marty said. "They all seem to think Jake was a stand-up guy. Apparently, he was always prompt with his pick-ups and deliveries. One of his clients—a guy at Myers Seafoods—said Maloney was always looking for extra work and suggestions for businesses that might need a shipper. The guy there—Henry's his name—had the feeling that Jake never had quite enough work to make ends meet. He said in the last six months to a year, though, Maloney seemed more relaxed about work, as if things were going better."

"Huh, interesting," Brie said. "Can you tell from his records if he had acquired any new contracts lately?"

"That's the odd thing. From his freight manifests, it doesn't look like he had."

"Have you had time to go over his mileage log?" Brie asked.

"Not yet. I think we need to sit down with all the paperwork and compare those freight manifests to the mileage log."

"Maybe later tonight or early tomorrow," Brie said. "I've got a number of leads to follow up on first. By the way, do you know if we'll be meeting with Lieutenant Fenton at all today?"

"Not sure on that, Brie. You might give him a buzz."

"Roger that, Marty."

Brie backed out of the driveway. It was time to seek out Nate Freeman and see what kind of a vibe she got from him. At the end of the block she turned right and headed up the highway. After about three miles, she spotted a dirt road coming up on her right. A small wooden sign, shaped like an arrow, said *Airstrip*. Brie slowed the car nearly to a stop and took a right onto the gravel road. It wound through a small patch of forest for maybe a quarter of a mile, and abruptly, she came out into a large cleared area. The grass landing strip stretched out as far as the eye could see. There was a good-sized hangar building up ahead with two aircraft inside—a Piper twin-engine Comanche and a single-engine Cessna.

There was a single-wide trailer to her left as she drove in. A couple of folded-up lawn chairs leaned against the side of it, and a wood picnic table and an older gas grill stood in front. Brie parked the car and got out. She saw a man approaching from the direction of the hangar, wiping his hands on a blue rag. She walked toward him. He was tall—six-three or six-four—and he was wearing a backwards ball cap. When she got close to him, she saw he had dark hair and a chiseled face. His black tee shirt hugged a pair of massive biceps, and his hawk-like eyes seemed to assess and evaluate her all at once. For some reason the phrase *target acquired* rolled through her mind.

"I'm looking for Nate Freeman," Brie said.

"Present and accounted for," he answered.

"I'm Detective Brie Beaumont with the Maine State Police." She showed him her ID.

"This must be about Jake Maloney," he said. His voice was cold, and Brie could see right away that he wouldn't be counted among the mourners.

"That's right," Brie said. "I'd like to ask you some questions."

"Shoot," Freeman said. He stuffed the rag in his back pocket, crossed his arms on his chest and brought his feet to parade rest.

"Can you tell me about your relationship with the deceased?"

"Didn't have a *relationship* with him," he said, hitting "relationship" with sarcasm.

"Okay," Brie said. "No relationship. But he was your sister's husband, which makes him your brother-in-law, i.e. a relative."

"I related to him as little as possible. I thought the guy was a waste of space."

"How'd that make your sister feel?"

Nate Freeman's eyes softened a bit at the mention of Nancy. He lowered his head, and for a moment, the arrogance disappeared. "It made her feel like shit. But I wasn't gonna pretend to like the guy just because she made the mistake of marrying him."

"Sounds to me like your dislike for him might have bordered on hatred."

"Now you're catching on," Freeman said.

"Why?" Brie said, looking him straight in the eye, temporarily ignoring his disrespect. "Why did you hate him?"

"My sister had it tough growin' up. I tried to protect her, not let her see what a mess things really were. But she saw anyway. I just wanted her to find someone who'd take care of her. Provide for her, so she wasn't worryin' all the time. Worryin' about how to make ends meet."

Brie's assessment was that Nate had become both father and mother to Nancy when the two of them were children. From that point on, in his mind he was the only one who could protect her. She doubted that any suitor or husband could have lived up to his scrutiny.

"Did it ever occur to you that things could have been much worse? That Jake could have abused your sister? If being short of money was a deal breaker in relationships, most of the middle class would be divorced."

"He may not a beat her, but there was other stuff."

"What other stuff?" Brie asked.

"The worthless shit was screwin' around with someone."

"Did you know who?"

"I knew and I told him if he didn't stop, I'd rearrange his equipment so he'd never screw anyone again."

"So you threatened him?"

"Damn straight."

"And within two or three hours of sleeping with Tara French, Jake Maloney is found dead. Killed with what I'd call military precision."

Nate Freeman's expression changed for just an instant from bird of prey to fish on a hook. He took a step back, and a chink opened in his wall of antagonism.

"Now you're catching on." Brie couldn't help herself.

"I had no idea they were together yesterday before he died."

"Really? And where were you yesterday morning between six-thirty and nine-thirty?"

"Where I always am. Right here."

"Can anyone corroborate that?"

"No. I live alone." He nodded toward the trailer. "That's what I call home."

"According to your sister, you're a former Navy SEAL. I'm assuming you own weapons. Guns, knives?"

"Both. I own what I need to protect myself. But the reason I could never have killed Maloney, even though I may have wanted to, is because I was a SEAL. I'd never bring dishonor to the SEALs or the Navy by making a stupid move like that." He looked her straight in the eye when he said it.

Brie got no immediate sense as to the truth or falsehood of his statement. Hatred is a strong motive, and she had no doubt Nate Freeman had hated his brother-in-law. In fact, he had almost bragged about it. Freeman knew about the affair between Jake Maloney and Tara French. What was more, he had threatened Jake with bodily harm should he find out the affair was continuing. *All that goes to motive,* she thought. *Then there's means.* That one was a no brainer. Nate had been a SEAL—part of an elite force trained to kill if necessary. She had no doubt he owned a weapon suitable for the job and the skill set to easily do away with the likes of Jake Maloney. Opportunity got the third check. He had known his sister was gone the night before Jake died. He might have figured Jake would make a move on Tara. He could have been watching either of their houses with just that thought in mind. Could have followed Jake, hoping there would be an opportunity.

Brie closed her notebook and put it in her pocket. "Well, that's all for now, Mr. Freeman. I need to caution you not to leave the area while the investigation is under way."

"I'm not planning any vacations."

"As things unfold, I may have more questions for you."

"You know where to find me." Some of the arrogance had faded into the background a bit. Brie placed his change in attitude under the heading *Self Preservation*.

She walked back to her car and was about to get in when curiosity stopped her. "Mr. Freeman," she called. He stopped and turned slowly around. "Whose planes are those? Who uses this airstrip?"

"These two belong to a couple of the summer rusticators," he said, waving a hand toward the planes in the hangar. "The Navy lands here, too, sometimes with parts or personnel for maintenance of the radio transmitter."

"Thanks," Brie said. She got into her car, backed up, and headed down the dirt road toward the highway, processing her thoughts about the case as she went. For whatever reason, Jake had wandered out the Heron Head trail, which would have given ex-SEAL Nate Freeman the perfect opportunity to do the deed. Another thought suddenly occurred to her. She wondered if someone had asked Jake to meet them out on Heron Head. She remembered what Nancy had said—that Jake would not have gone out there, that it was totally out of character for him, that he didn't like hiking, didn't even like taking walks. So, what if he'd been lured out there on some pretense? The killer would have been right in thinking that it was the perfect place to murder him. Even if a struggle had ensued, no one would have heard it.

Brie reminded herself to ask Marty if any of the neighbors or townspeople he had interviewed had seen anything at all. She thought about the houses that fronted on the harbor and the couple of houses along Final Reckoning Road. They'd have to interview those folks. She also thought about Varney's diner. The diner had a bird's eye view of the road that ran down toward the trailhead. Of course, Varney would have been busy with the breakfast crowd, if there was one. But it was worth asking him who was there yesterday morning and if, by chance, he had seen anything. She checked her watch. It was time for lunch anyhow. Now was as good a time as any to stop into the diner, have a chat with him, and grab a bite to eat.

Her cell phone rang. It was Dent Fenton. She answered the call. "Hi, Lieutenant."

"Hey, Brie. I just read your report on Tara French. Where are you now?"

"Just heading back to Tucker Harbor. I met with Nancy Maloney again. I wanted to see if she knew about the affair."

"Did she?"

"She said her brother had warned her about Tara French, but she didn't believe him. I also questioned her brother, Nate Freeman."

"Anything there?" Dent asked.

"He hated Maloney and made no bones about it. He knew about the affair and had threatened Maloney with bodily harm if he didn't end it."

"Oh, yeah?"

"He was also in the SEALs. Owns weapons. No alibi for the time of the murder."

"Think he's good for it?"

"It's a strong possibility," Brie said.

"We can get a warrant. Search his place."

"I'd like to interview Tara's husband. See what I find out. Or would you rather have Marty take that?"

"No, you do it, Brie. You interviewed Tara French, so you should question the husband. Marty's still working Maloney's client list and interviewing neighbors."

Brie told Dent Fenton she planned to ask Varney Simms some questions, since the diner had a bird's eye view of the road leading down to the trailhead. "The problem is, the fog was so thick yesterday morning you could have painted a wall with it. The killer had perfect cover."

"Nonetheless, you never know. Keep digging, Brie. And good work so far. I'm planning to make a trip down there later on this afternoon to meet with you and Marty. I'll call you when I have a better lock on the time."

"Aye, aye, Captain," Brie said, jokingly.

"Sounds like you've already had enough of shore duty."

She thought she heard something wistful in his tone. "I'm afraid I'm a woman between two worlds right now, Dent. But I can tell you, it won't affect my work on this case."

"I know that, Brie. I knew that when I brought you on board."

His comment surprised her, and she felt grateful for it. He had confidence in her abilities. "Thanks, Lieutenant. I appreciate that. I'll see you later." She ended the call, and just in time. She was coming up fast on the diner. She slowed nearly to a stop and turned left into the parking lot.

Brie got out of the car and stretched her arms above her head. The day was as fine as a day could be. Temperature around 70 degrees and a light breeze off the ocean. She wondered where the *Maine Wind* was. She hadn't heard back from John last night, which meant there was no cell phone reception where they had anchored. Not surprising. John had told her that the population really thins out when you get up along the coast of Nova Scotia. She knew he'd call when he was able.

She headed into the diner and stopped at the hostess station. She could see Varney through the serving window. At the sound of the bell, he looked up. "Hello, miss, or I guess I should say Detective." There was no sarcasm in the remark. In fact, his tone was respectful. He came out of the kitchen and around the lunch counter with his hitch of a walk and his enigmatic little smile.

"Where's the lunch crowd?" Brie asked.

"This may be lunchtime for the rest of the world, but here in Tucker Harbor we're on a different clock. Booth?" he asked, picking up a menu and walking along the front window as if he knew the answer.

"You bet," Brie said. "So when's your busy time?"

"Well, the old timers usually come down for coffee and conversation around ten o'clock. Some of them eat breakfast, some lunch, and some of 'em just have pie or donuts—those are usually the widowers."

Brie smiled at that.

"Then we start getting busy again around three or three-thirty. In a lobstering village everything runs on a different clock. Men come in to eat when they get back in harbor, which is mid-afternoon, or sometimes families come down for burgers and fries about that time. Mealtimes and bedtimes are all turned around when you keep the hours these folks do."

"I've noticed," Brie said. "It's like a ghost town by eight o'clock at night."

"Now, in the summer we get the tourists stopping in as they drive through the village. So, of course, at this time o' year, I make sure I'm open at regular people mealtimes."

"Boy, Varney, that makes for a long day."

"A-yuh," he responded, which was yes in Maine-speak. But Brie had already decided Varney wasn't native to Maine, since he didn't drop his "R's" the way the natives did. The Maine or Yankee dialect turned lobster into lobstah, butter into buttah and later into latah.

"How's the investigation coming along?"

This was the perfect opening, and Brie stepped through. "It's moving along," she said. "You know, Varney, being up on this hill, the diner has a decent view of Final Reckoning Road." She noticed his eyes got a little fidgety. "Did you see anything at all yesterday morning? Either Jake headed toward Heron Head, or anyone else on Final Reckoning Road between, say, six-thirty and nine-thirty a.m.?"

"There was no one in the diner at that time yesterday, so I took the time to do some inventory and some bookkeeping in the back. Would you like to see where I work?"

"No, that's not necessary," Brie said. She guessed that from the back area, where he did those things, he had no view out the windows.

"That fog yesterday was murky as a witch's brew. I doubt I would have seen anyone if they walked right by the windows decked out in lights."

"Well, thanks anyway, Varney. If you think of anything, anything at all that seemed unusual, please let me know." Brie took out one of the cards Dent had made for her and gave it to him. "My number's on there," she said.

"Will do. Now what can I get you for lunch?"

Brie opened the menu and scanned it. "How are your burgers?"

"Best in the land." Varney's tone left no doubt about it.

"Okay, then. I'll have the Varney Burger." It was basically a California burger with cheddar cheese and bacon added. It came with fries.

"Drink?" Varney asked.

"I'll have a Coke."

Varney took her menu and headed for the kitchen. In a few minutes Brie could smell the burger and hear it sizzling on the grill. Her stomach growled at that. She took out her notebook to distract herself and looked over the notes she'd made while interviewing Nate Freeman. It would still be too early to interview Steve French, Tara's husband. He wouldn't be back in the harbor till mid-afternoon. She decided she'd go back to the inn and fill out a report on the Freeman interview. She also wanted to start a file for herself. Thoughts and questions were beginning to percolate in her mind. She wanted to write them down. Doing so always helped her begin to see her way through the case, especially if it started to get complicated.

In a few minutes Varney set a fantastic-looking burger down in front of her. "Hope you like it," he said.

"There's little doubt of that, Varney, if it tastes as good as it smells."

He looked pleased, gave her a nod, and shuffled back to the kitchen.

Brie dove right in and savored every bite. She knew she was lucky that she could eat like this. She had been blessed with a good metabolism, and in her line of work—police work—she'd had to build up strength, which had meant weight training. Aboard the *Maine Wind*, her weight training regimen consisted of hauling up sails, lowering and furling them at the end of the day, carrying armloads of wood for the woodstove, raising and lowering the yawl boat and dories, and provisioning the ship before each voyage. All of it entailed plenty of lifting and kept her in shape. She thought about her friend Ariel back home, who gained weight if she looked at food. Ariel had always been amazed and a little jealous of Brie's ability to eat anything with abandon and never gain weight. But Brie had also never been cooked for the way she had in the past three months. Aboard ship, George turned out the most amazing meals she'd ever eaten, and she had decided were it not for all the physical work aboard the *Maine Wind*, that she might for the first time ever be fighting the battle of the bulge.

Varney checked in with her once or twice to see if she needed anything, which gave her a chance to sing the praises of his Varney Burger. There was the sense of something poignant about Varney, as if he soldiered on but maybe wasn't really happy with his life. When she was done, he brought the check and she gave him some cash. When he came back with the change, she thanked him and gave him a generous tip. He tried to give some of it back, but she insisted he keep it. With a sheepish expression, he nodded and stuffed it in his pocket.

"You sure I can't show you that back supply room?" It seemed important to him to prove to her that he'd had no way of seeing anyone pass by the diner yesterday morning.

"Well, okay, sure," Brie said. She got up from the booth and followed Varney through the kitchen into the back room. There was a cooler and shelves for dry goods, but it was a windowless space, lit from overhead by fluorescent lights. The door out to the kitchen area was positioned so there was no way to see out the front of the diner when you were back in the supply room. At one end of the room, Varney had a door laid out across two file cabinets. It served as his desk. There was a chair in between the file cabinets where he sat to do his bookkeeping.

"I see what you mean, Varney. No way to see the outside world from back here."

He nodded, looking satisfied that she was in agreement about that.

"Well, thanks, Varney. You've got my number if you do think of anything. I should be going, but I'll probably see you later for dinner."

He followed her back out into the diner. When she left, he was clearing the table, and his eyes were doing their ping pong moves around the diner.

Chapter 12

An onshore breeze came over the harbor, carrying the tang of decaying vegetation left by the tide. As Brie walked out of the diner and across the parking lot, she felt the August sun on her back. She paused at the car door to let the warm rays soak into her shoulders. Hailing from northern climes makes one savor such moments in a way southerners cannot, since they will seldom or never come face to face with the bite of a subzero wind chill.

After she had basked in the sunlight for a few minutes, she climbed into her car and sat thinking. She planned to walk down to the harbor about two o'clock, so she could catch Steve French when he came in for the day. She wanted to talk to him before Tara had a chance to run interference. That way she'd have the element of surprise working for her. She didn't know how he could have committed the crime, though, since he'd gone out on his boat early yesterday morning—before Jake Maloney had made his way over to the Tara's house, and hours before he was murdered.

Steve French certainly would have had motive and undoubtedly the means—she couldn't imagine a lobsterman not having a pretty hefty knife aboard his boat. What French didn't have was opportunity. In her mind there was no way he could have known Maloney would be out on that point yesterday morning. But being the cuckolded husband made him a person of interest, so she needed to question him. She also needed to question some of the other lobstermen to make sure they had seen French out on the water pulling his pots during that time.

Brie turned on the car, pulled out onto the highway, and followed it down through the village and up the hill to the inn. She got out and headed in the back door. She could hear a vacuum cleaner at work, and she walked to the front of the inn and looked into the parlor. Atticus Kane was behind the vacuum, rocking back and forth in a graceful rhythm as he worked the machine over the floor. Brie didn't want to disturb him, so she headed up the stairs and into her room. She took off her jacket and laid it on the end of the bed. The room had been made up, and there were two mints on the bedspread where it had been tucked into a bolster over the pillows. Brie picked up one of the mints and walked over to her laptop as she unwrapped it. She sat down, logged into the department and brought up a blank report form. She checked her watch. It was just short of one o'clock. Plenty of time to finish the report and get back down to the harbor before the lobstermen came in for the day.

Brie wrote a detailed report on Nate Freeman, putting in his relationship to the victim as well as his apparent hatred of Jake Maloney. She also detailed his military background, the fact that he admitted to owning an assortment of weapons, and finally his claim that he was innocent and why. By the time she had wrapped up the report, it was a quarter of two. She went in the bathroom, splashed some water on her face to freshen up, and brushed her hair. She grabbed her jacket and headed down the stairs and out the front door. Then she thought about something. She went around the inn, opened the trunk of the Impala, and put an evidence envelope in the inside pocket of her jacket, just in case. She pulled out a couple of latex gloves, stuffed them in her jacket pocket, and headed back around front.

As she started down the road, she had a good view of the water. She could already see one or two lobsterboats rounding the lighthouse out near the mouth of the harbor. By yesterday afternoon, everyone in Tucker Harbor had known about the death of Jake Maloney. The more horrible the news, the faster it spreads, and the news about Maloney had been plenty horrible. She and Detective Marty Dupuis had been around the village enough since yesterday that her appearance down on the docks would come as no surprise to anyone. Even so, she steeled herself for a certain level of resistance.

By the time she got down to the harbor, there were two lobsterboats pulled up at the dock, unloading the day's catch in large plastic crates. Out on the water, she could see a couple more boats making their way past the lighthouse. Brie walked out the dock toward the first boat. The captain was wearing a long, orange rubber apron that hung nearly to his sea boots. He had a round, weathered face, and his thinning hair was plastered to his head. He paused in his unloading as she approached and ran a forearm across his sweaty brow. She could see him take in the badge on her belt.

"You one of the police here about Jake Maloney?" His "here" came out *he-ah.*

"That's right," Brie said, looking down at him from the dock. "I'm Detective Brie Beaumont. Maine State Police." She showed him her ID.

"Howdy do, Detective." He held out a grimy, hand which she gripped without hesitation—a move he clearly wasn't expecting.

"Hugo Lemay," he said. "Terrible turn of events yestahday."

"It was, indeed," Brie said. "I'm hoping to catch Steve French when he comes back in today. Can you describe his boat? And do you know what time he's usually in with his catch?"

Hugo looked at her for a moment, probably cogitating on why she was looking for Steve French. Then he turned and held a hand up to his eyes as he looked seaward toward the harbor entrance. "I can do ya one bettah," he said. "That's

Stevo makin' his way in just now." He pointed to a white-hulled boat. "Right behind 'im—see the black hull—that's his BFF, Kevin Krumm. That's the kids' lingo for Best Friends For-evah." He dropped the final "r" as Mainers do. Brie heard a hint of sarcasm in his BFF remark, and there was hoot of laughter from the boat behind his.

"Thanks," Brie said. "I'll catch him after he's done unloading." Hugo Lemay gave her a little salute, and she moved off. There was a small building on the dock, and Brie walked around the shore side of it, out of sight but within earshot of the unloading boats. She sat down on the edge of the dock to listen to the goings on.

She heard the two boats at the dock—Hugo Lemay's and the one behind him—finish unloading and pull away. Then there was a rumbling of another engine as the next boat maneuvered up to the dock and tied off.

"Stevo," the guy on the dock greeted him.

"Jack-man," Steve French replied.

"Good catch today?"

"Ayuh," French said. Brie waited for the rest of the exchange, but there was none. She looked around the corner. The sorting and offloading of French's catch continued in silence, with Stevo lifting his crates onto the dock and Jack and another guy stacking and weighing them. She got the impression this taciturn exchange was business as usual for Steve French.

In the meantime, Kevin Krumm had maneuvered his boat up to the dock behind French's to a more enthusiastic greeting.

"K K." Jack-man gave him the rock-on sign.

"Toad!" Krumm roared. *Strange moniker,* Brie thought because Jack-man was a handsome guy.

Kevin Krumm launched into his act. Loud and jovial, he was a wisecracker who'd begun to run his mouth the moment he docked his lobsterboat. "Could 'bout wrung the fog outta my shirt this mahnin'. Got so turned around, thought I motahed into the goddamn Bahmuda Triangle." The guys on the dock laughed, and the banter ran nonstop as Krumm hoisted the boxes of lobsters off his deck.

Brie thought about Hugo Lemay's comment about French and Krumm being BFF's. *Apparently, opposites attract,* she thought. Steve French was as nondescript as a passing fog bank. And Krumm, at least during show time at the dock, was a boisterous clown.

She could see French finishing up, so she hopped up and headed over to him.

"Steve French?" she asked as she came up to his boat.

"Ayah?"

"Detective Brie Beaumont with the Maine State Police." She flashed her ID. "Can I talk to you for a few minutes?"

"I gotta move my boat off the dock. Come aboard if you like." He seemed neither startled nor flustered, which fit with what she'd already observed. But she also got the sense he'd rather talk to her out of earshot of nosy villagers.

"Fine by me," Brie said. She stepped onto the gunwale of his boat, and he offered her a hand as she jumped down onto the deck. Steve French pulled away from the dock and headed for his float. Brie stood next to him in the house, feet spread for stability on the deck. She'd been ashore for a little over twenty-four hours and was already losing her sea legs.

French motored toward his float and maneuvered up to it like a pro. He grabbed his gaff hook, snagged the float and hooked the line to his bow eye.

"Nice work," Brie said when he came back to the wheelhouse.

He gave her a nod. Steve French put the "a" in average. Neither tall nor short, handsome nor ugly. He had washed-out blue eyes and dishwater blond hair buzzed short. But what really relegated him to that no-man's-land of the forgettable was his apparent lack of a personality.

"I need to ask you some questions, Mr. French," Brie said as she took out her notebook and pen.

He nodded again but said nothing.

"I'm sure you're aware of the death of Jake Maloney. He was found yesterday out on Heron Head."

"Ayah. I heard." He looked her in the eye, but from a place of what felt like complete detachment.

"How well did you know Maloney?"

"Didn't know him at all, really."

"Were you aware that your wife was acquainted with him?" Brie watched his response carefully.

"Wasn't aware of that, no." He said it in the same dispassionate way, but her words ignited something in his eyes. It wasn't anger. Brie thought it was fear.

"I interviewed your wife this morning. We had received information that connected her to Jake Maloney." Brie waited for the question men always asked, not calmly but confrontationally. *Connected how? Acquainted with him how?* But the questions didn't come.

French just nodded but said nothing.

Time to drop the bomb, I guess, Brie thought. "Mr. French, your wife has admitted to having an affair with Jake Maloney."

He continued to look at her for a few seconds and finally lowered his head. "What do you want me to say?"

"I'm wondering if you knew about it? And I'm wondering how it makes you feel?"

He answered her two questions with four words. *No* and *Bad, I guess.* The last three were said with complete apathy.

Brie was beginning to understand why Tara felt like the background music. She was vibrant and full of life. Steve French seemed to be full of . . . smoke was the only word that occurred to her. His emotions were as insubstantial as smoke. Not merely evanescent—they were nonexistent.

"Do you love your wife, Mr. French?"

"Of course." But it was said in the same dispassionate manner.

"Where were you yesterday morning between six-thirty and nine-thirty?"

"On the water. Pulling my pots." There was a hint of something bordering on surprise in his response, as if to say, *Where else would I be? What else would I be doing?*

As she stood silently studying him, Brie did her MMO math—Motive, Means, Opportunity—to see if Steve French fit the equation in any way. There should have been motive. His wife was having an affair with another man. But in order for there to be motive in such a case, there has to be an instigating emotion. Jealousy, rage. On the surface French appeared devoid of these or any other emotions. She hadn't seen even a flash of anger in his eyes.

Moving on to means, although he was of average height, she was sure French was physically capable of the murder, and she was sure he owned a knife that would do the job. But what about opportunity? If any of his cohorts had seen him on the water during the timeframe of the murder, that cancelled out the third part of the equation. One out of three dropped him way down in the batting order.

Steve French would have been the most logical choice, all things being equal. The cuckolded husband is always the chief person of interest in such a murder. But all things were not equal. Motive, means, and opportunity were not there on his side of the scale, tipping it in his direction. Brie remembered Dent Fenton's words when he'd asked her to come on the case. *Just a gut feeling that this might be a tough one.*

Despite her own gut feeling that this was not their guy and the fact that he was missing two variables in her equation, Brie decided to dot the *i's* and cross the *t's*. "Mr. French, do you keep a knife aboard your boat?"

"Sure." It came out *Shu-ah.* "Lobstahman's gotta have a knife. Yu-ah life can depend on it."

Brie knew this. She'd heard the stories of lobstermen getting tangled in their gear and being pulled overboard. Lobster traps, or pots, as they are known, are weighted with bricks, and there are usually two traps on each line. Once thrown overboard, they sink fast, and so does anything attached to them.

"Could I see your knife, please, Mr. French?"

"Shu-ah." He opened a box attached to the wall of the house and took out a knife in a leg strap sheath.

Brie pulled a latex glove out of her jacket pocket. "May I?" she asked.

French handed the knife over, and Brie carefully removed it from the sheath and inspected it for any signs of blood. It was a type of dive knife known as a shark knife, and the blade was slightly serrated, which ruled it out as the murder weapon. Jake Maloney had been killed with a smooth-bladed knife. Brie saw no reason to take it into evidence. She put it back in the sheath and handed it back to French.

"I think that about does it for now," Brie said. "Do I have to swim back to shore?"

That actually got a half-smile from French. He signaled for a pick-up. Kevin Krumm was still at the dock shooting the breeze with Jack-man, better known as Toad. Krumm turned and saw there were no boats on their way in. He was out of his lobsterboat in a flash and untied one of the skiffs from the end of the dock and rowed in their direction.

Brie remembered something she wanted to say to French and turned back to him. "Your wife is waiting for you at home. She's eager to talk to you. It may not be too late to work things out."

French studied the deck and after a moment looked up at her. "Thanks, Detective. I'll keep that in mind." There was a hint of sincerity in his voice—a quantum leap toward emotion for Steve French.

Brie's phone rang. She pulled it out of her pocket and answered it. "Beaumont."

"Brie, Dent Fenton. I'm on my way down to Tucker Harbor. Can we meet about quarter past four?"

"Sure. I'm just finishing up an interview."

"Great. I'll let Marty know. Let's meet in the parking lot near Heron's Head."

"Copy that, Lieutenant. I'll see you at four-fifteen." She ended the call.

Kevin Krumm brought the skiff up to the starboard side of French's lobsterboat. French reached down to steady the small craft, and Krumm gave Brie a hand in. Her eyes met his, but there was no joviality there. Despite the fact that she was wearing a badge and there with official status, he gave her a look that was unquestionably menacing. She took the seat in the bow, and French stepped aboard and sat in the stern. Krumm rowed quickly back toward the dock. Brie could see he was in a hurry to get his boat off the dock. There were a couple more lobsterboats just entering the harbor. They pulled up to the end of the dock. Steve French climbed out first and offered Brie a hand up. Krumm tied off the skiff and came out last.

"I'll call ya latah, Stevo," Krumm said, heading for his boat. "Come on ovah. We'll have a be-ah."

French nodded. "Shu-ah."

Brie wanted to say, *He's not coming for beer. He's got fences to mend.* But she decided she'd better keep it professional. Krumm boarded his boat and pulled away from the dock. Steve French headed for home.

Brie walked off the dock and stood watching as Krumm maneuvered his boat out toward his float. It was clear to her that this character Kevin Krumm was some part of the picture—some factor in the Steve French equation. Indirectly, that made him a factor in the Jake Maloney equation as well. *Guilt by association,* she thought. Lobsterman Hugo Lemay had suggested that Krumm and French were bosom buddies. From what she'd seen, Krumm was pretty much the antithesis of French. But then again, maybe Steve French was the perfect straight man for Krumm. With French as his sidekick, he'd never have to worry about competing for the floor. She thought about the guys in the lobsterboat behind Hugo Lemay's guffawing about the French/Krumm friendship. *What was that about*? she wondered. *What was the big joke*?

Brie checked her watch. It was three-fifty. She started up the hill to the inn to get her laptop and her car. If she had a few minutes to wait when she got down to the parking lot for her meeting with Dent Fenton, she could get started on her report on Steve French. Suddenly something stopped her in her tracks. She turned back around and looked out at the harbor. Kevin Krumm was in the process of mooring his boat, and as Brie watched him, she had a weird *déjà vu* moment. When she and Scott had come ashore yesterday with the passengers, she had taken a few shots of the harbor with the *Maine Wind* lying at anchor. She hadn't thought anything of it then, but there had been one lone lobsterboat in the harbor. Based on the position of it in her mind's eye, she was pretty sure it had been this boat—Kevin Krumm's boat. The question was, why was his boat in the harbor when he should have been out pulling pots? Its presence there wouldn't have registered with her yesterday since she had yet to learn about the murder, the affair between Tara and Maloney, or the friendship between Steve French and Kevin Krumm. The words *guilt by association* ran through her mind again. She wasn't sure this piece meant anything or even if it belonged to the puzzle. But it was an incongruity, and detectives always pay close attention to incongruities.

Then she had another thought. She'd taken those pictures of the *Maine Wind* yesterday. It was quite possible if Krumm's boat *was* in the harbor, that it would show up in one of them. At least she hoped it would. That would be proof that it was there. She turned and headed up the hill. She was eager to get back to the inn and review those picture. *It might be nothing, but then again . . .*

It took Brie five minutes to walk back to the inn. She went in the front door and headed straight up to her room.

She pulled her camera out of her duffel and removed the SD card. She booted up the laptop, loaded her card into the SD slot, and opened the folder with her pictures. She scanned through them till she came to the shots of the *Maine Wind* taken from the shoreline in Tucker Harbor. There were several tightly framed telephoto shots of the *Maine Wind*. But she soon found what she was looking for. In two of the wide-angle shots of the harbor, there was a lone lobsterboat at its mooring. The boat had a black hull. Krumm's boat had a black hull. What's more, the position of the boat in the harbor matched that of Krumm's lobsterboat. *Bingo*, Brie thought. She enlarged the picture and wrote down the boat's registration number. She would compare it to the number on Krumm's boat just to be sure. But she knew it was a match.

Brie removed the SD card and returned it to her camera. She shut down the laptop, unplugged it, and put it in the carrying case. She slapped her pocket to be sure she had her car keys and notebook and headed downstairs and out the back door to her car. She climbed in, put the laptop on the seat next to her, and drove toward the other end of the village for her meeting with Dent Fenton and Marty Dupuis.

When she came to Final Reckoning Road, she turned left and continued down to the parking lot below the Heron Head trail. It was just before four-fifteen, so she decided there wasn't time to start her report on Steve French.

Marty arrived first, followed shortly by Dent Fenton in his SUV. Dent signaled for the other two to join him in his vehicle. When they got over to the SUV, Brie asked Marty if he'd like the front seat. He told her to take it and climbed in the back. Dent powered down all the windows so the late afternoon breeze could blow in. He had three coffees in a carrier and a bag of donuts. Brie and Marty each grabbed a coffee, and Dent sent the donut bag around.

Brie peeked in and saw a chocolate one with powdered sugar. "Anyone partial to the chocolate?" she asked.

"Sounds like you are, Brie. Go for it." Once the goodies were distributed Dent said, "So where are we at? Marty, why don't you go first."

Marty set his donut down and flipped open his notebook. "Well, as to the time of death, we can pin it down to sometime after four a.m. Maloney's next door neighbor saw him moving around his kitchen about that time."

"And we may get closer than that," Brie said. "Assuming Tara French is telling the truth, according to her, Maloney left her place sometime after six forty-five." Brie filled Marty in on her interview with Tara—the fact that she was the last one to see Jake alive and that she was having an affair with Jake Maloney.

"Did you get a chance to interview the husband yet?" Dent asked.

"I just came from interviewing him. Odd guy. He's introverted, but it's more than that. He seems apathetic. Claimed he didn't know his wife was involved with Maloney. And he had very little emotional response to me telling him about the affair."

"Could be keeping it bottled up," Marty said. "Until it finally came to a head and he killed Maloney in a fit of rage."

"You think that's a possibility, Brie?" Dent asked.

"Of course. It always is. He's hard to read. He almost seemed resigned to the fact when I told him. Like it wasn't that unexpected. The problem, though, is opportunity. He was out on his boat from four a.m. till mid-afternoon. If I can find any of the lobstermen who saw French out there during the timeframe of the murder, then that puts him out of it."

"Huh." Dent took a drink of his coffee and a bite of his glazed donut.

"There's something else, though," Brie said. "French has a close friend. Kevin Krumm. I met him briefly." She told Dent and Marty about remembering the lobsterboat in the harbor the morning before and finding that boat in her pictures before coming down to the meeting. "That boat belongs to Kevin Krumm. And coupled with his close association with French, I think he has motive."

"Revenge—righteous indignation," Dent said.

"Exactly," Brie said. "So that's motive and opportunity. And as to means, all of these lobstermen carry knives—and serious ones—aboard their boats. French wears one strapped to his leg when he's out hauling his pots. He explained to me that their lives can depend on that knife if they get tangled in their gear somehow and pulled overboard."

"Have you interviewed Krumm yet?" Marty asked.

"Not yet," Brie said. "I just had time to check my SD card for the pictures before I came to the meeting. I have photos taken around nine o'clock yesterday morning that show Kevin Krumm's boat in the harbor. I plan to find Krumm and interview him after we're done here."

"So, Krumm's a person of interest, and from your report, it sounds like Nate Freeman, Nancy Maloney's brother, is too. Also Maloney's former partner. What was his name again?"

"Dan Littleton."

"That's right." Dent turned in his seat. "Marty, what else have you turned up with Maloney's trucking clients?"

Marty flipped a few pages in his notebook. "I'll go over what I've got."

"If you don't need me to stay for this, Lieutenant, I'd like to go question Krumm before he heads for the bar or something. I'm keeping up with your reports though, Marty."

"Ditto that, Brie," Marty said.

"You go ahead, Brie," Dent said. "I'd like to know what sense you get from this Krumm character though, Brie. What say we all grab some dinner at Varney's up the road here before I head back for the day?"

Marty nodded his accord.

"Fine by me," Brie said.

"Great." Dent checked his watch. "Let's meet at the diner about six-thirty. Will that give you enough time, Brie?"

"I think so. I'll call you if I'm running late." She put her notebook in her pocket, got out of the SUV, and headed for her car.

Chapter 13

Brie drove back up Final Reckoning Road and turned onto the highway. She planned to go back to the inn, drop off her laptop, and ask Atticus—assuming he was around—where Kevin Krumm lived. But as she approached the center of the village, she saw Amber, the girl who waitressed at Varney's Diner, walking down the road. Brie had an urge to stop and talk with her. It had been her experience that young people often notice things that adults don't, as if their lack of communication somehow makes them keener observers of their elders. Anyway, she liked the girl, and this was a chance to talk to her. She'd ask Amber if she knew where Kevin Krumm lived and thereby open the door to receiving any comments or observations she might have.

She pulled her car to the side of the road, climbed out, and walked toward her. She saw a fleeting smile cross the girl's face before Amber got it securely back under lock and key.

"Hey, Amber. I saw you walking and just wanted to say hello."

"Hey," Amber replied in a tone that said: *There might just be a reason to live.*

"Brie Beaumont. Do you remember?" Amber had blood red fingernails today and matching lipstick. *Very vampirish,* Brie thought.

"Sure," Amber replied. "I remember." She pronounced it 'shu-ah' and 'remembah' like the lobstermen had—a fact that

Brie found somehow entertaining. *Hmm, a Down East vampire,* she thought. *Just what the tourists are missing.*

"Accident at the diner?" Brie said, nodding toward Amber's uniform. The front was smeared with what looked like barbecue sauce.

"Yeah," Amber said. "Plate slipped outta my hand. Barbecue sauce—a little greasy, I guess. I'm stopping back home to change my uniform. Then I gotta go back to the dinah."

"Listen, Amber, I wonder if you can help me. I'm trying to find out where a guy named Kevin Krumm lives."

A smile tugged the corner of Amber's mouth, trying hard to prevail. Brie saw an actual twinkle in Amber's eyes, as if the girl were privy to some private joke.

"He lives just up the end of the village," she said. "On Back Bay Road. Second house in from the highway."

"I was up there this morning," Brie said. "That's where the Frenches live." Now Amber's face morphed to an expression of intense curiosity. Brie could see her trying to put two and two together. Despite how hard the girl worked at appearing indifferent, Brie guessed Amber had a lively spirit and a sharp and curious mind. She also decided the girl had a sense of humor. *Very unvampirish,* she thought.

"Amber, did you ever get the sense that there was any bad blood between Kevin Krumm and Jake Maloney?"

"Like, I'd think if there was bad blood it'd be between Steve French and Maloney."

"Why do you say that?" Brie asked. She knew the answer, of course, but wanted to confirm that people in the village knew about the affair between Tara and Jake. People other than Maloney's brother-in-law, Nate Freeman.

Amber gave her an exasperated look as if to say, *I thought you were a detective.* "*You* know," she prompted. "Maloney and Tara French . . . Gettin' it on."

"Ahhh," Brie said, nodding as if she got it. "Do you think Krumm knew about that?"

Amber shrugged. "Don't know. But Krumm is like obsessed with Steve French."

Brie's ears perked up at that. "Obsessed how?" she asked.

"Well, they're always together. Krumm hangs on his every word."

Brie wondered which words those might be since French barely spoke. "Go on," she said, fascinated by this fountain of information spouting forth from one so taciturn.

"Krumm's wife divorced him. He like hates women now."

"Really?" Brie said.

"Yeah, you can tell." She paused and looked at Brie as if hoping for approval.

"Go on, Amber. I'm very interested in your perspective."

That gave Amber the infusion of confidence she needed. "Well, I guess I could see him bein' French's, you know, like avenging angel. Going after the guy that was screwin' his best buddy's wife."

"It's a possibility, I guess." Brie said. She thought about his buffoonish behavior at the dock and wondered if he'd have the balls to kill someone in cold blood.

Then Amber was speculating again. Brie could see that she enjoyed the mental challenge of all this. She leaned toward Brie in a conspiratorial way and lowered her voice. "Unless, of course, Krumm wants Steve French like all to himself. Then he woulda been celebrating the Jake and Tara thing."

"You mean all to himself as in . . ."

"You got it. Gay and lookin' to play." She winked one racoonish eye at Brie.

"Hmmm," Brie said. "Interesting." She thought about those guys in the boat behind Hugo Lemay's laughing about the French/Krumm friendship and wondered, for a moment, if there might be something to Amber's theory. It just didn't seem to hold water, though. If Krumm had designs on Steve

French, one would think he'd welcome the affair between Tara and Maloney. Maybe even hope the two of them would ride off into the sunset together in Maloney's truck. In that case, killing Maloney would be counterproductive.

"I think the avenging angel scenario might be a better fit," Brie said. "But Krumm would have to have a violent side. Plus, the person who did this struck with military precision."

Amber's eyes widened. "Don'tcha know? Krumm's like one of those militia freaks. He's got all kinda guns and knives."

"I didn't know," Brie said. "But that certainly is important information."

"Yeah. Me and my friends laugh about it. He's like one of those Doomsday preppers." She said it *preppahs*. "Maybe it's not so funny, though, huh?"

"Maybe not," Brie said. "This has been very helpful, Amber. But I should let you get home and change."

"Well, I'm here." Amber nodded at the white saltbox house they were standing in front of. It was directly across from the harbor, and Brie immediately had a thought. It was a long shot, but nothing ventured . . .

"Amber, one more thing. I know it was extremely foggy yesterday, but did you by chance see Jake Maloney go by your house? Or, if you were working at the diner, maybe you saw him from there. Someone would have to have followed him out to Heron Head."

"I didn't work yesterday morning. And I didn't see anyone go by the . . ." She stopped suddenly, and her eyes shifted to the side as if to capture some image just beyond her field of vision. "That's funny," she said.

"What is it, Amber?" Brie asked.

"I did see something. I'd like completely forgotten about it till now. I guess it didn't seem important yesterday. I mean, like, nothing bad had happened yet."

"What did you see, Amber?" If Brie had had a seat, she'd have been on the edge of it.

"There was a lobsterboat in the harbor yesterday. I thought that was odd since they're always gone during the day."

Brie felt a little let down since she already knew about the boat. "Do you know whose boat it was?"

"Yeah. It was Kevin Krumm's boat. But that's not all."

Brie's ears perked up. "What else, Amber?"

"I was looking out the upstairs window." Amber turned and pointed at her house. "My room is right there."

"Yes?"

"I got up to go to the bathroom. When I looked out the window, I saw Kevin Krumm rowing through the fog to his boat. He tied off the skiff and went aboard. I just figured he was going out late."

"Do you know what time that was?"

"Yeah. It was like five minutes to eight. I looked at my clock when I got up. I went to the bathroom, and when I came out, I looked out the window again, and I saw Kevin Krumm rowing the skiff toward the other side of the harbor."

"Toward Heron Head?"

"Kind of in that direction."

"Was it the same skiff?"

"I couldn't tell. But it must have been. I went back to bed and didn't get up for a couple of hours."

"Could you tell if the guy rowing the skiff was Kevin Krumm? Could you see his face?" Brie asked.

"Nah. It was too foggy, and he had on a gray hoodie with, like, the hood up. But it had to be him. He climbed right aboard the boat like he owned it."

"Amber, if necessary, would you be willing to testify to what you saw yesterday morning?"

Amber looked at the ground and her brows knit together. Brie could see her assessing whether doing such a thing fit with her persona. After a few moments she looked up at Brie, and there was fire in her eyes. "Yeah, shu-ah," she said. "Jake was a nice guy. Even though he and Tara . . . you know. He, like, didn't deserve what happened to him."

Brie remembered Amber saying almost the exact same words at the diner yesterday. "Good," she said. "It may not come to that, but I'm glad to know you'll help if needed."

"Well, I should get goin'." Amber backed up a couple steps, waiting for Brie's okay.

"You go," Brie said. "And thanks for helping me." She took a card out of her pocket that had her cell phone number on it and gave it to Amber. "If you think of anything else, Amber, give me a call. And you know what? I don't know your last name."

"It's Torgesen," Amber said, like she wished it wasn't. She looked down and scuffed her foot on the ground.

"Norwegian?" Brie asked.

"Yeah, why?"

"No reason. I've got some Norwegian ancestors is all," Brie said.

Amber nodded awkwardly, like maybe that made it more acceptable. Then she turned and ambled toward her front door.

"Hey, Amber," Brie called. "What's the special tonight? I'm eating at the diner with a couple other detectives."

"There's two. Baked haddock and beef stroganoff—one of Varney's favorites."

"Does he serve that on potatoes or egg noodles?"

"It's always noodles. I think that's best."

"Me too." Brie gave her a wave.

She walked back to the car, savoring the thought of egg noodles in her near future. That got her thinking about George and the *Maine Wind,* and she felt a pang of homesickness for her shipmates. She hoped she'd be able to reach John tonight and tell him how things were progressing. He'd been her confidant and helper on the other two cases she'd become involved in. Even though he was no part of this case, since she was working with the Maine State Police, still it felt odd not having him here to share her thoughts with.

She paused and looked out at the harbor before climbing into her car. She thought about Amber seeing Kevin Krumm rowing through the fog to his boat yesterday and then her seeing the skiff headed for the opposite shore near Heron's Head. It was damning for Krumm. He had motive, means, and opportunity. Now they had an eyewitness who had seen him heading toward the crime scene within the timeframe of the murder.

Brie got in her car and started it up. She pulled out and headed for Kevin Krumm's house. It was quite possible Krumm had seen Jake Maloney going to the Frenches' house yesterday. Jake wouldn't have known Krumm was home and would never have guessed that Krumm might see him. Maybe Krumm became enraged by the situation and decided to follow Maloney when he left the French house. Maybe he wasn't planning to kill or even harm him. *But why would he go to his lobsterboat*? Brie wondered. The only logical explanation was that he had followed Jake far enough to see that he was going out Heron's Head. Maybe he'd seen an opportunity—knew he could go back to his boat for a knife and cut across the harbor and intercept him in the forest on Heron's Head.

Brie turned onto Back Bay Road and stopped across the street from Krumm's house. She checked her watch. It was five-fifteen. She figured she'd have plenty of time to question Krumm and get back to the diner by six-thirty to meet Dent Fenton and Marty.

She got out, crossed the road, and walked up to the front door. Krumm's house was of the same Cape Cod style, but considerably smaller than the Frenches' house. She rang the bell, and within less than ten seconds Kevin Krumm opened the door. He had a smile on his face and started to say something, as if he were expecting someone. When he saw her, his expression soured like he'd just chewed up an aspirin. Brie could see that it took great restraint for him not to blurt out something rude.

"Hello again, Mr. Krumm. Brie Beaumont, Maine State Police." She showed her ID.

"What's this about?" he asked suspiciously.

"As you must know, we are investigating the murder of Jake Maloney."

"What's that got to do with me?"

"That's what I'm here to determine."

"Look, lady. You're barkin' up the wrong tree."

"Nonetheless, I need to ask you some questions. We can do it here, in earshot of your neighbors, or we can do it inside. Makes no difference to me."

"I didn't even know the guy."

"That may be, but we have reason to believe you may have had a motive to kill him."

"You're crazy, lady."

"Tread carefully, Mr. Krumm. You're addressing an officer of the law. If you persist in this vein, I'll have to bring you into headquarters for questioning."

Krumm let out a sigh of disgust, stepped back, and let her in. Brie had only seen him aboard his lobsterboat, wearing a ball cap, and then seated in the skiff when he had rowed French and her ashore earlier. She hadn't really formed a physical impression of him. As she stepped in the door, she sized him up carefully. He was a tall, strongly built man with feet big as platters and hands like serving bowls. He had a double chin, eyes the color of dishwater, and a receding hairline. Despite her attempts to stay in neutrality, Brie felt an instant aversion to him—the kind she always paid attention to. He was one of those men that women would label as "icky"—an assessment that had nothing to do with his physical appearance and everything to do with the vibe he sent out. The bravado she'd witnessed on the dock earlier, as he shouted back and forth to his buddies over the noise of his boat's engine, had been replaced by a sour, pouty expression and a whiny, nasal voice. He looked at her in a dismissive way as if she were a minor annoyance, like a hangnail, he had to tolerate.

Brie wondered if the scene she'd witnessed between him and his cronies at the docks was an act, and if in reality, he was a lot more like Steve French than she had suspected. But there was one major difference between the two men. While Steve French might be emotionally shut down, she had sensed no hostility in him. Krumm, on the other hand, reminded her of a nasty abscess about to burst and spread its poison indiscriminately.

Brie followed him into the living room. The furniture consisted of two shabby leather recliners in front of a giant flat-screen TV. The shelf unit that held the TV was stuffed with video games and gaming equipment. The décor seemed a perfect fit. Unfettered by a wife, he had crawled back into his man-cave, amply provisioned with microwave dinners and video games. Brie wondered if she was being too judgmental. But she liked to call things as she saw them, and in the realm of humanity, she had found that every coin did not have a flip side.

She took out her notebook and pen and started the interview. "Mr. Krumm, it's come to my attention that your boat was in the harbor yesterday. Why were you not out pulling your pots?"

"I got some bad grub somewhere. Must o' been the day before. I woke in the night with a bad case of the heaves. I was still upchucking yestahday maunin'. So I didn't go out."

"What is your relationship with Steve French?"

"Good buddies is all."

"And what about Steve's wife?"

Krumm narrowed his eyes and crossed his arms on his chest. "Don't got no truck with her."

"And Jake Maloney?"

"Barely knew the guy. We 'bout done here?" he whined.

"Not by a ways," Brie said. "Were you aware of Jake Maloney's involvement with Tara French?"

Krumm glared at her. "I didn't know nothin' about that. Figures though, she'd be just like all the othahs. Evil bitches. I nevah yet met one I could trust." He looked Brie up and down just to let her know she was included.

"So, that sums up your attitude toward half the human race, Mr. Krumm?"

"Pretty much," Krumm said.

"Healthy attitude, that," Brie said facetiously. She took a couple minutes to write in her notebook just to send a message about who was in control here. His scowl deepened with each passing moment.

"I understand, Mr. Krumm, that you are involved with certain militia groups."

"That ain't against the law. Gotta be ready when them assholes in Washington finally bring everything down."

"Is that so? Were you ever in the military, Mr. Krumm?"

"Marines. Ninety to ninety-four."

"Desert Storm?" Brie asked.

"That's right." He looked mildly confused that one of the *evil bitches* would have that fact at her fingertips.

Brie nodded and made a note in her book. "Tell me, Mr. Krumm, did you row out to your lobsterboat yesterday morning just before eight o'clock?"

"Did I what? Hell no. Didn't you hear me, woman? I told you I was pukin' my guts out."

"Once again, I need to remind you that you're talking to a law officer. If you can't remember that, maybe your memory of yesterday is even cloudier."

He glared at her, his face turning the shade of a well-cooked lobster.

Brie ignored his simmering rage and spread her feet to parade rest to let him see she wasn't going anywhere. "We have an eyewitness who saw someone row out to your boat and go aboard yesterday morning at around seven fifty-five, and then from there, row toward Heron Head on the other side of the harbor, near the time Jake Maloney was killed."

"That does it. We're through here."

"Actually we're not, Mr. Krumm. Unless you want to accompany me to headquarters and finish this interview there." Despite his indignation, she was inclined to believe he *had* gone to his boat yesterday morning. She looked him straight in the eye. "Are you saying you did not row out to your boat yesterday morning?"

"That's . . . what . . . I'm . . . saying." He pronounced each word separately, trying a new you're-the-village-idiot tactic.

"Any guess as to why someone would do that?"

"My guess is someone's lying to you. Wait, I bet you got that information from a woman, didn't you?"

"Who I got it from is not your business, Mr. Krumm."

"Ha. I knew it. Some crazy broad. Probably out to get me."

"Mr. Krumm, you're acting paranoid. It is the job of the police detectives to find the truth. Be assured, it is not our goal to build a bogus case against you or anyone."

At that, Krumm appeared to release a little steam. But just enough to drop below full boil. "Well, we're done here. I have to go to my boat and pull the radio out. It's been acting up." He headed for the door.

Brie stepped into his path. "Excuse me, Mr. Krumm, but I'll tell you when we're done."

"Look, Detective," he sneered. "I gotta go get that radio and get it repaired. If you got more questions, you'll have to tag along."

"Fine," Brie said. "I'll meet you down on the dock near the skiffs." She pocketed her notebook and headed out the door. *This is perfect,* she thought. *I wanted to have a look around his boat anyway*. Brie crossed the street to her car, got in, and hung a U-ey so she'd get to the dock before Krumm. She stopped her car beyond his driveway and waited till she saw him back his truck down. Then she headed for the lobster docks.

She was waiting next to the flotilla of skiffs when he came down the dock. He pointed to one and she climbed down the ladder, stepped aboard, and sat in the stern. Krumm came down and took the center thwart, and they rowed toward his lobsterboat. Even though he was facing Brie, he refused to look at her and focused his eyes on the harbor behind her.

Brie asked him some more questions about how long he'd known Steve and Tara French and how well he knew the Maloneys, but she was really just passing time, waiting to get aboard his boat and see if anything seemed suspicious. When they got to the boat, Krumm shipped the oars and floated up to the starboard side. Brie climbed aboard, and Krumm tied off the skiff and came aboard.

He made a beeline for the house—the enclosed part of the boat where the helm and the electronic equipment were located. He reached into the cuddy and started pulling stuff out. Brie guessed he was looking for a screwdriver so he could disconnect the radio unit that was screwed to the ceiling of the house above the wheel. Out came duct tape and some candy bar wrappers. When he pulled the binoculars out, the strap caught around the handle of a knife, and it fell to the deck near Brie's feet. It was a survival knife with a smooth blade, and Brie immediately saw there was blood on it. Krumm reached for it.

"Step back, Mr. Krumm. Don't touch that."

Krumm paused for a second, then reached for it again.

Brie's hand went to her gun. "Stop, Mr. Krumm, and back up."

Something in her tone got through, because his hand stopped in midair and he straightened up.

Brie pulled out a latex glove, put it on, and carefully picked the knife up by the very end of the handle. "There appears to be blood on this knife, Mr Krumm."

"What do you expect, lady? It's a fishing knife."

"Just one problem with that. You're a lobsterman and lobsters don't bleed. They crawl into traps."

"I don't know how that blood got on there." His face was red, and Brie could see he was agitated. He started to reach for the knife again.

"Step back, Mr. Krumm," she warned. She was pretty sure if she had to drop the knife and reach for her gun, he would grab the knife, and possibly throw it overboard.

"But I didn't do nothin'. You hear me?" His eyes turned mean.

Brie watched him carefully. "If that's the case, you need to prove it by stepping back and letting me bag this knife."

He hesitated for a moment. Volatility hung in the air, heavy and threatening. Finally he stepped back and stood glaring at her.

Brie got the evidence envelope from her inside jacket pocket. She unfolded the paper envelope against her leg, put the knife inside, and secured the top of the envelope. Then she folded it carefully in thirds and placed it back in her inside pocket.

She looked out the side window of the wheelhouse toward Heron Head. From where the boat was moored, it would be a quick pull to reach the shore near the trailhead. Even with the dense fog yesterday morning, it seemed foolhardy to her that Kevin Krumm would have risked being seen. But violent emotions drive people to make less than rational decisions. Krumm's anger at seeing Maloney leave the French house may well have been the catalyst for some very unwise choices.

"Let's head back to shore, Mr. Krumm." Brie nodded toward the stern where the skiff was tied off. He walked past her, and she watched him carefully as they boarded the skiff and pulled for shore. He didn't speak, but his eyes had darkened to the color of a dirty sky.

They docked the skiff, and Krumm went up the ladder first, followed by Brie. He started to walk down the dock but turned suddenly so Brie stopped right on top of him. Her hand went to her gun.

"I want that knife back. You hear?" He said it *he-ah.*

Brie stood her ground. "You'll get it back when we're done with it. Once I log the knife into evidence, there will be a careful chain of custody as it's processed through the crime lab. We don't lose evidence, Mr. Krumm." She was surprised he wasn't more concerned that the knife could incriminate him.

"Am I free to go or not? I gotta go back out for my damn radio."

"You're free to go, Mr. Krumm. But don't leave town."

Brie turned and walked off the dock. Kevin Krumm had motive, means, and opportunity. If Jake Maloney's blood was found on his knife, as she suspected it would be, Krumm's life was about to take a very unpleasant turn.

Chapter 14

Brie walked back to her car and climbed in. She pulled her laptop out of the case, turned it on, logged into the Maine State Police site, and brought up the case file for Jake Maloney. After putting in her badge number, she entered the knife into the evidence log, listing the date and time she had taken it into evidence. She also entered the details of where the knife had been found and that there appeared to be traces of blood near the hilt. After finishing the entry, she logged off and checked her watch. It was 6:20. She was supposed to meet Dent Fenton and Marty Dupuis at the diner at 6:30. She turned on the ignition and drove slowly through the village toward the diner.

At the far end of Tucker Harbor, she turned right, headed up the hill a short ways, and turned into Varney's parking lot. Since she was the first one there, she opened her windows and sat thinking about her interview with Kevin Krumm. While his motive may not have been any stronger than Nate Freeman's, in her estimation Krumm had had the best opportunity to see Maloney both arriving and leaving the Frenches' house yesterday morning. He was the only one who could have known Maloney had hiked out the trail on Heron Head. Unless, of course, Maloney had been going out there to meet someone.

While she was mulling, Dent Fenton pulled up in his SUV and waved to her. She put her windows up, got out and walked over to him.

"Hey, Brie."

"Hey, Lieutenant."

The beginnings of a smile warmed his blue eyes. "Dent's okay, you know. Especially when it's just the two of us."

"Sorry. Habit. You know."

He nodded his head in a resigned way.

Brie reached into her jacket. "I need to turn something over to you. I just took this into evidence." She filled him in on Kevin Krumm, the location of his house and his connection to Steve French. She also told him that Krumm's boat had remained in the harbor yesterday, and that Amber had seen someone rowing to the boat and then toward the opposite shore around the time of the murder.

"After I interviewed him, we rowed out to his boat. He had two knives aboard." She held up the envelope. "This one has traces of what appears to be blood. Based on what Amber saw, I decided it needed to be taken into evidence."

Dent's eyebrows went up. "I'll get that to the crime lab this evening. If by chance the blood is Maloney's, we'll bring this Krumm character in for questioning. Maybe we can wrap the case up quickly." Dent Fenton's prominent brow bone gave him a perpetually serious look. But Brie could see he was pleased that there was progress in the case.

"Unfortunately, Amber only saw the guy from a distance, and he had the hood up on his sweatshirt. With the dense fog yesterday morning, she couldn't swear to anything except that she saw a person rowing toward his boat, going aboard, and then rowing toward Heron Head."

"Still, it's pretty damning for Krumm. Did you log this in yet?"

"I did. And I'll sign it over to you right now." Brie heard a car and turned to see Marty Dupuis pulling into the lot.

On the envelope Dent wrote the time the knife changed hands, and Brie signed her name and badge number. Then he locked the envelope in his SUV and the three of them walked into the diner.

The place was empty except for one older couple sitting by the window, partway down the row of booths. When Varney came over to seat them, Dent asked if they could have the booth on the end. He obviously thought it would give them a little more privacy to discuss the case.

Brie sat down first, and Dent sat next to her. Marty went to the other side of the table and slid in to the middle of the seat. Brie looked around but didn't see Amber, and Varney quickly appeared with three waters. He told them what was on special—baked haddock and beef stroganoff—and went to get them coffee.

Brie and Dent decided on the stroganoff. Marty opted for the Varney Burger. Varney came back with their coffees, took the order, and shuffled back toward the kitchen. Dent watched him as he walked off.

Dent filled Marty in on their new prime suspect. They quietly discussed the other two possible suspects—Nancy Maloney's brother and Dan Littleton, Jake Maloney's former partner. Brie talked about the logistics of where the other two lived and pointed out that the location of Krumm's house would have given him the greatest opportunity to follow Maloney and kill him.

"What about motive?" Dent asked.

"On the surface, it's no stronger than Nate Freeman's motive. Maybe not as strong. Freeman is fiercely protective of his sister. He knew about Maloney's affair and seemed to flat out hate Maloney. But there's something about Krumm."

"What is it, Brie?"

"I don't know, really. He's got a special kind of creepiness." She turned and looked at Dent. "You know, sometimes you just get a vibe."

Dent nodded.

"Then there's this whole militia piece." Brie filled them in on that part. "If you ask me, he's a loose cannon, just waiting to go off. My guess—he saw Maloney sneaking into the French house yesterday morning. That and his distrust of women probably got him simmering. I think when Maloney left Tara's, Krumm followed him. He may not have been planning anything at that point. Maybe then he saw Maloney head down Final Reckoning Road and start up the trail on Heron Head. I think that's when he made a decision. He figured he had plenty of time to go back to his boat, get a knife, and intercept him in the woods, where there was no chance of being seen. And with his military training, I believe he would have felt confident attacking Maloney with a knife." She took a drink of her coffee. "I guess we'll know more after we get an analysis on the knife."

"The chances of him being framed seem slim," Dent said. "No one could have known that he'd be sick yesterday or that his boat would be in the harbor."

"And of the three suspects so far, he's the only one who could have physically seen Jake Maloney coming from Tara's that morning and decided to follow him," Brie said.

"I'll see if they can give that blood typing priority at the lab."

Brie nodded. She saw Varney approaching with a large aluminum serving tray. "Here comes dinner," she said.

Varney set their plates in front of them. "I'll bring more coffee," he said, seeing that, in proper police fashion, they had already drained their cups.

Brie waded into her stroganoff.

"How is it?" Dent asked.

"Good," she said. But to be honest, it wasn't as good as George's beef stroganoff. How could it be? It hadn't been cooked on Old Faithful, aboard the *Maine Wind*. On the other hand, though, Brie had never met an egg noodle she didn't like, so she munched away contentedly, savoring every bite but deciding she'd add a mile or two to her run this evening.

Marty set his burger down and took a drink of coffee. "So, Dent, you going fly fishing this fall?"

"Wouldn't miss it. I've got vacation scheduled for the fourth week in September."

"Rapid River?" Marty asked.

"You bet. My annual pilgrimage."

"Dent here's quite the fly fisherman," Marty said to Brie.

"I heard about that when we met out on Sentinel Island earlier this summer." Brie turned to face Dent. "I read Louise Dickenson Rich's book, *I Took to the Woods,* this summer while aboard the *Maine Wind*. She and her husband lived on the Rapid River. The story of her years there is amazing. What a woman she was."

"That area of Maine is just as pristine, just as remote and hard to get to as when she lived there in the 1940s," Dent said.

"Her story reminds me of Justine Kerfoot, a legendary woman who, in 1928, moved to the Boundary Waters Canoe Area of Minnesota as a young woman and worked as a canoe guide there for many decades. Talk about strong women, both of them. Pioneers, really."

"And such great role models for girls," Marty said.

"The house where Dickenson Rich lived is now called Forest Lodge. It's one of only two fishing camps on the Rapid River. I stay there every year on my fishing trip," Dent said.

"Wow. That is so cool. So, tell me, how did you get into fly fishing?"

"Well, my dad started taking me with him when I was about ten years old. I loved it from the first. I like being right out there in the river or stream with the fish. Being part of their environment. I feel free every time I wade out into a river with my gear." Dent's blue eyes seemed to deepen and take on a reflective quality, like the rivers he so loved.

Brie nodded like she got it. "Police work is hard, and homicide work is particularly stressful. We see a lot of death. We deal with the darkest, ugliest side of human nature. For me, going out into nature . . . well, it restores me. Especially when water is involved. It's why I love the sea and sailing. I guess there might be some interesting philosophical parallels in all of it. You know, the river—death—rebirth."

"Your education is showing, Brie," Dent said, ribbing her.

"I certainly hope so, or my parents struggled for nothing," she said.

Dent nodded at that.

"How about you, Marty? Do any fishing?" Brie asked.

"Dent and I go for day trips and weekends sometimes to the Passadumkeag and the Piscataquis Rivers. I don't get out as much as Dent. Family, you know. Seems like the kids've always got stuff going on the weekends."

"He's no slouch with a rod and reel," Dent said. "He landed a trophy-size brook trout—over five pounds—up on the Piscataquis in May."

"It may sound weird, but I find some interesting parallels to detective work and to criminology in the sport of fly fishing," Marty said.

"Really? How so?" Brie asked.

Marty slid his plate aside and rested his forearms on the table. He wore a short-sleeved blue sport shirt, and his brawny arms filled out the fabric above the elbows.

"As a fly fisherman, you are the predator, the stalker. You wade into the fish's environment in order to catch it. You learn its habits—what it eats, where it holds. You use flies or nymphs to mimic its food, to trick the trout into taking the bait. I think the more a detective learns to think like a predator—the more he himself becomes the predator, intent on his catch—the more successful he will be."

"Interesting," Brie said.

Marty took a drink of his coffee. "The detective stalks the killer, perhaps just as the killer stalked the victim. The detective is out to catch a murderer. In a battle of wits and wills, he follows the killer. He wades into a stream of evidence—of possible suspects. Catching a killer is often a process of elimination, a process of narrowing the field using a range of tactics, just as the fly fisherman goes to the right part of the river and fishes at the right depth. Wits, reason, logic, powers of observation, tenacity, and patience. These are the detective's nymphs. They are his rod, reel, and line. If he uses these nymphs skillfully, he will catch his prey."

"And fish are cagey," Dent said. "They are not easily caught or fooled."

"Like the killer, they will fight you. Sometimes to the death. They want their freedom, and you are out to deprive them of it."

Marty's words hit home, and Brie felt a chill run through her soul as she remembered the night Phil had died, and also the mortal battle she had waged for her life at Granite Island in May.

"It's a fascinating analogy, Marty," Dent said respectfully. "You know, in all the years I've been fly fishing, I've never thought about the parallels to police work."

"Maybe it's because I learned the sport after I was already a detective. But to me the parallels are striking."

"Dang, more education showing," Brie joked.

Marty's dark eyes twinkled at that. "You know the famous fly, the Gray Ghost, invented here in Maine in the 1920s?"

"Sure," Dent said.

"Well, as a detective, even that name resonates with me. There's always the case that goes cold—the killer who can't be caught. Like a gray ghost, he seems to slip away into the shadows, not unlike the monster salmon that eludes the best fisherman."

Dent shook his head in admiration. "Marty, I think you need to write a book."

"Nah, I'll just keep fishing."

Varney stopped by to see if they wanted dessert and to pour one more round of coffee. They all decided to pass on dessert.

"So, I guess we're kind of in a holding pattern until the labs come back on Krumm's knife," Brie said.

"Hopefully, we'll get the results some time tomorrow," Dent said. He reached for the check and insisted on picking up the tab for the dinner.

"Thanks, Dent," Brie said, and Marty seconded.

Dent nodded and gave her a warm look, clearly pleased that she'd dropped the formality temporarily.

They took a last sip of their coffee, got up from the booth, and headed for the door. Brie turned to give Varney a wave good-bye. She could have sworn she saw a look of apprehension on his face as his eyes followed them toward the door. She took note of it but didn't put much stock in it. Any kind of police presence tended to make people nervous. *Just drive down a highway where's there's a police car or highway patrol in the flow of traffic,* she thought, *and watch everyone fall in behind him.* She'd seldom seen any driver bold enough to pass that police car. People pussyfoot around the police, and she thought Varney was probably no exception to the rule.

As they opened the door to leave, Varney called out, "Could you flip the sign over when you leave."

"No problem," Marty said and turned the cardboard sign to *Closed*.

The three of them walked across the parking lot together.

"I'll let you two know as soon as I receive any word from the crime lab on the knife," Dent said. "In the meantime, Marty, I want you to follow up with the rest of Maloney's shipping clients. Do you have his mileage log?"

"I collected that from his truck when I drove Nancy Maloney to the morgue yesterday."

"Good. I want you to check the mileage entries in the log against the dates and locations of pick-ups and deliveries."

"Sure," Marty said. "I can get on that tonight."

"No need. Take the rest of the night off. You too, Brie. You can work those angles tomorrow while we wait for the labs to come back on Krumm's knife."

With that they headed for their separate cars. Brie was the first one out of the lot. She was eager to get back to the inn, change her clothes, and head out for a run. She was glad Dent had given her permission to kick back tonight.

Chapter 15

Brie pulled in behind the Whale Spout Inn. It was just past seven-thirty. She got out with her laptop, walked to the back of the car, and locked her gun in the trunk. She wasn't about to leave it in her room with no lock on the door. She headed over to the clothesline to retrieve her pajamas she'd hung there after breakfast and then went in the back door of the inn. She had plenty of time to get in a nice run and still be back before dark. She planned to try John again tonight and hoped the ship would be anchored somewhere with cell phone reception.

In her room, she pulled on a snug-fitting yellow tee shirt and a pair of black leggings to keep her muscles warm in the cool evening night air. She brushed her hair out, returned it to a ponytail and twisted it into a bun so it would stay put while she ran. She pulled on a clean pair of running socks, sat down on the floor, and went through a series of stretches she had learned in dance to loosen up hamstrings, inner thighs, and quads. She put on her running shoes and headed downstairs. The inn was quiet. Atticus was nowhere to be seen.

She walked out the back door. The highway ran right past the side of the inn, and Brie took it down through the village. As she passed Amber's house, she looked to her right to see if the girl might be outside. No luck. Tucker Harbor had rolled up its sidewalks, and as she ran down past the harbor, she didn't encounter a soul. It was a fine evening. A light breeze carried the refreshing tang of salt off the ocean, and the ebbing evening light cast a silver net across the waters of the harbor. Brie ran on through the village and up the hill at the other end. Through the window of the diner, she could see Varney closing out the register and getting ready to leave.

She continued on up the hill. It was a fairly steep grade, but she was already warmed up from her run through the village. In a few minutes she passed a road that led down to a gate, half mile or so in the distance, that allowed access to the Navy's VLF transmitter, which was used for submarine communication. A sign next to the road said *Authorized Personnel Only*. A very old graveyard lay at the intersection of the two roads. Weather-washed headstones, their granite shoulders sloped and bowed with age, leaned at precarious angles trying to hold their own against the march of time.

Brie ran on and now she could feel a mild tingling in her hands and a sweat just beginning to break. The exertion felt good after hours of standing interviewing suspects or sitting either discussing those interviews or filing reports. She emptied her mind, trying to be in the Zen of the moment, as her friend Ariel always advised. She focused on her breathing and on the inner rhythm of her heart. As she did so, she became more aware of an array of sounds that accompanied the closing of the day. Crickets were starting to chirp, and she heard the high-pitched buzz of cicadas from the trees along the highway. In the distance she could hear the mournful call of a gull as it circled over the ocean, searching the waters below for its prey.

Now that the road had leveled out and her heart rate was up, Brie lengthened her stride and began to feel a pleasant burn in her calves and thighs. To her left, topping the bluff that overlooked the sea, was another small graveyard. Flags and flowers were placed by some of the headstones. She decided this must be the current cemetery for the village of Tucker Harbor and the surrounding area. She thought it was a lovely final resting place.

She ran on and soon passed the road leading to the airstrip where Nate Freeman lived in his single-wide. She thought for a moment about her interview with Nate Freeman, the former Navy SEAL, and about the knife she had turned over to Dent Fenton. Freeman would have been skilled with such a weapon. No doubt about that. Then she thought about Kevin Krumm. Lots of killers are caught because they are careless, arrogant, or just plan stupid. The arrogant part of the profile sure fit Krumm.

Brie ran on. Based on her watch and the lay of the terrain, she figured she'd covered about four to four and a half miles. She saw signs of life up ahead. She was coming up on the old Navy base. She had passed it on her drive into Machias yesterday but hadn't stopped. She decided she'd integrate it into her run tonight. Atticus had told her there were now some condos on the grounds of the old base, and she was curious to see them.

The Tucker Harbor fire station sat at the intersection of the highway and the road into the base. As she approached, Brie saw two guys sitting out front. They had their legs stretched out in front of them and were shooting the breeze. When she got close, they stopped talking and watched her instead. Brie took it as a sign she hadn't lost it. She slowed her pace as she came to the intersection and jogged over to where they were sitting.

"Hey, guys," she said.

"Hello, miss. Nice evening for a run," the guy on the right said. He was a husky fellow about her age, with freckled arms, a bull neck, and rust red hair.

"It's a perfect night," Brie said.

"Storm movin' in later, though," the second guy said. With his Yankee accent, storm became *stahm* and later became *latah*.

"You guys must be firemen," Brie said.

"You got it," the husky guy said.

"Volunteer?" she asked.

"A-yuh," said number two.

"So, I'm staying in Tucker Harbor for a few days," Brie said. She didn't tell them she was a cop. "This must be the old Navy base I've heard about."

"That's right," Husky said. "There's still a number of the original buildings." He nodded toward a group of buildings across the road and down a ways. "And down the end of the road here, you'll see what used to be housing for officers and base personnel. They've been converted into condo units, but those are the original structures. They date back to when the base was built."

"I see the sign here," Brie said, turning and nodding at the fancy wood sign behind her. It said Misty Harbor Homes. "So what year was the base built? Do you know?"

"Nineteen sixty and sixty-one."

"The height of the Cold War," Brie said.

"That's right," Husky said. "Our sub fleet was at its most active in those years. The transmitter—that's the antenna array south of the base here—was built to communicate with the fleet."

"You seem to know something about it," Brie said.

"I'm kind of a naval history buff. And this was such an important facility. Still is, for that matter. While the base is gone, the transmitter is still fully operational, sending one-way communication, in a continuous encrypted signal, to the United States strategic submarine forces."

"Very interesting," Brie said. She could see Husky was just hitting his stride.

"It's the most powerful VLF, or very low frequency, transmitter in the world. It operates at 24 kHz, which is still within radio frequency, or RF, but at the very bottom end of it."

"I'd heard about the transmitter," Brie said. "So have there been any adverse environmental effects from all those radio waves?"

"There've been some questions about the ELF arrays and some studies done on those by the Navy. Apparently, there are more questions about the extremely low frequency waves."

"Huh," Brie said. "Well, I have to admit to ignorance when it comes to knowing the differences between VLF and ELF signals."

"That's okay," Husky said. "Most people don't know much about the technology."

Directly across the highway from them, the road continued in a straight line as far as the eye could see. A small cement island sat in the middle of the road, like there might once have been a gate there or maybe a check-in station of some kind. A worn metal sign read, "No trespassing. Property of the U.S. Government."

Brie nodded across the road. "More of the old base down there?" she asked.

"Just a couple abandoned buildings."

"Well, guys, before I warm down too much and lose my light, I think I'll reconnoiter the old base a bit. Nice meeting you two."

"Same here," the husky guy said, standing up. "Name's Paul Riley," he said, shaking hands with Brie. He looked like he wanted to keep the conversation going but didn't know how. "This is Jack," he said, turning to his sidekick.

"I'm Brie," she said. "Thanks for the info, guys."

"Anytime, Brie," Paul said.

Jack nodded but didn't get up. "Feel free to take the jogging tour," he said, turning tour into *to-ah*. "There's some nice views of Holmes Bay from the bluffs down thata way." He nodded along the road to his right.

She headed on down the road, hung a left and looped around a group of one-story buildings that looked like they might have housed the base mess hall, commissary, and maybe some barracks. The old baseball diamond was still there, and she wondered if any kids lived in the condos and if they ever got up a ballgame there. She continued down the road toward the ocean bluffs to check out the revamped base housing—now Misty Harbor Homes. *Sure sounds like a nice spot to hang your hat,* she thought.

She was beginning to see the view off the bluffs now, and it was spectacular. She came up to the junction of Misty Harbor Trail that ran between two rows of condos. One row of homes sat directly on the edge of the bluff, with the other row across the street from them. All of the structures except one were double condo units. On the very end was one single family unit. It had a for sale sign next to it. Brie walked off the road and along the side of the home up toward the edge of the bluff. The land faced west, and the sun was dipping toward the treetops of Starboard Peninsula, which ran ten miles south and east of the town of Machias on the far side of Holmes Bay. The approaching sunset cast pale gold light across the wide expanse of water, and the wind carried the heady scent of sea roses that grew along the top of the bluff.

Brie stood for a few moments taking in the astounding view before walking back to the road. She ran south along Misty Harbor Trail between the two rows of condos. The exteriors had gray shake siding and white trim, perfectly suited to their seaside location. Brie tried to imagine them when they would have housed Navy personnel and their families; when children would have burst loudly out the doors on summer evenings after dinner for a game of baseball or capture the flag. *Being stationed here would have been nice duty,* she thought. It was a pretty spot, and as she passed Brie nodded or waved to a few people who were sitting out in their yards or gardening.

At the end of Misty Harbor Trail the road turned left, back toward the base buildings. She reversed course and ran back the way she'd come and down the other way beyond the condos where the road curved and dropped down a small hill for about a quarter of a mile. At the end of the road she came to another remnant of the old base. It was a square area about eighty feet wide and was surrounded by high fence topped with barbed wire. Within the fenced compound were three small buildings, each about six by eight feet, and in the center of the fenced area was what looked like an opening to a stairway. It was surrounded by a railing made out of pipe. But from her viewing angle outside the fence, Brie could not actually see a stairway. A sign on one of the buildings read, "Hazardous Noise. Caution, May Cause Hearing Loss. Hearing protection required." Brie cocked her head and listened but heard not a sound. She walked around the perimeter of the fenced area. The grass inside had gone to seed. Another sign read, "Caution, Restricted Space. Permit required."

Brie thought maybe the area gave access to utilities that ran below the condos. She wondered about the hazardous noise part, though, and decided whatever function these buildings had served was now defunct along with the rest of the base. She headed up the road and at the top of the hill turned left and ran back the way she had come toward the highway. The sun had set. It was time to get back to the inn.

At the entrance to the base, the firemen were nowhere to be seen. She hung a right and increased her pace along the shoulder of the highway toward Tucker Harbor. After she had covered a couple of miles, she noticed that the breeze had died, and it felt like the humidity was on the rise. *Storm moving in*, she thought, remembering Jack's prediction back at the firehouse. In a few more minutes, she passed the road to the airstrip. With no breeze to aid evaporation, she could feel the sweat on her back and upper chest. But the exertion felt good; it helped her to completely empty her mind and be firmly in the moment.

She saw the cemetery coming up on her right. Someone was walking among the headstones, pausing here and there to read one of them and occasionally turning to face the ocean. When she got closer she saw it was Varney Simms from the diner. There was a dirt road—really just a grassy track—that looped through the narrow cemetery and back out to the highway at the other end. Brie turned in at the northern end of the track and slowed to a walk as she approached Varney.

He looked up from the grave marker he was studying as she came toward him. He smiled at her, but Brie saw beyond the smile to the sadness in his eyes.

"Hello, Varney," she said.

"Hello, Detective. Looks like you've had quite a run." She saw him make a conscious attempt to brighten up a bit.

"You can call me Brie, Varney. I ran as far as the old base and around there a bit. I'm on my way back now. I hope I'm not disturbing you."

"Not at all," he said. "I can't run. Bum leg and all." He patted the side of his right leg. "But I like to take a walk up the hill at night for some exercise. And I find this a peaceful spot."

She looked down at the marker that was decorated with a small American flag. She saw it was the final resting place of a young soldier who had died at twenty-three. It made her instantly sad and a little angry as well.

"Someone you knew, Varney?" she asked.

"Not well. But he lived in Tucker Harbor, so of course we all knew him. Such a waste. Died in the war. IED."

Brie reflected on the fact that such a terrible phrase as Improvised Explosive Device had become a part of the American vernacular. They turned from the marker and walked on down the row.

"Do you have any children, Varney?" she asked.

"Nope, never married. Guess I never found the right girl. How about you, Miss Brie? You married?"

"Just to my job, so far. But I'm learning to broaden my horizons a bit lately."

"That's good," he said with sincerity and glanced shyly at her eyes. "Work isn't everything. Or shouldn't be. You realize that more and more the older you get."

"I think you're right, Varney."

"Do you ever wish you could just chuck the whole thing? Start over?" His eyes slid sideways as if he could glimpse that other life just beyond his field of vision.

Brie knew he must be referring to his own life, but she felt the irony of his words in relation to the last few months of hers. "I think everyone feels that way sometimes."

He looked a little disappointed, like maybe he was hoping for a different response.

"I've had a couple of chances to talk with Amber Torgeson, who works for you. I like her."

Varney smiled and seemed to brighten. "Hard not to like that girl. She's kind of a misfit. But with a heart of gold."

"In my work I've found that's not uncommon with the ones who are considered misfits."

"Kind of makes you wonder about our society. Seems things are upside down somehow."

"That's as true a statement as I've heard recently," Brie said.

"Kind of makes you hope the aliens land some day and maybe straighten us out."

Brie let out a laugh, which got a big smile from Varney. "They could always home in on that gigantic tower array." She nodded toward the southwest, where the tops of the naval transmitter towers were visible. "Or maybe pick up on the signal beaming toward the center of the galaxy," she joked.

"You got it. And fly right down through that ozone hole some of the Mainers think is up there. I mean, who knows what all those transmissions are doing?"

She was glad to see that Varney had brightened up a bit. *Amazing what a little human companionship can do,* she thought. They followed the arc of the track back out toward the highway. A car horn beeped as they came up onto the road, and Atticus Kane waved as he passed in his pickup truck. He had a couple of small trees in the back that were obviously headed for habitation near the Whale Spout Inn.

The air had gone still as death as they walked along the road toward Tucker Harbor. "You run on ahead, Miss Brie," Varney said. "I'll just slow you down."

"You sure, Varney? I don't mind walking back."

"Nope, there's a storm comin'. No point getting caught out in it."

As if on cue, the growl of distant thunder rolled across the ocean from the east. She said goodbye to him and picked up her pace. As she ran toward the inn, the air felt heavy and close around her. She thought about Varney walking among the headstones and the sadness she had seen in his eyes. She remembered the dream she had had the night before—the graveyard, the rain, the black umbrellas. The words *quiet desperation* played through her mind.

Chapter 16

Brie dropped down the hill and took Third Street, which intersected with the highway on the west side of the village and ended on the east side just above the inn. She was trying to beat the rain and picked up her pace. The percussive sound of thunder enveloped her. She felt strangely vulnerable and was happy when the inn came in sight. She slowed up a bit in order to warm down, and when she came to the corner of the inn's property, she cut across the yard, retrieved her gun from the trunk of her car, and went in the back door.

Atticus was just coming out of the parlor with his coffee mug in hand. "Sounds like we're in for a blow," he said. "There's a flashlight in the top drawer of your dresser, in case we lose power, and there's also an oil lamp and matches in each room."

"Thanks, Atticus, I saw that," Brie said. "I'm just glad I got back before it hit."

"It's still a ways off. Tucker Harbor sits in a kind of bowl surrounded by the hills, so storms moving in from seaward always sound closer than they are."

"Well, I think I'll go grab a shower, and then maybe sit out on the porch and watch it roll in."

Atticus nodded, and she headed up the stairs and into her room. She went in the bathroom and undressed. She put her tee shirt, leggings, and sports bra into the sink's wash bowl and filled it up with soapy water. Then she turned on the water in the shower and hopped in. She stood under the hot spray for a few minutes, feeling her muscles relax, before washing her hair and scrubbing off. In about ten minutes, she climbed out, wrapped her hair in a large soft towel and dried off with another one. She pulled on jeans and a long-sleeved pink tee shirt and stuffed her feet into her deck shoes. She combed out her hair but didn't dry it and went out into the bedroom to get her cell phone. She picked it up off the top of the dresser and headed downstairs and out the front door onto the porch.

The storm was still a ways off, so she sat down in one of the wood rockers and pulled up John's number in her log. The call went immediately to his voicemail. She listened to the message, lonely for the sound of his voice. She couldn't believe it had only been a day and a half since the *Maine Wind* had sailed out of Tucker Harbor without her. She put the phone in her pocket and rested her head against the back of the rocker as she worked the chair gently with her feet. Onshore, darkness was setting in, but there was plenty of light out on the harbor. In fact, the sea still reflected the dying sunset and appeared unusually bright before the wall of blackness advancing from the east. Despite the approaching storm, the evening air felt warm, and after a few minutes, she started to yawn. She laid her head against the back of the rocker, fighting the urge to doze off.

An explosive thunderclap jolted Brie awake. The porch floor seemed to vibrate beneath her feet, and the smell of ozone told her the lightning had struck close by—too close. A vicious sky rolled over Tucker Harbor, sending spears of lightning into the sea and sealing off the village with a cloud deck thick and black as volcanic ash. Brie stood for a moment at the edge of the porch, riveted by the drama and danger unfolding around her. She pulled herself away and headed for the door just as the sky opened up.

Inside the door, she listened as the torrent hammered the porch roof. She walked into the living room where a fire was burning in the fireplace. Wave upon wave of rain assaulted windows darkened by nightfall and the blackness of the storm. Brie walked up to one of the windows. She could see her reflection in the glass—an image of safety and sanity superimposed on a background of turmoil. The grandfather clock in the corner ticked off the seconds in calm and ordered cadence as lightning racked the room and thunder shook the walls. The time on the clock read nine thirty-five.

Brie headed for the stairs and climbed the double flight up to the second floor. She opened the door to her room and flipped the light switch that turned on an overhead light. As she closed the door, the power flickered twice and went out. Hands out in front of her, she felt her way across the room to the dresser. She ran her hands over the top, feeling for the box of matches she'd seen there. When she found them, she slid the box open, took out a match, and slid it closed. She stuck the match and it flared to life, casting ghostly shadows around the room. Brie lifted the glass on the oil lamp and held the match to the wick. As she replaced the chimney, the room glowed softly from the amplification of the flame on the glass and the lamp's reflection in the dresser mirror behind it. Long shadows leaned in from various angles, jockeying for space in the lamp-lit room. The play of light and darkness made her think of Varney in the cemetery—the sadness she had seen in his eyes and how it had shifted to mirth as they joked about the aliens flying through the ozone hole.

The storm howled around the Whale Spout Inn like a disembodied soul, and the wind brought long fingers of rain rattling, tapping against the window panes. Brie went into the bathroom but left the door open. There was enough light for her to see, and she brushed her teeth and put on her pajamas that were hanging on the back of the door. The nor'easter had brought with it a front of cold, damp air, and the warmth of the knit pajamas felt good against her skin. She brushed out her long pale hair. She'd gotten a haircut in Rockland a month ago and the girl had talked her into bangs. She hadn't had them since childhood, and she remembered that it had seemed like a monumental decision. But the stylist had been right—Brie liked the way they set off her blue eyes and her cheekbones. John liked them, too, and had taken to playing with them sometimes as he held her in his arms during their secret moments. She closed her eyes, trying to conjure up the feeling of her head against his shoulder. After a few seconds she opened her eyes and let out a sigh. Just then she heard the generator start up behind the inn, and the lights came back on.

She walked back out into the bedroom and stood at the desk, looking down at the laptop. Dent had told her to take the night off, and she was inclined to do so, but she needed to write her report on the Kevin Krumm interview. Resisting the urge to let the report wait till morning, she turned on the laptop, sat down, and started. Twenty minutes later she was done. She noted the internet was up and working despite the storm. She filed the report and shut down the computer.

Brie wasn't quite ready to go to sleep, but she turned the lights out and the oil lamp down low and crawled into her bed. Thunder echoed through the halls. A high-pitched moan whistled along the eaves outside, like an errant banshee begging for shelter. She pulled the covers up to her chin and lay there feeling safe as a schooner in a hurricane hole.

She listened to the ravages of the storm outside, but in her mind's eye she was far away from the Whale Spout Inn, aboard the *Maine Wind*. They were sailing overnight on their way back to Maine from a music festival, on an exceptionally fine night in late July. Brie had the middle watch, and Scott was at the helm. She stood at her post in the bow, feeling the motion of the sea, as the ship leaned into a fresh, steady breeze. The crescent moon rose off the starboard bow, a candy orange slice hung in a coal black sky. The summer wind was like velvet on her face—cool but so lovely. The *Maine Wind* had its own special music—its above and below deck sounds.

In the dead of night, with all the shipmates abed, she took them in on a different level. On those long night watches, she liked to think of the ship as her confidant. It would whisper all manner of things to her with the creak of a boom, the slap of a halyard or the sudden snap of a sail. The *Maine Wind* was a sea-kindly vessel, and to Brie the groan of her timber with the rise and fall of the sea was the sound of a ship at ease in its element.

Brie could almost feel the motion of the ship as she drifted off to sleep. The sudden ringing of her cell phone startled her from her reverie. She jumped out of bed and grabbed the phone off the desk. It was John calling.

"Hey, John," she said, her voice already in sleep mode.

"Did I wake you, Brie? You sound a little groggy."

"I'd just dozed off. I was thinking about our night sail back from Connecticut."

"Ah, I remember," John said, his voice soft as the wind had been that summer night.

"I tried to reach you last night." She headed back over to the bed and crawled under the covers. "Where are you anchored?"

"We're in Port Mouton." John pronounced it Ma-toon as the Nova Scotians would. "It's a beautiful natural harbor with a little village along the southwestern coast of Nova Scotia."

"It sounds wonderful. But is it blowing like crazy there?"

"Not too bad. I think we're just a little north of the worst of the storm. How about you?"

"I'd say Tucker Harbor is pretty much dead in its path. We just lost our power about a half hour ago. But I was on my way to bed, anyway. So no big deal." She paused for a moment. "It's good to hear your voice, John."

"I miss my second mate," he said. "George told me tonight that our chemistry is off without you aboard."

"Yeah, I know. I miss you guys, too, and the *Maine Wind*."

"Any breaks in the case yet?"

"We might get one tomorrow. We're waiting for some blood analysis to come back."

"So, how do you like working with Dent Fenton?" he asked tentatively.

"Well, now that Dent's been promoted to lieutenant, I'm working the case mostly with Marty Dupuis."

"Oh, I see."

Brie thought he sounded pretty happy about that development.

"But we all met for dinner tonight to go over things. It was nice."

"That's good." But he didn't say it like it was, and Brie could hear him struggling to keep an even tone. "So should I be preparing for you to jump ship and throw in with the Maine State Police?"

"Well, it seems I already jumped ship. But no to the second part. I can't wait to go back to sea."

There was a short silence at the other end, but she read relief into that silence. Finally he spoke. "You've been through a rough patch the last year and a half, Brie. I want you to do what's best for you. I think whatever that is will be best for *us*, too."

"Thanks, John. That shows a bigness of spirit. Makes me miss you even more."

She could almost feel him smiling at that, though he said nothing. They talked for a few more minutes about the cruise and the passengers. He told her that Hurley Hampden was full of wild speculations about why the guy had died on Heron Head. "I think Hurley would have liked to stay ashore and work the case with you," John joked.

"That certainly would have added a dimension," Brie said.

"I don't think accountants get to stumble on dead bodies too often. It sounds pretty ghoulish, but Hurley is over the moon about the whole thing. He said this has been the adventure of his life. He can't wait to get you back aboard. Learn all the details."

"Oh, my," Brie said. "That sounds exhausting."

John laughed. It was a good note to end on, and they said goodnight to each other.

Brie got out from under the covers just as lightning filled the room. She counted, "One thousand-one, one thousand-two, one thousand-three," before thunder rumbled through the walls. *Storm's moving off,* she thought. She laid the phone on the nightstand next to the bed, walked over to the dresser and turned the oil lamp all the way down. She hurried back to the bed as the light died in the room. As she pulled the covers up to her ear, she thought about the sound of John's voice. The memory created a nice vibration along her heart. The rain on the roof was just what she needed to drift off. She imagined she was aboard the *Maine Wind,* the rain falling on the deck overhead as she slept below.

Chapter 17

The sound of her cell phone brought Brie up from the depths of sleep. She reached over to the night stand, fumbling for the phone, wondering if it was John calling—if something was wrong. She heard rain on the roof and saw the time on the phone was six forty-five, but didn't recognize the number.

"Hello," she said tentatively.

"Hello, Brie? I mean, Detective."

Brie recognized the voice immediately. "Amber, is something the matter?"

"I'm . . . I'm at the diner." Her voice shook. "It's Varney. He's . . . he's on the floor. He's dead, Brie."

"Amber, don't touch anything. I'm on my way. Turn the sign on the door to Closed. I'll be right there." Brie was already out of bed, grabbing her clothes.

"Okay," Amber answered in a tone that said: *I just pretend to like death, but really I'm terrified of it.*

Brie threw on her jeans and a cotton sweater, clipped on her service pistol and badge, and pulled her rain slicker out of her duffel. She shoved her bare feet into her deck shoes, grabbed her camera and keys, and shot out the door and down the stairs. Atticus was in the kitchen. He turned as she came down the back hall and was about to say something. He must have seen the look on her face, though, because he stopped dead, spatula in hand.

Brie pushed out the back door and ran for the car, pulling her hood up against the heavy rain. She hadn't taken time to ask Amber any of the details, so she had no idea what kind of a scene the girl was dealing with. She turned left onto Third Street and drove as quickly as safety allowed toward the other end of the village. When she pulled into the diner parking lot, there was no one around. She saw Amber standing at the door looking out. She was the color of an incarcerated ghost. Brie grabbed her camera and hopped out of the car. She opened the trunk, picked up the bootie box, pulled a pair of latex gloves out of another box, and headed for the door.

Amber opened the door as she approached. The girl was still wearing her raincoat. Brie stepped inside onto the gray floor mat that covered the tile floor next to the door. She set down the bootie box.

"Where is he, Amber?"

The girl raised a shaky hand and pointed toward the end of the lunch counter.

"Wait here," Brie said. She set her camera down on top of the small hostess station, stepped each foot into the bootie box for a shoe cover, and pulled on the latex gloves. She picked up her camera and walked to the end of the lunch counter. Varney was sprawled on his back on the floor. There was no blood, no wounds, no signs of assault. It looked like he had just lain down on the floor and died. Brie could also see from the stiffness of his limbs that Varney had been dead for a few hours. His body was in rigor mortis. She flipped open her phone and dialed 911. Then she called Dent Fenton to alert him.

"Was he murdered?" Dent asked.

"There's no sign of struggle. Looks like death due to natural causes," Brie said. "Either a heart attack or a stroke." She was silent for a few moments.

"What are you thinking, Brie?" Dent asked.

"I'm thinking I'd feel better if we had the Evidence Response Team go over the scene. This is probably a natural death, but two deaths in three days . . ."

"I hear you, Brie. I'm calling Joe Wolf now, and I'll get the crime lab team down there, too."

"Thanks, Dent. I'll stay here and wait for Dr. Wolf."

"Copy that, Brie." Dent ended the call.

Brie squatted down next to the body. She could see that Varney had a piece of paper crumpled in his left fist. There were a couple of business cards on the floor next to his body. Her eyes travelled up to a bulletin board on the wall above where he lay. Pinned to the board were a few village announcements, a map of the area, and a number of business cards for handymen, carpenters and the like. There was a tack on the board with a fragment of paper attached. Brie guessed the rest of it was clutched in Varney's hand. When he started to fall, he must have grabbed for something to steady himself and hit the bulletin board.

Brie walked back to where Amber stood huddled next to the door. As she approached, she could see tears in the girl's eyes. Below the eyes, her eyeliner ran into two small black pools of sadness. "I'm so sorry about this, Amber."

"What happened?" Amber asked.

"It looks like he had a heart attack or a stroke," Brie said. "The medical examiner is on the way. We'll know more later."

"Varney was kind of an odd guy, but he was always nice to me." A sob escaped. "Not everyone in this village is."

"I know, Amber. It's hard. He seemed like a nice man." Brie reached out and took hold of the girl's arm. "I just talked to him last night when I was out for my run. I wonder if he came back here to the diner instead of going home."

"Why does he look like that?" Amber shivered when she asked the question.

"He's been dead long enough that his body is in rigor mortis."

"Is that normal?"

"Yes it is, Amber. It starts a few hours after death and sometimes can help us figure out the general time that a person died." Brie could hear sirens in the distance.

"Amber, did anything at all seem different or unusual when you came in this morning?"

Amber thought for a minute and shook her head. "Everything was completely normal. But when I walked to the end of the counter, I saw him there." She lowered her head and her voice. "I could tell he was dead. That's when I called you."

"This may sound like an odd question, but did you know of any connection between Jake Maloney and Varney?"

"Other than the deliveries Jake made a couple times a week, I don't think so," Amber said. "I mean, I never, like, saw them together."

Brie nodded. She could have asked more questions but decided to save them till Joe Wolf had done the autopsy and established cause of death.

"Why don't you head back home, Amber? There'll be lots of law enforcement arriving soon. I'll talk to you later."

Amber nodded, looking lost.

"Is there anyone at your house right now?"

"Yeah, my mom's home today."

"That's good, Amber. You tell her what has happened."

Amber nodded again. Brie opened the door and the girl stepped out. She pulled the hood up on her coat and walked down the hill, her head bowed against the rain.

Brie picked up her Nikon and walked back to where Varney lay. She popped up the flash and took some shots of the body from different angles as she looked carefully for anything that might seem amiss. She had brought her camera, not knowing whether the situation would warrant a visit from the Evidence Response Team, but knowing she would want photos of the scene no matter what. In her mind the occurrence of two deaths in three days demanded that care. The detective in Brie always chose to err on the side of caution, and there is no such thing as too many pictures of a death scene. But there can be too few.

Brie zoomed in on Varney's left hand that held the crumpled paper and took several shots. She took some close-up head shots and a few shots of his other arm and hand. She straightened up as she heard the first squad car turn into the lot. It was a Washington County Sheriff's patrol. The car door opened and Sergeant Jeff Starkey stepped out. Brie had met him two days ago when they had found Jake Maloney's body.

She went to the door and opened it. "Hello, Sergeant Starkey."

"Ah, Detective Beaumont." He stepped inside the door out of the rain. "I heard you were working the Maloney case with the state police. I was headed in to the Sheriff's office when the call came through."

"I've been staying here in Tucker Harbor, so I was the first to get called," Brie said.

"What've we got here?" Starkey craned his neck and looked around the diner.

"Victim's the owner of the diner—Varney Simms," Brie said, nodding toward the far end of the lunch counter. "It appears to be a heart attack or stroke. No signs of struggle. Lieutenant Fenton is sending the Evidence Response Team, though, and the ME is on the way."

"Who found the body?" Starkey asked.

"Amber Torgeson. She works at the diner as a waitress. Lives here in the village. She's just a kid and was pretty shaken up by the whole thing. I'd say it was her first close encounter with a dead body. There didn't seem to be any reason to keep her here, so I sent her home."

Starkey nodded. He looked down at Brie's feet. "You're bootied and gloved up, so I'll let you deal with the crime scene guys. I'll wait outside and direct traffic."

"Thanks, Sergeant."

Marty Dupuis and Joe Wolf, the ME, arrived at the same time and came into the diner. Wolf's jet black hair glistened with rain. He slipped off his rain slicker and hung it on a hook to the right of the door. Both men stepped in the bootie box and put on latex gloves. Brie directed Joe Wolf to the end of the counter and walked behind him.

Wolf squatted down and visually surveyed the body. "Nothing to indicate a struggle. No apparent marks on the hands or body." He checked the victim's back for signs of lividity. "Looks like he died right here," Wolf said. He pressed on the purplish color on the back of Varney's shoulder, and the skin blanched. "Lividity isn't fixed yet," he said. "He's been dead less than twelve hours."

"I saw him last night around quarter of nine when I was out for a run," Brie said. "He had walked up the hill to the cemetery. The storm was fast approaching, so maybe he came back to the diner to ride it out."

"May have gotten winded hurrying back. Could have led to a heart attack," Wolf said.

"So you're thinking heart attack or stroke?"

"I'll know more after I do the autopsy, but if it walks like a duck and talks like a duck . . ."

"Ockham's razor," Brie said.

"That's right," Wolf said. "The simplest explanation is usually the right one."

"Will you be running a tox screen, though?"

"I will," Wolf said. "I like to err on the safe side when someone dies suddenly and alone like this. The results won't be back for a few days, though."

Wolf noticed the piece of paper crumbled in Varney's hand. Brie pointed out the tack on the bulletin board with the fragment attached. "I think he grabbed for something when he started to fall," she said. "I'd like to know what it is, though, when the evidence team gets around to removing and bagging it."

Brie heard a commotion up front and turned to see the Evidence Response Team entering with their kits. "Well, I think I'm about to be in the way, so I'll let you get on with it, Doc." She stood up and took a step back.

"You can call me Joe," he said, looking up at her. He held her eyes for a moment, and Brie felt a little thrill run though her. *My goodness, but my world is suddenly populated by handsome men,* she thought.

Wolf was surveying the body again. "I'll call you with the autopsy results later," he said.

"Thanks, Joe." She turned and headed for the door as the Evidence Response Team spread out and started working the scene. One of them had already attached a powerful flash to his camera and was shooting pictures of the scene.

She and Marty stepped to one side of the door to talk to each other.

"This is an unexpected twist," Dupuis said.

"The timing sure is weird," Brie said. "But Varney wasn't young, and there's no sign it was anything but death by natural causes." She looked around the diner trying to make sense of the situation. "By the way, Amber said Jake made deliveries to the diner a couple times a week. You're interviewing Maloney's clients. Had you talked to Varney yet?"

"Just yesterday, as a matter of fact, and yes, what Amber said tracks. Varney said Maloney made deliveries once or twice a week. Mostly meat and eggs—sometimes produce. I got the impression Varney liked Jake."

"I got that too," Brie said.

"It's a long shot, but just for the heck of it, I think I'll drop by Nancy Maloney's house and see if she knew of any connection between Jake and Varney. Other than the deliveries, that is."

"May as well," Marty said. "But the Maloney murder is still our main focus, and Kevin Krumm is still our most likely suspect. Hopefully we'll hear something on the knife and the blood by this afternoon."

"After I talk to Nancy Maloney, I'm heading back to the inn. When you're done here, we could spend some time going over Maloney's truck log and check it against his freight manifests."

"I'm supposed to stay here till the evidence team is finished," Marty said. "But I could head over to the inn after that."

"Sounds good," Brie said. "So I'll see you a little later."

She was about to leave the diner when Joe Wolf called her back over to the body. One of the evidence techs was just beginning to remove the piece of paper Varney had clutched in his hand. Brie squatted down and watched.

With a tweezers, the tech carefully pulled the paper from Varney's stiffened fist. Taking hold of the opposite corner, he opened it just enough to see what it was. Brie recognized it immediately. It was a monthly tide table that showed the times of daily high and low tides.

"Well, nothing earth shaking about that," Joe said.

"That's for sure," Brie said. Common as lobsters in Maine, tide tables could be found on counters and bulletin boards in restaurants, grocery stores, and gas stations. It came as no surprise that Varney would have had one hanging on his bulletin board. The tech shook open an evidence envelope and, using the tweezers, carefully slipped the crumpled tide table inside and sealed the envelope.

Brie stood up. "Thanks, Joe," she said. "I'll talk to you later."

"I'll call you once I've established the cause of death," he said.

Brie walked back to the door and said goodbye to Marty. She pulled her hood up, ducked out the door, and ran for her car through torrential rain.

A classic nor'easter had driven in from the sea, blanketing the coast with heavy rain and muscling out the sunny, moderate temperatures of the last two days. Brie's short experience in Maine had taught her that these storms could linger for days, lashing the coast with gale force winds, sending down relentless rain, and driving tourists into small villages to dine and shop. Weather that was bad for sun-seekers was good for coastal businesses.

The fact was that nor'easters were a quintessential part of Maine. Like slow-moving leviathans, these systems were intrinsically different from weather in the Midwest that would come to a sudden and violent head, often culminating in a string of tornadoes. The Midwestern low would slash its way through a city, town, or rural community like a spree killer, then be gone as quickly as it had come, often leaving utter devastation in its wake.

Nor'easters, on the other hand, were a sustained but far less violent presence. One was forced to settle in with them for the long haul. They drove people inside, and for Brie, they always drove her to a more metaphorical inside—an inner space where she was inclined to focus on issues that were sometimes hard to see in the harsh light of a sunny day. And so, she had come to embrace the storms—a fact that made complete sense to her. She knew herself to be a contrarian. Often what delighted her left others lukewarm and vise versa.

She started her car and carefully backed up, avoiding all the emergency vehicles. As she pulled out onto the highway, she thought about Varney walking among the headstones in the cemetery the night before. A shiver ran through her. It seemed such an odd foreshadowing of what was to come. She had to wonder if he had had some sense of his own impending doom.

Chapter 18

Brie turned right onto Third Street and pulled into the Maloneys' driveway. She went to the lower door and rang the bell. Before long, Nancy opened the door. She wore a pair of old jeans and a baggy gray tee shirt. Brie was shocked at her appearance. Nancy's face was pale and gaunt, and there were dark bags under her eyes. She looked like she had aged ten years in the past two days. *The price of grief,* Brie thought. At such moments, two emotions always vied for control of her heart: hatred of the perpetrator who had brought such pain, and sadness for the ones left to struggle alone. She had trained herself to tamp down the hatred—knew that that emotion is no friend of the truth seeker. And a detective is, above all, a seeker of truth.

"Hello, Detective," Nancy said. She held the door open for Brie to enter. "Please come in out of the rain." She stepped back to let Brie in and then closed the door against the strong wind.

Brie looked around the formerly cluttered family room. It was immaculate. The carpet had been cleaned, and the room smelled fresh, like every surface might have been scrubbed. "How are you holding up, Mrs. Maloney?" she asked. She knew this kind of frenetic activity was sometimes how women dealt with grief. And Nancy was alone now, which made her situation worse.

"I'm all right," Nancy said. She looked down at her hands that were red and raw from cleaning. "Some of Jake's family are coming from out of state for the funeral. I told them they could stay here."

Brie wondered about the wisdom of that, but on the other hand, Nancy would have people close around her, which was probably good.

"Is there any news, Detective? Do you have any suspects?"

"I can only say that we are making progress. I hate to be the bearer of more bad news, but Varney Simms who runs the diner was found dead this morning."

"Oh, no," Nancy said. "Please God, not another murder."

"No," Brie said. "It appears he died of natural causes. Probably a heart attack."

"Oh, that's so sad. What is happening to our village?" Nancy's eyes filled with tears. "I'm sorry, Detective. Where are my manners? Would you like to sit down?"

"I'm fine. I just wanted to ask you if Jake had any connection to Varney. I know he made deliveries to the diner a couple times a week, but did he have any other connection to him either through his business or personally?"

Brie could see Nancy trying to read between the lines. "Why would you ask that? Do you think Varney's death could somehow be connected to Jake's?"

"There's no reason to suspect that," Brie said. "But it's my job to look into any connection they might have had, since their deaths have occurred so close together."

"Well, Varney was a client of ours. And of course we knew him—but just casually. Jake and I ate at the diner a lot, but Jake had no other connection with him. At least none that I knew of. Varney always seemed a little lonely to me. He wasn't married, no children." Nancy stopped suddenly, reflecting on what she had said, maybe realizing that she was also describing her own condition. After a moment she looked up at Brie. "I'm very lucky to have my brother so close by," she said.

"Yes you are," Brie said. "He seems to care deeply about you. I'm sure he'll be a great comfort to you during this time."

"He already has been," Nancy said. "I just wish he and Jake had gotten along better. He was never able to see the good in Jake for some reason."

To Brie, the reason was pretty obvious. Nate Freeman had known about Jake's affair with Tara. "Well, thank you, Mrs. Maloney. Detective Dupuis and I will be going over Jake's log and manifests this morning. Will you be around if I have any questions?"

"I should be here all day. I still have lots of cleaning to do, and it's not much of a day to go anywhere." She looked out the window at the driving rain.

"That's for sure," Brie said. "When is the funeral scheduled for?"

"Next Tuesday. It's a little over a week, but we had to wait for some family members to come in from out of town. And the funeral home in Machias had a pretty full schedule this week."

Brie nodded. "Well, the house looks wonderful. Just be sure you get your sleep."

Nancy ran a hand through her hair, looking suddenly self-conscious. "I must look like a mess."

"You look like a woman who just lost her husband." Brie reached out and squeezed her arm gently. "Well, I should be going." She walked back to the door and then thought of something. "Do you know where Varney Simms lived?" she asked.

"If you go to the other end of the village, he lives up the highway a bit. It's a little way out of Tucker Harbor. I'm sure Atticus Kane, over at the inn, could direct you to his house."

"Thanks," Brie said. She pulled up her hood. "I'll make a speedy exit. We don't want to let the rain in."

Nancy opened the door, and Brie made a dash for her car and dove inside. She backed out of the driveway and headed down the street toward the inn.

She parked in back and sat for a few minutes, thinking there might be a break in the rain, but soon decided she was being foolishly optimistic. She pulled up her hood, opened the door, and made a dash for the inn. She stopped inside the door to hang her dripping rain slicker on a hook there. She slipped off her wet shoes and carried them with her toward the stairs.

Atticus popped his head out of the kitchen when he heard her. "You left so suddenly this morning. Is everything all right?"

Brie told him the news about Varney.

Atticus shook his head. "Poor Varney. It's unbelievable. Two deaths here in three days." He stuck his hands in his pockets and rocked back and forth on his heels. "It's a real loss for the village too. Varney's place and the inn here comprise the sum total of our hospitality industry. His diner will be sorely missed by the townsfolk."

"Atticus, there's another detective coming over to help me go through some details on the Jake Maloney case. I wonder if you could put another chair in my room and possibly a small table."

"Of course. No problem at all. I could also set up a table in the living room if you'd like to work in there. I've got a fire going, so it's warm. And there's no one else in the inn, so you'd have the room to yourselves. Unless you prefer complete privacy, that is."

Brie shivered at the mention of the fire. She hadn't realized how cold she felt. The combination of the wind, rain, and no breakfast had caught up with her. She considered Atticus' offer. They were just checking Jake's freight manifests against his log—nothing top secret, certainly. "You know what, Atticus, the living room sounds great. We'll just need a table."

"I'll get that set up for you."

"I think I'll go up and freshen up a bit. Could you let me know when Detective Dupuis arrives?"

"Of course. Might I ask if you've had anything to eat?"

"Actually, I haven't. But I missed the breakfast and don't want to put you to any trouble."

"Well, technically you haven't missed breakfast, since it runs till ten o'clock. Let me whip something up for you."

"That would be most appreciated, Atticus. Thank you."

"I'll bring it up to your room if that's all right."

"That would be wonderful." She started for the stairs and then paused. "I'm not sure how to ask this, but is the inn making it? I mean, you don't seem to get very many people."

"Well, believe it or not, this isn't our busiest season. We get super busy in the fall when the leaves come out. We're always totally booked a couple months in advance of the fall foliage season. You checked in on Monday and just missed our weekend traffic. At this time of year we're almost always full on the weekends. If you're still here on Friday, you'll see things pick up."

"Huh, well, that's good to hear. The economy is still off—I know businesses are struggling."

Brie started up the stairs and then stopped. "One more thing, Atticus. Do you know if Varney has any relatives in Tucker Harbor?"

"Not that I know of. He moved here about ten or twelve years ago, and he's always lived alone."

"Do you know where he lived before?"

"No idea," Atticus said.

"Nancy Maloney told me his house is up the highway, a ways out of the village."

"That's right. Just follow the highway north out of the village here. His place is about a mile or so up the road. It's a dark red two-story house—the only one of that color along there. It'll be on your left."

"Thanks, Atticus."

Brie continued up the stairs and into her room. The power was back on in the inn, and she flipped on the bathroom light. She brushed her teeth, then washed her face and hands with hot water and held the towel against her face as she listened to the rain assaulting the roof. The wind was literally howling, and just the sound of it made her feel colder. She went into the bedroom and got a pair of wool socks out of her duffel. She pulled them on and exchanged her cotton sweater for a wool one.

She took the grayed length of thin line out of her duffel and walked over to the window. As she stood looking out, she began to work the line into an intricate Monkey's Fist. It was a useful knot, typically placed at the end of a heaving line to give it weight and help it sail out over the water. She always carried the line with her—her lucky rope, as she called it. Over the past few months, she had found the tying of knots to be a somewhat Zen-like pastime. It was a good way to empty the mind, and the activity seemed to work on her PTSD as effectively as any psychologist she had found. John kept a copy of *The Marlinspike Sailor* aboard the *Maine Wind*. After joining the crew, she had applied herself to the study of it in earnest and had refreshed her knowledge of her sailors' knots. She had also learned to splice line and create intricate sennit braids.

The window where she stood was totally clouded with rain which helped her vision turn inward. She thought again about Varney walking in the cemetery the night before, and also the dream she'd had her first night at the inn, about being in a graveyard with the rain coming down and the black umbrellas. The imagery felt oddly connected to what was unfolding.

A knock at the door brought her up out of her thoughts. She went and opened the door. Atticus was there with a tray of hot food that smelled amazing. He carried it in and set it on the dresser.

"Thank you, Atticus. You have no idea how hungry I am."

"I think I do," he said. "You enjoy, and I'll let you know when the other detective arrives." He left the room and closed the door.

Brie went over to the tray and lifted the metal serving lid covering the plate. There was an omelet stuffed with an assortment of veggies and covered with a delicate hollandaise sauce, two meaty strips of bacon, and a serving of pan fried potatoes. There was also a plate of whole grain toast with a side of rhubarb preserves, and a small metal pot full of coffee.

She carried the tray over to the bed, where she sat with her legs folded Indian style, the tray in front of her. She poured a cup of coffee and started into the omelet. The first few bites of food and first sip of hot coffee began to warm her. She put her thoughts of the case aside and focused on enjoying the meal.

By her third cup of coffee, she had begun to feel human. She finished the remaining quarter of the omelet and enjoyed the last piece of toast with her final cup of coffee. Dent Fenton was taking care of procuring a warrant for Varney's property, and he planned to head down to Tucker Harbor once he had obtained it. They were also waiting on the blood analysis on Krumm's knife. They were in a holding pattern of sorts, so it was the perfect time to finish the work on the freight manifests and Jake's mileage log.

Brie drained her cup and climbed off the bed. She placed the tray on the dresser and went over to the desk, where she closed and unplugged the laptop. She put the computer in the carrying case and slipped it over her shoulder. Then she picked up the tray and headed out the door and down the stairs with it. Atticus was in the kitchen when she came in. She set the tray down. "Atticus, that was a delicious breakfast. Thank you again."

"Well, no need for thanks. It's included in the price of your room."

"I know, but still, it was nice of you."

"The diner will be closed now, so please feel free to make yourself a sandwich in the kitchen here if you get hungry."

"Thanks."

"I usually whip up something for dinner. I'd be happy to make a little extra for you."

"Well, I'm not sure how the day will be going. But thank you for the sandwich offer. I might take you up on that later." She heard the bell ring and then the front door of the inn open. "That must be Detective Dupuis." She headed out of the kitchen and down the hall.

Marty was just taking off his coat and hanging it up in the front entryway. "Hey, Brie," he said as she approached.

"Hi, Marty. How's it going up at the diner?"

"The Evidence Response Team is still at work, but they've removed the body and Joe Wolf just left the scene. I had a call from Dent. I told him there were two officers from the Washington County Sheriff's Office on the scene, and he said, in that case, I could leave. I told him we'd be here, going over Maloney's log."

"Atticus said we can work in the living room. Do you have all the documents?"

"Right here." Marty held up two manila evidence envelopes.

"Great. Let's get started."

Brie led him into the living room. There was a large fire blazing on the hearth, and Atticus had moved a square wooden table in front of the fire and brought two of the padded dining room chairs in and placed them at the table. Brie found an outlet nearby and plugged in the laptop. They settled down at the table and took out the paperwork. She had the chair closest to the fire, and the heat radiating into the room felt good.

"Why don't you bring up Google maps, and we can input the addresses from the manifests for Maloney's pickup and delivery locations and then check that figure against the mileage log."

"Sounds like a plan," Brie said. She brought up the Google screen and typed in the first two addresses as Marty read them off to her. They had a year and a half's worth of freight manifests. If there was anything irregular going on with them, Brie assumed they'd identify a pattern over the last eighteen months.

After about a half hour they got in a good flow with the work. Brie would input the addresses and get a mileage figure, and Marty would check that figure against the log. They had made their way through several months of freight manifests. So far, the mileage tracked very closely with what Jake had entered in his log.

By the time they had made their way through nine months of manifests, something began to emerge. About once every month, they found a mileage gap in the log. The gaps occurred at different times of the month, but it was always roughly the same number of miles that were unaccounted for.

"What do you think, Brie?" Marty asked.

"It's odd," Brie said. "If it were just a trip here and there, one could assume he was simply using the truck for something personal. But it's too consistent—always the same number of miles."

"What do you suppose he was running?" Marty asked.

"Well, there's the obvious stuff—guns, drugs, or human beings."

"The problem is, all we have is a round trip distance. The delivery could have been made anywhere along the line, and the rest of the mileage would be getting the truck back to home base."

"Using the mileage, we could establish a radius of the area in which the deliveries had to take place," Brie said. "But that's as close as we can get."

"What if it wasn't a criminal activity? What if someone just requested that he not keep a record of the delivery?" Marty asked.

"Why would they care what he wrote down if it's not illegal?"

"I don't know."

"And of course, there's the fact that Jake Maloney's been murdered in a very premeditated way. If these discrepancies in his records have anything to do with the murder, it's a fair assumption that he was involved in something illegal."

"You're right," Marty said.

Brie leaned back in her chair and rubbed her eyes. They'd been working for two and a half hours. "Let's take a break, Marty. Clear our heads—see if we can rustle up some coffee."

They got up and walked down the hall to the kitchen. Atticus had left a note that he would be gone for a couple of hours and that they should feel free to make coffee and sandwiches if they wished. He had left the coffee out on the counter next to the coffee maker. Brie went ahead and ground the coffee while Marty filled the carafe with water and emptied it into the coffee maker. In a couple of minutes, the machine was sputtering and hissing and emitting a rich, comforting aroma.

"You hungry for a sandwich?" Brie asked.

"I could definitely eat one," Marty said.

She went to the refrigerator and got out the sandwich fixings, and Marty put together a ham and cheese sandwich. Brie opted out since she was still full from breakfast.

Lieutenant Dent Fenton arrived at the inn around quarter past one, got out of his car and made a dash for the porch. He rang the bell before stepping inside. He saw Marty heading down the hall toward him.

"Marty, hi," he said.

"Hello, Lieutenant, how was the drive down?"

"Slow. There's so much rain the roads are flooded in spots." They walked into the living room, where Brie and Marty had their work spread out. "Where's Brie?" he asked.

"She's rustling up some coffee," Marty said.

"Rustling, eh?"

"Well, she's from west of here, remember," Marty said.

"So, how do you like working with her?" Dent asked.

"Oh, she's sharp. So smart—reads between the lines. Thinks outside the box. I'd guess they're missing her back at the Minneapolis PD."

"That's been my sense of her since we met on that missing persons case out on Sentinel Island in July. Frankly, I'm a little jealous of you getting to work with her."

Dent said it in a joking way, but Marty figured there was probably a bit of truth in the remark. "Ah, the trials of being a lieutenant," he said.

"I know she has to go back to her job aboard the *Maine Wind* when we've closed the case, but I'd really like to keep her attached to the force in some capacity," Dent said.

"Well, she's been deputized. Maybe we could use her on a case by case basis, or even as a civilian consultant."

Brie finished making the coffee and put it on a tray along with three cups. As she carried it toward the living room, she heard Marty and Dent talking about keeping her attached to the Maine State Police in some way.

"You two planning my future?" she asked as she came through the door.

Dent and Marty whipped around. They hadn't heard her come into the room and were clearly flustered. Brie smiled at catching them off guard.

"We were just commenting on what a good detective you are, Brie."

"And stealthy too," Dent smiled. "You shouldn't sneak up on people that way."

Brie looked down at her feet. "Well, I'll admit, socks are quiet. Next time I'll bang on a pot or something to announce my arrival." She set the tray down on the coffee table near the fire.

"Dent, would you like a sandwich? I can make you one," Marty said.

"No, I'm good."

"Want some coffee?" Brie asked. "I put an extra mug on the tray."

"Sure," Dent said. "I've got the warrant for Varney's property, but we're still waiting on Joe Wolf's ruling on cause of death. Although, from your assessment of the scene, it sounds like a death by natural causes." Dent took a sip of his coffee, and his eyebrows went up. "Nice and strong—just the way I like it. Any leads on Simms' next of kin?" he asked.

"Ironically, I ran into Varney last night while I was out for a run. He was walking in the cemetery at the top of the hill above the village. I stopped when I saw him, and we talked."

"Go on," Dent said.

"Well, it somehow came up that he lives alone. Never married—no children. And judging by his age, his parents may be gone too. I asked Atticus Kane, who owns the inn here, if Varney had any relatives in the village. He said no. Apparently, Varney moved to Tucker Harbor twelve years ago. Atticus didn't know where he lived before that. I'll ask around the village, though. See what I can find out."

"Good," said Dent. "We'll have to check public records to see where he lived before moving here. And we'll collect phone records, bills, and any correspondence when we visit his property. I also plan to bring his computer in, just in case."

"Kevin Krumm is still our main focus, though," Marty said. "We should get the lab findings sometime today on the knife Brie confiscated."

"That may blow the case wide open," Dent said. "As far as we know, Krumm's the one with motive, means, and opportunity in the Maloney slaying."

"It just seems odd to me that he wouldn't throw the knife in the ocean or at least wash the blood off completely," Marty said. "I mean he had to come back across the water in the skiff."

"Criminals don't always think of what they should," Dent said. "Their arrogance tends to get in the way."

"He surely is arrogant," Brie said. "Plus, there was just a trace of blood up near the hilt of the knife. He may have wiped it off, but not inspected it carefully after doing so. Like you say, arrogance sometimes cancels out caution."

"And as to this second death—Varney Simms—it's probably just an odd coincidence," Dent said.

Brie stayed silent, and she was aware of the lieutenant regarding her. "You getting a different vibe on any of this, Brie?" he asked.

"No," she said. But the truth was she didn't like coincidences. She changed the subject. "You want me to come with you to Varney's place or stay here and keep working on Maloney's records?"

"Why don't you press on here, and Marty and I will head over to Simms' property."

"Works for me," Brie said. She was quite happy to stay in out of the elements.

"We'll stop back when we're done," Dent said. The two of them headed for the front entry, and she heard them pulling on their coats. Then the door opened just long enough for her to hear the wind and rain lashing the front of the inn. The door closed, and sanity was quickly restored.

Brie walked around the lower level of the inn for a few minutes, looking out various windows at the storm as she sipped her hot coffee. She ended up back in the living room and poured herself a second cup. She walked over to the bookcases and studied the photos of Atticus with his friends and family. WHOMP. Something hit the side of the inn, hard. She hurried to the window and saw that a large limb had broken off the maple tree in the side yard and walloped the inn as it fell. Like Varney, it had been struck down unexpectedly. *Lucky it didn't hit the window,* she thought. *It would have come right through.*

"Luck. Coincidence." She said the words aloud as she walked back and sat down at her work. As a detective she had always been wary of coincidence in the same way she was wary of answers that came too easily, or solutions that appeared too obvious. *Just work the case, Brie.* She recognized the tempering voice of her own inner wisdom. She picked up the next freight manifest and compared it to Jake Maloney's mileage log.

Chapter 19

Brie had worked her way methodically through Maloney's trucking log for another hour when a thought occurred to her. She considered it for a moment as she got up and poured herself more coffee. She sat back down and signed into the Maine State Police database, where she accessed the death records for Washington County, of which Tucker Harbor was a part. Her goal was to see if anyone else had died in the vicinity of Tucker Harbor in the recent or even not so recent past. Anyone whose death might seem out of the ordinary. There was no concrete reason for her search, but rather a growing sense of something they weren't seeing even though it was there to be seen—like the subtext in a novel. She thought about Dent's words at the crime scene when she had asked him why he wanted her to work the Maloney case. *Just a gut feeling that this might be a tough one,* he had said. Over the past couple days those words had played through her mind more than once. And while she had remained in neutrality, she had by no means rejected the premise.

Brie limited her search to a fifteen-mile radius around Tucker Harbor. As she scanned through the death certificates, she noted specific things on each one. Cause of death, manner of death—whether accident, suicide, homicide, or natural causes—location of death, and age of victim. She worked her way backwards in time and was about to abandon her search when something caught her eye. It was a four-year-old death certificate for a man named Everett Fein, age 52, who had died in July of that year in the vicinity of Tucker Harbor. The manner of death was listed as accidental. Time of death—9:10 p.m. Cause of death was multiple blunt force injuries that occurred when the vehicle he was driving left the road and went over a cliff. Fein's occupation was listed as professor of physics. He had lived in Ellsworth, Maine.

"Huh," Brie said to herself. Something about the case made her pause. Tucker Harbor was quite a ways from Ellsworth. She wondered why the professor had been there that night. "This might warrant looking into." She was about to pull up the accident report that the state troopers would have filed and also check the weather data to see if it had been raining or foggy that night, when her phone rang. It was Dent Fenton.

"Beaumont," she said into the phone.

"Brie, I just had a call from the crime lab. The blood on Kevin Krumm's knife is a match to Jake Maloney. We're on our way to his place now to arrest him."

"Are you done at Varney Simms' residence?"

"We've collected what we need for the time being. We didn't find any computer, though."

"Well, could be he didn't use one. He seemed like kind of a simple guy."

"I guess that's what we'll have to assume," Dent said.

"Do you want me to meet you at Krumm's place?" Brie asked.

"Actually, I'd like you to stay here until we get word from Joe Wolf on the COD on Varney Simms. Could you also do a search in the DMV, property records, etc., to see if you can find out where Simms lived before coming to Tucker Harbor?"

"No problem," Brie said. She told him about her search of the death records in the vicinity of Tucker Harbor, and the death of the professor four years earlier.

"Interesting," Dent said. "What are you thinking?"

Brie stood up and walked to the window. "Nothing concrete. Just a feeling that there could be a missing variable in the equation. But I have nothing to base it on, really."

"Nothing but good instincts," Dent said. "Why don't you follow up a bit while we're waiting on the Simms ruling. See if you can talk to next of kin—get any information on why this professor was in the area when he died."

"Will do," Brie said. "I'll keep you posted."

"Do that." Dent ended the call.

She stayed at the window for a minute. The storm was persistent as a petulant child, and she wondered how the roads were faring. Atticus hadn't returned yet, but he had said he'd be gone for a few hours. Brie added a couple of logs to the fire and sat back down at her computer. She did a search for the accident report on Everett Fein.

With such a death, one could only speculate as to what had happened. Either the professor had fallen asleep at the wheel or had become distracted and lost control of his vehicle. Weather could also have been a factor. Dense fog or heavy rain could reduce visibility enough to cause such an accident. But there was nothing noted on the accident report to suggest the weather had been a factor.

There was no spouse listed on the death certificate, but she found the name of Miriam Fein in the file. She was identified as the next of kin. Brie guessed she might be Fein's daughter, or possibly his mother. There was an address and phone number for Miriam Fein, and Brie recognized the address—it was the same one that was on the death certificate. She took a moment to collect her thoughts and then dialed the number.

The phone rang seven or eight times before an elderly voice answered.

"Hello," Brie said. "Is this Miriam Fein?"

"Ye-e-e-s." The word was drawn out in a tremolo.

"Miriam, my name is Brie Beaumont. I'm a deputy detective with the Maine State Police."

"Oh, dear-r-r. Is something wrong?"

"Nothing is wrong, Mrs. Fein. I'm sorry if I alarmed you." There was silence at the other end, so Brie continued. "I'm working on a case in Tucker Harbor, and in going over some records, I found the accident report on Everett Fein. Was he your son?"

"Yes. My only son." She said it slowly, and Brie could hear the despair in her voice.

"I'm so sorry, Miriam," Brie said. She suddenly had a heartbreaking image of the old woman left alone in the home she had shared with her son.

"What kind of case did you say you're working on?"

Brie hesitated for a moment, not wanting to upset the old woman. "It's a homicide case," she finally said.

"And you think it's somehow connected with my son's death?" she asked, her voice shaky again.

"Not necessarily, Mrs. Fein. But I like to look at things from all angles. And in going over the death records, I found the report of your son's accident. Do you know why he was near Tucker Harbor when he died?"

"Some k-i-i-nd of research," Miriam said haltingly.

"Do you know what he was working on?" Brie asked.

"No. But Everett had a friend and colleague at Baines College, where he worked. He might know. His name is Stephen Wells. He calls me regularly to talk. He's a very nice man."

"Would you happen to have his phone number nearby?" Brie asked.

"J-u-u-st a minute," Miriam said.

Brie heard a drawer open and then pages being turned. "Here it is," Miriam said.

Brie wrote the phone number down. "Thank you, Mrs. Fein."

"Detective?" she said, clearing her throat.

"Yes?" Brie said.

"What happened to my son has always seemed wrong." Miriam's voice was suddenly stronger. "He was a very careful driver. I always felt there had to be some other reason for the accident."

"Like what, Miriam?"

"I don't kn-o-ow. It's just a feeling." Her voice dropped off again, and she sounded completely exhausted. "Will you look into it, Detective . . . I'm sorry, I've forgotten your name."

"It's Brie, Mrs. Fein. Brie Beaumont." She gave Miriam her phone number. "I'll talk to your son's colleague and see if I think there is any reason to investigate further."

"Thank you, Detective Beaumont. That's all I ask."

Brie said goodbye to Miriam Fein and sat feeling drained. The rain made a constant barrage on the walls and windows of the inn. She closed her eyes and thought of the *Maine Wind*. In her mind's eye she was standing in the bow of the ship on a day when sea and sky vied for who was the bluer. She smelled the salt air and felt the spindrift hit her face as the big schooner beat upwind into a fresh breeze.

She opened her eyes and looked down at the phone number Miriam Fein had given her for Stephen Wells. Before she went off in another direction, she knew she had to do some checking on Varney's previous place of residence. She also felt she should talk to Joe Wolf and see if anything unusual had turned up in the autopsy.

She accessed the DMV database and did a search under Varney's name and date of birth. What she found surprised her. There was no record of him having a driver's license before he lived in Tucker Harbor. She searched property records, state employment records, and finally Social Security data. There was no trace of Varney Simms existing anywhere before he had shown up in Tucker Harbor twelve years ago.

She picked up her phone and called Dent Fenton.

He answered on the second ring. She could hear road noise. "Fenton," he said.

"Lieutenant, it's Brie. I did that search on Varney Simms you requested. Here's the thing, though. I can't find any records on him whatsoever before he moved to Tucker Harbor. It's like he just appeared out of thin air."

"Really?" He was silent for a moment as he mulled over what she had said. "This just keeps getting stranger."

Brie also told him about her conversation with Miriam Fein and that Everett Fein was doing some kind of research when he died.

"What's your gut telling you, Brie?" he asked.

"I'm not sure, but I've had a growing sense of something going on here—something that may be of greater scope than petty disputes and illicit affairs. Not that those things don't lead to murder. As we both know, they are the most common causes of it."

"We'll go ahead with the Kevin Krumm interrogation. See if he changes his story, or if it tracks with your questioning of him. A lot hinges on what we get from him. As you pointed out, though, the evidence against him is circumstantial."

"Meaning the knife could have been planted," Brie said.

"That, and the waitress—Amber—saw someone rowing to his boat, but couldn't swear it was Krumm. But we'll cross that bridge with the DA when we get to it."

"I'm going to call Joe Wolf. Ask how the autopsy is proceeding—see if he's found anything unexpected. I'll also read over my report on Nate Freeman, Nancy Maloney's brother, and see if I could have missed anything there."

"Otherwise, I guess we keep digging. Go deeper—study the strata," Dent said.

"Problem is, in Varney Simms' case, there's not much strata to study," Brie said.

"I'd like you to do some follow up on this accident case—the professor from, what was it, Baines College? You said you got the name of a possible contact at the college?"

"That's right. Dr. Stephen Wells. He was a friend and colleague of Everett Fein."

"See if you can talk to him; find out what he knows about the research Fein was working on."

"Will do," Brie said.

"Stay in touch, Brie." Dent Fenton ended the call.

Before trying to reach Stephen Wells, Brie decided to call Joe Wolf and see where he was at on the autopsy. She found his number in her call log and punched it in.

He answered on the second ring. "Hi, Brie. I was just getting ready to call you and Dent."

"What have you found, Doc?"

"Varney Simms died of cardiac arrest," Wolf said. "However, the blood work showed an unusually high level of insulin in his bloodstream."

"Was he diabetic?" Brie asked.

"He was, but even if he had just given himself an injection before he died, the levels are too high."

"So, you're saying he may have given himself an overdose of insulin."

"That's how it looks. Is there any reason to think he was suicidal?"

"I don't know, but I did see him last night before the storm rolled in. He was walking in the cemetery, oddly enough. I stopped to talk to him. He did seem pretty down. He even said something like, 'Do you ever wish you could just chuck the whole thing? Start all over.' "

"Huh," Wolf said. "That's not a good sign."

"He brightened up as we talked, but still, I guess, thinking back, it wasn't a good sign." Brie thought for a moment. "Dent and Marty did a search of his property. I wonder if they found any prescription drugs—anything that might indicate he was being treated for depression?"

"I'll asked Dent that when I call him."

"So Simms could have overdosed on the insulin, in which case the COD would be suicide."

"That's right," Wolf said.

"Or someone else could have given him the insulin, in which case we're talking murder."

"Also a possibility, I guess, assuming someone had a motive for killing him."

"If that were the case, though, there should have been signs of struggle," Brie said.

"Unless he was taken by surprise," Wolf said.

"That's true."

"The real problem is, because Varney Simms was diabetic, it would be virtually impossible to determine whether his death was a murder or a suicide."

"But that would be the beauty of it as well, if it was murder," Brie said.

"That's right. There would be absolutely no way to prove it was anything other than suicide."

"Well, thanks, Joe."

"It's not much help in the investigation. It just raises another unanswerable question."

"Still, too many unanswerable questions tend to lead to an important conclusion."

"Which is?" Wolf asked.

"That there's more going on than meets the eye," Brie said. She thanked Joe and ended the call.

There was now a large and unanswerable question surrounding Varney Simms' death. Nor did the possibility that Varney had committed suicide lessen the size of the question mark by much. Even if it was suicide, she had to wonder why now, why two days after Maloney's death? Coincidence? She didn't buy it. No, she believed Varney's death was a game changer. It was time to readjust her focus to a broader playing field.

Chapter 20

Before placing the call to the number that Miriam Fein had given her, Brie did a Google search for Baines College. She found it was near Ellsworth, Maine. She looked up Dr. Stephen Wells and saw that he was the current chair of the Physics Department. She checked the distance from Tucker Harbor to the college and saw that it was about an hour and forty minutes' drive on a good day. Today, she figured it would take her at least two hours to get there. *It could be worse,* she thought. If she found she needed to meet with him, she'd still have time to get to Ellsworth and back before dark.

She picked up her phone and punched in the number Miriam had given her.

On the third ring a man answered. "Hello."

"Is this Dr. Wells?" Brie asked.

"Yes it is."

"Dr. Wells, I got your number from Miriam Fein. My name is Brie Beaumont. I'm a detective with the Maine State Police."

"Yes?" Wells said.

Brie could hear the apprehension in his voice that the word "police" always triggered. "Dr. Wells, I'm working on a homicide case in Tucker Harbor, and in checking through death records, I came across the accident report on your colleague, Everett Fein."

There was a moment of silence at the other end of the line. "Yes," Wells said hesitantly.

"Everett's mother Miriam told me that he was working on some sort of research when he died. Do you remember what he was working on that summer, or why he was in the area of Tucker Harbor?"

"I'm afraid I really can't tell you much, Detective. It's been a number of years, and I don't really remember what Dr. Fein was working on or if he was merely on vacation when he had the accident."

After the "I'm afraid" part, Brie didn't pay much attention to the rest of what Wells said. She had zeroed in on his tone of voice. He sounded terrified.

Brie hadn't the slightest idea why he was upset, but she made a split second decision. "Doctor, I wonder if you'd be willing to meet with me. It's really just to cross some t's and dot some i's to satisfy my lieutenant. Is there somewhere we could meet in Ellsworth? Possibly on the campus?"

"The campus is closed down for the summer, but I'd be happy to meet you in town."

Even stranger, Brie thought. Now he actually sounded eager to meet with her.

"There's a Thai place, the Bangkok Restaurant, on Downeast Highway, just as you enter Ellsworth." He gave her the address.

Brie checked her watch. "I can make it by four-thirty," she said.

"I'll meet you then." He hung up before she could say anything else.

Brie sat and looked at her phone in bewilderment. The professor had seemed borderline paranoid about saying anything to her over the phone. And yet she sensed that he wanted to meet with her. It piqued her curiosity about what she might learn from him in person. She called Dent Fenton to let him know that she was heading to Ellsworth to meet with

Stephen Wells. She got his voice mail and told him she'd report in later on what she had learned.

She piled up the paperwork she and Marty had been checking, shut down and unplugged the laptop, and carried everything up to her room. She put on the Maine State Police jacket for extra warmth under her rain slicker. Unconsciously, she patted her gun as she decided what she needed to bring with her. She put her small notebook in her jacket pocket, along with some money, and left the room. Downstairs, she pulled on her rain slicker and stepped out the back door into a wind that seemed determined to send her airborne. Hunched over, she leaned against it and headed for her car.

Inside the car, she wriggled out of the wet slicker and tossed it in the back seat. She turned on the ignition, put the address of the restaurant into the navigation system, pulled out onto Third Street and headed for the opposite end of the village, where she would pick up the highway toward Ellsworth.

Rain sheeted Highway 191 as Brie drove northwest toward Machias. Banks of fog rolling in off the ocean came ashore along the steep bluffs of Holmes Bay. She navigated in a gray soup that narrowed her world to the abbreviated ribbon of road her fog lights could penetrate. By the time she reached the outskirts of Machias—normally a mere thirty-minute drive from Tucker Harbor—she could already feel the tension in her shoulders from the hairy road conditions. She rolled her shoulders several times as she turned west onto Highway 1 and made her way through the outskirts of Machias to the small downtown business district. She crossed the Machias River just upstream of Bad Little Falls, swung up the hill past the campus for the University of Maine, Machias, and headed out of town, passing Blueberry Ford and Cranberry Motors on her right—two business names that brought a smile to her face. *Colorful names on a colorless day,* she thought.

Beyond Machias she followed the road west toward Columbia Falls and Cherryfield, and from there, across vast tracts of blueberry barrens shrouded in mist. From pictures she'd seen, she knew that in little more than a month, the autumnal barrens would morph into a blanket of show-stopping crimson. And in little more than a month, they'd be bringing passengers aboard the *Maine Wind* for their fall foliage cruise. A moment of panic gripped her heart as she thought about the windjammer season drawing to a close and the decision she would have to make about whether to stay in Maine or go back to where she had always thought she belonged. It was a decision that seemed as unclear, as ill-defined as the fog-bound road on which she drove.

"Darn choices," she said aloud. "Why is life always about choices? Damn free will anyway!" Tears came to her eyes, and she felt irrationally angry. Then she thought about something her grandmother had always said. *Pain is the cracking of the eggshell of life.* Brie had always thought it was just another tired cliché that old people seemed to love so much. With a roll of the eyes—the hallmark of imagined superiority—she had ignored the phrase in the way that youth loves to ignore wisdom. But suddenly she was struck by the symbolism of new life emerging from pain. Had it not been the story of her past eighteen months? She drew in a deep breath and let it out, feeling a little calmer about the decision she faced. She listened to the hypnotic sound of the wipers, back and forth. They seemed to be saying this or that, this or that. She wondered if choices might be as easy as breathing in and out if one just knew the secret of how to look at them.

The hard rain on the roof of the car made her think of sitting inside a large metal drum. She turned on the radio, and the voice coming over Maine Public Radio reminded her that she wasn't alone in this gray, soggy, windswept world. It was fast approaching four-thirty when Brie came into the outskirts of Ellsworth, behind a line of cars that crawled through the fog like blind ants feeling for their nest. She followed the prompts from her dashboard navigator and, within ten minutes, arrived at the Bangkok Restaurant, where she had arranged to meet Stephen Wells. She put on her rain slicker, opened the car door, and made a dash for the restaurant entrance.

Inside the door stood a short man wearing a belted trench coat and an Irish rain hat. He was lurking next to a potted palm bush, as if it might provide cover for his apparent discomfort. As she approached, he removed the hat, revealing a head as bald as Cadillac Mountain.

"Dr. Stephens?" Brie asked softly, moving over next to him.

"Why, yes," he said. "Are you the one who called me?"

"Yes I am." Brie started to take out her state police I.D.

"Oh, that's not necessary. I see your badge." He looked around uncomfortably, as if the palm bush might suddenly have grown ears.

"Shall we sit down, Doctor?" Brie suggested.

"Yes, let's." He shook the water off his hat, rolled it up and stuffed it in his pocket.

They walked forward to the hostess station, and before long, a small Asian man came to seat them. "Table for two, Dr. Stephen?" he asked.

"Yes, if you would, Sam."

They were shown to a table by the window. They removed their coats and sat down across from each other in a pair of ornately carved wooden chairs. The table had a white linen cloth and napkins. Sam laid down a pair of menus. "Tea?" he asked.

"Yes, please," Brie said.

"And for you, too, Dr. Stephen?"

"Yes, Sam, as always."

Sam made a little bow and went to collect the tea.

"What a nice place," Brie said in way of an icebreaker.

"Yes, and if you're hungry they have wonderful food."

"I am hungry, so maybe you can suggest something, Doctor. It seems you're a regular here."

"You can call me Stephen," he said. "And yes, I come here often. You might like the coconut soup—on the menu it's called Tom Kha Gai. Or the massaman curry is wonderful if you like flavors of pineapple and cinnamon."

"The curry sounds just right. Perfect day for it."

Sam came back with tea and took their order. Brie went for the massaman curry, and Wells ordered the chicken pineapple.

After Sam walked away, Brie got right to the point. "Can you tell me what Everett Fein was researching when he had his accident?"

Wells leaned forward as if sharing a secret. "He was investigating a phenomenon known as *The Hum*."

"The hum?" Brie said, a little nonplused by his answer.

"Shh, shh, not so loud." Wells brought a finger to his lips.

"Dr. Wells, the place is empty," Brie said, looking around the room. She stared out the window, wondering if her hours of driving to and fro in treacherous weather would be for nothing.

"I can see you're skeptical." Wells leaned toward her. "But the *Hum* is a real phenomenon that has occurred in various places around the world. Scientifically, it's very intriguing to physicists and geo-physicists."

"Can you describe it?" Brie asked.

Wells looked over his shoulder. "Not here. You'll find all of that in Dr. Fein's notes."

"Where has it occurred?" Brie asked.

"I must insist that we talk no further about it, Ms. Beaumont. I advise you to read the notes."

He kept talking about the notes, but Brie saw no evidence that he'd brought anything with him. "You say this phenomenon has been reported near Tucker Harbor."

"That's right. For a number of years. So Everett—Dr. Fein—decided to go and spend some time there. Talk to the people; do research. He was on sabbatical and hoping to collect enough material for a peer-reviewed article—maybe even a book."

"And then he had the accident."

"Yes. Tragic," Wells said, almost in a whisper.

"Do you know how long he had been in the area before the accident occurred?" Brie asked.

"A couple of months." Wells leaned toward her in a conspiratorial manner. "Obviously long enough to discover something that led to his death."

"So you believe he was murdered?"

"I didn't say that." Wells held up his hands and glanced nervously around the room.

"I believe that's what you are implying, Doctor," Brie said. She wondered if he had shared his theory with Miriam Fein, leading her to believe her son's death was something other than an accident.

"I don't want to get involved in this in any way," Wells said.

Brie heard the same fear in his voice she'd heard on the phone earlier.

"I must ask you not to call me again once I give you Dr. Fein's papers."

"Dr. Wells. We're in the middle of a homicide investigation. We may have to contact you again," Brie said.

Wells practically squirmed in his chair. Brie was worried he might bolt for the door, but thankfully the food arrived just in time to defuse the situation. Sam set the plates down, did his little bow, and went back toward the kitchen.

"All right, all right," Wells said. He gave his napkin a hard shake before placing it on his lap. Brie could see anger in his eyes. "Just don't call me on my cell phone. I'll give you a different number. If you need to talk to me, you can leave a message and I'll call you back."

"Why all the cloak and dagger?" Brie asked.

"I just like to be careful. Look what happens when you're not." He took out a pen and small notebook, wrote down the number and pushed the piece of paper across to her.

Wells appeared to harbor an Orwellian kind of paranoia about cell phones. Brie wondered if he felt the same way about the government. "I'll respect your wishes, Dr. Wells," she said.

They ate in silence for a few minutes before Brie broke the ice by commenting on the wonders of the massaman curry and thanking Wells for recommending it. He encouraged her to try his dish, which she did, and they ordered another pot of tea when Sam came to check on them.

When it was apparent they were wrapping things up, Sam appeared from the kitchen with a hard-sided leather briefcase, which he slipped against the wall on Brie's side of the table. She smiled to herself. *So much cloak and dagger*. But then she decided caution was usually the better part of valor. She'd reserve judgment of the situation till she'd had a chance to delve into Everett Fein's notes and see what was what.

"Thank you for your help in this matter, Dr. Wells."

"You'll find a picture of Everett Fein in the top folder. It's the only one I have of us, so I'd really like it back."

"Of course," Brie said. "I'll be sure everything is returned."

"You can just leave it here with Sam when you're done. He'll get it back to me."

Brie nodded but refrained from comment.

"Everett was a fine man—a brilliant scientist. I just hope he didn't die for nothing," Wells said.

"Dr. Wells, if there's a connection to the homicide case we are working, rest assured I will find that connection."

"You sound rather confident."

"I'm good at what I do."

Wells studied her carefully for a moment. "I'm inclined to believe you, Detective. You seem like a person of scientific mind."

"You of all people understand the importance of logic. And logic is the backbone of criminal investigation. Once you have all the pieces, there's no way for them not to fit together."

Wells nodded and reached for the check. He insisted on paying for the meal. "It's the least I can do to thank you," he said. "But I really hope I'll be able to stay in the background through all of this."

"I'll do my best," Brie said. Then she thought of something. "Dr. Wells, one last thing. Do you know where Everett Fein stayed while he was doing his research?"

"As a matter of fact, I do. He stayed with a friend who lived in Machias. An elderly man who had been one of Everett's professors in college. Dr. Andrew Richmond. He and Everett became close friends in Dr. Richmond's declining years."

"Would you have an address or phone number for him?"

"Sadly, Dr. Richmond passed away about a year ago. Too bad, because he might have been able to help you."

Brie nodded. "Another dead end. Sorry, unfortunate choice of words."

Wells paid the check in cash, and when Sam appeared back at the table Wells told him to keep the change.

"Thank you, Dr. Stephen," he said, giving his small bow. And then he was gone.

Dr. Wells stood and put on his coat and, with a single nod to Brie, left the restaurant. Brie watched him—a stooped figure against the wrath of the wind—as he made his way to an old blue Volvo and climbed in. A minute later he was gone. She stood and put on her raincoat, zipped it up, and snugged the hood to her head with the elastic ties. She picked up the briefcase and headed out the door to her car, clutching the attaché to her chest as if it contained secrets of state, when really she was just trying to keep it from being whipped out of her hand.

Inside the Impala she wriggled out of her wet coat and put it in back. The rain was a blinding beast, and she decided she'd wait this wave out. She fired up her onboard computer and put in Jake Maloney's case number and her badge number and started to write a report on her interview with Wells. It took her a little over twenty minutes, and by then the rain had slacked off a little. She filed the report and then pulled out her cell and punched up Dent's number.

"Fenton," he said, over a static-laden connection.

"Lieutenant, it's Brie. Can you hear me?"

"Barely."

She spoke loudly. "I've just finished interviewing Dr. Wells, and I sent you my report. He gave me all of Everett Fein's notes from his research in Tucker Harbor."

"Anything interesting?"

"Not sure yet. I'm headed back to Tucker Harbor now. I plan to spend the evening reading this material. Anything new on Krumm?"

"We're still interrogating him. We won't be charging him till the DA looks at everything."

"I'm planning to stop on the way back and interview Nate Freeman again."

"Maloney's brother-in-law."

"Right," Brie said. "I want to be sure I'm not missing anything there. He had M, M, and O and is about the same height and build as Krumm. In a boat in the fog, one could easily be mistaken for the other."

"Well, watch your back, Brie. And take it easy on the drive. The roads are a bitch."

"Will do. I'll check in later and bring you up to speed on what I'm finding in Fein's notes."

"Roger that, Brie." He ended the call.

Brie buckled her belt and turned left onto Route 1, also known as Downeast Highway. The road was filled with tourists and campers who had either left Acadia National Park or, despite the rain, were venturing toward the park. Ellsworth was the gateway to the national park, and for three or four months every year, congestion along High Street and Highway 3 heading toward Acadia and Bar Harbor was epic.

Brie crept out of town with the traffic. Her brain was in neutral. She'd become one with the rain and the yellow and white lines on the highway. When she came to the junction of Highways 1 and 182, she took 182 heading east. In spots the highway skirted Taunton and Hog Bays, and like settlers landing on the shores of New England, wave after wave of fog rolled in off the Atlantic. She thought about Jake and Nancy Maloney, Varney Simms and Amber, and she thought about Everett and Miriam Fein. *All the lonely people. And Brie Beaumont.* The thought surprised her. She remembered the dream she'd had—the black umbrellas. The anonymity of those black umbrellas with each person isolated beneath one. She suddenly felt terribly alone. It wasn't the isolation of the place or even the desolation of the weather or the landscape. Nor was it missing John or the *Maine Wind*. It was something deeper than all of that. Something that went to her very core—a truth that had evaded her, possibly for a very long time.

Quiet desperation. The words lingered in her mind like they wanted resolution. She wondered if desperation wasn't the result of missing some truth in oneself or, more universally, within existence. For many years her stock in trade had been uncovering the truth, and yet, she often felt utterly divorced from the universal concept.

She thought about Dent's words—*study the strata.* She guessed she needed to do more of that on a personal level at this crossroads in her life. *We're all such works in progress.* She turned the idea in her mind, looking at it from different angles. She found it interesting that until eighteen months ago, she hadn't thought much about such things. Oddly, it felt as if she were still growing up. *Or maybe just growing.* A sudden gust of wind rocked the car. She refocused her mind on the road ahead of her and on the case before her.

She thought about Kevin Krumm, not yet charged but being held. Jake Maloney's blood had been found on the knife aboard Krumm's lobsterboat. Motive—righteous indignation.

Maloney had been having an affair with his best friend's wife. Opportunity—he lived next door to the Frenches. Could easily have seen Maloney both arrive and leave his clandestine meeting with Tara French. And then there was Krumm's general MO—militia type, Doomsday prepper—kook. The kind of crazy who might take the law or meting out retribution into his own hands.

Was it too perfect? Maybe. Or maybe Krumm was just what he appeared to be—guilty. But Varney's death certainly raised questions. Two big ones that Brie could think of. *Murder or suicide? Game changer or not?* There was no way to know right now.

Brie considered the other suspects. First, Dan Littleton, Maloney's former partner. Supposedly no opportunity. He'd been at the coffee house that morning, and several witnesses could corroborate that fact. Steve French—Tara's husband. No opportunity. He'd been out hauling his lobster pots when the crime was committed. That left Nate Freeman. Now, he was a different story. He had the full deck—motive, means, and opportunity. He was a former Navy SEAL—easily capable of killing someone with a knife. He could have been keeping an eye on Maloney that morning. Freeman could have followed him and, seeing Krumm's boat in the harbor, decided he could easily frame Krumm for the murder.

She planned to stop at Freeman's place on the way back into the village. Although he had had no alibi for the time of the murder, she had believed his initial testimony. But she was eager to see if a second interrogation revealed any chinks in his suit of honor—honor that seemed somehow compromised by his hatred of his brother-in-law.

But there was other information she hoped to gather from him as well. This whole situation with Dr. Fein's death and the odd, rather sci-fi focus of his research troubled her. And then there was Stephen Wells' unmitigated fear at being connected with Fein's research in any way. Maybe she was losing her mind, but this part of the investigation made her think about some kind of covert government operation. There had been a naval base at Tucker Harbor, but that had been shut down two decades ago. "Oh, come on, Brie," she said to herself. "You're acting as paranoid as Wells now." Still, she couldn't help thinking again about Nate Freeman—former SEAL—holding forth out at that airstrip. It wasn't totally inconceivable that he could be connected with some kind of military operation. She reminded herself to watch her back around him. She believed there was an invisible thread that connected three deaths. All she could do was keep feeling for it, and hope, when she found it, it wasn't a tripwire.

Chapter 21

Brie had been driving for an hour and a half, feeling her way along the fogbound and rain-sheeted highway. MPR was doing a show with acoustic guitar, and it had been nice company during the long drive. She rolled her shoulders, sat up tall in her seat, stretching her back, and twisted to the right and left, unleashing a couple of pops in her spine. She wished she'd gotten coffee for the trip back and reminded herself to stop at the coffee house in Machias—where she'd interviewed Dan Littleton—and grab a cup.

The thought had no more than occurred when she realized she was entering the outskirts of Machias. Within five minutes she was approaching the bridge that crossed the Machias River and brought her into the small downtown business district. She got lucky and found a spot right in front of the coffee house. She grabbed her rain slicker, climbed out, and pulled it on as she headed for the door. Inside she saw Molly Harrigan, Dan Littleton's girlfriend, whom she'd interviewed the first day of the investigation. There was a younger girl also working the counter, but she saw no sign of Dan.

"Hello, Detective," Molly said as Brie came up to the counter. Her thick dark hair was pulled back today, and she wore a pair of black-framed glasses which seemed to intensify her green eyes. "If you're looking for Dan, he's not here right now."

"Actually, I'm just looking for a cup o' joe," Brie said. She noted that Molly looked relieved. In the midst of a homicide investigation, the arrival of a detective at your establishment is bound to be a stressor.

Molly took Brie's order for a tall black coffee—the house blend. "How's the case going, Detective? Any luck yet?"

"It's coming along," Brie said. "I'm not really at liberty to discuss the details." She tried not to sound too stern when she said it.

"Oh, sure. I understand," Molly said. Then the girl looked like she'd just remembered something. "I got the names of those two students who were in the coffee house the morning Jake Maloney died." Molly lowered her voice as she spoke, as if the unsavory topic might taint the ambiance of the establishment. "They came back in this afternoon." She opened a drawer beneath the counter, took out a slip of paper, and handed it to Brie.

"Thank you," Brie said. She noted that Molly had written down phone numbers for the students.

"I'll go get your coffee now."

Molly was back with Brie's java in just a few seconds. Brie paid her and stuffed a dollar in the tip jar.

"Thanks," Molly said. She looked like she wanted to say something else but had no idea what that might be. Brie nodded and picked up her coffee. As she headed for the door, Molly called out, "Have a nice day."

"You too," Brie said over her shoulder and pushed the door open against a wind that seemed intent on keeping her inside the building.

She headed for the car, pulled the door open, and climbed in. She put her coffee in the holder and got her leg in just as a giant gust of wind slammed the door closed. It was a little after seven p.m., but all the atmospheric gloom made it seem later. She enjoyed a few sips of her coffee and then pulled out her cell phone and called the two students whose names were on the slip of paper. They both confirmed that they'd been in the coffee house early on the morning of Maloney's death and that Dan Littleton had been there the whole time. Brie decided she could pretty much close the book on Littleton as a suspect.

She turned the car on, pulled away from the curb, and made her way through Machias and picked up Highway 191. She estimated she'd get to Nate Freeman's place right around 7:30. She felt it was important to re-interview him, but she was also eager to get back to the Whale Spout Inn and dig into Everett Fein's notes. It was probably a long shot, and maybe she was totally out in left field, thinking there was some connection between his work and the other deaths. But there was something eating at her—something about Varney Simms' death. She had no idea why—it was just that familiar feeling of something important hanging out there, just beyond her grasp, not mocking but pleading with her, like a ghost trying to be heard.

As Brie drove the last leg toward Tucker Harbor, she mentally formulated a list of questions she wanted to ask Freeman. In several places the road skirted the bluffs of Holmes Bay, and she lost her train of thought as she looked out over the Atlantic. The curtain of rain and fog lifted occasionally, offering glimpses of turbulent seas as the tide rushed into the Bay of Fundy. The nor'easter had the coast in a tight grip, and there was no way of knowing when it might relinquish its hold.

The highway bent away from the ocean, and Brie started to watch the left side of the road ahead for the single slate of wood that said *Airstrip*. It was mounted on a thin post about three feet off the ground and would be hard to spot through the rain. After a couple of miles, she saw it and slowed the car to a crawl to make a left onto the gravel road. She watched the track carefully for any spots where she could get stuck, but so far, the road had held up to the storm. She came clear of the trees and saw Freeman's pickup parked next to the trailer where he lived. She drove forward toward the hangar and stopped. She left the engine running, got out of the car, and walked into the hangar.

"Mr. Freeman," she called. "Are you in here?" There was no answer, so she got back in the car, looped around, and headed for the trailer. She parked in front and got out. She pulled the hood of her slicker up, walked over to the door, and knocked three times.

In a few seconds Freeman opened the door. He had a beer in his hand, and the TV inside was blaring. He looked surprised to see her, and Brie could see his guard go up. "Hello, Detective. What brings you out here tonight?"

"I have some more questions, if I could take a few minutes of your time."

Freeman pushed open the screen door that separated them. "Come on in," he said. He turned and clicked off the TV and set the beer and the remote on the coffee table in front of the couch.

Brie climbed two metal steps and entered the trailer. To the right of the door was a small kitchen. It wasn't fancy, but it was clean and tidy. The living room she was standing in had a sofa covered with tan fake suede and a coffee table that had seen better days. Across from the sofa a giant flat screen TV—way out of proportion to the size of the room—usurped most of the opposite wall. The only other piece of furniture was an old recliner covered in dark green leather. To Brie's left, behind the sofa, was a locked gun case. She turned around to study the contents. Freeman had enough firepower to hold off a small army single-handedly.

"That's quite a gun collection. Planning for World War III?"

"What can I say? It's a hobby of mine. I'm ex-military. I like guns."

Not everyone who's ex-military feels the need to own his own personal arsenal, Brie thought as she surveyed the collection. There were a pair of Sig Sauers—the weapon carried by Navy SEALs—three Glocks of different calibers, and a Smith and

Wesson .357 Magnum revolver—a cannon of a handgun. There was a Browning Lightning BLR lever action rifle with a scope, and a Bushmaster AR-15 semi-automatic rifle. Freeman had two shotguns—8 and 12 gauge—both pump action, an HK submachine gun, and an AK-14.

While the collection was in what looked like a bulletproof Plexiglass case, Brie couldn't help glancing at the flimsy lock on the trailer door. "Not a very secure location for all that firepower," she said.

Freeman just shrugged. "I'm not concerned about it, so you shouldn't be either."

Brie raised her eyebrows but decided not to enter into a discussion about the number of weapons he owned. She had other objectives in questioning him and wanted to keep the communication lines open.

"So, I hear you got the guy who offed Maloney. That crazy man, Krumm."

"We're holding him. He hasn't been charged yet," Brie said.

"Why the hell not? You confiscated his knife, and it had Maloney's blood on it. What more do you need?"

"How do you know about that?" Brie asked. "We didn't make that information public."

"No, but Krumm sure did. He blabbed to his buddy Steve French and French's wife—that slut Tara."

Brie nodded. Juicy news like that would have travelled through the village like wildfire. "He hasn't been charged yet because all the evidence is circumstantial. The DA won't bring charges unless he thinks the case against Krumm is strong enough. On the surface the murder weapon being on his boat is damning. But it could have been planted there by someone else. Someone who knew they could frame him for the crime. Someone who might have been following Maloney that morning, when he went to Tara's, and saw a golden opportunity with Krumm's boat in the harbor that day."

"You think I did it. And then framed Krumm. That's it, isn't it?" Freeman's voice had gone up 20 or 30 decibels.

"I think there's more than one way to look at this," Brie said, watching him carefully to see if his disbelief morphed into behavior either telling or threatening. "The fact is, you have no alibi for the time of the murder. You admitted that you hated your brother-in-law and that you knew about his affair with Tara French. That's a pretty strong motive. And as to means—well, there's no need to elaborate on that one."

There was no bluster, foul language, or indignation. Freeman's gaze never wavered from Brie, and if either rage or guilt was simmering inside him, it created not a ripple on the surface. Having been a member of a Special Forces unit, he would have known all about interrogation and what signs the interrogator was watching for. Freeman was a tightly locked book, and his complete lack of a reaction sent a chill through Brie. For a moment they stood face to face, the space between them so negatively charged you could almost see the electron field emission. It was a classic showdown—no weapons, just nerves of steel equally matched, which Brie found terrifying on one level, oddly exhilarating on another. Danger is a powerful catalyst.

At that moment Freeman's cell phone rang, ending the stalemate. As he went to answer it, Brie regrouped mentally. She knew one thing. Freeman was quite capable of killing. Had he killed Maloney? Quite possibly, but without forensic evidence, they'd never prove it. Plus, in her mind, there were too many unanswered questions, too many odd coincidences. While she did not, for a second, assume Freeman was innocent, there were other questions she wanted to ask him, and she was eager to finish an interview that had become increasingly uncomfortable. So when he came back from the kitchen, she took a different tack.

"Mr. Freeman, a few years ago there was a scientist who was in the area doing research. His name was Dr. Everett

Fein. He would have been staying in the area of Tucker Harbor for a number of weeks. Do you recall him?"

"As a matter of fact, I do. Real odd guy—a true geek. Stuck out like a sore thumb in a lobstering village. Looked a little like a mad scientist version of Gregory Peck. You know that actor from the old movies."

"He would have been talking to people in the village, conducting interviews" Brie said. "Did he talk to you, by chance?"

"He picked up the word that I was ex-military. Stopped out here to talk to me. Guess he thought that gave me a pipeline to God about unexplained phenomena."

"What kind of phenomena?" Brie asked.

"Why do I get the sense you already know?"

"Just answer the question, Mr. Freeman."

"Something called *The Hum*. People in the area have been claiming to hear it for years."

"Have you ever heard it?" Brie asked.

Freeman's gaze shifted microscopically. If Brie had blinked, she would have missed it.

"No," he said, returning to his impassive stare.

Brie decided he was lying about that.

"It's public hysteria, if you ask me," he said. "Wherever there's any kind of military installation, people cook up stories about strange occurrences. It's gotten worse in recent decades because folks just don't trust the government."

"It's the information age," Brie said. "There's a lot of spin out there about everything. And frankly, it's harder than it used to be for the government to keep things hidden."

Freeman's eyes turned hard, and Brie thought she saw a flicker of defiance or arrogance, which told her he might not agree with what she'd just said.

"Look, Mr. Freeman. Nate. I know you're a former SEAL, and I have no doubt you come down on the side of the government in most instances. But I have to ask you, as a member of this community, if you've ever had the sense of anything odd going on here? Anything unexplainable?"

"I wouldn't read too much into that scientist's death if I were you. There are some dangerous spots along this road." He gestured with his hand in the direction of the highway. "I think the good doctor just had an unfortunate accident." He gave her that impassive look. The brick-wall stare.

The thing with brick walls—they're put in place to keep people out. Brie wondered what lurked behind this particular wall. Guilt or innocence? Or just more desperation. She knew one thing. When a dangerous man becomes desperate, it's a deadly combination. She moved her personal threat level from yellow to orange.

Chapter 22

Brie was happy to leave Nate Freeman and his arsenal behind. She wanted to get back to the inn and study Dr. Fein's notes, and even though total darkness was a good hour away, she was eager to get off the rain-soaked highway. Within ten minutes she entered Tucker Harbor and turned onto Third Street. She passed Nancy Maloney's house and headed for the inn at the far end of Third. She pulled in next to Atticus' pickup truck, got out with the briefcase Stephen Wells had given her, and went in the back door.

It was warm and cheery inside. There were lights on in both the parlor and the living room. Shadows leapt and darted up various walls, which told her there was a fire burning in the fireplace. She set the case on the stairs and walked down the hall. Atticus was in the living room, by the fire, reading.

"Hello, Brie. Finally back for the day?"

"Let's hope so. It's been a long one."

"There's some coffee and blueberry pie in the kitchen if you're hungry."

"That sounds great. I think I'll head up and take a shower first, though."

"You'd better enjoy the peace and quiet. Tomorrow we'll have a full house."

"That so? Well, you know what they say. Forewarned is forearmed." She turned and headed for the stairs, picking up the case at the bottom.

She hung her rain slicker on the back of the bedroom door and turned the lock. She went in the bathroom and started the water in the shower. Within twenty seconds she had peeled out of her clothes and climbed under the hot spray. *So comforting,* she thought. She let the hot water beat down on her head and back, dissolving every thought in her mind. She lathered up her hair and body and then stood a few extra minutes breathing in the warm steam, letting it relax her back that had been too many hours in the car today.

She climbed out, dried off, and put on a cozy sweatshirt and a pair of soft, well-worn jeans she had pulled out of her duffel. She took a towel and cleared the steam off the mirror, plugged in the hair dryer the inn had provided, and blew her hair dry. When she couldn't put it off any longer, she opened the door and stepped out of the bathroom, which was warm and moist as a steam closet. The bedroom felt cold by comparison.

Now would be a good time for that coffee, she thought. She walked downstairs to the kitchen and poured herself a large mugful. She cut herself a piece of the blueberry pie and headed back up to her room. Setting the coffee and pie on the desk, she put the leather briefcase on the chair and slid the lock buttons sideways. The locks on either side of the handle sprang open with a sharp clack-clack. There were a number of manila folders inside that she took out and set on the desk. It looked like a lot of reading, but she was game. She picked up her coffee and took a sip. The room was chilly, and the hot coffee warmed her.

She went over to the end of the bed and picked up an L.L. Bean wool blanket that was folded there. It had a plaid pattern of muted rose and gray tones. She shook the blanket to unfold it and swung it around her shoulders like a bullfighter maneuvering a cape. The wool was thin but oh so comforting, and she felt herself begin to warm up immediately. Decked in her Sitting Bull garb, she took her place at the desk and opened the first manila folder, labeled *The Hum*.

There was the picture that Stephen Wells had mentioned. She recognized Wells immediately. But it was the other man who interested her. Dr. Everett Fein. He and Wells were standing next to each other in what looked like a college lecture hall. Behind them was a large pull down board covered with math formulas. Fein was wearing jeans and a blue plaid shirt. He was considerably taller than Wells and wore heavy, black-framed glasses. He looked nothing like Gregory Peck in her estimation, and she wondered what Nate Freeman was thinking. He did have a strong jaw line, but that's where the resemblance ended. Still, even though he didn't look like Gregory Peck, there was something vaguely familiar about his face. Brie had no idea why. She had to agree with Freeman, though. With his bushy eyebrows and his deer-in-the-headlights expression, he did look like a mad scientist.

She set the picture aside, wondering if looking into the Fein's research might be a giant waste of time. But she had nothing else to do tonight, and they were in a holding pattern with Krumm's arrest, so what could it hurt to delve into this stuff? See if anything jumped out.

She leafed through the first folder. Everything in it pertained in some way to the phenomenon known as *The Hum*. There was a long list of Tucker Harbor residents that Dr. Fein had interviewed. Next to each name he had noted whether or not that person had heard the hum. If a person had, then next to his or her name Fein had placed a page number referencing notes from the interview of that person. The research was well organized.

Brie cast her eye down the list to see if she recognized any of the names. There were several she knew. Amber Torgeson and her mom, Heidi, were both on the list, as were the Maloneys, and Steve and Tara French. Brie recognized Hugo Lemay's name—one of the lobstermen from the docks—and the fireman she'd met named Paul Riley. While more people had heard the Hum than not, Brie thought it curious that about thirty percent of those interviewed claimed to have experienced nothing at all. She saw Kevin Krumm's name on the list under those who claimed to have heard the hum. Curious, she pulled out the corresponding interview. Krumm not only claimed to have experienced the phenomenon, but had several wild conspiracy theories about what was causing the hum. Brie was not at all surprised considering his militia connections and all his doomsday prognosticating.

Based on his interviews, Fein had written a summary of how the hum manifested—what it felt like and sounded like to those who had experienced it. There was research on where else, geographically, it had been heard. Brie read all of this material with interest. She started with Fein's description of the hum.

The phenomenon, as described by those in the area of Tucker Harbor, Maine, manifests most frequently at night, although some people thought they had heard it during the day. The phenomenon is described by residents in a number of different ways. As a vibration, sometimes heard audibly, sometimes felt in the body, like a very mild electrical current. "The Hum" does not seem to have directionality. Those who had experienced it said there was no way to determine where it originated. When it starts, it just seems to be everywhere. And it stops as abruptly as it starts. Some described it as one single tone alternating with a heartbeat.

Brie stopped reading. This last description triggered a memory of the dream she had had that first night at the inn. All those black umbrellas in the cemetery and the people humming that one note—that one single tone. *Oh my gosh,* she thought. *Is it possible I heard this "Hum" that first night?* She thought back on the night she had arrived in the village. On how she had awakened in the middle of the night, the odd dream still with her. She had felt nauseated, but now she remembered that feeling of the heartbeat. The single tone and the heartbeat. She had been half awake and had thought it was her own heart beating in that odd rhythm—had thought her PTSD had caused both the dream and the nausea. She remembered she had stumbled over to the window and pushed it open, and the sound had stopped abruptly.

Brie sat for a minute feeling stunned. Suddenly Fein's research took on a reality it hadn't had a few minutes ago. She had asked Atticus if he had heard anything strange in the night. So the experience *had* registered on some different level with her. But when he said he hadn't heard anything, she'd written the whole thing off to her post-traumatic stress. She wasn't surprised he hadn't heard it. Apparently some people didn't. She also knew that when any sound, odd or not, is heard over a long period of time, people adapt to it and may actually cease to be aware of it. When it becomes a commonplace occurrence, they just filter it out.

She took a drink of her coffee and set the interview file aside. With growing interest she read Fein's notes on where else *The Hum* had been experienced. Taos, New Mexico; Clam Lake, Wisconsin; Woodland, England; Auckland, New Zealand. Clam Lake, Wisconsin caught her eye because it was so close to Minnesota, where she had lived until four months ago.

"Let's see what the heck is going on in Clam Lake, Wisconsin," Brie said to herself. She opened her laptop and Googled Clam Lake, Wisconsin and *The Hum*. Up popped a bunch of sites about the Navy's extremely low frequency transmitter facility in Clam Lake, Wisconsin. She learned that, located deep in the Chequamegon National Forest, the site is home of the world's largest ELF transmitter that is operated in conjunction with a second extremely low frequency transmitter in Republic, Michigan.

"Well, who would have guessed," Brie said. For a moment she thought the facility must be just like the Navy's antenna array near Tucker Harbor. But after doing a couple more searches, she learned that the two kinds of transmitters were not related at all. While the ELF transmitters in Wisconsin and Michigan and the VLF transmitter near Tucker Harbor both sent one-way encrypted signals to the submarine fleet, the mechanisms by which they functioned were entirely different. The VLF transmitter near Tucker Harbor operated within the RF, or radio frequency, range of 9 kHz – 300 GHz, with transmissions broadcast from a standing antenna array. Transmissions could only be received by submarines very near the surface of the ocean.

The ELF transmitters in Wisconsin and Michigan were a much more recent invention. Brie read about the amazing technology. A powerful electrical current is generated and sent through above-ground antenna cables along a path dozens of miles long. The current is then passed deep into the earth through a system of copper grounding cable and well-type electrodes sunk 100 – 300 feet into the granite bedrock, thereby turning the bedrock underlying Lake Superior, Wisconsin, and the Michigan UP—an area known as the Superior Upland shield—into a giant antenna. An antenna that can transmit an encrypted signal, via electromagnetic pulse, to deeply submerged submarines around the world.

She sat back, flabbergasted. The technology sounded almost unbelievable. She tried to think of who she knew with Navy connections. Someone who could verify this information. She took a drink of her coffee and sat for a few moments. There was Nate Freeman, former SEAL, but in her mind he was a suspect. She'd prefer not to go to him for information. Suddenly she had a thought. She could call Ben Rutledge.

Ben was John's friend who lived on Sentinel Island. Ben had inherited a decommissioned lighthouse on the island from his friend Harold. Brie and John had gone out there to visit him in July, and Brie had become involved in a missing persons case while there. Ben had been a career Navy man. He might be able to answer some questions about this ELF technology that seemed somehow connected to Everett Fein's research. She brought up his number in her phone log but noted that she had no reception. Probably interference from the storm. But Ben had a landline, and she was sure the inn had one as well. She went downstairs to see if Atticus was still in the living room. He was.

She knocked on the wood archway to get his attention.

"Brie. So quiet. I didn't hear you come down. What's up?"

"Just wondering if the inn has a landline. I need to make a call, but . . ." She held up her cell phone. "No reception."

"We do have a landline, although with the nor'easter blowing, you may get some static on the line. There's a phone in the parlor across the hall and one upstairs at the end of the hall to the right. You'll see a little sitting alcove with a phone. You'll have a little more privacy on the upstairs phone if that's what you're looking for."

"Thanks, Atticus. Just throw a few extra dollars on my bill to cover it."

"Is the call going outside Maine, if I might ask?"

"No, but I'm calling someone on one of the islands."

"Well, don't worry about it. I'm not."

"Thanks, Atticus." She turned and headed up the stairs and down the hall to the right.

At the end of the hall she found the alcove. It was no more than four feet square. A green wingback chair and a small round table sat next to a tall window. The window had lace curtains. A lamp with an antique glass shade illuminated the space. On the table was a black handset phone with a rotary dial. Circa 1950s, Brie guessed. She smiled. *That's the charm of Maine,* she thought. She looked up the number in her log and dialed it on the rotary phone. As she waited for the call to connect, she checked her watch. She hadn't thought about the time. It was just after nine-fifteen. She hoped she wasn't being rude.

"Hello." It was Ben, and the line was pretty scratchy.

"Hello, Ben. It's Brie Beaumont."

"Brie, for heaven's sake. This *is* a surprise. Good to hear your voice."

"Have you talked to John lately?"

"Just the other day, as a matter of fact. He told me about the murder case you're working on with Dent Fenton. Tucker Harbor, right?"

"You got it."

"How's it going?"

"More twists and turns than a bowl of spaghetti," Brie said. "There's been a second death. What looks like a suicide. I'm also looking into the death of a physicist, Dr. Everett Fein, from four years back. He was doing research in the Tucker Harbor area. I met with a colleague of his who gave me Fein's research notes but made it clear he didn't want to be involved in any way. Frankly, he seemed scared witless about the whole thing."

"Interesting. What was this guy researching?"

"A phenomenon known as *The Hum*. Have you ever heard of it?"

"I may have, but fill me in."

"It's some kind of an odd vibration that has been heard by residents in the Tucker Harbor vicinity for quite a few years. The same manifestation has been reported in a number of other places around the world—Taos, New Mexico; England; Australia. Dr. Fein taught at a college in Ellsworth, Maine, and had decided to do research on the phenomenon during his sabbatical. That was four years ago."

"So what did he turn up?"

"Fein interviewed most of the residents. Apparently, lots of them had heard the hum. Maybe seventy percent. The rest said they'd never heard it. Here's the odd thing though, Ben. I think I heard it the first night I was staying here. I woke in the middle of the night experiencing an odd feeling like a heartbeat and a sound or vibration. It felt like I was a single string that had been plucked. I'd been having a strange dream, and I wrote the whole episode off to my Post-traumatic stress. But after reading Dr. Fein's research, I think I may have heard this hum."

"Interesting," Ben said.

It wasn't disbelief Brie heard in his voice, but something else. She wasn't sure what.

"*The Hum* has also been reported in the area of Clam Lake, Wisconsin. Well, that got me curious since I'm from Minnesota—right next door. So I looked up the location to see what I might find. Clam Lake, Wisconsin is home to the largest ELF, or extremely low frequency transmitter, in the world. According to my research, Project ELF, run by the Navy, consists of two transmitters—the one in Clam Lake and a second transmitter one hundred and forty-five miles away on the Michigan Upper Peninsula, near the town of Republic."

"I'm familiar with those facilities," Ben said. "They're referred to as WTF and MTF—Wisconsin Transmitting Facility and Michigan Transmitting Facility. The two ELF transmitters are used to communicate with the Navy's deeply submerged submarines around the world. The signals can even penetrate thick ice to reach subs under the polar ice cap."

"Well, I haven't gotten through all of Dr. Fein's research on *The Hum,* but in scanning through his notes, he's made several references to this ELF technology. Now, I'm no scientist, but what I've read about how the ELF transmitters work seems unbelievable. Almost sci-fi, in fact."

"And that's why you called me, right?"

"I thought you might be able to shed some light on the topic. If I'm to understand how the Wisconsin and Michigan transmitter works, an electrical current is sent around an above-ground antenna somewhat like a power line and then deep into the granite bedrock of a vast area known as the Superior Upland shield."

"You've got it exactly right, Brie. And yes, the amazing part of the technology is that the entire bedrock of that part of the Canadian Shield becomes a giant antenna for transmitting these extremely low frequency electromagnetic waves, which are bounced off the ionosphere and into the oceans. Tiny packages of information—usually no more than a three-letter encrypted code—are transmitted via an electromagnetic pulse whose wavelength is around 2500 miles long. It can take up to thirty minutes for a submarine to receive that three letter code."

"That's astounding," Brie said. "I don't know why, but that part about the bedrock becoming the antenna is mind-bending. So this technology actually turns the Earth itself into an antenna."

"Welcome to the world of military ops, Brie. Because of the composition and depth of the Lake Superior bedrock, that area of Wisconsin and Michigan is one of a very few places in the world where such a transmitter could be built."

"So you're saying there could be another transmitter somewhere else if the geologic conditions were right."

"Theoretically, I guess so. But the transmitters in Wisconsin and Michigan, which operate at 76 Hz—below radio frequency range—meet worldwide coverage requirements when they transmit simultaneously. So it seems another transmitter would be redundant. Of course, the Russians have a comparable ELF transmitter facility for communicating with their subs. The ZEVS transmitter operates at 82 Hz and is located on the Kola Peninsula near Murmansk. The peninsula is a part of Russia adjacent to Finland that lies mostly north of the Arctic Circle on the Barents Sea."

Brie sat thinking for a few moments. She had no idea what she was fishing for or why. She was just casting her line out there to see what would surface.

"Could the transmitters be used for anything else?" she asked. "I mean, it seems a technology that sophisticated might have applications other than just sending three-letter codes to submarines."

"The importance of that technology during the Cold War would have been inestimable," Ben said.

"But from what I read, Project ELF in Wisconsin and Michigan didn't even come online until 1989. By then the Cold War was all but over. So I guess that leads me to wonder if the technology isn't being used for something else. If it might not have other applications."

"I believe ELF technology has been experimented with for earthquake detection," Ben said. He was silent for a few moments. "Brie, I think you need to be careful. You may be poking at something that's better left alone."

"Ben, that sounds a little paranoid." She couldn't help thinking about Stephen Wells at the restaurant that afternoon.

"You know what, Brie? A little paranoia may be a healthy thing when you start nosing around in anything related to the military."

"What, Ben? Are you suggesting there's some kind of clandestine government operation going on? Something blacker than the sea on a moonless night?"

Silence spun down the wire.

"Ben, you there?"

"I'm here, Brie." There was resignation in his voice, but something else too. The connection between them seemed filled with unspoken words. Words that had been thought of but couldn't be let out.

"Look, Ben. I really have no choice. We've had two deaths here in three days. One murder, and one suicide with a question mark after it. My gut tells me Dr. Fein's death may be somehow connected as well."

More silence from the other end of the line. She didn't want Ben worrying about her, so she pressed on. "Look, Ben, all I'm doing tonight is reading Dr. Fein's research. And frankly, I have no idea how it could be connected to the death of a truck driver and a diner owner. If there's any deeper investigation, I'll be doing it with my team from the Maine State Police. So don't worry your mind, okay? And please don't tell John about any of this. He's got enough on his plate what with his passengers and all this bad weather."

"All the same, I'd like to touch base with you tomorrow if that's all right."

"That's fine, Ben. You've got my cell number. Call any time."

"I'll do that. And it's very nice talking to you, Brie. If you run into any more questions, give me a ring. You know I'm a night owl."

Brie was eager to get back to the rest of Everett Fein's research. See if she could find anything that might trigger a question about his supposed accidental death.

"Thanks, Ben, but I'm sure any other questions can wait till tomorrow."

Little did she know that tomorrow would be a very long way off.

Chapter 23

Brie hung up the phone and closed the small notebook she had been writing in. She walked down the hall to her room, went in and closed the door. She sat back down at the desk and had a few forkfuls of blueberry pie before returning to Fein's research.

Before setting the file aside that had the interviews on *The Hum,* Brie opened it and took out the picture of Everett Fein and Stephen Wells. She set it on the desk next to the laptop. She hoped having it in view would make her feel connected to Dr. Fein and help her find any clues there might be in his research.

"Talk to me, Dr. Fein," she said aloud. "Were you onto something? Something that got you killed?"

Brie reached for the next two folders, one labeled *7 Hertz Resonance* and the other labeled *Atmospheric Heating and Cooling and its Implications*. She opened the first one on 7 Hz resonance and started reading. From her research on the ELF transmitter in Clam Lake, Wisconsin, she knew that a 7 Hz resonance fell within the range of extremely low frequency waves or pulses. Fein's notes talked about the fact that during tunneling operations in World War I, the Germans had noticed a very low frequency noise that had a strong resonance at 7 Hz. Fein wrote:

They felt electrical storms were responsible for the noise. But in the 1950s the research of a German scientist—W.O. Schuman—

revealed that a cavity existed between the earth and the ionosphere. The cavity has a fundamental resonant frequency of about 7 Hz. This came to be known as the Schuman Resonance.

Brie read on.

Schuman discovered that an electromagnetic wave of the same frequency, broadcast into this cavity, would travel 25,000 miles around the world at the speed of light. As scientists discovered more about these resonances, they learned that frequencies below 100 Hz do not fade out, which set the stage for research and development of ELF technology.

"Hmmm," Brie mumbled. "Interesting. I feel like I've started down the rabbit hole and things are going to get curiouser and curiouser." She read the rest of the notes in the file which discussed another 7 Hz resonance that sometimes manifested before earthquakes. Fein considered this a natural phenomenon, but noted that conspiracy theories abounded claiming the resonance was generated by humans of Machiavellian intent, bent on using ELF technology to wreak havoc on the Earth.

It looked to Brie like Everett Fein had started researching *The Hum*, and along the way had made some connection, at least in his mind, between this ELF technology and the presence of *The Hum*. But why? The Navy's radio transmitter array near Tucker Harbor was a VLF or very low frequency transmitter. And from what she had read, there was no relation between how the two types of transmitters functioned.

Brie picked up the picture of the two physicists and studied it. "I'm feeling a little out of my depth here, Dr. Fein. But I may as well see where all this is leading." She set the file aside and picked up the one labeled *Atmospheric Heating and Cooling and its Implications*. In the file was a detailed chart of the layers of the atmosphere, which she studied carefully. There were five layers, starting with the troposphere and ending with the exosphere. Travelling upward, the layers of the atmosphere alternately cooled or warmed, unless the cycle was disrupted in some way. Brie read that the stratosphere, which contains the protective ozone layer, should be a warm layer, because ozone absorbs solar UV radiation, which heats the air in the stratosphere. But, with loss of ozone, this layer cools rather than warms. The ionosphere, two layers up, is another warm layer. But the presence of greenhouse gases trapped near Earth's surface affects the ionosphere, causing it to cool. From what she read, it was clear to her that the atmosphere was constantly engaged in a balancing act—one that was key in maintaining the Earth's temperature.

She sat back and rubbed her eyes. All of this information was interesting, but she was beginning to think that it had no relation to the case. Plus it was getting late. She turned over pages in the file and stopped with the penultimate sheet in midair. The breath caught in her chest as she stared down at the last line in the file. Amid Everett Fein's scribblings on the last page, Brie saw Varney Simms' name, phone number, and a date and time. August 5th, 8:30 p.m. The notation was in the left margin with a box drawn around it—its presence there as foreign to what surrounded it as Everett Fein might have been on a fishing trawler.

"August fifth," Brie said. "What are you doing in Dr. Fein's notes, Varney?" She picked up the file about *The Hum* and leafed through the sheets till she came to Fein's interview with Varney. The date on the interview was June 30th, more than a month before this notation. "Interesting," she said. Then she had a thought. She reached for her small notebook that held all her notes from the case and flipped through it. She found the page where she'd written notes from Everett Fein's death certificate and located the date of his death. It was August 8th, just three days after the meeting he had scheduled with Varney Simms. "Even more interesting," she said.

Suddenly she felt wide awake. She took it as a sign she was getting somewhere. *Could it be a coincidence*? she wondered. But, in her book—that would be the homicide detective's gut instinct handbook—coincidences were to be taken with a grain of salt. Her gut was telling her that this meeting between the two men and Fein's subsequent fatal accident were somehow connected.

She closed the folder, set it on the pile, and picked up the last of Everett Fein's manila folders, which had an odd title. The tab on the folder read: *Deep Water*.

Brie took a drink of her now cold coffee and opened the folder. There was a date at the top of the first page of notes. The date read August 5, the same day as Fein's meeting with Varney Simms. Brie wondered if these notes had been written after his meeting with Simms, but she couldn't imagine why.

She started reading what Fein had written, becoming more astounded with each paragraph. Everett Fein postulated that there could be an underground installation near Tucker Harbor that housed an ELF transmitter and monitoring facility. This installation would be comparable to the Navy's ELF transmitter in Clam Lake, Wisconsin, the difference being that this facility was part of a "Black Project." He further suggested that this clandestine operation was somehow connected to the Russian ZEVS facility on the Kola Peninsula. Brie stopped reading for a moment. Ben had mentioned ZEVS when they were on the phone together. He had said that ZEVS, the Russians' extremely low frequency transmitter facility, was the counterpart of the Navy's Clam Lake installation.

Brie thought about the wariness she had sensed in her conversation with Ben. And his words, *Brie, I think you need to be careful. You may be poking at something that's better left alone.* His concern about what she was investigating was beginning to make a bit more sense.

Brie went on reading. Dr. Fein theorized that this secret or "black" installation was being used to experiment with electromagnetic pulses in a coordinated project with the Russian ZEVS transmitter to heat and cool layers of the atmosphere, particularly the ionosphere. Fein suggested that the project's second objective was to experiment with opening and closing holes in the ozone layer within the stratosphere.

"That's completely crazy," Brie said out loud. Had Varney's meeting with Everett Fein really triggered the writing of these notes? If so, the implication was that Fein had gotten some or all of this information from Varney Simms. She thought about Varney shuffling around his diner delivering coffee and burgers, and the idea seemed absurd. But she decided to set those speculations aside. She wanted to keep reading. Unless Dr. Fein had completely lost his marbles, there had to be some rational explanation for why the experiments he was describing would ever be attempted.

Fein's notes revealed that, in the three days after his meeting with Varney Simms—the three days before his death—he had not only written down his theories on the clandestine government op, but he had discussed his speculations about uses of the ELF technology with a number of his physicist colleagues.

Dr. Fein's conclusions revealed the final shocking piece of information—the reason for the "Black Project." He wrote:

I believe the clandestine experiments with the extremely low frequency pulses are an attempt to use this technology to heat or cool the layers of the atmosphere as a means to control the effects of either runaway global warming or cooling. Furthermore, I believe this is accomplished through a cooperative effort between the Russian ZEVS facility near Murmansk and the covert installation here, the goal being to triangulate ELF pulses over the Greenland continent. By being able to control freezing and melting of the Greenland Ice Sheet, catastrophic rises in sea level could be averted.

But the power wielded by countries that would control such a technology is staggering; the potential for global chaos mind-bending. While their stated goal may be to stabilize the environment, in the wrong hands this technology could wreak havoc on global population by accelerating ice melt and sea level rise.

I find the name of this project to be particularly telling, he wrote. *Particularly ominous. I fear that, in the wrong hands, "Operation High Tide" could be used as a dynamic for population control—one with catastrophic consequences.*

"Operation High Tide." The words loomed off the page at Brie, but she wasn't sure why. She leaned back in her chair and closed her eyes. All of a sudden a thought lit up her mind like a Tesla coil. She had an image of Varney Simms lying dead on the diner floor, and the evidence tech removing a piece of crumpled paper from his clenched fist—the paper Varney had snatched off the bulletin board in his dying seconds. It was a tide table—a chart of times of high and low tides. *Operation High Tide,* Brie thought. No coincidence there. Varney was trying to leave a clue. A clue that his death was not a suicide. A clue to an operation he must have regretted being involved in.

Varney's involvement seemed outlandish to Brie, but then she remembered that they could find no evidence of his existence before he had moved to Tucker Harbor twelve years ago. She guessed he was an agent . . . spook . . . sleeper . . . call it what you want, for whatever military or government group ran the "Black Op." They would have wanted someone completely unobtrusive, and Varney Simms was that. She thought about his shuffling limp and wondered if he hadn't taken a bullet somewhere along the way—a good possibility in his line of work. And the way he had died—overdose of insulin—was definitely a CIA-like way to eliminate someone who had become a liability.

She remembered her encounter with him in the cemetery the night before he died. Knowing what she now knew, some of the things he'd said were surprisingly reckless. He'd joked about "the ozone hole some Mainers think is up there." And then he'd said something even more surprising. "I mean, who knows what all those transmissions are doing?" She had assumed he was referring to the Navy's VLF transmitter in Tucker Harbor, but now she realized he'd been referencing something quite different. In his line of work, saying things like that could get you killed. She wondered if he had known his days were numbered. Known his death was imminent.

Maybe he was tired of seeing people die because they got too close to the truth. Maybe Jake Maloney's death was the final straw. "Do you ever wish you could just chuck the whole thing? Start over?" he had asked. She hoped wherever he was now, he was getting to do just that.

Brie thought about the dramatic beauty of this remote part of Maine. Its rugged cliffs, its high tides and changeable weather. The "Bold Coast." For Varney, though, who must have longed to *come in from the cold,* it had literally been the "Cold Coast."

Thinking of Varney in the cemetery made her once again recall the dream she'd had. There was a final element in the dream that had bothered her. Those tombstones with the Roman numerals. She thought she now understood the symbolism. Since the night she'd had the dream, she had been trying to remember the sequence of the numerals. Now she realized those Roman numerals could have symbolized things encrypted or hidden. *Amazing,* she thought. *Things hidden. There's an understatement.*

She didn't know how Jake Maloney had become involved in a government "Black Project," but now she was certain he had indeed been involved. She thought about the gaps in Maloney's mileage log. Gaps that had occurred at regular monthly intervals. Her guess was he was transporting something connected with the operation. He must have gotten too curious, or maybe he'd seen something he wasn't supposed to. She didn't reject the idea that Varney could have killed Maloney or that he might even have been ordered to do so. But she thought there was another possibility.

If Varney Simms hadn't killed Maloney, it meant there was another operative in the village. Someone who had found out that Varney was leaking information—that Varney wanted out of the operation. Someone with even deeper cover status than Varney. She thought about Maloney's brother-in-law, Nate Freeman. The ex-SEAL. He also could have gotten Maloney involved in transporting whatever it was that had generated those missing miles in his log. And when Maloney got too curious, Freeman took him out. Freeman may also have been ordered to take care of Varney Simms, who was becoming a liability to the operation.

She thought about Freeman being in charge of the airstrip. That was convenient as well. Those involved in the "Black Op" could fly personnel and supplies in and out, and no one would be the wiser. She recalled her visit to Freeman's trailer earlier that evening. If he was indeed involved, it made her shudder to think how vulnerable she had been.

She wondered about the location of the secret government facility and ELF transmitter. It had to be somewhere in the vicinity of Tucker Harbor since the people here had been affected by *The Hum*, and Dr. Fein had made a connection between *The Hum* and extremely low frequency transmissions. She thought about the old Navy base she had visited on her run last night. It didn't seem like a plausible location, especially since the advent of the Misty Harbor Homes development. She thought about the fire station at the entrance to the old base and the two guys she had talked to there. Then she remembered seeing the abandoned road on the other side of the highway, and the old sign that said: Property of the United States Government. She had asked the guys about it, and they had said it had been part of the old base, but that there was nothing down there anymore. Now she wondered if they'd just been saying that. If maybe they were involved too. She took it as a sign she was becoming suitably paranoid.

She needed to call Dent Fenton. She checked her watch. Ten forty-five. She hoped she wouldn't be waking him up. She pulled out her cell phone and found she had a couple of bars. She brought up Dent's number and sent the call. A lightning strike outside lit up the window. A deafening crack of thunder followed. Brie heard a few moments of intense static. Dent's phone rang three times and went to his voice mail.

"Damn," Brie said under her breath. She heard the beep at the end of Dent's message. "Dent, this is Brie. It's ten forty-five. I need to talk to you tonight if you get this. I've come across some startling information in Everett Fein's research—a connection between Everett Fein and Varney Simms. And I think Nate Freeman is involved in the deaths. I know this will sound crazy, but I believe there's more going on down here than meets the eye. Literally. I wouldn't be surprised if we uncovered some kind of clandestine operation in the area of Tucker Harbor. Call me when you get this, no matter how late it is."

She hung up and walked over to the window. The nor'easter had been on the rampage a little more than twenty-four hours and was still going strong. Somehow it leant a suitably *noir* atmosphere to all the cloak-and-dagger developments in the case.

She walked back to the desk and sat down. She rocked onto the back legs of the chair and propped her right ankle akimbo on her left knee. Her mind had been cluttered with all the paraphernalia of the case. Crime scene details, testimonies, and facts. Unanswered questions and confusing dead ends. But now a number of significant pieces had fallen into place. And while there was still one big question to be answered involving Nate Freeman, her mind didn't feel like it was in overdrive. Which may have been why, when she picked up the photograph of the two physicists—Stephen Wells and Everett Fein—something dawned on her, something so shocking she almost tipped the chair over backwards. She righted her chair and sat looking at the picture, astonished.

Brie got up and clipped on her gun. Then, with the picture in hand, she headed out the door and down the stairs. She walked along the hall and into the living room. Atticus was nowhere to be seen, and she decided he had retired for the night. The fire in the fireplace had burned down to glowing embers. She crossed the room. A floor lamp dimly illuminated the corner of the living room by the fireplace. She lifted a framed photograph off the bookcase and held it under the light. There was no wild hair and the face was much younger, but it was the same face—the face of Everett Fein in naval uniform, standing next to Atticus Kane.

"Gotcha," she whispered.

Suddenly she knew she was not alone. As the hairs rose on her arms, a sudden sharp pain stung the base of her neck. *A hypodermic needle.* She reached for her gun as she turned but couldn't seem to pull it free of the holster. The room had begun to spin, the person before her a blur as her vision started to close down. Brie tried to lunge at the darkening figure but instead crumpled to the floor like a paper cup that had been stepped on. Then everything went black.

Chapter 24

Atticus Kane pulled Brie's gun from her holster, walked across the hall into the parlor, and locked the gun in the bottom drawer of his desk. Then he headed for the stairs and took them two at a time. He moved with decisive speed, knowing exactly what he had to do. He walked into her room and over to the desk where she'd been sitting. He took a moment to flip through a couple of the files, then gathered up everything that had been in Dr. Fein's briefcase. He checked the pockets of her raincoat, retrieved her car keys, and put them in his pocket.

He had started for the door when he heard Brie's cell phone ring. He walked back to the desk and picked it up. The caller ID said Dent Fenton. He was the lieutenant in charge of the Maloney case. One of the two policemen who'd been at the inn this afternoon. Atticus let the call go to voice mail and then listened to it.

"Brie, this is Dent. I'm returning your call. Where are you? Call me back. If I don't hear from you within ten minutes, I'll call again."

Damn, Atticus thought. *He's not going to let this go. If he doesn't reach her, he'll be sending in the troops.* But it didn't really matter. He was going to destroy the evidence and take her to the facility. Then he'd double back with one of the security guys and get rid of her car. And he knew just where he was going to put it. By the time Fenton got to the inn, he'd be back here and would tell him he had heard Detective Beaumont start her car and drive off around eleven o'clock. Still, for a moment Kane stood frozen, wondering if the top to Pandora's box had not been irrevocably damaged.

He put the cell phone in his shirt pocket and carried the files downstairs to the living room. He took the poker and stirred the embers back to life in the fireplace. Then he placed Everett Fein's files on the hot embers and watched them ignite and flame up. He looked over at Brie and noticed the picture lying next to her body. He went and picked it up and added it to the fire. He turned the embers over a couple of times to be sure all the files had turned to ash and then set the screen back across the fireplace.

Atticus dragged Brie's limp body out of the living room and down the hall to the back door. He put on his rain slicker, stepped out the door, and headed over to his truck. He got in and backed it up to within a few feet of the door. He climbed out, leaving the truck running, opened the tailgate, and went back inside.

The cell phone in his pocket rang again. He fished it out. It was the lieutenant calling back as promised, exactly ten minutes after the previous call. Atticus wondered if he would try to call the inn. He went outside to shut off the truck and came back in. It wouldn't look good if he called here and got no answer. *Maybe if he calls the inn's number I can buy some time,* Atticus thought. He stood waiting, and sure enough, within a minute or so the phone rang. He walked into the parlor and answered it.

"Hello, this is the Whale Spout Inn," he said, trying to sound hesitant, as one might be considering the hour.

"Hello. Is this Atticus Kane?" Dent said.

"Yes . . ." Atticus said, sounding suitably puzzled.

"This is Lieutenant Dent Fenton of the Maine State Police."

"Yes, Lieutenant. What can I do for you?"

"I'm trying to reach Brie Beaumont. She left a call for me a short while ago, and she's not answering her cell phone. Is she there?"

"I'm sorry, Lieutenant, but she's not here. She left in her car a little before eleven o'clock. I was in the living room reading when she came downstairs and said she had to go out. I asked her if whatever it was couldn't wait till tomorrow, but all she said was she'd be back in about forty-five minutes."

There was a moment of silence from the other end of the phone. Atticus sensed frustration and worry.

"I can't seem to raise her on her cell phone," Fenton said.

"Reception in the area has been bad tonight. She asked to use the inn's phone earlier when she couldn't get reception on her cell."

"What time was that?" Fenton asked.

"Around nine o'clock, I think. Maybe a little later."

"I'll keep trying her cell phone, but if I can't reach her, I'll need to call you back in forty-five minutes. I'm sorry. I know it's late."

"That's all right, Lieutenant. I don't have any guests except for Brie tonight, so I'll stay up in case you need to call back. And if she comes in before expected, I'll tell her to call you."

"Thank you, Mr. Kane," Dent said and ended the call.

Atticus went back to the hall and opened the back door. He picked Brie's body up off the floor. She was a tall woman, probably five-seven or five-eight, but she felt light to him. He looked at her face as he carried her through the door. She was beautiful, but he felt no qualms about what he would probably have to do. He thought she would understand. *In a way we're all soldiers at arms.*

He laid Brie's limp body on the tailgate of the pickup so her legs hung over the edge. It was raining hard again, and he could see her jeans were already getting waterlogged. He walked to the storage shed and came back with a tarp, which he dropped into the truck next to her. He climbed into the truck, pulled her body back along one side of the bed, and tucked the tarp under her. Then he rolled her body and the tarp toward the opposite side of the truck and tucked the excess material underneath her. It was secure enough. He didn't have far to go, and he would be driving slowly.

He climbed in behind the wheel, pulled out onto Third Street, and took an immediate left onto the highway, heading north. He planned to take the secondary road into the facility. It was rough, but he wouldn't risk driving through the village and up the highway on the opposite side where he might be seen.

A little more than a mile along the highway, Atticus slowed to a near stop and took a left onto a narrow dirt road. As soon as he entered the road, he leaned over to the glove box, took out a two-way radio, and pressed the send button.

"Four-Seven-Two-Echo-Whiskey-Delta-Niner-Niner-Zero." He looked at the clock on the dash. "Code: Papa-Sierra-India at Twenty-three twenty-five."

After a second the radio crackled with static and a voice said, "Bravo-Yankee-Victor."

Atticus set the radio on the seat and focused on the narrow track in front of him. Wind-lashed undergrowth beat against the sides of the truck as he wound through dense forest for a mile and a half. The terrain was becoming hilly, and a sudden flash of lightning showed the track ahead drop away. Atticus clutched and shifted the truck into first gear for the downgrade. The dirt road was rutted and potholed, but solid. In another half mile he rounded a bend, and his headlights revealed what looked like a large freight elevator sitting in the middle of nowhere. No matter how many times he'd seen it, the portal still looked like something straight out of *The Twilight Zone*. He drove the truck forward into the elevator that was lit with dim yellow hazard lights. As soon as he was inside, the elevator started to descend, and he heard the massive steel and granite door slide into place overhead.

The elevator descended a hundred and fifty feet and came to a stop. Atticus drove forward into the wide, brightly lit tunnel cut into the granite bedrock. The ceiling of the tunnel formed a perfect arch of gray rock. Atticus accelerated on the smooth surface. The tunnel ran straight as an arrow for two miles. He covered the distance in less than five minutes.

Two security personnel were waiting at the end of the line with General Fredricks. As Atticus pulled to a stop, he noted the general's impassive demeanor, but it didn't fool him for a second. If the wheels came off this wagon, it would be Fredricks' head on the chopping block.

Atticus climbed into the truck bed and pulled away the tarp, and the two security guards slid Brie's unconscious body out of the truck and onto a gurney they had waiting. Kane stepped over and had a few words with the general, and then he and one of the guards got in the truck and headed back down the tunnel to the freight elevator.

Chapter 25

Nate Freeman sat in his trailer listening to the rain drumming on the metal roof. What the female detective—that Beaumont woman—had said disturbed him. She had asked: "Have you ever had the sense of anything odd going on around here? Anything amiss?" He had pretended ignorance. Nor had he admitted to hearing *The Hum,* which was the same story he'd given that scientist four years ago. But the fact was he'd had a strong sense of something out of whack. *Why hadn't he acted on it?* Now Jake was dead, and even though he'd never liked his brother-in law—strike that, he couldn't stand him—still Maloney hadn't deserved this fate, and neither did his sister. He was troubled by the manner of the killing—up close and personal. It wasn't easy to kill like that. No one knew that better than he did.

In the last few years he'd spent plenty of time on his ATV exploring the back roads in the area around the old Navy base. And while he'd never seen anything outright, his gut told him there was something going on. He'd been a member of Special Forces for too long not to pick up the scent. Plus there were the occasional unexplained landings at the airstrip of individuals who had the unmistakable aura of spooks or G-men, sometimes accompanied by nerdy-looking individuals he'd pegged as either computer geeks or scientists.

And then Jake had gotten involved in something, and that was bad because, as far as he was concerned, Jake Maloney had been an idiot of the first order. Nancy had said she was worried and that Jake had become secretive. At first he'd just written it off to Jake screwing around with that bitch Tara French. But then Nancy had told him about the missing miles in Jake's log and the fact that Jake would be gone for whole days but never would tell her who she should bill for transport. Then he'd mysteriously show up with extra cash. And lots of it. Now Varney Simms was dead too, and while no information had been released on his death, Freeman thought the whole thing stunk to high heaven.

He sat for a couple more minutes thinking about what he should do. Finally, he decided the darkness and the rain were the perfect cover for a recon mission. He had had an odd feeling about a small fenced-in area on the old Navy base, just down the hill from the Misty Harbor Homes development. He decided it was time to check it out, and he swung into action.

He went to get his soft-sided weapons bag. He had no idea what he might encounter, so he opted for loaded-for-bear mode. Into the bag went a handheld VHF radio, a bolt cutter, flashlight, night vision goggles, a few tools, a flare gun, several frequency jammers, and a case containing a small amount of C-4, which he strapped securely inside a padded compartment in the bag. He added another small case with blasting caps for the plastic explosive. Then he went in the bedroom and put on his black camouflage gear and came back to the living room and unlocked the gun case. He took out the two Sig Sauers and extra clips. He loaded both, put one in his kidney holster and holstered the second one on his belt. He loaded his HK submachine gun, checked the safety, and put it in his weapons bag along with extra magazines for the HK and the Sigs.

He went to the closet and pulled on his black waterproof jacket and a black ball cap. He zipped the jacket, hefted the bag over his shoulder, and headed out the door to his pickup truck.

Chapter 26

Lieutenant Dent Fenton sat at the desk in his cramped home office, staring out the window at the blackness of the night. His heel tapped nervously on the worn pine floor as he shuffled papers around the cluttered desktop. Every few minutes he checked his watch. He'd tried Brie's cell phone several more times to no avail. None of this made any sense. Where would she be going at this time of night in the middle of a gale? She had mentioned Nate Freeman in the voice mail she had left him. But if she'd turned up evidence that Freeman was involved in the murder, Dent was sure she wouldn't go after him without backup. Unless she thought he was a flight risk. He remembered from her report that Freeman ran the airstrip, which meant he'd have access to a plane. He pulled up the Freeman report on his laptop, found a phone number for him and dialed it. The call went immediately to voice mail.

"Damn." He stood up and paced back and forth behind his chair.

Brie had told Atticus Kane, the innkeeper, that she'd be back in forty-five minutes. That meant another fifteen minutes before he'd know whether or not she had returned to the inn. Dent decided he wasn't waiting any longer. He picked up his cell phone and put through a call to Marty Depuis.

Marty answered on the second ring. "Hey, Boss, what's up?"

"Gear up, Marty. I'm heading over to pick you up. Brie left me an odd message, and now I can't raise her. I called the inn, and Atticus Kane said she left the inn to go somewhere."

"Pretty late for that. What do you think's going on?"

"Don't know, but I don't like the way it smells. Something's rotten in Tucker Harbor. I'll fill you in some more when I get there." He ended the call.

Dent picked his service weapon up off the desk, checked the clip, and holstered the weapon. He went to his locked ammo box and took out three extra clips. He grabbed his jacket off the back of his desk chair, put it on, and placed the clips in the left-hand pocket. He pulled on his Maine State Police cap, grabbed his keys, and headed out the door.

Marty Depuis was waiting on the front porch of his house when Dent pulled up. Marty ducked his head against the rain and ran for the car. He pulled open the door of the SUV and jumped in. The driveway was covered with crushed rock, and Dent was careful not to peel out. He didn't want to wake Marty's kids.

"So fill me in," Marty said. He pulled the hat off his head, shook it off down near the floor, and put it back on.

"Brie left a call for me at ten forty-five. I was in the shower so I missed it, but when I called her back a few minutes later, she didn't answer. Finally, I called the inn. That's when Kane told me she'd gone out. Here's the thing—she's found a connection in Everett Fein's research to Varney Simms."

"What's the connection?"

"She didn't say. Remember she was just leaving a message. She said she thought Nate Freeman was somehow involved. But here's the real shocker. She said she had reason to believe there might be some kind of clandestine operation underway near Tucker Harbor."

"Wait. You mean some kind of government or military operation? Like a 'Black Op'?"

"I know it sounds crazy. But remember Dr. Fein was down there investigating this *Hum* phenomenon, and he ended up dead."

"It was ruled an accident, though," Marty said.

"Believe me, if someone like the CIA wants to off somebody, it's going to look like either an accident or a suicide."

"Makes Varney Simms death pretty suspect if that's the case."

"I'd rather not get Brie killed while she's on my watch," Dent said. He took out his phone and punched up the number for the Whale Spout Inn. "I'm calling the inn again. If she's not back, I'm going to notify the commander of the Tactical Team. We may need to get them down here."

Atticus Kane and the security guard from the facility had just stepped in the back door of the inn when the phone rang. Kane ran for the parlor and caught the call on the third ring.

"Hello. Atticus Kane here." He tried to sound alert but calm.

"Mr. Kane, has Brie returned to the inn?"

"I'm sorry, she hasn't, Lieutenant."

"We're on the way to Tucker Harbor and may need to stop at the inn if we can't locate her."

"That's fine, Lieutenant. I don't think I could sleep with all this drama going on. I'll be up."

"Thank you. We'll keep you posted," Dent said.

Atticus Kane turned to the guard. "Let's go. We've got to get rid of her car, and I know just where it's going." He had the inn thoroughly bugged and had listened to the message she had left Dent Fenton telling him she suspected Nate Freeman. That's where the police would be headed, and that's where he planned to ditch her car.

"You follow me in my truck," Kane told the guard and handed him the keys. "I'll drive her car. No headlights until we get to the highway on the other side of the village."

They headed back out into the elements. Kane fished Brie's keys out of his pocket and climbed into the Impala. He turned left onto Third Street and drove the half mile to where it intersected the highway on the opposite side of Tucker Harbor. He switched on his headlights and did the speed limit for the few miles between Tucker Harbor and the turn for the airstrip. As he neared the turn, he checked his rear view mirror to be sure the guard was behind him and signaled a right turn. Two thirds of the way along the gravel drive leading to Freeman's trailer, Kane found a spot wide enough to pull Brie's car off to the side. It would look like she had parked there so as not to alert Freeman of her presence.

That should put the police off the scent, Atticus thought. *If they find Freeman at his trailer, they'll arrest him or bring him in for questioning.*

All he had to do for now was lay low. If necessary, Detective Beaumont's body would turn up in the woods near Freeman's trailer, in a shallow grave.

The guard pulled up behind him in the pickup, Kane climbed in, and they backed down the driveway to the highway.

"We'll head back to the inn and await further developments," Kane told the guard. But he planned to be in phone contact with the general via his secure line as soon as they got back to the inn. He didn't trust the bonehead military commander not to screw this up. Simms should have been liquidated several years ago—he had told the general so. Now they had a goddamn mess on their hands. He planned on making the decisions from here on out.

Chapter 27

Brie struggled to hang onto consciousness, but like a slippery eel, each time she reached for it, it slid back into the depths. When she came up to the surface this time, she willed herself to stay awake. The back of her head throbbed with a splitting headache. Her ears buzzed, and her vision was blurred as if she were staring through thick fog. She was aware of voices and bright lights. Really bright lights. She knew she was sitting in a chair and that her hands and feet were bound.

Slowly, slowly her vision began to clear, and she cast her eyes around the cavernous facility. She decided this must be the heart of the operation—the war room, so to speak. The space was basically round, and she judged it to be about 150 to 200 feet in diameter. There were two main banks of computers manned by what looked like scientists. Most of them were men, but she saw a few women scattered here and there. On the wall in front of these computers a giant screen showed a 3D image of the Greenland continent. Other smaller screens displayed what looked like aerial views of various glaciers. Brie wondered if these glaciers had been targeted for experimentation with the ELF pulses she had read about in Dr. Fein's research. Electromagnetic pulses that could affect melting and freezing.

Pods of four to six scientists worked in teams, each at his or her own computer. Several of these groups were speaking in Russian. Brie was seated off on the perimeter of the space with her arms bound behind her. When she craned her head around, she could see that there was a long narrow corridor behind her with a steel door at the end. The chances of escape seemed very remote, and although she saw only scientists here, she had no doubt the storm troopers were nearby.

She tried to focus on her last memory before she had been attacked. At first she couldn't recall what she'd been doing, but then she remembered she had been standing in the living room at the inn studying a photograph. It was a photograph of a young Everett Fein and Atticus Kane in navel uniform standing next to each other. She wondered if Kane had been in Naval Intelligence during his service years and had later moved underground to work as a government operative. Everett Fein, being a physicist, would have been a good candidate for Naval Intelligence as well.

Fein must have encountered Atticus Kane when he was doing research on *The Hum* in Tucker Harbor. As Fein progressed in his research, and certainly after he had the meeting with Varney Simms, he may have suspected that Atticus Kane was somehow involved in a clandestine operation. Maybe Fein had questioned him or even confronted him when he suspected the alarming nature of the project. The fact that Fein had died just days after his meeting with Varney Simms suggested that meeting was in some way the catalyst that led to his murder. Brie suspected he'd made the mistake of approaching Kane, even trying to reason with him. One thing was clear to her. The minute their paths had crossed in Tucker Harbor, Everett Fein's days were numbered.

Brie thought about that picture again of the two young naval officers. Why had Kane left it on the bookcase? It seemed like a gross oversight on his part. But she doubted it was. So why leave it there? Arrogance? Maybe he thought no one would ever put the pieces together. Or was it just a game of cat and mouse he'd been enjoying, knowing sooner or later she *would* put the pieces together? She wondered now if her own fate hadn't been sealed the day she checked into the Whale Spout Inn.

She was certain that Kane had the inn bugged, and that he recorded all calls on the inn's line. He would have known about her meeting with Stephen Wells in Ellsworth, and he would have listened to her phone conversation with Ben about Everett Fein's research.

She thought about Jake Maloney's murder in the light of all this. Maloney would have walked right by the inn on his way to Tara's the morning he died. It was a good bet Atticus had seen him and watched for him to leave her house. Atticus obviously knew Kevin Krumm's lobsterboat was in the harbor that morning and saw a way to pin the murder on Krumm. It was Atticus Kane whom Amber had seen rowing out to Krumm's lobsterboat that morning and subsequently toward the opposite shore where Maloney was murdered.

Brie felt a sense of satisfaction that she had put all the pieces together. But it was satisfaction underscored by emptiness, because she doubted she'd make it out of this alive. No one had any idea where she was. And Kane and his cronies would make sure they pinned her death on someone else. She guessed it would be Nate Freeman, since she had mentioned his name as a suspect on the message she had left on Dent Fenton's phone.

She thought about John and the *Maine Wind,* and that made her feel even worse. She had traded their future when she signed on to work this case. Was it selfishness or the call of duty? She wished she could say unequivocally that it was the call of duty, but that might be adding self-deception to selfishness. She felt tears sting her eyes, and she hung her head, suddenly overcome with emotion. When she looked back up, she noticed that one young man in the pod of scientists closest to her was studying her. She lowered her head again, feeling oddly exposed and vulnerable.

Chapter 28

Nate Freeman turned right onto the highway and followed it northeast for a little less than two miles. At the sign for Misty Harbor Homes, he turned left and drove past the fire station and into what had been the grounds of the old Navy base. At the end of the road he turned right onto Misty Harbor Trail, and even though the houses were all dark at this hour, he shut off his headlights. He drove down a short winding hill about a quarter mile beyond the condos and pulled the truck off to the side of the fenced compound. He got out, grabbed his arms bag, and shut the door. He checked to be sure his truck was not visible to the condos up the hill from him and then made his way to the back of the high fenced area.

The fence was topped with barbed wire, so going over was out of the question. He unzipped the bag and pulled out his bolt cutters. They had rubber grips, and he touched the fence lightly to see if it was electrified. It wasn't, and he cut vertically through the fence near one corner. He pulled the fence back, pushed his bag through, and then went through himself.

He fished the flashlight out of his bag and shined it around the compound. He judged the area to be about seventy by eighty feet. There were three very small cement block buildings. A sign on one read: "Hazardous Noise. Caution, May Cause Hearing Loss. Hearing Protection Required."

What caught his attention was a cement stairway surrounded by a pipe railing in the center of the compound.

He went down the stairs, but at the bottom of the flight, they dead-ended in a stairwell in front of a cement wall. Freeman looked around. Underfoot was a metal grate covering what looked like a piece of sheet metal. He pulled a screwdriver out of his bag and pried up the metal grate. He could see that the sheet metal covered a piece of wood. He took a small pry bar out of his bag, and holding the flashlight in his mouth, he wedged the bar under the wood and levered it up. Underneath he was surprised to see a round submarine-style hatch that looked like it dated back to the Cold War years. He expected it to be locked or jammed, and at first the bar on top wouldn't budge. He put his back into it, and after several tries he felt the bar move, and he was able to rotate the steel circle on top of the hatch.

He pulled the hatch open and shined his light on a ladder that ran straight down for about fifteen feet. Nate Freeman hesitated, wondering what he was getting himself into. But he was mightily curious. And something else. For some unknown reason, this had the feeling of a mission. He knew it didn't make any sense, but he couldn't shake the feeling that there was a reason he was doing this. He sat on his haunches looking down the ladder for a few more seconds. Then he crawled down the hatch, slipped his bag over his shoulders and descended the ladder, pulling the hatch closed after him.

At the bottom of the ladder Freeman stepped onto a heavy metal grate that formed a platform at the top of a spiral stairway. The bedrock had been bored out, and the stairway descended through the gray rock funnel very much like a spiral stairway in a lighthouse. It was hard to judge the distance, but he guessed it must go down 50 to 75 feet. He shouldered his bag and started down. Visibility was sketchy with only the flashlight, but even so he made it to the bottom in two to three minutes.

He now found himself on a steel landing of sorts. The spiral stairs continued downward in a second flight, but to his right about six feet away was a door labeled Exit. Freeman estimated that he had descended far enough to be at sea level and guessed that this door must exit near Holmes Bay, the bay that the old Navy base skirted. He walked over and tried the door. It was locked. He walked back to the stairway and shined his flashlight over the railing. The metal spiral disappeared downward farther than his flashlight beam could penetrate. "I wonder what circle of hell this brings you out at," he said aloud and heard his voice echo off the cavern below him. "Well, no point turning back now. I've hardly seen anything yet." With that, he noted the time on his watch and started downward again.

Approximately five minutes later Freeman reached the bottom and found himself in an area about eight by eight feet. It had taken him about twice as long to descend the second stairway, so he judged that he must now be about 150 feet below ground. There were two steel doors. The one to his left had a standard keyed deadbolt lock. Straight ahead of him was another steel door with a reinforced window. He shined the light through the window and saw that it was a giant storage area that contained huge spools of copper wire, pieces of machinery and various vehicles for lifting and moving supplies. He wondered what all this equipment was being used for 150 feet below ground.

He stepped back from the storage room door. So far no alarms had sounded, and Freeman decided that the hatch up top and the spiral stairways must be a secondary entrance that was never used. Secondary entrance to what, though? He guessed most of this infrastructure dated back to the '60s or '70s when the base was active. He walked over to the other door and tried it. It was locked. He considered using the C-4, but then decided there was no point in announcing his presence any sooner than he had to. He got out his lock picks and went to work on the deadbolt.

After a couple minutes of intense concentration, he felt the bolt slide back. He put his tools away, hefted his bag onto his back and slowly opened the door. There was a tunnel bored through the gray bedrock. It had an arched ceiling about ten feet high and was wide enough to easily accommodate the vehicles he had seen in the equipment area. Ahead on the right he saw an overhead door to that area. The tunnel ran in a straight line off into the distance. Nate had no idea how long it might be. He checked his watch, shouldered his bag, and started down the tunnel at a jog. The compass on his watch showed he was heading southeast.

Freeman had been travelling at a slow jog for about twenty minutes and estimated that he must have covered about two miles. The tunnel had run straight the whole way, with no apparent changes in grade. He came to a stop and took a couple of deep breaths. About 200 feet ahead the tunnel ended at a steel wall. Freeman moved over next to the side of the tunnel and covered the last couple hundred feet at a run. As he approached, he saw there was an oval-shaped door about a foot off the floor in the center of the wall. It resembled the door in a ship's bulkhead.

He approached with caution, took the arms bag off his back, and set it on the ground. He was deciding what his next move should be when the door slid open. He flattened himself against the wall just as a security guard came through. He reacted instinctively, moved swiftly up behind the guard, and disabled him. He dragged him back against the wall, pulled a roll of duct tape out of his bag, and taped the guard's wrists, ankles, and mouth.

Nate Freeman knew the clock was ticking now. He removed the key card clipped to the guard's pocket, pulled his Sig Sauer from his holster, and swiped the card. When the door slid open, he stepped through.

He found himself in a chamber about forty feet long. At the far end was another bulkhead-shaped door like the one through which he'd just passed. He ran to it, swiped the card, and leading with his gun, ducked through the opening into another identical space. It was like a chambered nautilus. But unlike the curving seashell beauty of the real thing, these chambers were gray stone and cold steel.

Freeman looked around. There were pipes running along the arched ceiling. He had noticed them in the previous chamber, but now he saw there were valves on the pipes. Suddenly, the bulkhead-like doors made more sense. These chambers could be flooded.

He swiped the card and with growing trepidation passed into the next chamber. Deeper into the heart of the beast. *Why am I doing this*? He thought about his sister Nancy. If he were killed, she'd have no one. He remembered their mother's words: *Don't go looking for trouble*. But it was what he had been trained to do, and he couldn't shake the feeling that he was down here for a reason.

Chapter 29

Lieutenant Dent Fenton and Marty Dupuis had been travelling with lights and siren as fast as the storm would safely allow. It had taken them a little over an hour to reach Machias, and they were now on Highway 191 heading toward Tucker Harbor with flashing lights only. Within ten more minutes their GPS alerted them of the upcoming turn into Nate Freeman's place near the airstrip. Dent Fenton shut off his flashing cherry light and pulled his speed down to 45 mph. Within two minutes they saw the driveway on the left, slowed to a stop, and turned in.

Dent switched off his headlights and drove slowly up the gravel road, using his parking lights only. A few hundred feet along the road they spotted Brie's Maine State Police issue Impala pulled off to the side of the road. Dent and Marty pulled up behind it, climbed out, and unholstered their weapons as they approached the car from either side.

"No one inside," Dent said.

"Freeman lives in a trailer near the hangar," Marty said.

They followed the road for a few hundred yards till they came in view of the trailer. There were lights on, and they approached with caution.

"I don't see his pickup truck," Marty said.

They stepped to either side of the trailer's front door, and Dent knocked loudly. There was no answer, and Dent gestured with his head for Marty to go around back. Dent knocked again and announced himself.

"Mr. Freeman. Maine State Police. Open the door, please."

There was no response, and in a few seconds Marty came back around front. "Nothing."

Dent went up the metal steps and tried the door. It was locked. He stepped back and gave it a hard kick, and it flew open. The two officers entered, guns drawn, and made their way through the trailer.

"Clear," Dent called from the first bedroom.

"Clear," Marty called from the back bedroom.

They went back to the living room.

"There are no signs of a struggle," Marty said.

"Looks like there are weapons missing from the gun case," Dent said, nodding toward the locked case against the living room wall.

"Do you think Freeman called her, maybe told her he had some information, possibly to lure her over here tonight?"

"Possible, but it's speculation. One thing's for sure, it doesn't look good for Brie." Dent holstered his gun. "Let's head back to the car. I want to get out an APB."

They left the trailer and jogged back down the road. The strong wind shook the trees, and the rain started down again just as they reached the SUV.

From his onboard computer, Dent ran Nate Freeman's vehicle registration and got the make, model, and license plate number for his pickup truck. He issued an All Points Bulletin on the vehicle and an Approach with Caution warning. "Suspect is armed and should be considered dangerous," Dent said. "Suspect may be holding Maine State Police Deputy Detective Brie Beaumont hostage." He relayed a description of Brie. Then Dent called the commander of the Tactical Team and told him they were needed in Tucker Harbor.

Dent turned the SUV around in the gravel road. "We need to go to Nancy Maloney's, see if she's seen or heard from

Freeman tonight." He headed back toward the highway and turned left. There was silence inside the vehicle. Each of them knew the dread the other was feeling.

Ten minutes later they pulled into Nancy Maloney's driveway and got out. It was nearly one in the morning, and after what she'd been through, Dent hated to wake her like this in the middle of the night. But they had no choice. He rang the bell and waited. He was about to ring it again when a frightened Nancy Maloney peeked through the blind.

Marty spoke up since he knew she'd recognize him. "Mrs. Maloney, it's Detective Marty Dupuis and Lieutenant Dent Fenton." He held up his badge.

When she realized who was at the door she opened it quickly and let them in. "I'm sorry, Detectives. I was afraid to come to the door at this time of night."

"That's understandable, Mrs. Maloney," Dent said. "We're sorry to wake you at this hour, but it can't be helped."

"What's wrong? Something terrible has happened, hasn't it?"

Dent could hear in her voice that terrible news had suddenly become her norm. "Mrs. Maloney, did you talk to your brother or see him any time after eleven o'clock tonight?"

"Why no," she said. "He'd have no reason to come here that . . . Oh, no! Has something happened to him? Please tell me he's all right."

"Detective Beaumont is missing, and we have reason to believe she may be with your brother," Dent said. He watched her reaction carefully, but so far he could tell that none of this was computing with her.

"Why would she be with Nate?" Nancy seemed astounded at the suggestion.

"We have reason to believe your brother may be involved in the events of the past few days and that he may have abducted Detective Beaumont."

"No. You're wrong. Nate is a good man. He may not have liked my husband, but he would never have killed him.

And he would never hurt Detective Beaumont. You've got this all wrong." She held her hands out in front of her, palms up, in a pleading manner—body language that said she had nothing to hide.

"Do you know where he might have gone tonight, Nancy?" Marty asked.

"Maybe to a friend's house. I don't know his friends, though."

"Thank you, Mrs. Maloney. We'll keep you posted."

They left and got back in Dent's SUV. "We need to go to the inn and collect all the files that Brie was working on," Dent said. He started the car, backed out of the driveway, and headed for the other end of the village.

He pulled in behind the inn. "You may as well wait here, Marty. I'll be right back. I just need to collect all of Everett Fein's files. They are now evidence." He reached in the drawer under the passenger seat and took out a couple of evidence envelopes. He climbed out, headed for the back door, and knocked. Atticus appeared at the door and let him in.

Dent was back out in a few minutes, empty handed.

"Where are the files?" Marty asked.

"Brie must have taken them with her," Dent said. "Kane said she was carrying a briefcase when she went out tonight."

"Does that make sense to you?" Marty asked.

"None of this makes any sense. But I can understand her not leaving key evidence here. There aren't even any locks on the bedroom doors."

Dent turned on the SUV, switched on the wipers, and pulled out onto the highway. He felt sick inside at what might be unfolding, and more powerless than he had ever been in his life.

Chapter 30

Brie opened and closed her hands and wiggled her fingers. The PlastiCuffs were too tight. Whatever idiot had put them on her didn't know what he was doing or else was trying to exact punishment. Likewise, her feet were starting to feel like two dead stumps, and she rocked them from heels to toes to try and keep the circulation going. She continued to wriggle her wrists in the cuffs and put pressure outward on them in hopes of working a hand free, but she knew her chances were slim.

The tone inside the facility had changed about fifteen minutes ago, and tension had spread through the room like a contagious bug. Two military types—one of them looked like he might be a general—stood far enough away from her to be out of earshot. They were having a heated argument, and it didn't take a rocket scientist to know that it was about her. She took it as a sign they might not be planning to invite her to tea. Most of the science guys within earshot of the argument had ducked their heads and become suddenly intensely engaged in their work. Now Brie knew what geeks flying below the radar looked like. Nothing against geeks, of course. She had the utmost respect for intellect.

One young scientist in a pod a short distance from her had glanced in her direction several times. He seemed agitated. *A man with a conscience,* Brie thought. The next time he looked her way, she made eye contact with him. She read two things there. Empathy, but something else that gave her hope. She read resolve in his eyes.

A short time later he got up and walked at a casual pace toward a corridor on the far side of the facility. He was gone for a few minutes—the length of an average bathroom break. Shortly after he returned to his pod of co-workers, the military types left the area. The man with a conscience immediately stood and moved in her direction. He squatted down behind her chair and cut the cuffs with amazing speed. He slipped a tool into her hand that felt like a miniature wire cutter.

"I'm a scientist," he said in a low voice. "I know people have already died. This isn't what I signed up for." He slipped something into her other hand that felt like a credit card. He repeated a number sequence. 9-9-4-5-7. "Don't forget. Nine-nine-four-five-seven. Now go before they come back. The hallway behind you will take you to an exit. It's all I can do."

"What's your name?" Brie asked.

"Fritz," he mumbled.

"Thank you," Brie said. "I'll send help." But he was already walking back to his work station.

Brie bent and cut the cuffs on her ankles, got up and moved as swiftly as she could down the corridor behind her. She expected to hear alarms sound, but none did. She wondered if the young scientist had done something to short-circuit the system. Brie knew one thing; there was no shortage of true heroes in the world. But she feared for young Fritz, knowing the ruthlessness of Atticus Kane.

In seconds she had reached the door at the end of the corridor. There was a card scanner and a keypad. *Card first or code?* she wondered, but there was no time for debate. She swiped the card and keyed in the number sequence 9-9-4-5-7. The steel door slid open and she rushed through.

Nate Freeman had just stepped through another one of the bulkhead-like doors and made his way to the center of the chamber when he saw the steel door ahead of him start to open. But before he could get behind the wall, someone rushed through the door. To his amazement he recognized the detective woman who'd questioned him. *Named Brie,* he thought.

"What are you doing here?" he said, stunned.

"What are *you* doing here?" Brie panted. "Never mind. No time. RUN!"

"Wait." Freeman dropped to he knees and pulled a small black box about the size of a pack of cigarettes out of the bag he was carrying. He ran forward and slapped it on the left side of the door. "That should buy us a little time." He rushed back and, to Brie's amazement, pulled an HK submachine gun out of the bag.

"Wow, you come prepared."

Freeman took the Sig Sauer from the holster on his belt and handed it to her. "Now we go," he said with surprising calmness.

Brie ran down the tunnel toward the next door, scanned the card, and vaulted through the opening. She heard Freeman right behind her.

"How far do we have to go to get out of here?" she shouted over her shoulder.

"Once we get through these chambers, it's about two miles to the first stairway. There's no cover along that stretch."

"How far underground are we?"

"I'd say about a hundred and fifty feet."

Brie swiped the card for the next door, and they rushed through. It was a race to put as much distance as they could between themselves and the guards she knew would be coming. Freeman had put some kind of an electronic jamming device on the first door, but even with the help of the young scientist on the inside, she knew it wouldn't take them long to override the system. And once each door sealed behind them, they had no idea what kind of a lead they had. It sounded to her like once they were past these chambers, it was going to be an all-out footrace. She was glad she'd kept up with her running.

As they passed through the third door, the valves opened and the chamber started to fill with water at a surprising rate. Brie ran for the door at the end and scanned the card. Nothing. She scanned it again.

"Damn. We're trapped." The chamber was filling fast, and she looked around like a caged animal.

Nate whipped the bag off his back. "No worries. I've got the solution. Hold this."

Brie held the bag by the handles, and Nate took out a box and opened it.

"C-4?" Brie said. "You *do* come prepared. That's not legal, but I'm awfully glad you've got it."

Freeman took out a blasting cap. "I think I'm starting to like you." He pressed the C-4 onto the center of the door and stuck the cap in.

"Everyone's got a good side," Brie said.

"Well, get yours over next to that wall."

They ran for the far end of the chamber, and Freeman pressed his body against hers just as the blast went off.

"Works like a champ every time," he said.

They headed through the door and waded through the next chamber. "I think this is the last one," he said. "Then we're in the clear, pending any Indiana Jones-like death traps they have for us."

Nate slapped the C-4 on the door, and they repeated their wall hugger huddle as the blast went off. They ran to the ruined door and climbed through. They were in the open tunnel now, and they took off at a dead run.

"They may have two flooded chambers to deal with if they were slow breaching the first door," Nate said.

"We had passed through two of them before they turned on the waterworks. So those chambers were still intact. They'll have to drain some of the water before they can get through."

"A fact that may well have saved our lives," Nate said. "We've got a ways to go. Best not to talk. We'll get winded."

"Roger that," Brie said.

They ran, not flat out, but close to it. They had to put distance between themselves and whoever was coming behind.

They had been going for almost ten minutes when they heard the first gunfire. Brie estimated they'd covered nearly a mile, which put them partially out of range of the fire, but not completely. Rounds whizzed past them or ricocheted off the rock walls of the tunnel. Now they ran flat out—ran for their lives. They were both in shape and they were both fast—a fact that had saved their lives up to this point. Still, Brie sensed the bad guys were gaining on them incrementally. For almost ten more minutes they raced through the tunnel, trying to vary their path enough to avoid gunfire but not enough to slow their progress. Occasionally, Nate turned and sent a burst from his HK down the tunnel behind them.

"I see a door down there," Brie panted.

"The stairs are on the other side. Keep going."

The sight of the door was like water in a desert. It gave them hope and they picked up their pace. Within another minute they were up to the door and through it. Nate looked desperately around for something to jam under the knob. There was nothing. "Quick. Up the stairs." Nate pushed Brie in front of him. "You first."

Brie started up the spiral stairs. After the two-mile run, she was winded, and climbing the stairs felt like trying to swim to the surface of the ocean with no air in your lungs and a weight belt on. *A hundred and fifty feet,* she thought. *The equivalent of fifteen stories. And they'd be completely exposed to gunfire all the way up.*

As if reading her mind, Nate said, "If we can just get up the first set of stairs, we can hold them off. They can only come up these stairs one man at a time. There's an exit door there, too. It must go out to the sea."

They climbed the spiral with all the speed they could muster, but with every step, every second that ticked by, Brie felt time running out. They were two-thirds of the way up the spiral when gunfire erupted from below.

Chapter 31

Dent and Marty scoured the roads in and around Tucker Harbor, but found no sign of Nate Freeman's pickup truck. They were coordinating their search with the state troopers and the County Sheriff's patrols. They were also waiting for the Tactical Team to arrive, and Dent was in radio contact with the team's commander. It was all they could do, but Dent Fenton had never felt so helpless. He knew they needed a major stroke of luck.

They were now systematically checking all roads northwest of Tucker Harbor and had gotten as far as the old Navy base. Dent turned left into what had been the base property. A sign read Misty Harbor Homes and showed a diagram of the condominium development in the structures that had formerly been Navy housing.

They looped around the now vacant base buildings and proceeded down the road toward the homes, where they turned left onto Misty Harbor Trail. They drove slowly between the houses on either side of the road, using their searchlight to check the license plates on any pickup trucks they came to. At the end of the row of houses, they turned around and headed back the other way. Past the homes the road dipped down a small hill. As they came around a curve at the bottom of the hill, Dent immediately saw a pickup fitting the description of Nate Freeman's truck. It was pulled off to the side of the road next to what looked like some kind of fenced-in utility area. Dent checked the plate and radioed in that they had located the vehicle. Then he contacted Tactical and gave them the location. They were about fifteen minutes away. He and Marty got out of the SUV, drew their weapons, and approached the pickup from either side.

"Empty," Dent said. He shined his flashlight around the interior. There were no signs of blood.

They turned their attention to the fenced area. Dent pointed out the high fence and the barbed wire. "Looks like another remnant of the old base," he said.

They started around the perimeter heading in opposite directions. After a few seconds Marty called out, "Back here, Boss. The fence has been cut."

Dent caught up with him, and they surveyed the situation. Then Dent held the fence back and Marty went through. He followed him, and they began to check out the small cinder block buildings inside the enclosure.

Marty emerged from behind one of the buildings and shined the flashlight around the small compound. He noticed the cement stairs in the center of the compound and went down them.

"Boss, over here."

Dent came and peered over the pipe railing.

"There's some kind of a hatch here. Like on a submarine."

Dent hurried down the steps. "Open it, Marty." Dent pointed his gun downward at the hatch as Marty turned the bar and pulled the hatch open. Dent shined his flashlight in and saw the ladder descending.

"Should we wait?" Marty asked.

"No telling what we'll encounter down there. Remember Brie mentioned some kind of clandestine operation. Tactical is just a few minutes out. We'll wait."

Marty closed the hatch, and they climbed back up the stairs to wait for Tactical. Dent knew it was the right call, but it killed him to hold back. Brie's life was at stake. He hoped he wouldn't live to regret his decision.

Chapter 32

Brie and Nate Freeman raced up the spiral stairs as bullets pinged and ricocheted around them.

"AHH! I'm hit." Freeman grabbed his leg and sent a burst from his HK down the spiral stairs.

Brie squeezed past him. "Give me the bag and the HK." She pulled the bag off his back and he handed her the submachine gun. "Keep going. We're almost there." She gave him her Sig Sauer. "Go! I'll cover you."

Using his left hand, Freeman grabbed the railing and hopped toward the top.

Brie sent a serious spray of fire down the spiral as she climbed the stairs backwards. Within twenty seconds she heard Nate say, "I'm at the top."

Brie turned and ran up the last few steps and onto the steel platform next to him. She handed him the HK. "Cover us."

She dropped to her knees and inspected the wound on Freeman's leg. "Through and through," she said. "Missed the artery." She unzipped the bag and grabbed the duct tape. She pulled off several feet, wrapped the tape around his leg to cover the wound, and secured it. He barely flinched.

"That should slow the bleeding till we get you out of here," Brie said.

"Optimist," Freeman said.

"Why not?" Brie said. "We got this far."

Freeman gestured with his head. "Get the C-4 out and blow that door. We may need to beat a speedy retreat."

Brie pulled out the case with the C-4 and a blasting cap. "We only need enough to blow the lock." She ran to the door behind them, slapped the C-4 over the keyhole and lock mechanism, and inserted the blasting cap. She ran back to Nate, and they turned away just as the door blew.

Freeman ejected the magazine from the HK, pulled a full one out of the bag, and slammed it home. He fired another burst down the stairs. They heard a shout and a thud as someone went over the rail.

Brie took stock of the ammo. The last magazine was in the HK. They still had the two Sigs and an extra clip for each. She knew it wasn't enough.

Rounds peppered the underside of the steel platform they were crouched on.

"How much ammo do we have left?" Freeman asked.

"You're on the last mag for the HK, and we've got two more clips for the Sigs."

"It's just a matter of time before they send a squad down the shore to flank us," Freeman said.

"My guess is we'll run out of ammo before then."

Two more guys came into view on the spiral, and Nate sent a spray of fire toward them. One went down and the guy behind climbed over. Brie aimed and dropped him with one round from the Sig Sauer.

"All that firepower at my trailer, and here we are running out of ammo." Freeman sounded angry and disgusted.

"Don't beat yourself up," Brie said. "There's a limit to how many guns one person can carry and still make time on foot."

"You're right, but I hate feeling trapped."

All of a sudden Brie had a thought. "Can you hold them off for a minute or two?" she asked.

"I think so," Nate said.

"I'll need the flashlight."

"In the bag. Don't be gone long."

"Don't worry." Brie headed for the door and disappeared into the darkness beyond.

They were close to the water. Cold rain slashed at her as she made her way down a small hill and shined the light along the shore. Lo and behold, she spotted what might be their salvation. There was a small dory pulled up beyond the tide line. She ran over to it and scanned the inside. It was old, but it looked sound. There was no way to know if it was watertight. There were no oars, but she wouldn't tell Freeman that. No point in alarming him. Anyway, she had a plan.

She ran back up the hill, in the door, and squatted down next to him. "You have a compass on that?" she asked, pointing to the sophisticated-looking dive watch he wore on his left wrist.

"Compass and global positioning," he said. "Why?"

"Come on, Freeman," she said, zipping up the black bag. "It's time to go to sea."

"What?"

"There's a dory. If we're quick about it, we can escape onto Holmes Bay. With the cover of dark and the fog and rain, we may just have a chance."

He studied her for a moment. "Well, our odds here are slim to none."

"The firing's stopped," Brie said. "That's not a good sign."

"My guess is they're ramping up for their next offensive."

"Let's go," she said. "I'll help you." She slung the bag of supplies over her back as Freeman struggled to his feet. She handed him the flashlight, put an arm around his waist to steady him, and they went out the door.

"The dory's just a short ways down the shore." Brie helped him down the hill toward the small craft.

Freeman shined the light into the dory. "There are no oars," he said, alarm ringing in his voice.

"Don't need 'em," Brie said. "Tide's ebbing. We just need to get out there and it'll take us toward Hog Island. You've got a radio and flare gun in that bag. The Coast Guard will find us." She pushed the dory down to the water's edge. "Climb in and take the middle thwart," she said. "I'll push off."

Freeman hesitated for a moment and then stepped aboard. "Something tells me you're more resourceful than the average bear," he joked.

She handed him her Sig Sauer. "Stay low." She pushed the dory out onto the water and waded after it, holding the painter. She spun it around so it would be headed bow first toward Hog Island. After a few seconds she felt the bottom drop away, and she swam pushing the stern of the dory out into Holmes Bay. The water in the bay was beyond chilly, but not nearly as cold as it would have been out in the open ocean.

"That should be my job," Freeman said over the side. "I'm the SEAL."

"Don't worry. I'm a strong swimmer," Brie said. "I grew up in Minnesota—Land of Ten Thousand Lakes."

Chapter 33

Brie swam in an ink black world of water. Between her efforts and the outgoing tide, she guessed they had covered a half mile or more. Nate found a coil of line under the stern thwart. He tied one end off and tossed it over the stern. "Tie that around your waist," he instructed. "If the current gets strong, you'll be tethered to the boat."

Brie did as she was told and then continued to swim, as fast as she could away from the shore. She hoped the rain and fog in the bay would provide enough cover so they wouldn't be spotted.

After a few minutes she called to Nate. "Time to use that compass."

"Roger."

She saw a dim glow from his watch.

"Can you direct us onto a south by southwest heading?"

"No problem."

Brie waited a few seconds.

"You need to steer us about twenty degrees to port," Nate said.

Brie made the adjustment.

"I see lights on the shore," Nate said quietly.

"Stay low," Brie said. "We'll hope they can't spot us."

"If they have flares, we're sunk."

Bad choice of words, Brie thought.

They saw muzzle flashes and heard rounds fired out over the water. Then the squad headed south along the shore.

Within a few minutes they heard another burst of fire and saw more muzzle flashes. Then a bullhorn blared. "This is the Maine State Police. Drop your weapons or we will fire."

"I think the cavalry has just arrived," Nate said.

"I knew the Maine State Police would be coming once they discovered I was missing."

The current was swift now, and Brie was having trouble steering the dory from behind. She called to Nate, and he pulled her up over the stern into the dory. He peeled off his jacket and insisted she put it on.

"We need to call the Coast Guard and then see if we can jury rig a rudder," Brie said.

"Any ideas?" Nate asked.

They sat in darkness black as a tomb, feeling the tidal flow carrying them toward the open sea out beyond Holmes Bay.

"Switch on the light," Brie said.

"You think that's safe?"

"I think the bad guys are occupied," Brie said.

Freeman switched on the flashlight and shined it around the dory.

"If we could take out that center thwart, it might work as a rudder. It's long enough."

"I've got just the thing." Freeman pulled what looked like a large-scale Swiss Army knife from a sheath on his belt and folded out a miniature saw blade. He took off his watch and handed it to Brie. "Here, you'll need this." Then he went to work, cutting through the thwart next to the starboard gunwale.

Brie studied the watch's display for a minute, then pulled the radio out of the bag, pressed the Channel 16 button, for the Coast Guard channel, held down the transmit button and spoke.

"Mayday, Mayday, Mayday. We are two people adrift in a small dory in Holmes Bay, somewhere north of Hog Island. Our position is forty-four degrees, forty-one minutes, thirty-seven seconds, north, by sixty-seven degrees, nineteen minutes, twenty-one seconds west. We are drifting with the tide. I say again, Mayday, Mayday, Mayday. . ." Brie repeated the message a second time, released the button and waited.

"Drifting dory, this is the United States Coast Guard. Please go to channel twenty-two-A. Over."

"Acknowledge." Brie tuned to channel 22A and hailed again.

In a moment the radio crackled to life. "Drifting dory, this is the Coast Guard. Repeat your coordinates. Over."

Brie checked the watch and sent the coordinates again.

"Drifting dory, we have your coordinates. You are currently north of Hog. Can you correct course? Over."

"Negative. We have no oars and no rudder. We're trying to jury rig something. Over."

"Unless you correct course soon and sail due east, you will pass west of Hog Island and be caught in the main tidal flow draining from the bay. Over."

"Roger that. Over."

"Is anyone injured? Over."

"One man. He has a gunshot wound to the leg. Over."

"Is he conscious? Over."

"Affirmative. Over."

"Please give us your names. Over"

"Brie Beaumont and Nate Freeman. Over."

"Brie and Nate, we will be coordinating your rescue with the Canadian Coast Guard. They will be dispatching a rescue helicopter out of St. John, New Brunswick and should be over your location in approximately thirty-five minutes. Please update us on your coordinates every five minutes and inform us if you make landfall on Hog Island. Over."

"Roger that. We have flares. Over."

"That will help. We will let you know when the chopper is approaching your coordinates so you can fire your flare. Over."

"Acknowledge. Over."

"We will continue monitoring your calls on channel twenty-two-A. Over and out."

"The Canadians are coming for us," Brie said. "Is that normal?"

"The U.S. and Canadian Coast Guards collaborate fully in these waters. And the Canadians have the rescue helos—six of them at bases in New Brunswick, Nova Scotia, and Prince Edward Island." Nate finished sawing through the thwart on the starboard side and moved over to port.

"St. John, New Brunswick must be the closest." Brie braced the slat of wood while he sawed the other end next to the port gunwale.

"St. John is about seventy miles straight up the coast."

"You seem to know a lot about the Coast Guard in these parts."

"Kind of a hobby, I guess. I'm interested in the Coast Guard's rescue work. Those guys are a bunch of unsung heroes in my book."

"So, if you had it to do again, would you join the Coast Guard?"

Nate thought about that. "You know what? I just might. I like the idea of saving lives."

Brie reflected on the fact that he had saved hers and that she'd been wrong in her assessment of him. His sister was right. Nate Freeman was a good guy.

Just then the thwart came free. "I'll move to the stern and see if I can steer us," he said. "You track our heading with the compass and place the calls on our position."

He scooted back and pushed himself up onto the stern thwart. He put the makeshift rudder over the side into the water vertically, holding it in a tight grip so the current wouldn't pull it out of his hands.

Brie could immediately feel the dory respond as Nate angled the board one way or the other. "Works like a champ," she said. "You must have paddled stern in a canoe."

Nate chuckled. "I'm flattered you noticed."

Brie checked their heading using the compass on Nate's watch. "We need to sail due east or miss Hog Island. You need to come a hundred thirty-five degrees to port. I'll tell you when our heading is correct."

Nate braced his good leg against one of the cross members on the sole of the dory for leverage as he steered with the makeshift rudder. With strength and skill he was able to bring the dory around to the right heading. Brie felt the cold northeast wind on her face and chest now, but immediately realized that they were still being pulled west. She knew there was no way they could make headway against both the wind and the tide.

"We're still being drawn west," she said. "I think reaching Hog Island will be impossible."

"We had to try," Nate said. "The problem is, when the tide flows out of these bays, it's like pulling the plug on a bathtub. In some areas of the Bay of Fundy, the tidal current can reach six to eight knots."

Brie had read somewhere the astounding statistic that twice daily the Bay of Fundy fills and empties a billion tons of water—more than the flow of all the world's fresh water rivers combined.

"Well, I guess we'll be going with the flow," she said sardonically. She checked the watch. Five minutes had passed. She picked up the radio. "U.S. Coast Guard, this is drifting dory in Holmes Bay. We can't make Hog Island. Over."

"Drifting dory, you say you will miss Hog Island. Affirmative?"

"Affirmative." She sent their coordinates. "Over."

"Brie and Nate, the helo is on its way. ETA twenty-nine minutes. Over."

"Coast Guard, I am a deputy detective with the Maine State Police. Can you notify Lieutenant Dent Fenton of the Maine State Police that you are in contact with us and that I am safe? Over."

"Copy that. We will inform Maine State Police of the situation. Please continue to update coordinates every five minutes. Over."

"Copy. Over and out."

"May as well save your energy, Nate. Seems we're headed for the open sea."

Nate pulled the rudder back inboard and moved off the seat onto the sole of the dory next to Brie. The gunwales were high enough to break a little of the wind, and they huddled together in the bottom of the boat with the light of the single flashlight their only company in the midst of a cold, dark realm.

Brie guessed they might be travelling at about three to four knots.

"Do you know how long this bay is?" she asked.

"From where we are now, I'd guess it's about two and a half miles to Machias Bay, which will be much more exposed. From there we're headed straight out into the Gulf of Maine. At least the wind is behind us, so we won't swamp as easily if the seas get higher. On the down side, it's increasing our speed toward open water."

"Maybe they'll reach us before we drift out of Holmes Bay. How's the leg?"

"Hurts like hell, but the taping you did seems to be controlling the bleeding some."

Brie picked up the radio, hailed the Coast Guard and gave them their coordinates.

Their response came back. "Brie and Nate, our ETA is twenty-four minutes. What is Nate's condition? Over."

"Conscious. He appears stable."

"Any signs of shock?"

"Negative. Over."

"The pilot will be airlifting you both to Eastern Maine Medical Center in Bangor. We are in contact with the Maine State Police and are keeping them informed. Over."

"Copy. Over and out."

Brie had just set the radio back in the bag when—WHOMP. Something hit the underside of the dory hard.

Nate shined the flashlight over the side but saw nothing. When he turned the light back onto the sole of the dory, Brie's heart sank. The impact must have opened a seam in the old wood planking. Water had already pooled in the bottom of the dory.

"We've sprung a leak."

"Damn. What's next?"

Brie pulled the bag open and rummaged inside for something to bail with. Then she realized the only solution was in Nate's hand.

"Give me the flashlight."

Nate handed it to her, and she unscrewed the top and dumped the batteries into the bag. She knelt on the sole of the dory and started bailing with the handle of the flashlight.

Nate grabbed the roll of duct tape out of the bag to see if they could slow the leak by taping the seam, but they soon realized it was hopeless. The surface was too wet and the water was coming in too fast. Brie kept bailing. Nate foraged in the bag again, found the small plastic case of C-4, emptied it and started bailing.

They worked frantically side by side for the next five minutes. "Is it working?" Nate asked.

"Some, but we'll never keep up with the flow. It's like trying to empty a washtub with a thimble. Eventually we'll swamp." She sat back on her heels. "Hand me the radio."

Nate handed it over and kept bailing.

"Coast Guard, this is drifting dory. We've sprung a leak. What's your ETA? Over."

"This is the Coast Guard. Give us your coordinates, Brie. Over."

She consulted the watch and read them into the radio.

"Brie and Nate, the helo is nineteen minutes out. Can you stay afloat?"

"We're bailing but can't keep up with the flow. Can't estimate how long before we sink. Over." She kept bailing as she spoke.

"Do you have PFDs? Over."

"Negative."

"Can you both swim?"

"Affirmative. Both strong swimmers, but Nate is weak from leg wound."

"Copy. Please inform us if sinking is imminent. If you go in the water, stay together. Try to keep the radio and flare gun with you. Over."

"Roger. Over and out."

The next few minutes things happened fast as the situation began to unravel. They kept bailing at a valiant pace, but the leaking increased as another seam opened. The old craft had reached the end of its days and now seemed in a rush to find its watery grave at the bottom of the sea.

As Brie bailed, Nate started to prep for the inevitable. The radio was submersible, so he didn't have to worry about that getting wet. He put a flare in the handle of the flashlight, taped it shut to keep it dry, and zipped it and the flare gun into the inside pockets on the jacket Brie was wearing. She tried to take the jacket off and give it to him, but he refused.

"I've got a lot more insulation than you do. You're wearing the jacket." He ran the duct tape around her waist to cinch the jacket to her body. He untied the piece of line he had used to tether Brie to the dory and tied it around their waists so they couldn't drift apart. Brie gave Nate the watch, and he strapped it back on his arm. It was a dive watch, so the salt water wouldn't hurt it.

As the dory sunk lower in the water, they began taking water over the bow and knew sinking was imminent. Brie picked up the radio. She felt the same inexplicable calmness she had felt before in moments of extreme stress or disaster.

"Coast Guard, this is Brie Beaumont. Sinking of our craft is imminent." She read off their coordinates. "We have taken measures to keep the flares and flare gun dry, and we have tethered ourselves together. What is your ETA? Over."

"Brie and Nate. This is the Coast Guard. We are patching your call directly through to Captain Baker aboard the rescue chopper. Go ahead, Captain."

"Brie and Nate. We are approaching your coordinates and will be over you in thirteen minutes. Your job is to stay together. Try not to expend too much energy in the water, and keep talking to each other. Over."

"Copy that. We will do our best till you arrive. Over and out."

"I think we should load the flare gun," she said. "It's going to be hard to do it once we're in the water."

"You're right. Let's do it."

They retrieved the flare from inside the jacket, and Nate loaded it into the gun. "You handle the radio," he said. "I'll make sure the flare gun stays above water."

At that moment they felt the dory sink beneath them and they were in the ocean being swept along with the tide.

The darkness around them was total, the cold paralyzing. For the first couple minutes Brie struggled to breathe. Nate locked an arm around her waist so they floated as a unit. They each held their outside arm high enough to keep the radio and flare gun dry as they treaded water. The glow from Nate's watch, now strapped to his right arm, was the only light in a coal black universe. As the minutes passed, Brie thought of all the men and women who had died at sea and knew how terrifying and helpless those last moments must have been for them. No one mentioned the "H" word. Hypothermia. Now their greatest enemy.

"I guess this was a pretty bone-headed move," Brie said. "I shouldn't have brought us out here. We should have taken our chances ashore. I'm sorry, Nate."

"Survival, especially in battle, is all about fast thinking and adaptation. You assessed the situation and took action. I support that. Anyway, now who's being the pessimist? Look, we're still alive, aren't we?"

There was no response.

"Brie?" Nate shook her. "Brie, stay awake."

"Yeah, I'm here."

"Keep talking," Nate said. "Tell me more about that ship of yours. I've always wanted to sail on one of those old ships. Maybe when my leg heals up, I'll come aboard for a cruise."

They kept each other talking, but minutes stretched out. Thirteen minutes can be an eternity in the north Atlantic where temperatures average forty-four degrees. Every couple minutes Captain Baker's voice came over the radio checking their coordinates, telling them to hang on, that help was almost there.

When it was five minutes to their ETA, Nate suddenly said, "Listen. Can you hear that?"

In the distance Brie could hear a rhythmic whump, whump, whump—the sound of the chopper's rotor. The pitch continued to get louder and higher. *The Doppler effect,* she thought. *They're coming toward us. They're getting closer.*

"They're coming, Nate," she shouted. "Listen to that beautiful sound." She launched into a scientific explanation of the Doppler effect and why the sound was getting higher and louder. Then Nate was laughing.

"That's nice, Brie."

Only later did she realize how punch drunk she had been from the cold, and how funny she must have sounded.

The radio squawked to life. "Brie and Nate, this is Captain Baker. Give us your coordinates. Over." Brie held the radio toward Nate, and he read the coordinates off his watch.

The whine of the rotor grew louder and louder. "Brie and Nate, fire your flare. Over."

"Roger that."

Nate held his arm up high and fired the flare gun, and all of a sudden it was the 4th of July overhead. They could see the rescue chopper now with its search lights turned on the water, and in another minute Brie and Nate found themselves bathed in a heavenly glow. And then an angel in an orange suit was coming down through the light on a cable. It was the most beautiful thing Brie had ever seen. And then the orange angel was putting a harness on her, and she was being lifted through the light toward heaven. *Heaven is such a noisy place,* she thought. *Who knew?*

Then she looked out and saw the angel in the orange suit bringing Nate up. And then they were winging, beating through the night wearing special silver robes the orange angel had wrapped them in. Brie wished John could see her in her special silver robe. *He would never believe this,* she thought.

Chapter 34

Brie woke up not in heaven as she might have expected, but in a hospital bed. There was an IV in her left arm and a sleeping Dent Fenton slouched in the chair next to her bed. The clock on the wall read five minutes to nine, and from the sunlight streaming in the window she knew it must be nine in the morning. She was under a lot of blankets, and there was some kind of an inflatable apparatus around the sides of her body pumping up and down and putting pressure on her.

She tried to remember where she had been last. And like that, it all came rushing back. Her last memory was of the dory sinking out from under her and Nate Freeman. She knew there should be something after that, but she could recall nothing.

Just then a nurse came into the room. Her name tag said "Tess." She was fiftyish, round and jovial, with dark brown hair cut very short.

"Well, good morning. It's Brie, right?"

"That's me," Brie said. From the corner of her eye she saw Dent Fenton stir in his chair. "Where am I?"

"You're at Eastern Maine Medical Center in Bangor. You were mighty cold when you came in and just semi-conscious. We've been treating you for hypothermia." She popped a thermometer in Brie's mouth just as she was about to ask about Nate.

"That's more like it. Ninety-seven point eight." Tess nodded with approval. "We're getting up toward the right number now."

Dent had stood up next to the bed and was smiling down at her with those surprising blue eyes of his. "Well, good morning, Sunshine. Nice to have you back on dry land."

"Hey, Dent."

"Say, I know you miss the ocean, but there are better ways to get back out there, you know."

"Yeah, well, it worked, didn't it?"

"Just barely. But you get an 'A' for thinking outside the box."

"How's Nate? And how's the case?"

"Nate's doing fine, and there's lots to report, but we'll wait till Tess is done here."

Tess removed the blood pressure cuff. "Ninety over sixty. Does your blood pressure always run that low?" she asked.

"That's a pretty normal reading for me," Brie said.

Tess shook her head. "You must have had an angel on your shoulder to survive in that cold water."

All of a sudden Brie had a flash of memory. "I did," she said. "He was wearing an orange jumpsuit."

Tess smiled and nodded. "I heard the Canadian Coast Guard airlifted you to the medical center. You're a lucky girl." She made a few notes on her chart, then disconnected the pumping apparatus and removed it.

"Could I sit up?" Brie asked.

"Sure," Tess said. She raised the head of the bed to bring Brie into more of an upright position.

"Are they releasing me soon?"

"Once we know your vital signs are stable," she said.

"By the way, that's pretty much my normal temperature, too. It runs about a degree low."

"Good to know," Tess said and made a note on the chart. "They're bringing some breakfast up for you, and the doctor should be in within the hour."

"Thanks, Tess," Brie said.

Tess walked out, and Dent pulled his chair forward and sat facing her.

"So, tell me about Nate Freeman's condition," Brie said.

"They treated him for the gunshot wound and hypothermia. He's up in surgical recovery. I brought his sister Nancy into the hospital with me once the situation was under control in Tucker Harbor."

"We heard the Maine State Police from where we were out on the water," Brie said.

"Once the Tactical Team arrived, things really livened up. We were able to arrest all of the shooters who'd left the underground facility in pursuit of you and Freeman, because they were no longer on government property."

"Any sign of Atticus Kane? He killed Maloney, you know. And I'd guess Varney too."

Dent nodded. "We finally figured that out. After Tactical arrived, Marty and I still weren't sure what part Nate Freeman played in all this. I mean, we found your car abandoned on his driveway. His sister swore he was a good guy, but we had no way of knowing that until the call from the Coast Guard came into the Maine State Police about you and Freeman."

"He saved my bacon, you know. He and a young scientist named Fritz."

"I'm grateful to them," Dent said. "It should have been me."

Brie shrugged. "Things work out how they work out. I'm happy."

"Me too," Dent said.

"Anyway, back to Atticus Kane."

"Well, after we got word on you and Nate Freeman, we began to suspect something was fishy about Kane's story. He had told us you had driven off in your car around eleven o'clock. So Marty and I headed back to the inn. We found Atticus Kane dead next to his desk in the parlor at the inn. The skin on his face was cherry pink. I didn't need Doc Wolf to tell me it was cyanide poisoning. Marty and I figured it was self-administered."

"He was some kind of deep cover operative," Brie said. "That certainly is a spy's way to die. Wow, what a night."

"I called Joe Wolf and the Evidence Response Team. They're thinking of taking up residence in Tucker Harbor," Dent joked. "Anyway, once Joe and the lab guys got there, I left Marty in charge and headed for the medical center here. I'm sure the woods will be crawling with government spooks before long."

Just then a girl came into the room carrying a tray of food. She set it on the bed caddy and rolled it over Brie's lap. There was oatmeal with fruit and milk, two slices of whole grain toast, coffee, and juice. As Brie ate, Dent finished filling her in on how things had proceeded at the inn.

At a quarter of ten, the doctor came in and examined her, studied the notes on the chart, and wrote the release orders. Tess came back in and removed the IV and gave Brie her instructions. Brie took a nice hot shower in the bathroom, and Tess located a hair dryer so she wouldn't go out with wet hair. Her jeans and sweatshirt were still quite damp and the nurse didn't want her putting on wet clothes, so she found her a set of hospital scrubs to wear home. By ten thirty, Brie was ready to go.

Before leaving the medical center, she and Dent headed to the surgical recovery floor to see Nate Freeman. Nancy was there by his bedside, and Nate was awake and seemed to be doing really well. He told them the doctor was keeping him one more day, to watch the leg wound for infection.

Brie and Dent both thanked him for his role in saving her life.

"I was serious about sailing on a windjammer," he told Brie. "Once I heal up, you plan on seeing me aboard."

"I bet Captain John will give you a nice discount," Brie said. "After all, you saved his second mate."

"I'm not sure who did more of the saving," Nate said. "If you hadn't gotten us in that dory and out to sea, I think our respective gooses might have been cooked."

"I'm just glad we're alive to tell the tale."

Dent offered to bring Nancy back to Tucker Harbor so she could get her car. Nate encouraged her to do that, and by ten minutes of eleven, the three of them were on the road headed southeast toward Tucker Harbor.

Chapter 35

Dent phoned Marty Dupuis at the Whale Spout Inn to tell him when they would be arriving. Marty told him that the Evidence Response Team had wrapped things up and that he was just waiting for them to return. He also told Dent he'd found the list of the inn's upcoming visitors and called to tell them that the inn was closed for the foreseeable future.

It was shortly after one o'clock when Brie and Dent arrived back. Marty had made sandwiches and coffee, and the three of them sat down to discuss the situation over lunch.

Dent said he planned to schedule a meeting Monday with the governor to brief him on what had occurred in Tucker Harbor. He asked Brie to write a thorough report describing the underground facility and summarizing what she'd read in Dr. Fein's notes.

Next, Dent phoned Dr. Stephen Wells, the professor who had given Brie all of Everett Fein's research on *The Hum*. Although Wells had claimed he had given Brie the only copies of the documents, he admitted to Dent Fenton that he had made copies of everything. Dent made an appointment to pick up the documents from Wells the next day.

"Did the lab guys find my service weapon and shield?" Brie asked. "Atticus would have taken them."

"We found them locked in his desk along with your cell phone."

Brie looked relieved. "That's good. I'd hate to not be able to return them to the department." She looked from one to the other of them. "I've really enjoyed working with you two on this case, even though things got a little hairy at the end there."

"I'd like to maintain your deputy status and use you on a case by case basis, if you'd be interested, Brie. You wouldn't be on regular duty or be paid unless a case comes along where we need you and we call you up."

Brie was silent for a minute as she mulled over Dent's offer. "Well, I'd be amenable to that if it doesn't interfere with my responsibilities on the *Maine Wind* too much. Let's see how it works out for the rest of this summer. I'd like to return my service weapon, though. I'd be more comfortable if I wasn't responsible for a department weapon when I'm not on active status. I plan to acquire a personal firearm to replace the one I lost on Granite Island."

"That's fine," Dent said. "Suit yourself. But keep the laptop for now. You'll need it to file your reports. It's an older unit that we weren't currently using."

Brie gave both of them a hug, then walked with them out onto the front porch and watched as they headed for their cars. Dent climbed into his SUV, and Marty drove the Impala that she had had.

After they left, she spent the next couple hours filling out her final reports on the case. She also took time to walk down and visit Amber Torgeson, and to call Nate Freeman at the hospital to see how he was doing.

Then she went upstairs to freshen up and pack her belongings. John had left her a voice mail early that morning, saying that the *Maine Wind* would be anchoring in Tucker Harbor by the end of the day and that he hoped she'd be done with the case and able to come back aboard.

Brie changed into a clean pair of jeans and a white tank top. She had been busy upstairs for about a half hour, and when she looked out the window, she was thrilled to see the

Maine Wind just dropping anchor in the harbor. She picked up her duffel and the laptop case and headed down the stairs. She checked to be sure the back door was locked, then went out the front door, ducking under the crime scene tape, and walked down toward the harbor.

Someone had lowered *Tango,* the small dory, and was pulling for shore. Brie's heart skipped a beat as she got closer and saw it was John. As she passed the lobster docks, she watched him give one more strong pull on the oars. He moved to the front of the dory, climbed up on the gunwale, and jumped the three or four feet to dry land. Brie dropped her stuff and ran toward him. He turned from beaching the dory and caught her in his arms, lifted her off the ground and spun her around.

"I've come to rescue you from your miserable landlubber existence," he said.

"And not a minute too soon."

Brie stepped into the dory, and John loaded her things and pushed off.

"We've missed you, Second Matey. Some of us more than others."

"I'll have to figure out some way to make that up to you, Captain." She gave him a sly smile.

"Well, we'll see about that now, won't we?" He fixed his brown eyes on her in a most disconcerting way. "Of course, I'll have to pry you away from Hurley Hampden. He has a list of questions as long as the mainsheet for you. I think he may be planning a novel with you as heroine."

Brie laughed. It felt good to laugh, good to feel the sun on her face. It felt good to be alive. She looked toward the *Maine Wind* and then back at John. It felt good to be going home.

Epilogue

After an unsuccessful but exhaustive search for Atticus Kane's next of kin, Washington County, Maine sold the Whale Spout Inn to Nancy Maloney and Nate Freeman for the amount of the taxes due. Nate wrote to Brie several months later to tell her that Nancy had sold her house and moved to the inn to become the new proprietor. Nate said that he made himself available any time she needed help with repairs or upgrades. Together they had gotten rid of Atticus Kane's personal belongings and any furniture that seemed to relate directly to him, and had thereby exorcized his ghost from the Whale Spout Inn. Nate told Brie that adopting the inn was just what Nancy had needed. Not only was the Whale Spout an important fixture in Tucker Harbor, but owning it had brought purpose to her life and helped her to deal with the loss of Jake.

As for Varney's Diner, another fixture in Tucker Harbor, following Varney's death a lawyer from Machias contacted Amber Torgeson to tell her that she had been named in Varney Simms' will. Varney had left the diner, which he had owned free and clear, to Amber. Amber was delighted since she had yet to stumble on her career path. She and her mother Heidi decided to run the place together but kept Varney's name on the establishment. At last notice, Amber was taking cooking classes and employing her new talents at Varney's Diner.

And the underground ELF transmitter installation? After a shakeup that made its way to the highest levels in Washington, D.C., the clandestine operation, code named "Operation High Tide," located near Tucker Harbor, Maine, was aborted, and the secret facility was closed. At least, that is what everyone was led to believe. But the fact remains, whatever one wishes to make of it, that the federal government owns a lot of land and therefore a lot of underground territory in the United States.

Acknowledgements

Thanks, as always, to my family for supporting me in my work and to the following people. To my friend and fellow mystery author, Christopher Valen, for reading and editing the manuscript. To my friend Jeanette Brown for her careful reading of the manuscript and for her input. To my wonderful editor, Jennifer Adkins, for catching all the little incongruities and for polishing the manuscript to a professional finish —you're the best. And many thanks to Nicole Aimée Suek for her hard work and excellent cover design. I've really enjoyed working with you.

I would like to thank Bill Gillies of Wiscasset, Maine, for talking to me about his time in Naval Intelligence at the Winter Harbor military base and for explaining the work of the Navy's radio listening outposts during the Cold War, as well as the function of the Navy's VLF transmitter in Cutler, Maine. And also for assuring me that it would be hard to come up with a plot that was too far-fetched.

Thanks to Gary A. Borger, author of *Nymphing: A basic Guide to Identifying, Tying, and Fishing Artificial Nymphs.* It was delightful meeting you at the author get-together in Wausau, Wisconsin. Many thanks for your very interesting thoughts on the parallels between fly fishing and detective work.

Thanks to the Maine State Police for helping me with questions on the structure of the force, as well as details on firearms, vehicles, and jurisdictions.

I would also like to extend a special thank you to all my faithful fans for supporting my work, for your words of praise that often humble me, and for telling others about my books. You are the ones who keep me writing.

As a final note, I would like to say that while *Cold Coast* is a work of fiction, it is underpinned by much technological and scientific veracity. While the military base at Winter Harbor, Maine (Naval Group Support Activity or NGSA

Winter Harbor) was closed in 2002, after 67 years as a radio listening outpost, the Navy's VLF transmitter at Cutler, Maine still sends encrypted communication to the U.S. strategic submarine forces. Part of the land that housed the former naval base at Cutler is still owned by the U.S. government. The Russian ELF transmitter, ZEVS, really exists near Murmansk, as do the U.S. Navy's ELF transmitters in Clam Lake, Wisconsin and Republic, Michigan. As described in the book, these extremely low frequency transmitters send encrypted messages to deeply submerged nuclear subs in the Russian and American fleets.

It is also a fact that electromagnetic waves in certain frequency ranges are absorbed or refracted by the ionosphere, an electrically conductive region of the atmosphere beginning at an altitude of approximately 80 km. Ongoing government research and experiments involving ELF/VLF and other ionospheric transmissions are jointly sponsored by the Office of Naval Research, the Air Force Research Laboratory, and DARPA, the Defense Advanced Research Projects Agency.

Author's Note

Visit the author's website at:
www.windjammermysteries.com

An Invitation to Reading Groups/Book Clubs

I would be happy to visit your reading group or book club, either in person or by phone (speakerphone required), and join in your discussion of my work.
To arrange a book club visit, please email me at:
info@windjammermysteries.com

Glossary of Sailing Terms

Aft—Toward the back of the boat.

Abeam—At right angles to the boat.

Alee—Helm's alee or hard alee is the command for tacking or coming about.

Amidships—In the middle of the boat.

Bald-head rigging—A gaff-rigged sailing vessel that carries no topsails.

Ballantine—To coil a halyard into three overlapping piles. The finished pile of line looks like a 3-leaf clover. Ballantining keeps the line from fouling as the sail is doused or lowered.

Beam reach—Also "reach." To sail across the wind, or with the wind abeam.

Bearing—The angle from the boat to an object.

Beating—Sailing close-hauled, or as close to the wind as is efficient.

Boom—The spar that extends and supports the foot of the sail.

Bow—The most forward part of the boat.

Bowsprit—Permanent spar attached to the bow, to which jib-stays and forestays are fastened.

Close-hauled—Sailing as close to the wind as is efficient; also beating or on the wind.

Come about—Also "tack." To bring the boat across the wind to a new heading.

Confused seas—A highly disturbed water surface without a single well-defined direction of wave travel.

Cut—The shape or design of a sail.

Danger Sector—The fixed red part of a lighthouse's light shining over shoals.

Glossary

Davits—Outboard rigging for raising and lowering the ship's yawl boat or dory.

Dory—A small multipurpose craft usually propelled by pulling (using oars) or sailing.

Downwind—Away from the direction from which the wind blows.

Fore—Prefix indicating location near the bow.

Foremast—On a schooner, the mast closer to the bow.

Foresail—The sail that is rigged on the foremast.

Gaff—The spar that supports the top edge of a four-sided sail.

Gaff-rigged—A boat with four-sided sails rigged to gaffs.

Galley—A boat's kitchen.

Grabrail—A handrail running along the edge of the deckhouse or cabin top.

Gunwale—(pronounced "gunnel") A boat's rail at the edge of the deck.

Hatch—An opening in a deck, covered by a hatch cover.

Halyard—A line that hoists a sail and keeps it up.

Head—A boat's bathroom.

Heading—The course, or direction the boat is pointing.

Heaving line—A line thrown outboard to another vessel or to a person in the water.

Heel—The tilt or laying over of a boat caused by wind.

Helm—The tiller or steering wheel.

Hurricane hole—An area for safe anchorage, with good protection from the wind on as many sides as possible.

Jib—A sail carried on the headstay or forestay.

Jibe—To change tacks by heading off, or turning away from the wind, until the sails swing across the boat.

Knot—1 nautical mile per hour.

Lace-lines—Also reefing lines. Used to secure a sail to the bowsprit or boom.

Lazarette—A small hold, usually in the stern, for stores and gear.

Lee of the island—The side of the island sheltered from the wind.

Leeward—Away from the direction of the wind. Pronounced "lu-ard."

Longboat—The longest boat carried by a sailing ship.

Make off or Make fast—To secure a line to a belaying pin or cleat.

Mainmast—Mast farthest aft on a schooner. Carries the mainsail.

Mainsail—The sail attached to the largest mast on the boat.

Mainsheet—The line that controls the mainsail.

Middle watch—0000 – 0400, or 12:00 – 4:00 a.m.

Nuns and Cans—The most common types of buoys or aids to navigation. Nuns are red and conical-shaped, like a nun's hat. Cans are green and shaped like a can.

Painter—The bow line on a dinghy.

Peak halyard—Raises the end of the gaff farthest from the mast.

PFDs—Personal flotation devices.

Port—The left side of the ship when facing forward.

Port tack—Sailing to windward with the wind coming over the port side of the boat.

Pulpit—A railed structure at the bow or on the bowsprit. Only seen on historic schooners that were fishing vessels and used harpoons for catching big fish such as swordfish.

Quarter—The side of the boat near the stern.

Ratlines—System of tarred rungs used to climb to the top of the mast.

Rode—The anchor line.

Running—Sailing with the wind astern.

Saloon—The main cabin on a ship.

Scandalize the forepeak—On a gaff-rigged vessel, lowering the peak of the sail to slow the vessel.

Schooner—A boat with two or more masts: the foremast or forewardmost mast is shorter that the mainmast.

Scuppers—Holes in the rail or gunwale that allow water drainage.

Sea-kindly—A vessel's ability to move comfortably, or without undue strain, in rough seas.

Sea-worthy—A vessel able to survive heavy weather.

Sennit—Braided small stuff or cordage of many varieties. Used for everything from lanyards to chafing gear.

Sole—A cabin or cockpit floor.

Starboard—The right side of the ship when facing forward.

Starboard tack—Sailing to windward with the wind coming over the starboard side of the boat.

Staysail—A small headsail set between the jib and the foremast.

Stem—The forward edge of the bow.

Stern—The aftmost part of the hull.

Throat halyard—On a gaff-rigged boat, the halyard that raises the luff or forward edge of sail along the mast.

Glossary

Thwarts—The seats in a dory or dinghy.

Upwind—Toward the wind.

Windward—Upwind.

Yawl boat—A small, powerful motorized boat used to push a motorless vessel.